No Memory Unturned

Printed in the United States of America
Cover design by: MiblArt

First Printing, 2023

ISBN-13: 978-1-966238-03-4

No Memory Unturned

ARIANA TOSADO

Contents

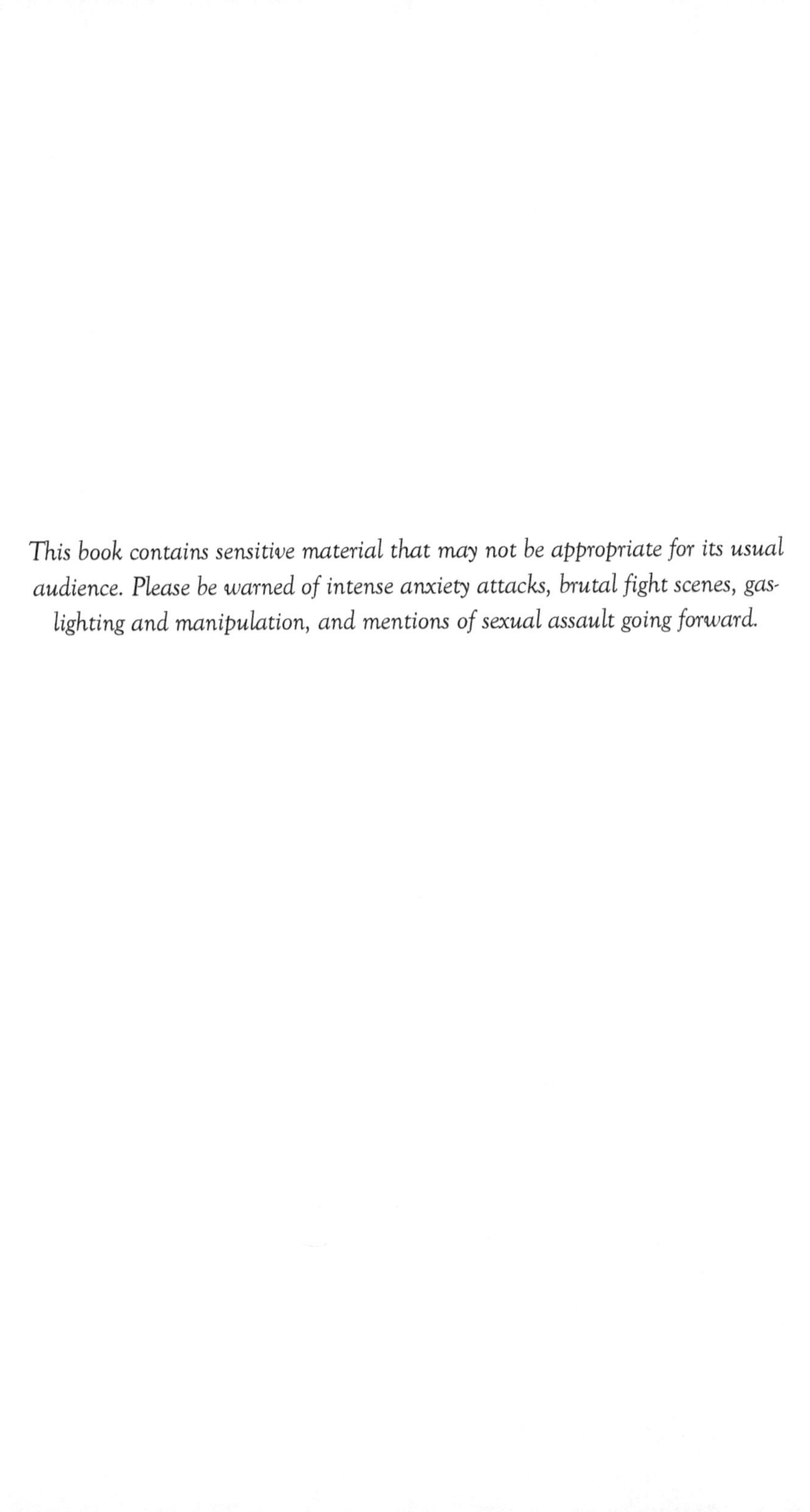

This book contains sensitive material that may not be appropriate for its usual audience. Please be warned of intense anxiety attacks, brutal fight scenes, gaslighting and manipulation, and mentions of sexual assault going forward.

ONE

"How are you, Amy?"

I heard that gentle, sonorous voice first. Then the beeping. Then the ticking. Then a woman softly crying.

"I want my baby girl back," she whispered.

I pried my eyes open, surrendering to the fact that I was waking up whether I liked it or not (which I *really* didn't—headaches of that intensity are outside the laws of reality). The beeping was coming from a heart monitor standing on my left. The ticking was coming from the clock on the wall in front of me. My mother was the woman softly crying.

Whoa. Why was my whole body throbbing?

A man with rugged, handsome features was standing next to

Momma. I knew this man. I definitely knew this man with icy-blue eyes, who had one arm wrapped around my mother's waist. Upon meeting my gaze, they both scurried to the right side of the hospital bed.

Wait—*hospital* bed?

"Emma?" Momma squeaked. Dozens of chestnut flyaways stuck out in the fluorescent light. The sleeves of her sweater were too long, covering most of her beige hands. "How do you feel, honey?"

For a split second, I wondered who Emma was as I shut my eyes against the harsh lights in the ceiling. A majority of the people in my life and my own identity were foggy in my mind, and the headache I had pulsed harder at my brain trying to recover it all from the mist.

"Em," Dad—*Oh, right, he's my dad!*—said, resting his hand on the light-blue sheets, "can you talk?"

My throat felt like it had been storing wet sand in it for the past decade, but my need for answers overpowered that: "Why am... I—here?"

My parents shared a disappointed glance with each other. My body almost made the mistake of locking itself in defense.

"We were hoping you'd know the answer to that," Momma told me. "You have a couple of broken ribs, a moderate concussion, a Grade 2 ankle sprain, and severe bruising on your stomach and arms."

Wow. I was surprised that *she'd* been the only one crying when I'd woken up.

The longer I stared at my parents, the more information—the more memories—that poured into my head. I remembered why seeing my parents *together* was so significant, why I should've been jumping out of that hospital bed and dancing with him. But I doubted I could move a finger without it snapping off, so the hot tears running down my face were the only things that could tell him how I felt.

"Dad," I whispered. "You're here."

"Of course, kiddo." He brushed an ever-so-light finger against my cheek. "Nothing could keep me away."

His olive-green T-shirt under his invisibility cloak complemented his lightly tanned skin—how had he managed to tan since the last time I'd seen him? His arms had earned a nice tone after months of consistent workout. But his dark, usually combed-back hair now stuck out in a ruffled mess. That wasn't normal for him.

"And as long as we know when the nurses are coming in and he puts the cloak on in time, he can stay for as long as you need him," Momma assured me, mustering a smile.

Well, *that* was great news, but now I was remembering a much bigger problem that had stopped me from even seeing him after school anymore: he and Aunt Becca had had to move all over North Carolina, even utilizing a few magician hideouts, because of Alexa's pack tracking them down—

Oh, right—their new apartment Mr. Dawson had managed to snag for them through his real estate friend. Did they already move in?

Hang on. What *did* I last remember? There was Opal finding out that she was a druid, her and me going through the rest of second semester keeping her secret together, me and my best friends prepping for finals week... The school year was about to end. Was it finals week? Was I missing my finals right now?

"Finals," I choked out.

Momma tilted her head, her brows furrowing and Dad's mimicking hers. "What about finals?" she asked carefully.

"Next week."

Dad's hand went to Momma's arm, whose eyes glazed over with opaque worry.

"Honey," she said, even quieter now, "finals were three months ago."

Wait. *What?*

I tried remembering yesterday. I tried remembering the day before, the weekend before finals week, anything I'd done this summer. It was all blank. Nothing but darkness, a gaping pit, in my memory.

"I..." I stared down at where my feet were hiding under the hospital sheets. "I don't—remember... anything. From summer."

Silence fell over us like a downpour. Nothing could be said or done to answer any of my questions or fix any of the current issues at hand—whatever those even were now!

I couldn't stay here. I needed to get answers as soon as possible. "What's—today?"

"Friday," Momma said, a melancholy dragging down her inflection. "August 24."

August. August? The *end* of—?

I gasped, a sharp pain in my ribs shooting in my chest. Not even amnesia could bury my mother's birthday.

"Happy—birthday," I whispered, fresh tears spilling over. A piercing jab at my ribs accompanied every shallow breath. "I'm—sorry—"

"No, honey, no!" she rushed to say, ever so gently taking my face into her hands. "Baby girl, all I wanted today was for you to be okay. I just wanted to know that I would have the rest of my life with you. You just gave me that. It's okay."

"I didn't—get you—"

"Yes, you did." Her honey-like voice soothed my crying with every word. "You did."

"You know what else she'd probably love?" Dad said beside her. "If you remembered anything in the last twenty-four hours."

I swallowed, cringing. "No."

I looked up at Momma. She exhaled, gripping the plastic bed rail. "Okay. Wednesday night, you and Opal were having a sleepover while I was out shopping. Then you texted me saying that you two were going out to get me a present. Does that sound familiar?"

I softly shook my head.

She bit her lip before continuing. "Well, I came home to an empty house with your phone on the couch, so I had Mr. Dawson telepathically call you. He didn't get an answer from either of you. He came over and used your phone for a locator spell, and you were in the Callistro Forest."

In full honesty, it sounded like she was making it all up as she went. How had any of this happened when I had no memory of it?

"When we drove up, we saw two silhouettes disappear into the forest the second they saw our headlights. We found you and Opal unconscious and took you here."

"Opal's here?" I rasped.

"Yep." Dad grazed my right hand with his thumb. "In the room next to you."

Opal Dubois: a druid. A destined-to-be high priestess, I found out, which her purple eyes exposed. (They *weren't*, in fact, contacts.) And she hadn't even known any of that until the end of March this year.

She was also the Callistro Academy gossip girl. Most surprisingly, though, she'd become one of my closest friends.

There came another memory: every afternoon we'd spent hanging out after she'd found out about herself—and Mr. Dawson. But as far as she knew about me, and hopefully still only knew, I was a mortal friend she could entrust the truth to. After all, how bad could the goddaughter of her uncle be?

Sarah and Breanne didn't know about Opal's magic but still enjoyed hanging out with her. She wasn't just the school gossip girl to us anymore, though, especially not to me—not when I finally had a magician friend who was my age. Even if I still couldn't *tell* her that I was a magician.

But what had Opal and I been doing in the Callistro Forest Wednesday night? Why would we go there alone? Why had we been attacked? Who would attack us?!

Did Opal...?

"Does she—know?" I asked, ready to close off my ears to the answer.

"No," Momma said. Before I could swallow with relief, she cocked her brows at me and tightened her grip on the bed rail. "Not that *we* know of. But you've kept a lot of secrets from us this year. I love you, Emmy, but the possibility of you having told Opal the truth and swearing her to secrecy is likely at this point. Only she and you can answer that question."

I knew that I definitely hadn't told Opal the truth during the school year; my family and I had agreed that it was in everyone's best interest, especially hers, to keep her uninvolved in the Atera situation. But hanging out during summer vacation, let alone sleepovers by ourselves without Sarah and Breanne, more than gave the opportunity...

Would I betray myself like that? Was I the same girl I had been at the beginning of summer?

"What happened this summer?" I whispered.

Dad put his hand on Momma's shoulder, taking the burden of that question off her. "We'll tell you everything we can later. Right now, you have guests, and we don't wanna tire you out before you see them."

Wow, thanks a lot, I thought. He'd only been in my life for almost a year by then, but that was *not* how to tell his injured, terrified sixteen-year-old daughter that whatever had happened in the past three months was anything but good.

It was a bit of relief, at least, when Mr. Dawson came in minutes later, his dark-brown hair in an unfamiliar disarray like Dad's. Gray subtly touched his roots now like a ghost had shyly painted them on. Aunt Becca came almost immediately after. Well, I had to assume that it was Aunt Becca when the door cracked open and nobody slipped through. The perks of magic.

Her hood popped off, exposing her unnaturally platinum-blond hair first. The rest of her faded into view, and she walked to the foot of the bed. Her blue eyes that Dad's matched squinted with pity. "Geez, kiddo. How'd you get yourself into this one?"

"Question of—the decade." My chest punished me for almost every breath in. Despite the stiff ache all down my backside, I didn't dare adjust my position. "Everything—hurts. A lot."

"Who knows?" Mr. Dawson remarked, taking a seat in front of the window on the left side of the room. The curtains had been pulled shut, but the yellow glow of the streetlights against the night sky shone through. "Maybe being a hybrid also gives you the power to heal yourself."

If only he weren't joking—healing is another phenomenon that not even magic can manage.

A magician isn't supposed to be all seven classes of magic, either.

"Um..." I kept my eyes on Mr. Dawson's sharp chin, unable to note his expression when I dared to ask, "How's Opal?"

"Unconscious," he replied, crossing his arms. "In pretty bad shape."

"I'm really sorry."

"Unless you were the one who attacked her, you have nothing to apologize for."

That was just it: I couldn't help but feel that, somehow and in some way, this *was* my fault—that I'd sparked whatever had happened Wednesday night. Like Momma had said, I'd kept secrets from my family all year: Cara and Steven when they first started texting me, an anonymous Hunter testing my DNA, even our school nurse really being Alexa undercover. Not to mention meeting Annisa, who was meant to become the world's most powerful druid and had the impossible ability to time travel. What if I really *had* told Opal the truth and had kept that from my family, too? What if I'd done things I couldn't take back, and I couldn't even remember them?

I wanted to run away from the reality that the hospital room was shoving down my throat. "I wanna go home."

"School starts next Wednesday, and you're not gonna be off of crutches by then," Mr. Dawson warned. A dark brow arched above his deep-set eyes. "You think you're ready to deal with all the gossip and rumors that'll be floating around campus when you and Opal show up on the first day like you will?"

Disappointment thrust through me like a sword—because not only was he right, but I'd missed out on my *entire* summer!

"Can't I—drop out and—be homeschooled again?"

"Atta, girl!" Aunt Becca beamed from the foot of the bed. "I think that concussion actually made you smarter."

"*Becca.*" Momma scolded her from my bedside, rolling her eyes and burying her head in her hand. "How many times do I have to—?"

"I *know.*" Auntie held up her hands, putting on a high-pitched mocking tone. "'Becca, Callistro isn't evil because the founder actually liked magicians!'" She scoffed, scrunching her face skepticism. "The founder's dead. They reopened the Hunter's Room for a reason! You're a walking reminder of why it's here today, and the only people there who *aren't*—"

"I'm not pulling her out." Momma loosely gestured to me. "Can you show some optimism?"

Auntie looked back at me, took a quick scan up and down, and then shrugged. "You're not dead."

I suppressed the urge to laugh; she was the worst person to have in the room during a time like this.

"Emma," Mr. Dawson started warily, like he'd been waiting his turn to speak to me. He laid his arms on the armrest of his chair. "What's the very last thing you remember?"

"The last im—*portant* thing is... we were looking around Dad—and Auntie's new apart—ment."

Okay. Yes. They definitely have moved in.

"Friday night," I said next. "After dessert, Sarah, Breanne, and I... went to bed. Then I woke up—here."

"The entire summer is gone from her memories," Momma told him, arms crossed. "The nurse said that based on her damage, it could be due to a number of things."

"The nurse probably doesn't know about memory-wiping spells," Mr. Dawson said, pressing the tips of his fingers together. "The break is too clean and *convenient* for it to be anything else."

Was this anxiety what it was like not knowing something crucial to our situation? Was this what I always put my family through?

"We have three options," Mr. Dawson said. "You can spend the next hour telling her everything we know, I can reverse the spell and she remembers on her own, or we can wait until Opal is here so I can recover their memories at the same time."

"We're definitely doing this with just us," Momma was quick to say. "We have no idea what Emma experienced that Opal can't know about. Or if either of their memories will expose us."

"I'm with you," Dad said, his rugged jaw clenched and a lump passing in his throat. His kind eyes landed on me. "Do you think you're ready to remember?"

My gaze rested on the light-blue sheets in front me, my brain searching for the truth to my answer: "Yeah."

It didn't matter what I wanted; I was in survival mode, and I needed my memories to survive.

Mr. Dawson stood from the chair and walked to the other side of my bed, across from my parents. "Close your eyes, take a deep breath, and relax yourself as much as you can. There's a chance you'll see something you don't expect to, but no matter what happened, you should stay calm until we figure things out."

"I know," I said, fingers fiddling with each other. I wanted my locket, if I even had it on, but I wasn't about to look for it or ask where it was. "I'm ready."

Mr. Dawson gave me one more chance to change my mind. When I didn't, he placed his warm fingertips on my forehead. "*Converte.*"

All in a deep, resounding echo in my head, cry after cry, scream after scream—soon my own joined them in that cold hospital room.

C H A P T E R

Two

Three months of memories hurtled to the front of my mind like a car flipping over and over. As August rewound into July and July rewound into the beginning of June, the dashboard of my own car faded into view as I opened the driver door. I stepped into the parking lot and then walked onto the grass of Capperson Park.

I know I've mentioned it before, but the white gazebo there is sacred. It's where Sarah, Breanne, and I formally met; where we swore our friendship for life; where they and the guys had surprised me for my sixteenth birthday; and where Jak had taken me to commemorate the Redway Boys leaving the day after... and have what was technically our second date. I prayed that it would stay a happy spot as I prepped the conversation in my head.

Sarah and Breanne had sent me away a little too eagerly when I'd left our dorm. It wasn't that they *wanted* me to break Nolan's heart, but I guess I'd postponed asserting the friend zone longer than I'd intended to. Even though his father had prohibited him from seeing me at all, he sneaked in hangouts so often that I almost didn't notice a difference.

But I *had* to do this. If he was never going to be my boyfriend, I couldn't let him think that he had a chance like I'd been doing since the night we met last year.

No boys unless necessary. That was my new motto.

Nolan's voice cut through my thoughts like a knife as he approached the gazebo steps, a darling smile already on his lips. "Hey, Emmy."

I internally cringed. "Hi."

He took a seat next to me, a baby-blue beanie covering most of his shaggy, dark hair. Soft leaf-green eyes bored into me with a sweetness I'd come to know as unique to him.

"How've you been?" I asked.

"The same," he said, shrugging. "You?"

"Good."

I had to get this conversation going in a direction that would close all the bad roads it could turn down. Straightforward yet slow: "Do you think you could ever hate me?"

Slower!

A playful scoff formed in his throat. Then he realized that I was being serious, and his brows scrunched into what almost looked like offense. "Never. Why would you ask that?"

"No matter what I do?"

"No..." He shrugged again, his eyes falling to the green park in front of us. The setting sun was lenient in warmth, especially under the shade of the gazebo and considering the fact that summer was around the corner. "I mean, you'd have to be a crime lord or something. But you're—" He abruptly turned to me, pausing. "You're not a criminal, are you?"

Technically, I was a criminal on more than one offense, but I obviously couldn't say that.

"No," I said, laughing it off, "I'm not. So, you wouldn't hate me even if... even if I—?"

Burning nerves popped in my chest when his shoulders relaxed in realization. "Even if you rejected me?"

I exhaled so shallowly that even I didn't hear it.

Nolan leaned back in his seat. "I guess I'm... kinda relieved."

My head caught back. "What?"

"You flat out ran away after I kissed you a few months ago, you barely text me anymore, and you hesitate to touch me whenever we hang out. I just figured. But I'd still rather be shot down instead of holding on to a nonexistent chance... Is it me?"

"No, you have nothing to do with it. It's all me, it's..."

Just days after Nolan had kissed me for the first time, Alexa told me that I was a hybrid. And when I remembered that, Marcus's words when he'd kidnapped me and Momma echoed next: about how gifted Ateras were. About how picky Nolan was and that was why I was special.

My next sentence was a long time coming—because, in full honesty, I *wasn't* good for him, just like his dad believed.

"Your dad's right, okay? It's best for you if we don't—"

"Wait. Wait a sec, *that's* what this is about?"

I sped up my words, anticipating his rebuttal. "Please, believe me when I say it's best for you—"

"How?" he snapped, startling me. "Did you ever think to get my opinion on that? Like, what part of 'I really wanna try this' isn't clear to you?"

"It's not that I don't wanna try it—"

"Ha, okay, sure. You say you feel the same way and even show it sometimes, but how am I supposed to believe you? I've been so into you since we became friends, all I want is a chance. That's literally all I want, a chance to explore something beyond what we have right now, but I can't even trust you when you say you do, too! Why does it feel like you're always lying to me?"

"Because she is."

Nolan and I sprang from our seats. At the entrance of the gazebo, Marcus was climbing the three steps up and stopping in the entryway. His voice was as rough and rugged as his features, his green eyes so aflame that I'd never been more scared of the man in my life—and that said something.

He stuck a firm finger at us like he was commanding us to be still. "I told you to stay away from this girl, Nolan."

"Why?" Nolan loosely gestured to me. "You liked her when you first met! *Nothing's* changed since, she hasn't done anything wrong—"

"She's a criminal, and I told you to stay away from her!"

Nolan whirled on me, gawking like I was a completely different person. "You literally just said you're not a criminal!"

"Not just that." Marcus marched up to me, grabbed my arm, and pulled me toward him. "Much worse."

"Whoa, hey!" Nolan reached for me, but his father yanked me behind him. "Stop, what're you doing?"

"You stay right there, I'm not telling you again!" Marcus's grip on me tightened as he glanced between the two of us, finalizing his glower on Nolan. "I'm protecting you, and that's all you need to know."

Wait. Was he... keeping his side of the deal of not exposing me and my family?

He wasn't telling my secret—he was remembering my threat. He knew that I was willing to carry it out. At least, I had been back then. But he didn't know where I stood now, and I had a strong gut feeling that, despite his rationality telling him the truth, he wouldn't take a risk on his son's life.

"Let her go!" Nolan tried to step forward, but one glare from Marcus sent him back. "Dad!"

"Money on it, she's been lying to you since the day you met! I can bet your college savings she's—"

His stare fell onto mine, and he shut his mouth. The vengeful thrum that had made my threat that night was resurfacing, coming up for air after spending months underwater, and I felt it on my face. The threat itself was empty now, but the passion behind it had been fully restored. Finally, my anger and fear were working *together*.

It was enough to make Marcus curtly exhale and rephrase. "You just never know if—"

"I said let her go." Nolan's anger was a side of him that I'd barely received a taste of, but seeing him in all his emotion and, well, teenage-ness then made me feel the most normal I'd had in a long time.

"You don't get it," I told Marcus, sounding a lot braver than I felt.

"I don't?" he snarled, tightening his grip on my arm again. "Really? Go ahead, tell me what I don't get."

"I was saying goodbye." I swallowed, forced to face what I was too scared to say to Nolan directly. Marcus, though, wasn't giving me a choice: "I promise—I swear—I'll stay away. Just let me go and I'll leave you alone."

"You rejected me because of him?" The weight in Nolan's solid tone fell against me like a swinging anchor. "You won't be with me because of *him?*"

Marcus's hold on me loosened as he turned his attention to Nolan. "Why did you come out here?"

"Emma asked me to meet her. I didn't know why, we started talking and then she rejected me because of what *you* said!"

"What did I say?"

"It's 'best for me' if we weren't together. Are you kidding me? You can't make that decision for me!"

A stifling silence overtook us for a few seconds. Not even the wind came by to say hello, nor was anyone out with their family, friends, or pets to provide some kind of ambiance.

I almost jumped when Marcus suddenly released me. A firm finger pointed at me and forced me down the steps of the gazebo as he growled, "I never want to see you again. If you *ever* show your face around my son, or *anyone* in my family,"—he leaned in closer, now on the first step while my feet had reached the grass—"your family's blood will be on *your* hands."

I'd spoken those words to him after almost strangling him in midair. They rang in my head, with my voice, in a vicious cycle, daring me to stay for a second longer.

The sunrays glared on my back, fueling my desire to throw

Marcus across the park. And yet, I couldn't help but think of all the ways he had of following through on *his* threat, even without being a magician.

"Deal," I said. "If you keep our first one."

Then I turned around. I ran away. I didn't look over my shoulder once.

†

Coming home that night, I didn't have anyone who could know of the full situation between me and Marcus, not even Momma—I'll never forget the fear engraved in her face the night I almost choked him to death and threatened his family. I didn't want her to know about today's deal, where he'd blackmailed *our* family. I couldn't put her through that again, not when we'd finally reached a ceasefire.

So I was alone, even as my best friends ran to me when I walked into our dorm, embraced me in a group hug, and held me when I wouldn't cough up the story.

Sitting against the door, Sarah and Breanne leaned their heads against mine, sharing grief despite the absence of words. They knew what I'd finally set out to do this evening, they'd been pushing me to do it for weeks. Maybe I didn't have to worry about Nolan anymore, but it was little weight off my chest. I had to pray that Marcus would continue believing my empty threat.

And now I had finals week ahead of me. The tests never stopped.

THREE

We couldn't believe where we stood when Monday morning came around: the last week of school, of our sophomore year. Callistro Girls were scrambling to get their final projects ready for presentation this week. The seniors were graduating this week.

The big pass-or-fail hunt for Momma's class was this week.

We'd spent all semester wondering about it, but her lips had stayed as shut tight as a watertight door whenever I'd tried to get even a *hint* out of her. Now I sat on the green bean bag chair in the secret room next to Monsieur Goubeaux's classroom, needing another plan to lure something out before tomorrow. Unfortunately, the last time my baby doll eyes worked on Momma was when I was six, and that was because she let me have the win.

(Masters really are trained to withstand *anything*.)

The entrance of the small room slid open. Opal Dubois dramatically groaned as she walked through, holding her bookbag's strap. After closing the entrance, she turned to face me. "I don't wanna do Perketti's final! Even the review packet sucks. When do you have her?"

"Wednesday." I sighed with the same dread, sinking into the bean bag. "Thanks for the pep talk."

Opal fell into the purple bean bag across from me, giggling. "Sorry."

I scrunched my brows, feigning curiosity. "Isn't it gonna be easy for you, though, with—y'know—superpowers?"

"Nope! Not even magic is gonna help, trust me." She dropped her bag down next to her, pushing her straight black hair behind her ears. "But I'd give you some of mine if it could."

It actually could; a lookout spell would give her a bird's-eye view of everyone else's papers (not that I was planning on doing that). But Opal was still new at exploring the possibilities.

The guilt from lying to her was adding up, but my family and I knew that it was safest. After what had happened to Steven in the forest a few months ago, we couldn't make Opal another lead to me and the Ateras by telling her the truth. Even if she wouldn't tell anyone about my *magician* identity, it'd only be a matter of time before she found out my Atera identity—and I didn't want to know if that would somehow lead to her piecing together the Adara story. Especially with Alexa now likely on the hunt for Adara, the truth would only paint a massive target on Opal's back.

So all she knew was that Mr. Dawson was my godfather and Momma and I knew his druid secret. But for some reason, I didn't feel like that was enough of the truth to leave her with, but I refused to let something happen to her just because of my secret.

I *was* gonna have magical mischief with her while I could, though. "Hear me out," I began, leaning forward. "For Mr. Hartman's class, see if you can mess with the printer."

"Why?"

"Because he always prints out his tests RIGHT before we take them to make sure nobody can get the answers beforehand. He might even give his classes a curve because of 'technical difficulties'."

She gawked at me with a grin, her purple eyes shining with amusement. "You're bad!"

We shared a laugh as I leaned back in our bean bags. "I'm kidding," I assured her. "For homework, though, it would've been awesome. I should've thought of that a lot earlier."

I stared up at the vintage lantern hanging in the center of the ceiling. What else would Opal probably want to hear from a friend who knew about her?

"Geez. It's crazy that you went through half a semester with magic."

She shrugged, twiddling her pale thumbs. "It's not really hard to hide. It's just fear getting in the way at this point. Like, the more I know, the more I'll have to hide because the more opportunities I'll have to use magic."

Exactly.

She breathily chuckled. "It's still *so* weird saying that."

What was crazy to me was how close this girl and I had managed to get solely because I was the only Callistro Girl who knew the truth. And that was dangerous on its own because, for the first

time in my life, I doubted how long I'd want to keep my identity
a secret from her.

"Hypothetically speaking," I mused, shifting my weight to the
other side of the bean bag, "what if you found out that Amelia or
Caroline had magic this whole time?"

She took a few seconds to think about it. Then, dimples
formed in her pale cheeks as she sighed. "Wouldn't that be weird?
You *never* know who does or doesn't! But it's not like I can blame
them for not telling me. They're my *roommates* and I don't think
I'd tell them about me unless I knew for a *fact* that they were magicians, too."

I forced a smile. I didn't like this—this was different. She was
nothing like what Momma had raised me to be careful around.
She wasn't a situation that Momma had trained me for: where a
friend, a magician, would without a doubt understand why I'd
kept the truth from her.

That's not why you haven't told her, I had to tell myself. *It's not
for your sake, it's for hers.*

"Makes sense," I said, fiddling with the silver locket around
my neck.

"Let's just—drop it for now," Opal said, her thumbs furiously
twiddling.

I opened my mouth, but that instinct built by magic called
me back: let sleeping dogs lie.

"Opal."

Her eyes met mine like I was scolding her.

I chewed on the inside of my lip. I knew I meant the words,
but I wasn't sure that I had the right to say them: "You can talk to
me about anything. I promise."

I'd always wanted to hear those words from my friends in the context that Opal now had them. Saying them to her, I could live vicariously.

Smiling tightly, she put her gaze back on her twiddling thumbs.

I pressed my lips together. That was okay. I guess finals week, secrets we felt pressured to keep to ourselves, and the overwhelming stress of hiding our identities had left us exhausted beyond the comfort of a close friend for now.

My phone graciously buzzed, and I took it out from my backpack's side pocket. Looking down at the screen, I was thankful that Cara's and Steven's messages were now attached to a *name* and no longer an anonymous number stalking me.

C: Hope finals week is going well! You got this!

S: And if it's not going well we have "overly frosted" cinnamon rolls waiting for ya

I inwardly smiled. *He will never let that go.*

That night, Sarah, Breanne, and I had every textbook and notebook we owned sprawled out in front of us. Breanne's laptop sat on the desk in the corner of the room between her notes, and Sarah's phone rested on her lap as she sat on her bed. I had mine in front of me on the purple circle rug in the middle of the room. Bedtime was half an hour away and our fingers had blisters from writing, but we kept scribbling like our grades depended on it (because they did).

Eventually, I exhaled and gave my eyes a break, stretching out my legs. I looked up at a hyper-focused Breanne softly clicking her tongue in concentration, and then went to Sarah. Her pear-green eyes were stuck on one of her textbooks, her mauve lips pressed into a tight, thin line. Her flawless bronze cheek rested in her hand again.

Sarah *never* touches her face because it causes acne, but her hand had taken more trips there this semester than Alexa had taken to kidnap me since she entered my life (including when she was Hunter). Like Breanne had told me in the Grand Foyer a couple of months ago, something was wrong and had been since the start of the semester. But even now, Breanne and I weren't brave enough to be direct and ask. Sarah had changed the subject every other time we'd even hinted at it—meaning it was bad enough for Sarah Duncan, of all girls, to hide from.

"Studying's a lot easier when you're not staring, Em." She kept her intent gaze on her book, the words shattering the dead silence that had enveloped us since we'd gotten back from dinner.

An apology was missing from my lips. I couldn't apologize for my concern anymore.

Just as I opened my mouth to speak, my eyes snagged on the glisten in Sarah's eyes. Part of me knew she wanted me to ignore it, to at least pretend that I didn't see anything—but I've never been able to ignore my family's pain, even for their sake.

"No," Breanne whispered to me from the desk, so gently that I had to meet her gaze to make sure that she'd actually said something to me. Earlier this semester, I'd had to persuade *her* to wait on asking, but our roles had switched within a second.

The girl's crying, I told myself. And with that, Sarah's anger wasn't an obstacle for me anymore.

I looked back at her. "What's wrong?"

Her eyes, lined with thin black eyeliner and tears, rose to mine. For a second, I wanted to regret the question, but her well-being was more important.

"I'm stressed," she replied simply. She looked back down at her textbook. "Study."

I didn't take my stare away, and hers began to blink rapidly. A tear dripped onto her page.

Only twice in Sarah Duncan's life has she willingly broken down in front of me. The first was her fourteenth birthday, when someone at the mall accidentally spilled their beetroot smoothie on the dress she'd been saving for the day *and* the spa had closed down—only for her parents to tell her when we got back to her house that the bakery would be a day late on the cake. The second time was freshman year, the night that Breanne's ex-boyfriend went to jail: Sarah's rage had finally subsided to sympathetic pain and she cried with Breanne. And if tonight was going to be the third time, it would be because of me—but if she was suffering, I couldn't let her do that alone. I was her best friend for a reason!

"Just study," she whispered. "Let me fail in peace."

I recalled those words from every other Callistro Girl today, and it was only Monday. "Please, not you, too—"

Dragon-like eyes shot up to mine. "Yes, me, too!" she snapped, her bed creaking as she leaned forward. "Actually, just me! Your mom's class is the only one I'm not struggling in! I have three C's and two B's, and if I manage to pass ANY of the AP exams, it'll be the best early birthday present ever!"

Breanne and I couldn't help the glance in the other's direction: THREE C's? We didn't even know Sarah had *a* C!

"So I'm sorry if I'm stressed out of my mind because I'm probably gonna fail my finals and get the lowest grade in the history of my school for freak geniuses, but I'll do my *absolute* best to accommodate you and change into whatever smiley personality you're used to! Happy?"

A fuzzy silence trailed her last word. I didn't feel safe looking at Sarah anymore—yet it felt like that was the best thing I *could* do then, especially when she flung the textbook off of her bed and buried her face into her hands. She raggedly drew in airy sob after airy sob, tears saturating each one.

I swallowed, my fingers tracing the edges of my locket. At Sarah's next exhale, my own tears brimmed in my eyes. I hadn't known that the situation ran *this* deep, that it was beyond a simple unloading. I'd just wanted to comfort her, I hadn't meant for any of this...

I stood up from the floor and carefully made my way to her bed. Words felt dangerous as I sat myself next to her and tried to wrap my arm around her, but she threw me off.

"Don't." She sniffed, then wiped her eye with the ball of her hand, smearing her mascara and eyeliner. "Don't—don't baby me like that."

My head caught back, breath hitching in my throat. "I wasn't trying to—I'm sorry."

Dull green eyes stared ahead at the closet door. I'd never seen them so heavy in the almost ten years I'd known the girl. She tiredly shook her head. "Don't bring it up. Just forget it."

I locked stares with Breanne again. Behind closed, thin lips, she ground her teeth, her doe-like eyes steady. She was already theorizing, but I wasn't going to hold my breath. Sarah Duncan has always been more cut out for the Hunter game than the two of us; her ability to keep a secret—and a cover—is a testament to that.

CHAPTER

FOUR

*S*ince when is the wall on my left side? Did Sarah and Breanne rotate my bed in the middle of the night again?

Realizing that the wall ran all the way down to my closet door in front of me—and upon the twisting of my bedroom doorknob—I sat up in bed. My bed. Not the one in my dorm—home.

I'm not supposed to be back home yet. What happened to–?

Flash.

Alexa Delphine, red hair and emerald eyes and all, stood in the middle of my bedroom with a black cloak around her shoulders. A Grand Hunter was standing in my bedroom.

—catch me that quickly.—

A shudder crawled through me at her voice in my head. Her

next words were cut off by another flash.

She had my wrists. She was dragging me out of bed, and I was kicking at her with every pull.

"Are you really gonna make—?"

Flash.

I thrashed in Alexa's grasp in the middle of my room, screaming for Momma. A gloved hand clamped down over my mouth, but the word still ruptured from my throat.

"Shut up!" Alexa hissed. "You—"

Flash.

"—of my daughter—!"

Momma crumpled to my carpet, her satin pajamas reflecting the moonlight from my bedroom window.

Instinct urged my feet to trip Alexa standing behind me, but another flash cut me off.

"Good night, Atera."

With a single prick to my neck, strength drained from my limbs. Alexa picked me up, stepping toward my bedroom door.

"Dad…!" I cried, using the last of my strength. "Dad—!"

My eyes closed, thrusting me awake.

Wednesday. Wednesday morning. Wednesday morning. It was Wednesday morning.

Those words beat like a drum in my head as I shot up in bed. Either because those words were the only part of reality that I had and that meant that they were safe, or they reflected something just as emotionally scarring as my nightmare—vision—whatever: Momma's final was now one day away.

What if that *had* been a vision? I was a hybrid wielder of magic, and I'd already had one vision this year that had come true!

What if that was warning me about what was going to happen after the final tomorrow? Or what if I just had the setting wrong and Alexa was going to steal me straight from the hunt?

Wednesday.

Believe it or not, until that early morning, I'd never used a sleeping spell on myself before; I'd never felt the need or overwhelming curiosity to, but there was no way I was getting back to sleep otherwise. And I needed as much sleep as I could get for this week.

†

I can't believe this.

Day one of finals hadn't been *awful*—but Thursday morning, it seemed like the end of the school year was determined to taint the image of the white gazebo in Capperson Park. It had never loomed so large as Momma stood tall on the top step and gazed down at her class—in our casual clothes for once—on the grass. Casual clothes, though, did nothing to alleviate the tension in my chest. In fact, wearing the reminder of what life would look like if I weren't a magician kind of made everything worse.

"This is quite literally your biggest hunt of the year, ladies." Momma's voice carried over to just us, even though it didn't matter because of the empty park. "You have the entire town of Capperson, the Callistro Forest, and the school at your disposal. The only place off limits is the forest on the other side of town.

"As you know, the best Hunters fully understand their targets. That means they understand what it's like to be hunted—they know exactly what goes through their targets' minds when they're trying to escape. That's why today, ladies, you become the hunted. Your mission is to simply not get caught: if you have no means of escape, you're done."

I'd been grateful for the cloudiness of today because it meant a cool morning. Now? The gray sky and tepid breeze weren't exactly contributing to an exciting atmosphere.

"However," Momma added, "I recommend identifying your Hunter as soon as you can. It'll make avoiding them that much easier. Meanwhile, I'll be taking note of your progress and checking in with our agents. They're the ones reporting back to me the quality of your work in detail. But be careful with your Hunter, ladies."

Why? We're just teenage girls.

"They're federal agents for a reason."

A chaotic chorus of gasps and "What?" rippled through us. We turned to each another like one of us was a wolf in sheep's clothing and we were trying to figure out who before we were eaten.

Sarah, next to me in a mint-green sweater dress, raised her hand. "We're being hunted by *real* Hunters? Not our classmates?"

"Yes, Miss Duncan," Momma replied, only affording one nod. "One per Callistro Girl. The school hired them specifically for this final, meaning you'll be given the most accurate simulation of what it's like to live as your enemy."

Yeah—*no kidding!* What was next? She was going to tell me that Alexa was the Hunter assigned to me?

My nightmare from Tuesday night flashed in my memory. I barely suppressed a gasp in time. Alexa had tried to take me from my bed in my childhood home—what if I *had* gotten the setting wrong? What if it was going to happen here, after all?

"I'll be at the school ten minutes before class ends," Momma said next, straightening. "It's your job to get back on time. Once you check in with me, you'll pass."

She turned around, to the table in the middle of the gazebo, and grabbed the black box of earpieces sitting on it. The same table my friends and I had used for my birthday celebration last year, and that Jak and I had shared afterschool snacks on.

Chills.

"The second I give you your earpiece, your hunt begins."

I'd dealt with Alexa and William for what felt like my entire sophomore year. This hunt shouldn't have had my stomach in knots and chest on fire with anxiety, but it did. The grade did. And if a real Hunter caught me using magic for whatever reason, a passing grade wouldn't be the only thing I'd lose today.

A proud smile lifted the corners of Momma's lips. "It's been a privilege teaching you all this year, ladies. Work hard, remember your training, and have a great summer."

She started with Ava Baleen. Then Teresa Darci. Then Jackie Cortez. And she went down the line until Breanne was gone, then Elizabeth Moody, then Sarah. Then me.

"You'll do great, baby girl."

"Mom..." I said, too quietly, too timidly, for her daughter. "This isn't what we planned. This isn't what you signed me up for when you told me—"

"Yes, Emma. It is." She held up my earpiece. "I brought you to the Callistro Academy to prepare you for the real world—for what you're destined to run into throughout your life. To train you for a life of being hunted so you'll be able to survive without me one day."

I hesitantly took the earpiece from her like it would explode the second I touched it.

"This is the everyday life your people endure. Now it's time for you to see exactly what they go through."

"I already *have*. I—I don't know."

"Trust me," she said, bringing my eyes to look up into hers—her hopeful, brave, and confident eyes that were promising me that things would be okay. "I wouldn't put you through this if I knew you weren't ready."

I brought the earpiece up to my ear and secured it, turning it on.

Momma just as quickly brought her hand up to it and muted it. "You can do this," she whispered. "You've been through much harder. And a lot worse."

I stared up at her—beautiful Momma with amber eyes, chestnut hair I'd been fortunate enough to inherit, skin as warm as her heart, and a confidence I still envied. For the first time since I started my sophomore year, I saw her as my teacher instead of my mother. And that was how I knew exactly how much she believed in me.

I swallowed at the thought of going. That vision. Knowing that my dreams could actually be visions of the possible future, no part of me wanted to risk that nightmare coming to pass today. Unfortunately, I didn't have a choice.

I took a deep breath in, unmuted my earpiece, and then ran through the field for the town square.

CHAPTER

FIVE

Nothing else was known about this hunt besides our mission. We'd been thrown into it with no manual or warning beforehand, just like how it would be out there.

I didn't know when Capperson High was having their finals or if they already had, but considering that it was 8:30 on a Thursday morning, the streets and town square were nearly vacant. Most kids were in school, most parents were at work, and most people were at their jobs. There weren't many pedestrians to blend in with, but it wasn't like I'd be guaranteed that luxury in the real world, either.

I skipped the main shopping center and went straight for the lot where the mall was. Still all good in my peripheral vision, even as I reached the front entrance. A mild breeze blew through my hair as I opened the glass door and started down the right side of the center aisle. Clothing, jewelry, and kids' stores passed by on my way to the elevator. I'd yet to hear footsteps, and yet to see anything change in my peripheral.

"Miss Lowe," Momma began in my ear, "why did that jogger set you off guard?"

Oh, right—our outfits had hidden cameras that let Momma see everything we did.

She still can't stop me from using magic—or "cheating", as she liked to call it.

"She's wearing a purple tank top that's sheer in the sun," Hannah replied, almost whispering. "There's a black strand around her waist underneath it. It's too thick to be anything else but a utility belt. And she has headphones in, but the wire is tucked away and her phone is nowhere to be seen."

Momma said nothing. On this hunt, she was only focused on whether we had the right answers to her questions.

The "up" button stayed lit as the steel elevator doors opened in front of me. I walked inside, pressed the button to the second floor, and almost got away scot-free before a man in a denim coat and cargo pants caught the doors. I nearly jumped back, leaning on the steel railing behind me. He flashed me a smile and said the most casual "hi there" I'd ever heard.

I failed, I thought. *I failed. I failed, I failed—*

"Come on, Dustin," the man called to his left, holding the elevator doors open. "You're making someone wait."

I never thought I'd be so grateful to be referred to as just "someone" as a little boy in a red T-shirt and shorts trotted into the elevator. The man stepped inside after him.

Then the wave of relief was over. And it was a tsunami of awkwardness.

It wasn't my first time experiencing the "elevator" moment, but I'm pretty sure it's one of those things that you never get used to. Just as Momma had said earlier this semester, schools like the Callistro Academy aren't built to help us get used to the worst moments of our careers; they're built to help dull the shock from them as much as possible.

Still, I made a mental note to propose a "most awkward social situations" chapter for next year.

The doors finally dragged open. The man allowed me out first, holding his son by the shoulders. I nodded a polite thank-you and stepped out, the food court sitting in front of me.

What am I supposed to do now?

I wasn't at the mall to shop or browse or even pretend that I was. Somehow, *I* had become the one hunting my Hunter. Shouldn't they have shown up by now? Was I really complaining that they hadn't?

I tuned in to the blenders mixing smoothies, a couple of people discussing their upcoming meetings, the footsteps walking in and out of the food court and down the center aisle of the mall, my own steps as I headed into the food court...

A beeping watch from a customer sitting in front of the Chinese restaurant I was about to pass.

I changed directions and started walking the width of the food court, toward the tables in the center. I took a seat a couple of rows back and diagonally across from the man with short black hair and a Bluetooth in his left ear, dressed in jeans and a brown leather jacket. With his back to me, he looked down at his watch like he was checking the time. I rested my elbow on the table and leaned forward, letting myself relax.

The intervals of the beeping changed every few seconds; the watch was a tracker, or at least a sensor detecting how close his target was to the receiver. He wasn't hunting me; he was hunting one of my classmates.

The blue light on his earpiece blinked on. A few seconds later, he said, "Yep, I gave her a brief run-through of the movie this morning."

The Language of Ambiguity, chapter three: using a play on words to flat out say what you mean. Hunters will either use words that are synonymous to the ones they mean, or they'll use the actual word but it'll be hidden in a bigger word or phrase.

The only person he could be reporting to right now was Momma. "Her" had to mean a Callistro Girl—his target. "Run-through" meant that she'd just run or walked by something. "Movie", based on context, had to mean the movie theater. Time unit conversion can vary, but right now, I had to assume that "this morning"—the current time—meant a second or minute ago.

After all, even though it was Momma on the other line, who would say "My target just walked by the movie theater a second ago" in public?

I kept my mouth shut and breathing even. He wasn't the Hunter who'd been assigned to me, but he was nonetheless a Hunter who could catch me and make me flunk.

"Sure. I'll get on it tomorrow," he said. The light on his Bluetooth switched off.

I can't leave while his attention is on his mission.

I looked dead ahead of me at the smoothie stall, where an employee was blending another order. After a prayer that she'd forgive me, I waited until she took her hand off the lid to move a strand of blond hair out of her face. My telekinesis popped the lid clean off.

A fountain of sunset orange erupted from the blender. The employee sprang back, grabbing the attention of what few people were scattered around the food court. Juice splattered across the counters, and the short woman who had ordered it.

Hunter (a nickname permanently ruined for me) sprang up like the explosion had been an attack meant for him.

"Ma'am, I am *so* sorry!" the employee exclaimed, grabbing a bunched handful of napkins from behind the counter and giving them to the customer. "I'm so sorry, is there anything I can—?"

"No, no, you're fine." The short woman chuckled awkwardly, accepting a napkin just as Hunter arrived. "I have accidents all the time at work. I'm a nurse, so something always manages to stick to me."

"Are you okay, miss?" Hunter asked, taking a few offered napkins and wiping blended fruit from the woman's neck.

I tuned out the rest, waiting until the passerby continued with their lives. With Hunter's back still to me, helping the employee clean the pick-up counter, I made a beeline for the elevator.

Huh, I couldn't help but think as the doors slid open again. I pressed the downward arrow. Who knew a Hunter could be such a gentleman?

Probably because he was the closest one around to help. He'd probably been scouting and making sure that a Callistro Girl wasn't trying anything funny, but any other thought was comforting at this point.

I walked out of the elevator back on the first floor and actually pondered what to do next. Momma had recommended identifying our Hunter ASAP to help us escape more easily, but how was I supposed to do that if I still wasn't being hunted?

Well, I'm not gonna wait *for them to find me here.*

I continued down the center aisle, taking note of the window reflections as I walked. A few months ago, Jak had caught his father in the Forever 21 window right before I went to help Ava Baleen escape three rotten teenage boys—I didn't want to make the same mistake twice and miss something in the reflections.

What about... the back exit that led to the alley? And it'd be my most discreet path back to the square.

I looked down at the watch Momma had warned us to wear today: a little less than an hour and a half to go before the end of the period. For a second, I thought about heading back to Callistro and hiding in the underground secret passageways the whole time. Seriously. I mean, I'd played the hunted last September and played Hunter for the first half of this semester! Every single day was already a fight to protect myself no matter what I did. An hour and a half was plenty of time for my assigned Hunter to find me if I stayed out in the open. I wanted that break, I wanted the *rest.*

Could I...?

Sighing, I shook the thought away. It had felt like cheating during the first hunt we'd ever had this semester, and it would definitely be cheating for the final. I couldn't be so unfair to my classmates. They were taking this test, too, and they didn't have an easy way out like I did.

Reaching the Kohl's at the back of the mall, I turned right

and into the hallway that led to the emergency exit. I pushed open the heavy door, the cold morning air carrying a breeze of sulfur-like odor. Heat was caught at the tail end of it, hinting at summer just around the corner. I reminded myself of the time I had left for the most difficult part of the week, and then I only had three more finals before my sophomore year would come to an end.

Wow.

I don't know why I'd expected to pass through this area without pausing. I'd stood in this same alley mere months ago and fought off a sinister group of boys who'd taken Ava Baleen hostage. The leader of which had been a magician and implied things I only wrote down in my last journal because I couldn't forget them but didn't want to keep them inside.

I shoved the memory down. That wasn't why I was here.

I sneaked down the alley and then around the back area of the mall. Nobody was around, but I hid behind the dumpsters and semitrucks unloading into Kohl's like a kid with a wild imagination. It wasn't like I'd have the opportunity to do this again—at least, not somewhat recreationally—any time soon. The school year was *over*. Despite the eternal days, it had flown by, and I was already facing my first real summer vacation.

The whole Alexa business actually fit into just one school year... Wow. And now I wasn't even sure if I'd ever get a semester without her. What if I ended up spending the rest of high school with her in my life? Would she really drag this out for that long?

Where had she been ever since I'd almost strangled her in the forest a couple of months ago?

I rounded a corner, turned left, and faced another back area. The garage for semitrucks was next to me, dumpsters sitting on my right. The large garage doors were all closed and nobody was around. With my peripheral vision still clear, I took the liberty to walk straight across...

Something was wrong.

A mass moved in the corner of my right eye. I whirled around just as a figure emerged from behind the dumpster and darted toward me.

I shifted my weight and threw a jab toward their nose. They parried with their left hand, grabbing my earpiece with their right. Just as I was ready to swing my leg to trip them, my mind identified his features. In the same second, Jak grabbed my hand and started dragging me back the way I'd come.

"What're you doing here?!"

We weaved in and out of the rows of vans, trucks, and boxes—but all Jak did was shush me. We stopped, facing an exit in the fence gate on our left that would take us into a dry field. The Callistro Forest lay just beyond it. Up ahead was the alley leading to the emergency exit door.

"You need to hide." Jak glanced between our two options, but it wasn't his words that scared me: it was the trace of worry in his tone that I'd hardly ever heard before. Like he was *actually* afraid that I wasn't safe. "I know you're taking your final right now, I know the school hired these Hunters, but you need to tell your mom that there are people here"—he glanced left at the field and kept his gaze there, like he'd made his decision—"who shouldn't be."

"How did you—what're you—?"

I couldn't finish before he shoved my earpiece back into my hand and then dragged me left, out into the open field. Instantly, we headed right, back in the direction of town square.

I barely managed to secure my earpiece back in and unmute it before Mom's anxious voice cut through. "Emma?"

Right. She was seeing Jak through the camera on my jacket button. That couldn't look good.

She sounds worried, too, I thought as we sprinted down an alley between two shops and came out into the east side of the square. *Does she know what's going on?*

"Mom," I said, "are you still in contact with the Hunters?"

The cloudy sky didn't inhibit the sun shining down onto the square. Fifty feet away, the water in the fountain winked in the light, but I couldn't shake the dark atmosphere that had de-scended—because Jak squeezing my hand right now wasn't him being cryptic or romantic. He was scared. And his fear was what I could trust most about him then because Jakson Bleu doesn't get scared unless something is actually wrong.

"I just checked in," Momma replied, impatience swelling in her voice. "They're all on track, but that doesn't tell me why Jak is there!"

I glimpsed him surveying our surroundings, at the few people walking around the square. In a situation like this, though, one witness was too many if we were caught in a fight.

As if running on nothing but instinct now, Jak let go of my hand and stepped toward the street, craning his neck to gaze down the road. The sunrays poking through the clouds beat down on my head as I glanced at the water in the fountain. I wondered if Momma was still in the park as I told her, "Jak says there are other people here."

Her voice lowered in my ear. "Emma. Magic is necessary."

She didn't need to tell me twice: *Prospectus.*

A bird's-eye view of the square projected itself in my head, exposing its layout—and the all-black figures hiding all across it. Whether on a roof or around an alley corner, they were all closing in on us.

Jak was right. He'd been spying on me, he'd known that they were coming. He knew that I wasn't safe.

I wondered if he'd seen something down the road, because just as I muted myself again, he spun back around and grabbed my hand. "Come on!" he exclaimed. Desperation clawed at his words, like he was begging me to run faster as we started down the alley we'd just come from.

There are Hunters down here!

"Jak, no—!"

We were halfway down when he yelped and grabbed his shoulder, dropping to the ground.

Six

"Jak!" I cried as I kneeled next to him, his back against the brick wall. My eyes snagged on the sedative dart that had sunk deep into his shoulder—as in the-needle-wasn't-even-visible deep.

"Go!" He panted, eyes fluttering as he tried to keep himself awake. "Emma, go, *now!*"

Two Hunters dropped down in front of us from the roof. Black masks covered half of their faces, matching suits concealing their arsenals. In a blur, one pinned me to the wall by my arms while another shoved a rag over my mouth.

I kicked back the guy pinning me, slamming her into the other wall. My elbow flew into the one with the rag, and I prayed that my knuckles wouldn't crack as I threw an uppercut at them.

Jak tripped the woman from his spot on the ground. I flung the man's head against the wall he'd held me against, knocking him out. When Jak missed the second time, the woman and another agent shoved his arms behind his back.

"Emma!" he cried with a wavering voice. His round brown eyes alone were begging me to listen to him. "GO!"

Please stay awake!

He rammed the woman into the wall while I sprinted out of the alley, back in the direction of the town square. The public suddenly felt a lot safer.

"This can't..." I whispered beneath my breath as I sprinted through the square, desperate to get back to the park and the gazebo. I'd seen those faces in the alley before. I'd seen them in my worst nightmares when I was little and I dreamed of Hunters capturing me and my parents. I'd seen them in the nightmares that had terrorized me the month after my sixteenth birthday. I'd seen them the day I met Alexa for the first time, and I'd seen them when she came for me at the carnival last year.

"Marie?" Amelia Baker whispered in my ear. "Is that you?"

Shoot. She can't see any of this!

"Emma," Momma stated. "What's going on?"

I fumbled unmuting my earpiece. "The hunt is breached," I said as I glanced around the edge of the square, daring the other Hunters to show themselves. The dose of the gas from the rag was just enough to make me dizzy and drag me down with tiredness, but I didn't know if it was enough to eventually knock me out. I had to get every piece of information I had (which weren't a lot) to Momma as soon as possible.

I approached the sidewalk, looking both ways down the

street. "Some of these people aren't just Hunters, they're from—"

On the left side of the street, a black sedan with a tinted windshield sped down. The closer it drew, the more it slowed—like it was planning to pick up something as it went.

"Emma, keep talking to me!" Momma demanded. "The Hunter cameras are going down one by one, where's Jak?"

I didn't answer, sprinting across the street. The last thing the car was probably expecting was for me to cross, and these people wanted me *alive*—as far as I knew and hoped.

The sedan flew into a U-turn and headed in my direction again, but I darted into the alley between two shops and ran as far down as my palpitating heart would let me go. When I turned left and down another alley, it was beating too fast, too hard, for me to keep going. My chest was on fire. My legs had turned into Jell-O. My head felt ready to implode, my breath unable to slow.

None of it mattered—I was at a dead end, stuck between two doors.

Cara and Steven, I thought. But I refused to risk their safety, too, especially since Cara was due in only a few months.

"Mom?"

No response.

"Hello? Mom!"

Footsteps beat down the alley. When I turned around, a man with red hair and glasses was coming straight for me.

I glanced between the two doors: the one on the left belonged to a toy store, and the one on the right led to the mechanic. I really didn't want to scar any children today, so I turned to the mechanic door and closed my eyes.

Exsolvo.

I swung open the unlocked door and dashed inside.

A long hallway with beige walls and concrete floors stretched out in front of me. With no time to stop and smell the roses (or the awesome rubbery smell of new tires), I hurried all the way down the hall, passing an open, empty office. The garage door stood dead ahead. I rounded the corner and pressed my back against the wall, just in time to hear the alley door open and footsteps approach.

I pictured the office door I'd passed: *Cado.*

The door clicked shut. I walked a few steps farther down the short hallway. Now in front of me sat the help desk and waiting room. And the floor-to-ceiling windows sandwiching the front door, putting me on display for the world to see.

"Good morning, miss," the middle-aged blonde at the desk said, leaning away from her desktop computer to look at me. "Can I do something for you?"

I glanced at the TV above her in the corner of the room. An episode of *The Flintstones* was playing. I couldn't help but wonder how many kids were safe at home watching it right now. Only two people sat in the padded chairs by the windows: a young brunette dully flipping through a magazine, and a businessman in a pressed suit having a quiet conversation on his phone.

Man, this place smells amazing.

"I just came in from the garage," I said, walking toward the front desk. I only had so much time before my Hunter would see that I wasn't in the office. "My mom wants to know if you guys do smog checks."

"No, I'm sorry, we don't," she told me sympathetically. "There's a place right next to the gas station down the street, I'm pretty sure they do."

Yep. Corner of Lincoln and Bark.

"I'll tell her, thanks!"

I turned around and left through the garage door at the end of the hallway. It was as nice of a break as any to play pretend, but I had to remember that the professionals were on my tail now. This wasn't a test anymore; I was out there.

"Good morning, miss." A lanky mechanic greeted me as he walked up, his navy cargo uniform stained with oil and grease. "What all are you looking for?"

"Hi, the woman at the front desk said there's a station down the street from here that does smog checks."

"Yep, next to the gas station on the corner of Lincoln and Bark."

"Thanks!"

I walked across the garage, needing a plan and needing it now. There had to be a place in Capperson that could offer even the slightest bit of safety! Didn't anyone else in this town build secret passageways or top-secret underground rooms to keep the enemy out?

When I stepped onto the sidewalk, the black sedan that had barreled toward me earlier was nowhere to be found—but I was out in the open and needed a hiding spot. I ran farther down, then across the street, and then into a café. There was a one-person bathroom at the end of the side hallway, where I promptly locked myself inside.

Finally, I could take my first few deep breaths. *I have to calm down. I can't freak out. I can't freak out, I'm literally not allowed to freak out.*

Whether that was Momma's rule or my own was another question that I didn't have the answer to.

"Emma," Mom finally said in my ear, "are you safe?"

She's okay. A breath of relief flooded out of me.

"For now," I whispered, trying to quiet my panting. "What's going on?"

"This wasn't supposed to happen. I've lost contact with the Hunters, I don't know where they are. The girls are freaking out."

I couldn't even begin to imagine. This wasn't new to me, but it was brand new to them.

"Did you see that black sedan?" I whispered, cursing the acoustics of the tiled bathroom.

"Yes."

"What about the guy chasing me down the alley?"

"Yes. That was your Hunter."

He finally found me.

I swallowed hard, fingers trembling as they gripped my locket. My body heat roared against the cold of the bathroom. "I lost him, but there are more. They caught Jak, they sedated him, I don't know how I'm gonna—"

"Requesting immediate backup!" Sarah cried in my ear, stealing a beat from my heart. "Stuck in the belly of the diamond, *under a spell!*"

It sounded crazy—to be honest, I didn't even know what she was talking about until she said "spell"—but the play-on-words method works. Sarah had just warned us that she was in the abandoned diamond mine (now a historical landmark) that was older than Capperson itself. We also now knew that it used to be a magician hideout. And a Hunter had run her into the ground.

"Sarah, what happened?" Momma asked as I opened the bathroom door.

"With all due—respect—Mrs. Marie," Sarah whispered, breathless, "I don't think we're—we're dealing with—friendly agents."

"I'm on my way," Elizabeth Moody replied. She sounded just as focused on her surroundings as I was as I paced to the end of the café's back hallway and turned right. "I think you're right," Elizabeth said. "I'm seeing them, too."

What? Wait, no—Hunters never reveal anything about themselves or their missions, let alone Grands! They're not supposed to expose themselves while they're on a mission!

But if they need help from an outside source, as exclusively rare as it is... they have no problem exposing their targets.

That can't be what Alexa's doing, can it? Would she really execute her plan right now of all times? Is this her plan?

She'd definitely been quiet long enough to *have* a plan, and that was enough to make me run.

Pushing open the backdoor of the café, I stumbled into another alley. I remembered exploring these alleyways when I was younger and then bringing Sarah and Breanne along with me so we could pretend to have an adventure. Now I couldn't stop expecting a Hunter to jump down from the roof and force a rag onto my face.

I could either go right and deeper into the alleyways, or I could go left and blend in with the public. After the black sedan, though, I wasn't convinced that these guys were worried about avoiding the public.

"Sarah," Momma said in my ear as I ran down the back alley,

"are you okay?"

I wondered what Momma saw then, if Sarah was stuck in a position where her camera was covered—because Sarah didn't respond.

No. Forget hiding. I had to help her.

I went back to the front of the café and stopped on the sidewalk. The field where the mine entrance should be was a straight shot from here, at the edge of the Capperson Forest. The one place we were forbidden to go...

Well, Breanne wasn't here to stop me from breaking the rules this time.

"I lost my tail about a minute ago." Teresa Darci's voice crackled in my earpiece. "I'm at the diamond. It's bare."

So the mine (or the entrance, at least) was empty.

I crossed the street and then sprinted to the field. Off to the right, at the edge of the forest, I caught Teresa checking her surroundings before taking off her cardigan.

"Sorry, Mrs. Marie," she said, walking to a tree and hanging the cardigan on one of the low-hanging branches. She briefly waved at one of the buttons.

"The Russo Diversion is a wise choice right now," Momma replied. "Go, be careful."

Teresa bolted to the mine entrance yards away.

I followed, pressing myself behind a tree at the edge of the forest. "The diamond is still bare on top. Requesting positions of backup."

"Passing the mountain range," Ava Baleen whispered (she was at the mountain bike store), "but I have a tail. She's waiting until I'm cornered."

"'She'?" Momma asked. "Ava, your assigned Hunter isn't…"

Alexa, I instinctually thought. *No, stop. Alexa wouldn't expose herself so carelessly.*

But then what if she's tailing me right now? What if this is when she's gonna come for me?

I forced myself to shake it all away. My best friend needed help.

The rusty metal door of the mine sat ajar. At that point, we'd learned to pick everything from the front door of a house to large industrial locks built to keep the country's most dangerous criminals out of the national bank, but the rusty remains of the mine's lock lay next to my feet like it had been kicked off. I slipped inside.

Dirt, pebbles, and dust fell from the ceiling as I crept farther in. My palpitating heart seemed to echo throughout the dead-quiet tunnel. At the end of it, a long, old wooden staircase sloped down.

I eased my foot onto the first step, the board pushing up against my weight with a surprisingly sturdy resistance. Discrepancy number one: after having at least three people walk down before me, the boards were way too durable to be three centuries old without maintenance. One of them would've broken by now, especially if Sarah had *run* down here to get away quickly.

I paused, cursed the fact that Mom wasn't a magician and couldn't hear telepathy, and then took a deep breath. "Mom? Are you okay?"

"I'm on my way, girls. Please, please be careful."

I swallowed and then forced myself to skulk down the rest of the steps, noting the multiple tunnels I passed. The temperature dropped and the atmosphere dampened with every step. Sarah had said that she was in the "belly", which had to mean the bottom of the mine.

"Walker and I are in," Elizabeth announced. "Both Hunters have disappeared."

"Something's wrong," I said, reaching the last step. "A few agents and a black sedan have come after me, I even saw a Redway Boy—"

I wasn't sure what was worse: that the mine had opened up and I was now in a room that branched off into five different tunnels, or the twelve other Callistro Girls saying, "Me, too!" in my ear.

My heart shoved itself into my throat. How was this possible? What was going on? Why was I starting to doubt that Alexa and William were actually behind this?

Elizabeth Moody and Caroline Walker approached behind me. I turned to them as I asked, "Which tunnel, Darci?"

"Far right," Teresa replied, the three of us following her directions. "Positioned under the dome."

We had no idea what she meant by that—I didn't even know if it was code. But we continued treading through the tunnel on the far right, passing wooden boards and receding walls. Dust rained down with every swift step we took, so abundant that it clung to our clothes and I had to suppress a couple of coughs.

Soon that dust and dirt gave way to stone, which constructed a kind of study area at the end. An old table sat against the stone wall in front of us, aged books, papers, and binders lying across it like carefully positioned props. Where there should've been a wall on our left, a wooden bridge stretched out instead to what looked like the end of a cavern. Two dusty armchairs sat in the center of the space, and a portrait of a colonial man hung on the wall in front of us.

He looks familiar...

"This *was* a hideout," Caroline whispered, slowly stepping farther in as she glanced around her. Her dirty-blond side braid had loosened, strands flying every which way atop her head. "I wonder if this guy founded it."

Elizabeth walked up to the portrait, her short black ponytail elegantly swaying. She leaned in toward the print in the bottom-right corner. "'John Melicent-Marie Atera, 1787'."

Wait. What?

I stared at the painted icy-blue eyes of the colonial man: slim face, oak-brown hair... This man was probably *Grandpa's* fifth-great grandfather! He founded a wielder hideout over two centuries ago? Decades after the mine opened?

This mine was Atera family history.

"Wow. An Atera founded this place," Elizabeth said, tracing her dark-brown fingers along one of the dusty armchairs. "They've been hiding for that long?"

A lot longer, I thought.

"Wait," Caroline stated, in the middle of the room and directly underneath a vintage lantern. Her hazel eyes dragged themselves up from the ground to us as she pushed a stray blond lock behind her ear. "Something's off. It's not pitch black in here."

Elizabeth and I looked up at the lantern hanging above Caroline's head. Looking down the tunnel we'd just come from, I realized that lanterns hung all the way down there, too. Each one was lit.

"Supposedly nobody's been here for decades," Caroline

mused. "So who turned on the lights?"

We surrendered to silence, glancing back and forth between one another.

I quickly shook my head, snapping myself out of it. "Darci, where are you?" I said into my earpiece, but nothing came back. "Darci?"

"Marie, Walker, and Moody," Amelia Baker cried, "I'm heading toward the diamond but I'm not alone. Callistro Girls, branch out and get ready for a phantom circle."

A phantom circle was the only Grand Hunter tactic Momma had taught us this year. A pack starts at the outskirts of their hunting area and slowly closes in around their target. They almost *try* to be seen before they disappear again, like a ghost, to put the target on high alert—to where they don't even realize that they're standing in the dead center of a Grand Hunter circle until it's too late.

In other words, we were spreading out.

Elizabeth turned with worried black eyes to me and Caroline. "Guys—"

"We'll be okay," Caroline whispered, like she wouldn't give herself the time to be afraid. She unmuted her earpiece. "Baker, once you're down, take the far left. I'll be next to you."

"And I'll be next to you," Elizabeth said, then facing me. "Will you be okay on your own here?"

"We were *supposed* to be on our own for the whole hunt." I offered her the best smile I could muster. "Hurry. I'll see you in a few minutes."

They went back down the tunnel, and I bolted to the bridge stretched out in front of me. The ground was only about six feet below, but Caroline's words were echoing and my mind was conjuring too many questions: why were the lights on? *How* were the lights on? Why were the staircase and bridge still in great shape? What had happened to my two classmates who'd gone completely silent after—?

After going the way I was going now?

Teresa went silent after telling us to go this way.

I stopped in the middle of the bridge and closed my eyes. *Prospectus.*

An image of the remainder of the opening burst through my head: someone was waiting for me at the end of the bridge, hiding behind a stone wall. Ready for me. If I knew enough about hunting at this point, they were listening for the sounds of my footsteps to know when to jump.

The opening at the end of the bridge gave way to a grand cavern, abundant with caves drilled into its sides and stalactites hanging from its ceiling. To my surprise, a lake lay across it, its bank on the far-left side. A staircase led down into the space from the end of the tunnel I was walking down now.

A cavern. "Dome".

My vision flew down the bridge in the other direction, into the tunnel Caroline and Elizabeth had run into. The spell showed me the room at the bottom of the stairs we'd taken to get here.

My Hunter had finally caught up. He was turning into the far-right tunnel, on his way to me.

SEVEN

own there! Down!

A small cave entrance sat in the trench below me, in the corner and hidden by a boulder. I took off my flats, slipped under the wooden railing, and jumped down the six-foot gap with my knees bent. Throwing myself behind the boulder, I slid inch by inch into the freezing cave. The only thing warning me of my Hunter's and the other Hunter's proximity was their footsteps resounding on the wood of the bridge.

I hid in the dark, prayed that there wasn't anything hibernating in here, and pressed my body tighter against the icy-cold stone wall. I covered my mouth, tight and strained breaths seeping through my fingers.

This is real. They're actually after us.

Calm down, calm down. I didn't know if I was telling my throbbing heart or myself, but it wasn't working on either.

I dragged my eyes to the opening of the cave. *Prospectus.*

My assigned Hunter now stood in the study area. The other agent, still standing on the bridge, motioned for my Hunter to go back the way he'd come. Turning around, they raced back to the stone wall they'd been hiding behind and then to the staircase leading down into the cavern.

I waited until both agents disappeared in the spell's vision before uncovering my mouth, letting my breath flood out of me.

Minutes passed of repeating the lookout spell until my Hunter and the one that had been waiting for me dropped their new hiding spots. Go figure, I managed to miss the timing of casting for the exact moment they left. If I wanted their new locations, I'd have to venture deeper into the mine.

I hate this. I hate this so much.

I dusted off the dirt and pebbles from my feet before slipping my flats back on. "Baker," I whispered into my earpiece, stepping out of the cave and into the trench.

I started to climb the wall, making my way up to where the second Hunter had been waiting for me. "Baker. Lowe, Shaw, is anyone still there?"

Fear prickled my every last nerve. Nobody was responding. "Mom?"

She'd gone silent long ago. I was alone.

This wasn't happening. This couldn't be happening. Where were my classmates? Where was my teacher? Where was Jak?

"If *anyone* can hear me," I whispered desperately, standing at the top of the staircase and looking down at the lake on the left side of the cavern, "the ocean—there's an ocean nearby. Come to shore."

Prospectus.

My mind projected an overview of the cavern: large and glorious in all its creation and natural state. Stone and rock built the walls and floors. Misshapen boulders and caves dotted it on the first and second floor. The lake glistened even in the dim light, its water scarcely rippling as people dressed in black came marching down its sides—

Oh no.

I darted into a nearby tunnel, reaching the entrance just as the Hunters arrived at the other side. They stormed into every hidden tunnel, throwing boulders of every size aside in an attempt to find someone.

No, I realized bitterly. *Me. I'm the only one left.*

Prospectus.

This wasn't right, there were too many of them. There were exactly...

One, two, three, four, five—

No—there weren't *enough.* Nine Hunters, ten Callistro Girls.

I was pretty sure I'd even caught the face of the Hunter I'd seen at the mall. He'd changed outfits to match the uniform the rest of them had on. But when I'd found the redheaded man making his way toward me while I was on the bridge, he was still in a suit...

Where was *my* Hunter? And why wasn't he dressed like the other agents?

"Please, if anyone can hear me!" I whispered-screamed, scurrying down the tunnel before turning left. "Requesting backup, stand on top of the diamond—"

Turning down another tunnel, I slammed into a tall figure.

No. This was it. I was caught, I'd been caught by—

"Jak!"

His bottom lip had been busted open. A bruise was forming on his cheek, and blood peeked through his white dress shirt on the front of his shoulder.

He didn't seem to care about any of that as he whispered, "You tracked them down here, too?"

"What? You were tracking my class?"

With a curt sigh, he grabbed my hand and pulled me down the tunnel. "No," he said, stopping at an intersection. He glanced left and right but never at me. "I was tracking mine."

"Redway *is* here?"

"To our surprise, too," he replied, pulling me right. "Last I heard from Wyatt, he was heading down the third tunnel in the main entrance. But he's gone silent since, so has everyone else."

"All the Hunters are in the cavern." Dirt drizzled down despite my quiet voice. "But they came from the other side of the lake. Our friends have to be there, in, like, a hidden room or—"

Jak spun around. Before I could open my mouth to ask, he cupped my face with his hands, pressed his lips together with a wince, and then met them with mine. Blood smeared across the left side of his mouth as he released his lips, and those round brown eyes flamed with an angry determination.

"In case they rip us apart when they catch us."

"You think they're gonna catch—?"

He grabbed my hand again and started dragging me down the tunnel, which was just as well. I was pretty sure that I didn't actually want the answer to that question.

"Did you get any hints from Adrien or Wyatt?" I asked.

"Wyatt said there was a lake inside a cavern. We never heard from him again after that."

"But we're upstairs."

"So we go down."

He started bounding down a flight of stairs with me right on his heal. Momma's voice resonated through my head with every step: *Make yourself lighter and move with your knees, not your whole leg. Lean slightly forward. Embrace the momentum you build and use it to stop yourself from hesitating. Balance. Center of gravity.*

When we reached the bottom, we were standing at the lake on the other side. The bank traveled a few yards up and gave way to a rocky slope that transitioned to the second floor of the cavern.

Creeping up to the edge of the bank, we looked out. Giant stalactites hung from the ceiling, dripping water onto the lake. The walls and ledges around us seemed to be closing in as Jak and I shared a glance, and one thought with it: we were running out of time.

His eyes traveled far somewhere behind me. "Merlin," he whispered, pointing at a torch—not a lantern—mounted next to another cave entrance on the second floor.

"Discrepancy," I noted.

We stalked up the slope, my hand still in Jak's as we hurried to the wall and pressed our backs against them. I followed his lead in inching closer and closer to the cave entrance. The second we were close enough, we dashed inside.

I tried my earpiece one last time. "Cortez? Duncan?"

"McRein," Jak whispered, gently tapping his own earpiece as

if to wake it up. "Zhang, Charles—!"

"Emma?"

I froze. I knew that voice. I'd grown up with the warm quality of that voice, but not once had I ever heard the terror my mother had spoken my name with until that morning. That wasn't her, that couldn't have been her.

"Jak." I grabbed his arm with a firm hand, staring into the dark room we faced.

He stopped, his concern scanning me like I was having a panic attack. I was almost ready to. Then, he turned his stare to the black room.

A single lightbulb turned on in the center of the ceiling, leaving the outskirts dark. It hung directly over my mother, who was tied to a chair.

"Mom!" I cried, ready to run, but Jak held me back in the entryway like he knew what she was about to say.

"Go back, Emma!" she exclaimed. "Get back to the school, go get help—!"

"Nobody at Callistro has the authority to stop this," another voice—another familiar voice—rumbled from the shadows.

My Hunter emerged from the back of the room, tall and proud. Thin black-rimmed glasses now concealed his deep-set brown eyes, with strawberry-blond hair that sat gelled back on his head. A jawline strong enough to cut a diamond drew attention to the burn scar on the left side of his face—and, well, not to be judgmental, but the man had quite a nose on him.

His gray suit only boasted his triumph as he smiled at me and said, "Good morning, Miss Marie. Looks like we'll be recruiting you and Mr. Bleu, after all."

"What?" I spat, fighting to sound more angry than terrified.

"You're the only ones who *found* this room instead of being taken to it. Unlike your classmates—"

Rage shoved me forward, but Jak kept a firm hold on my wrist. "Where are they?" I exclaimed.

"Easy!" Almost perfectly white teeth gleamed at me. "They'll be sent back to the school, and they won't remember anything about today. Actually, they're watching us right now." He pointed at the cameras positioned in all four corners of the room. "Say hello!"

"Are you kidding me?" Jak snapped. "This was a recruitment gig? You're telling me this whole final is just to find new young agents?"

"Fine." My Hunter briefly rolled his sharp eyes. "This was never really a test for your class so much as it was for the two of you."

He prowled around my mother, who kept glancing back and forth between the three of us. I hated how much she resembled the woman Marcus had tied to a chair earlier this year in her and Dad's first home.

"Before the schools converted to strictly self-defense instruction, they hired real Hunters every year for the spring hunting final. It's a win-win situation: the school accurately tests the competence of the students, and we're able to scout for fresh talent."

"How does that give you the right to tie up my mom and kidnap our friends?" I spat. "Why were Jak and I singled out?"

"We received an anonymous tip at the beginning of the year that we had two particularly skillful agents-in-training this year at Redway and Callistro."

I cursed the nausea that tossed my stomach left and right, that set my nerves on fire, that dropped my throbbing heart to the floor as my Hunter took off his glasses—and scar. His contacts came next, revealing diamond-blue irises underneath.

"And that anonymous tip"—the headmaster of the Callistro Academy threw his red wig to the ground and finished with the fake nose—"was me."

EIGHT

That was how he'd found me so easily after losing his tail on me: magic. That was how he so pristinely played his role as the headmaster of a Hunter school while protecting his identity at the same time. That was why he'd gotten so close to my family...

Was that why he had risked his life in the beach house fire to save me and my dad?

No. I didn't believe it. I *couldn't* believe it! He wouldn't do this to me, he'd *never* be this cruel to me!

"You're lying," I said, stunned beyond my ability to process. "You'd never do this, this isn't you."

"Oh, really?" Mr. Dawson said curiously, cocking his head to the side. "Really?"

I stared at the man in front of me like I no longer knew him—because he was actually suggesting that I didn't. This wasn't who he was. He wasn't evil, he was a magician—

He was a magician. Telepathy.

—Come on. What's going on?—

He smirked. He'd heard me, and he was smirking. Not in his I'm-proud-of-you-for-figuring-it-out way, but in an it's-cute-that-you-think-I'm-joking way.

No, he couldn't... Was he...? He wouldn't—!

I listened to my surroundings, praying that my senses would give me an answer of some kind. Silence echoed off the walls and pierced my ears with a vile, taunting ringing.

Mr. Dawson wasn't telling me that things would be okay, that this was an act. He wasn't telling me that none of this was true, that my mother and classmates weren't in danger.

—Mr. Dawson...?—

He rolled his eyes. "I think we need a recap." He rested his hands on the back of the chair Momma was tied to. A knife twisted in my gut. "You have an army of ten Master Hunters on one side,"—Jak and I turned our heads at the agents coming up behind us—"and a Grand and helpless Master on the other—"

Wait. *What?*

"You're *not* a Grand Hunter." Momma scoffed, turning her head as much as she could to meet his eyes. "You were never... No, we became Masters together—"

"Amy, you're tied to a chair with *two* sophomore classes that couldn't even pass a high school final, and your daughter and her boyfriend are about to be taken to a professional agency for recruitment. You really think I'd lie about this right now?"

"That's not true!" I said, turning to Jak. "Jak, that's not true, he's not...! This is an act, he's always been—!"

"Em," he muttered, glancing at the group of Hunters behind us blocking our exit. "I don't—I don't know. I don't even know if we're still taking a test."

"Emma, come on," Mr. Dawson said in a familiar manner that made me shrivel up inside. He used that casual tone with me during mentoring sessions to alleviate the pressure, to encourage me to try a failed spell again. Now he was using it to manipulate me. "I've known you for your entire life. You were practically *born* for this career, I'm just giving you a leg up."

I stuttered with every word that came to mind. Why was he doing this? Why was he just now revealing that he'd been a Grand Hunter this *whole* time, threatening us with an army of Master Hunters—?

Wait a minute.

"Did you say those are *Masters* behind us?" I asked, pointing behind me and Jak.

"We need to sharpen your listening skills, but yes," Mr. Dawson said. "The Masters your school hired for your final, remember?"

With heat rising into my cheeks at the mockery in his voice, I met my eyes with Momma's. "You said the school hired regulars," I told her.

"Masters, regulars, close enough." Mr. Dawson snapped his fingers. Two agents grabbed me and Jak by our arms.

If he'd said that that had been another lie, fine—but regulars and Masters were far from being "close enough". And Momma had warned us that we'd have to remember *everything* she'd taught us this year. She'd warned us about details—about how the tiniest ones sometimes mattered the most and revealed the big picture.

She'd also taught us how to escape from being caught from behind.

As Jak tripped the agent behind him, I threw my head back against the woman grabbing me and then elbowed her square in the chest. Grabbing her arm, I twisted it behind her back and then slammed her into the ground. Jak had kicked his captor into the wall and was already using a scissor takedown on the next Hunter coming for him. I set my right foot into place to twist my body and throw a backspin blow on the lanky agent charging toward me. He parried my shot, twisted my arm behind my back, and threw me against the wall.

A dull ache shot across my chest as I collided with the stone. With the agent's body heavy against me, pressing me to the wall, I swallowed down the rage threatening my control. This would *not* be what took me down; I wouldn't lose to a pillow fight when I'd dealt with Alexa Delphine so many times.

"Jak!" I shouted. In my peripheral, Momma writhed in the ropes keeping her captive. Mr. Dawson held her down by the shoulders, smiling at the whole scene.

The agent behind me flew off me, caught in Jak's rear naked choke. I threw Momma's jab-hook-uppercut combo at the Hunter coming to stop it.

I knew from the get-go that there were too many, so I ran into the room. Mr. Dawson lunged to grab me, but I ducked and landed behind Momma's chair, feet almost skidding across the dusty floor.

My head stayed down as I focused on the thin rope around

Momma's wrists. *Exsolvo.*

The rope unwound and fell to the floor. Momma went for the ropes around her ankles.

"You're getting cocky!" Mr. Dawson growled, grabbing me by the shoulders. I shook free and swung a roundhouse kick at him. He flew into the wall on the other side of the room, twinging my heart.

Don't. He hurt you, and Mom.

Banging. Banging was faintly echoing from the back of the room. I followed it to a metal door in the right-hand corner.

Head down.

Exsolvo.

An instant click sounded, and I pulled the heavy door open. A horde of Callistro Girls and Redway Boys poured out, almost knocking me over as they bolted past me.

"Emma!"

Sarah and Breanne broke through the crowd and threw their arms around me.

"You guys did it!" Breanne cried, tears brimming her swollen blue-hazel eyes. The poor girl had probably been sobbing about failing her final.

"Come on!" Sarah exclaimed, already sharpening her focus and leading Breanne to the entrance of the room. The tides had drastically turned: each Callistro Girl was fighting her Hunter with a Redway Boy at her side. Our enemy was outnumbered, and Sarah and Breanne jumped in with confidence because of it.

"And then there was one."

Mr. Dawson had never worn such a sinister tone before. A fast, mechanical snap followed.

"Your turn, Emmalynn."

I turned and looked over. Standing at the wall across from me, Mr. Dawson had a switchblade to Mom's throat.

"Mr. Dawson," I said with a cruel tremble. My anger wanted to drop the formality, but that name was the last piece of familiarity, comfort, I had left to hold on to. "Don't, please don't, just tell me why you're doing this—"

He laughed, almost indignantly, like his patience had snapped. "Okay, never mind, maybe you're not right for the agency. Your intuition is painfully weak."

"Why?" I cried over the grunts and panting resounding in the tunnel next to us. I dared myself to take a few steps forward, stopping behind the chair. "*You* were the one showing me how to be good. How to fix the world so we don't have to live like this anymore! What about your niece? What about your best friend, what about all those years you spent helping—?"

—I've known about you for a long time, Emma.—

I never thought I'd be so furious to hear Mr. Dawson's telepathic voice. Another familiarity he had ripped to shreds.

—I've known about your fate for an even longer time,— he told me. *—Why do you think I planned this? Why do you think I want you on our team?—*

I froze, dumbfounded. *—What're you talking about? What could you possibly get out of doing this?—*

—My entire life, I've sacrificed everything I know and love for the sake of keeping other magicians a secret! Ever since I met Tristan, it's always been HIS needs, HIS life, YOUR family above my own!—

Every sentence twisted a sword in my gut. I gripped the back of the chair with one hand to steady myself.

Momma's lip quivered as she eyed me with every warning she'd spent my whole life giving me. For some reason, part of me was ready to throw them all away if it meant I had the truth of what was going on right now.

I swallowed hard, my locket around my neck feeling miles away. —*You said you*—

—*Of course I did! Why do you think? I gave up everything for you guys: my chance at a normal life, the one and only woman I've ever loved, I even almost let you cost me my life at that stupid beach house! I let your family use me all these years, all just so you could keep your power a secret? I don't think so.*—

My jaw trembled with fury. A Hunter in the tunnel went down in my peripheral. A Redway Boy and Callistro Girl were eyeing us.

Mr. Dawson didn't seem to care. —*Not anymore, at least. Because the world is going to know our power. They will know it, and they will fear it.*—

—*No. That would endanger... That would—your people*—

—*That's the best part: my people, your people, are the Hunters fighting your friends right now. Don't you get it? We're not here to wipe out magicians. We're just here to make sure disobedience isn't an option when we step into power. We're here to build our power. And you, Adara, are perfect for that.*—

My fists clenched at the name. How could he use it as a weapon against me like that? If any part of this *were* an act, which I honestly couldn't believe I was starting to doubt, how could he so easily play the role? Like... like part of him actually believed it?

The commotion next to me was slowly dying as I said, —*But Jak doesn't have magic, how could he fit into all this?*—

A devilish smirk slid across Mr. Dawson's lips. —*Easy fix. What, you thought I actually gave Tristan's magic back to him?*—

"Shut up!" I cried, half of the voices next to me pausing. "No, I don't care what you say, you're lying!"

"I'd rethink your pride right now." Mr. Dawson huffed, pressing the blade against Momma's skin. I almost apologized for my words. "Repeating it won't make it magically come true!"

"Put that down," Adrien stated. When I looked over, he was stepping over an unconscious Hunter.

No way.

Every last agent had been knocked out. An army of Callistro Girls and Redway Boys now stood in the tunnel, blocking the entryway to the room. Mr. Dawson was trapped.

"Oh." A smile twitched on his lips, his eyes barely affording mine. "So we did need more backup."

This was nothing but a mission to him.

I shoved the surging, stinging tears far down. Fine. If I really meant so little to him—if anything at all—if everything we'd been through had been false, I refused to grieve it in front of him. If all he wanted was to make me a weapon, he deserved my anger. He deserved the vengeful magician he wanted out of me.

"He said to lower the knife." With my weight finally steady underneath me, I finally let go of the chair. "I know you're not stupid enough to test an entire pack."

He raised the switchblade, throwing my challenge right back at me. "Wanna make a bet?"

No, but I did want to end his game, end this stupid final, and I only knew one way to do it: I closed my eyes.

"No, seriously, go ahead!" Thomas said. "Give me your worst,

Emmalynn, I—!"

The room jerked around us, startling him and my classmates. I opened my eyes in pretend shock and stumbled into the chair, dirt sprinkling onto us. Mr. Dawson instinctually lowered the switchblade from Momma's throat.

Well, I had to use the warlock part of me eventually.

I sprang forward and kicked the switchblade out of Mr. Dawson's loosened grip. Momma leapt out of the way as I lunged for the blade. When Mr. Dawson reached for me, I used our momentum to twist his arm behind his back with my free hand, my other pressing the blade against his throat.

I swallowed, heart split by clashing emotions: *I* was holding a blade to Thomas Dawson's throat.

Both classes held their breath (as much as they could for a bunch of teenagers who'd just been scarred for life). Momma faced us all from the middle of the room, panting—but then her breaths became laughs. And a smile slid onto Mr. Dawson's face, too.

Then—unbelievably—Momma started *clapping*. And Mr. Dawson was *laughing*! And the Hunters behind my classmates were getting up!

The mob in the entryway collectively shuffled inside the room upon realizing it, but Momma held up her hand and stopped them. She tilted her head up slightly to address the Hunters rising from the dead. "Thank you, agents. You're dismissed. I'll take a look at your evaluations when we get back."

No. No way. No way.

"Yes, ma'am," the man I'd monitored in the mall replied, standing at the front. A large bruise was forming on his cheek, blood dripping from his eyebrow. He split his group of colleagues down the middle, leading them out of the tunnel and back into the cavern.

Like none of this had been real. I still refused to lower the switchblade. And Mr. Dawson stayed still in my grip.

"What's going on?" Jackie Cortez exclaimed for us, her heavy breaths falling in rhythm with everyone else's.

Momma turned to my classmates. "Ladies and gentlemen, the only way any of you will experience the magnitude of our pride right now is if you follow in our footsteps one day and become a Hunter instructor."

No. This can't be fake. Not after what Mr. Dawson told me—

I commanded myself to shed the formality again as Momma walked over to me. She placed a gentle hand over mine gripping the switchblade for dear life. Mr. Dawson carefully stepped over to the side, Momma holding my gaze with comfort.

"Em," she crooned when my grip didn't falter. "It's okay."

How... how could she say that?

She slid the weapon out of my hand and then closed it. Her other hand rubbed my arm as if she could really console me about this.

Lip trembling, heart struggling to decide between rage and relief, I looked from my mother to my classmates and then back. "Wh—what're you talking about?"

She beamed at me. "Your final is officially over, and you all passed."

You can imagine the chaotic, breathy chorus of "What?" and "What do mean?" and "Are you kidding me?" that followed, but Momma simply chuckled. She wrapped her arm around me and then walked me over to stand next to my classmates.

Mr. Dawson stepped up to the center of the room, in front of the chair. "Your mission was simply to not get caught. In this field, you're not caught until you have absolutely no means of escape. Until your only option is... well, death."

"But we... we were all locked—in the room—with no way out," Kimia said, breathless, pushing a thin blond braid over her shoulder. "If it wasn't for Emma and Jak—"

"Exactly, Miss Holland." Mr. Dawson nodded. "You still had a means of escape. You had someone from your pack."

This had all just been part of the final.

"Your schools want you to thrive in your careers," Mom said, taking her place next to Mr. Dawson. Her voice echoed off the frigid stone walls. The temperature seemed to drop. "We want to set you up so that you eventually reach the top. There's only one key difference with Grand Hunters versus regulars and Masters: teamwork. Some see it as a disadvantage, and in a lot of cases, it is. But that's why Grand Hunters hunt in a pack: they're the ones who have proven that they're even better when they work together. When one member of the pack is captured, the rest come to their rescue. Every person in this room has proven that they're capable of that."

Bafflement swelled in the room, but I could bet my magic that anger was no stranger to any of us in that moment.

"Did the Redway Boys know this was a final?" Elizabeth asked. Stray strands of black hair from her ponytail stuck to her face with sweat. "Were they graded, too?"

"Yep," Mr. Dawson replied. "They just didn't know that this was their final, too. Instructor Yang told them early this morning that an 'enemy organization' planned on breaching the Callistro final as a means to infiltrate our schools, and they drove over. He's been monitoring their progress alongside us."

"But why combine us?" Sarah asked, hands as confidently on her hips as ever. She must've been suffocating in that sweater dress by now.

"Because it proves my previous point," Momma said, folding her hands together. "Everyone here had a common goal: to stay safe and protect one another for the greater good. You allowed that goal to unite you into one pack, and you were successful."

"So then why the disguise?" I spat, glowering at Mr. Dawson. My jacket encased my body heat, but for some reason, the idea of taking it off felt like surrender in a way. "Why couldn't you just hunt me as yourself?"

So I wouldn't feel like I hate you like I do right now.

"I think you'd agree that that would've made things too easy on my end," he said, his slightly upturned lips twitching with a caged laugh. "The second I pulled off the disguise, you froze, hesitated, and started doubting that this was real. Albeit you were right, but if you saw me running toward you back in that alley, you would've stopped and questioned me just the same. I would've caught you, and you would've failed."

I hated him for being right about that. I hated that he knew me that well. He had no right to know me that well.

"So you..." I began, fighting an uphill battle to keep my voice from biting, "*planned* for the final to happen here?"

Momma smiled softly as if to comfort me. "I quizzed you girls on the Svobada Maneuver multiple times on our simulation hunts for a reason. All it took was one Hunter to use it on one of you, and the rest came following to protect a member of their pack. Only school authority knows that this mine used to be a magician hideout. We just fixed it up to accommodate our needs."

"And we were ready to stop the test at any time if necessary," Mr. Dawson added. "With that said, you all just experienced the life of an active agent in this field. I hope this will help you accurately decide if you want to pursue this career after graduation, after all, when the time comes. It's not a decision to take lightly."

Ha. Except, I didn't get a decision. Maybe we'd never been in real danger, but that didn't mean that this final had been any less real to me. My mother and Mr. Dawson should have known that.

"Then," Breanne squeaked next to me, "we passed?"

"You passed," Mom and Mr. Dawson said, radiating with pride.

My classmates hugged and squealed and high-fived and congratulated each other, but I was frozen in my spot, mindlessly gazing at the stone under my feat. I'd been numbed from the inside out. Despite the cold underground, my body was on fire. My mind was finally acknowledging the effects of the last hour lingering in my head. It was hard to breathe for more than one reason.

"Emmy!" Sarah cried, throwing her arms around me. "We passed, everything's okay!"

I pushed her away. "You think it's okay?" The tears stuck in my throat were preventing me from snapping, which I couldn't decide if I was grateful for or not. "After everything that's happened, after...!"

I helplessly glanced back and forth between the two of them, my words lost to confidentiality.

I shook my head. "I couldn't—no. *None* of this was okay."

"Emma..." Breanne placed a delicate hand on my shoulder like she was scared to touch me.

"I thought Alexa was here," I whispered. "I thought... I thought she was gonna expose me, I thought we—I thought my mom was gonna die."

My best friends knew how to fill in the blanks. They didn't know that my terror rooted from the fact that Alexa was still actively in my life, but they didn't need to.

It's usually hugs, no matter how gentle, that manage to squeeze the tears out at the last second if your thoughts or feelings don't do it first. Maybe I shouldn't have been angry that tears started racing down my cheek once Sarah and Breanne held me in their arms, but I was.

My head rested on Breanne's small shoulder. I eyed Mr. Dawson, almost wishing that my stare had the ability to shoot double-edged swords. I mean, he'd used magic against me like one.

—*Who do you think you are?*—

He jumped, glimpsing me for a nanosecond. I hadn't meant to speak the words to him, but seeing that I'd reached him fueled the fire in my head. —*Who on this planet told you this was a good idea? Why would you EVER do that to me? How could you be that cruel to me, how?*—

—*Not here. At school.*—

—*No!*— My jaw quivered as I hugged Breanne tighter. —*You owe me something now—!*—

"Emmy," Sarah said as Breanne released, resting a bronze hand on my arm.

I forced myself to face her.

"It's okay," she whispered, noting the burning tears lining my eyes. "You're okay."

It was all I could do to nod and suck it up. I fell into another group hug with them, forcing myself to accept that none of the bad was real and only the good existed right now. My chest felt just as heavy, but at least the anxiety of impending doom wasn't pressing down on it anymore. Just red-hot rage. Betrayal.

"Ladies and gentlemen," Momma called over my buzzing classmates, "if you would please follow me and Headmaster Dawson out of the mine, we'll be heading home now."

I would've relaxed with everyone else had I not still been tempted to throw Mom and Mr. Dawson down the second-story ledge of the cavern.

We collectively moved down the tunnel, our footsteps scraping against the dirt and stone. I lingered in the back and told the girls to go on without me—I needed to be alone to give my mind the freedom of thought it needed.

Apparently, Jak felt the same way.

"Are you mad, too?" I asked, keeping a six-foot distance between us and David Martinez with Amelia.

"A little bit," he said, eyes loyal to the ground. He was refusing to let me see them, and he kept any emotional inflection from his tone. Okay, so he was almost as furious as I was. He'd stayed in the back of the group when Momma and Mr. Dawson had come clean, so I hadn't been able to see his response to it all, but sometimes actions speak louder than expressions.

"Well, you did a great job," I said as we started down the slope to the bank of the lake. We now faced the cavern in all its damp air and rocky beauty. Walking past it now, it almost felt more like a class field trip. "Holding your own while I got to my mom and our friends."

"Thanks. You, too."

And then, like a boulder off a cliff, awkwardness squashed the air between us. I couldn't remember the last time a conversation had been awkward between me and Jak. All the silences were usually filled with hugging and holding and kissing, and the actual conversation part was mostly just Jak flirting with me. What was going on? What reason did he have for being as angry as I was?

"You really helped me," I assured him, trying to gain his eyes with my own. "You *know* I wouldn't've been able to do any of that without you. Nobody would have."

"Thanks," he said. His chuckle sounded way too forced, a smile going with it.

"Then why are *you* so upset? Thomas and my mom are gonna get it from me when we get back, but at least we passed. And the people you said shouldn't be here were hired by the school. When you first found me, I thought you were talking about Alexa and William."

"I was."

I froze just before we reached the staircase that would take us back up to the wooden bridge. Jak stopped with me like my reaction was right on time, facing me in full.

Uh oh—my heart was trying to shove itself into my throat again.

"What?" I whispered, swallowing it back down.

Jak's brown irises finally started tearing down every brick of the wall he'd put up to hide what I realized was his fear. "I was," he said again. "I *did* think that the 'enemy organization' was after you. But only when I saw my parents around town at the same time we were."

NINE

Lunch had been served in the Dining Hall, but need-less to say, I was nowhere near in the mood to eat. If anything, I was ready to go into the Hall just to spoil the final for Opal, who had it tomorrow.

First, though, I had to scream at Mom and Mr. Dawson in his office—because what had happened in the mine was miles be-yond not okay.

"Well?" Momma grinned at me, standing next to Mr. Daw-son in front of his desk. "You passed. I couldn't be prouder of you—"

"What were you thinking?" I snapped, shooting daggers at them both. Mr. Dawson's grip tightened on his desk as he leaned against it, like he knew this conversation had been coming. "What made you think that was a good idea? You know how big a threat Alexa still is, and you made me think she was coming back today!" My vision two nights ago flashed in my memory, setting my anger ablaze. The air grew a little thinner. "I thought she was here to expose me, I thought I was—I was gonna—!"

"We get that, Emma," Momma said with crossed arms, officially entering mom mode. "But I told you at the beginning of the hunt, I've been telling you since I first enrolled you here, that you need to understand your enemy. You need to know firsthand what your people deal with on a day-to-day basis—"

"I *do!*" I told her, gripping myself, because I wasn't going to show weakness by going for the locket around my neck. "That's how I've been living the entire year!"

"You've been hunted, yes," she said, "but you've never been part of an active escape with a pack on your tail. And I'd much rather your first experience with that be an exam for school than the real thing."

"You were never in any real danger," Mr. Dawson added all too calmly. "We planned the whole thing out to a T, why do you think I was your Hunter?"

"I'm the one who assigns the agents to each student." Momma rested one hand on her hip, her other holding her up on Mr. Dawson's desk. She was using her confidence against me, and I needed a solid argument all the more because of it. "You had to think that you'd been assigned to an actual Hunter so that we would get real results out of you."

My fingers dug into my arms as I squeezed myself tighter. "Like everything Alexa's done to me hasn't given you enough?"

"You've grown since the start of the semester." Mr. Dawson

was still infuriatingly calm. "In more ways than one. That's why I didn't telepathically tell you that the entire thing was just the exam. Then you'd be able to relax and have the luxury of knowing that your mom's life wasn't in danger. But what if your mom were a magician? Or it was your family captured today instead? What if I were Alexa or William or any other—?"

"Stop."

It was the firmest I'd ever spoken with either of them—the furthest I'd ever tested either of them—but not an ounce of me said that it was wrong. For once, I felt like I'd earned my anger.

"You don't get to use that." I cursed the hot tears blurring my vision the longer it stayed on him. "You became my biggest enemy in a single sentence. You used your involvement in my life against me."

"I needed you to—"

"Did you mean anything you said?"

"No," he said, offense sharpening his features. "None of that was true, I just needed a—"

"For you to have come up with a lie of that degree, it had to be at least a *bit* true!"

"No, Emmalynn!" he retorted, even startling Momma as he stood from his desk. "You know me better than that."

I thought I did.

"I went with the only realistic excuse I could find. Actually turning against you would make sense if I wanted power and were as crazy as Alexa. But power's never been my motivation. My family *always* has been. And you and your family have been that to me since I was fourteen at Redway." His gaze briefly left me, and he shook his head. "You're more family to me than my brother is."

I swallowed.

Alexa. Now I knew why Moren had asked Mr. Dawson a few months ago if he still had feelings for her: nores can only see external, present circumstances. Mr. Dawson didn't have feelings for Alexa anymore, but he *had* given everything up, including the only woman he'd ever loved, for the Ateras. That was still true. Who was to say that not even a mustard seed-sized part of him had meant what he'd said in the mine?

"Was it easy for you?" I whispered.

"No," he breathed. Momma watched us with a stare that seemed to mourn our situation. I wondered if Mr. Dawson had told her what he was going to tell me to make me believe him. "That was the hardest cover I've ever had to keep up. I knew I'd betrayed you. I knew I'd become an Alexa to you in that moment. That was a coat I wanted to rip off the second I put it on. But..." He trailed off, like even he couldn't find something that would justify his actions.

"But we needed to test you on priorities," Momma said for him. At least her authoritative tone had been replaced by gentle assurance. "We wanted to know if you'd be able to make one of the hardest decisions on the battlefield and fight someone you thought you could trust. It took you a second, but once you were convinced that he was a threat, you took action against him. You didn't let past experience or relationship cloud your judgment."

She stepped up to me and rested her hands on my shoulders. "You focused on what you were seeing in the present. For that, I'm beyond proud of you."

I stepped away from her hold. "You forced me back into the worst moments of my life and replaced everyone with the people

I love the most. You betrayed me in a way that *wasn't* an act. That final was real to *me*."

Mr. Dawson's head stayed down in thought, keeping his arms crossed. Even Momma was quiet, waiting for his mind to finish.

"I'm not sorry for doing it," he finally said, "because you learned and proved a lot. But I *am* sorry for not doing it better. We could've... toned it down a bit."

I didn't know what to say. All I knew was that they didn't have to go that far. I didn't *want* them to have to go that far. And I hated that that exam had been so successful to the extent that even I knew now that I could trust myself out in the field.

Momma carefully took me into her arms, rubbing my back. Whatever remained in me, inside that messy ball of emotion in my chest, made sure that I only wrapped my arms around her halfway. She'd never not known me better before. This hunt had been *approved* by her. How could she have thought that it was the best way to go about testing me? How could Mr. Dawson have agreed with her on it?

His eyes refused to look at me, whereas I tried burning a hole through him. That telepathic conversation we'd had down there still felt too real.

When did my closest relationships—when did magic—become the greatest weapon against me?

"I'm sorry for not doing it better," Momma said when she broke away. "But we got a lot more out of it than we thought we would—did you cause that small earthquake?"

All I could do was nod.

Mr. Dawson's head shot back. "You know a spell for one?"

Fine, let them try to move on so quickly; that didn't mean I had to.

"It was my will." I shrugged. "Now that I know I'm part warlock, it was easy-ish."

Mr. Dawson hummed, and Momma turned to him with curiosity. Then he approached the glass coffee table in the middle of the room, picked up the orchid plant sitting on it, and then walked over to me.

"How about we do another test?" He smiled like he was trying to take my mind off of things. But the worst way to do that to someone you've just traumatized is to treat them like a science—or magic—project. Needless to say, the *last* thing I wanted to do for either of them was perform again.

"I don't really feel like..."

I couldn't continue with the stifling silence that lay beyond my voice. I looked up at them both, wanting some kind of direction, an excuse to leave—because, honestly, part of me hated being mad at them for something they hadn't intentionally done, which was hurt me. I just wanted to go upstairs to my room and forget the rest of the day with a nap.

Momma placed her hand on Mr. Dawson's shoulder, shooting him a look of understanding that passed some kind of message to him. He lowered the plant.

"Okay. Understandable," he said. "I just—I have a theory. And if any part of you is willing to test it out with me right now, I'd like to. If you'll let me."

He had to go there, didn't he?

"Fine," I finally said. "What do I have to do?"

"Exactly what you did before to cause the earthquake. But this time, I want you to grow another flower from the stem."

Okay, I thought. If an earthquake was possible, how could a flower take me down?

My fingers lightly brushed against the stiff main stem of the orchid. I cupped one fully blossomed flower. Each petal had a white base that stretched into a rich magenta. Strong yet delicate, fragile petals. I told myself that I could create something just like it, and closed my eyes.

I opened them again. Nothing.

I crossed my arms as if to protect myself from the embarrassment. "I can't do it unless I feel pressured. Adrenaline helped me last time."

"I think you're overthinking it." Mr. Dawson lowered the plant to see me better. "Try just touching the stem with your magic's will to grow a new flower."

Oh, that's all? I thought, tempted to roll my eyes, but I took another breath and uncrossed my arms.

Will is a strange but powerful thing. I'm a walking example of that. It's difficult to describe, but when you use it, it's because every part of you believes that something will happen solely because you want it to. And I really wanted that orchid to grow because I really wanted to know what Mr. Dawson was on about—and I also really wanted to leave so I'd feel less guilty about being mad at him. That flower had to submit to my will, and I commanded my magic to embody its warlock class to grow it.

A fresh bud blossomed from where my index finger released, its petals unfurling into white and purple. Just before I could exhale with my awe, Mr. Dawson stepped back and Momma backed into the coffee table, nearly tripping over it.

"What?" I said, my senses back on alert.

"There it is again," Momma said, pointing loosely at me. "Did you see that?"

"So you're *not* crazy." Mr. Dawson marveled at me, setting down the orchid on the glass table. "They do—"

"*What?*" I firmly repeated.

"Last time, you said amethyst." Mr. Dawson turned to Momma like I wasn't even in the room. "But now—"

"Emerald," she murmured. "Em, your eyes turned emerald."

Okay, I seriously needed to start practicing these other classes of magic in front of a mirror. At this point, especially after this morning, I wouldn't have doubted for a second that Momma and Mr. Dawson were messing with me about my eyes turning any other color but amber when I used magic. It was *literally* impossible in every sense of the word!

"Like..." I said carefully, "like—"

"Like an emerald," Momma said again, because *that* clarified things.

"But..." I began, dumbfounded, "what—what does that mean?"

Mr. Dawson shrugged, pressing his lips together. "I don't know. I can only tell you when they change color—whenever you activate a different class in you—not why. And to be honest, we can't expect the answer any time soon, either. *Nothing* like this has happened in the history of magic. So if you really want answers, we have to play it by ear and be patient."

"Is there any chance that this is dangerous?" Momma asked him cautiously.

"Actually, I'd say it's a benefit." He crossed his arms. "It's not like Emma's never going to have an enemy again after Alexa and

William. Ha, we still have Caldwell to take care of. And then we have people we don't even know about working behind the curtain—"

"I'm so glad to know that my daughter will always be a walking target." Momma rolled her eyes, sitting herself down on the white sofa sitting against the wall.

"Amy." Mr. Dawson sighed, but I knew how to finish.

"Magicians in America will always be in danger until Adara happens. But we know that's what I'm meant to accomplish, we know that future's a strong possibility. And I'm already dead set on making it happen."

Momma curtly exhaled, crossing her legs. She was the classiest, most beautiful I'd seen her in a while, her chestnut waves elegantly framing her narrow face. "You sound so grown up," she said, softly smiling. "I guess I just don't want to let you go yet."

I had to set aside some of my remaining anger. The little girl in me wanted to run to Momma.

"You'll never have to." I walked over to her as she stood, and wrapped my arms around her. Her sweet, nostalgic perfume wafted into my nose. "I'll always need you for something."

Her hold on me tightened. "I know."

I let myself crack a smile. But I still wanted to spoil the final for Opal.

The final... Right. There was one more thing we had to discuss, but I really didn't want to worry Momma and Mr. Dawson about Alexa and William just yet. That didn't mean, though, that I could go long without info, especially since I didn't have Steven's locator spell that let me find someone with just the thought of them; Steven had to destroy it because, as difficult as it was, it was a weapon in the wrong hands.

Besides, I wouldn't be able to text next year since phones were being banned from the Callistro Academy. No more communicating with my family during school, no more watching funny cat videos if I woke up from a nightmare. No more texting Jak for updates. I had to take advantage of that while I could.

E: When are we talking about today?

J: Whenever you can meet

That's not helpful, I thought. The next time I'd be able to meet him? Without consequences or suspicion? That'd take a decent amount of consideration and time to figure out…

"What's wrong, honey?"

I looked up at Momma, slipping my phone back into my pocket. At least I wouldn't have to hide texts anymore, either. I needed more information on this before I could share with either of them what Jak had seen.

"Nothing." I plopped down onto the couch. "But Jak's mad at you for today, too."

"Figures." Momma smiled, her hand loosening on my shoulder. "How can I ever make it up to him?"

The question curdled in my stomach. How could I? How could I make up for putting him through this for this long? All because of lying to him, because he couldn't know anything.

How would I ever make it up to him—or anyone?

TEN

The craziest thing that happened that week was obviously Momma's final, but the second craziest? Friday afternoon, the last day of school, when Sarah, Breanne, and I got back to our dorm and finished packing.

"This is insane…" Sarah sighed as she put another set of neatly folded pajamas into the cardboard box on her bed. She gently tossed her long black hair over her shoulder. "You guys. It's over."

"Sophomore year is over." Breanne packed her decorative pillows and stuffed animals into her box. "At least we get to keep this room next year!"

"Next year…" I took out the trinkets inside my bedside table drawer, shaking my head in disbelief. "Wow."

"We're gonna be juniors," Sarah sang, speaking a mile a minute. "We're moving up in the Hunter game, we're gonna be *juniors*—!"

A knock on the doorway cut off her squeals. We looked over at the pale, purple-eyed girl standing in the entrance of our dorm.

"Hey, hey!" Opal chimed.

"Opal!" Sarah dashed across the room, grabbing the girl's wrists to pull her inside. "Good, you can help me convince Emma to take my hair curler!"

"No!" I said, closing the box in front of me. "I don't need it!"

She huffed, placing her hands on her hips. "I got the one of my DREAMS as an early birthday present from my aunt in Egypt. Breanne won't take my old one because she burned herself last month, so now she's scared of it. But Emma's scared to take it because of her mom."

Opal faced me with her brows furrowed. "Your mom won't let you have a hair curler?"

I rolled my eyes, refusing this conversation and grabbing the packaging tape next to the box.

Sarah was more than happy to answer for me. "No. She'll just think Emma's trying to *impress* someone."

"*Oh,*" Opal said. Unfortunately, pulling a new piece of tape wasn't loud enough to drown her out when she said, "Mr. Bleu would love you in curly hair!"

That's the problem, I almost said.

"I've never seen you with curly hair," Breanne mused, meeting Opal and Sarah in the middle of the room. "You should take it!"

Opal fiddled with her thumbs, looking over Sarah's shoulder

at our bathroom. The hair curler sat on the marble vanity top. She shrugged. "I wouldn't mind taking it."

"Yay!" Sarah skipped to the bathroom, grabbed the curler, and then ran back to shove it into Opal's hands.

"Thanks!" Opal twisted the device, pushing a strand of her black hair out of her face. "So I stopped by because my mom is gonna be here soon to pick me up. Our first vacation starts tomorrow and our flight is in a few hours. I wanted to hear about your plans for summer, though."

"Your *first* vacation?" Sarah asked, arching a brow. "How many do you plan on having?"

"Just a couple for the first half of break," Opal replied. "My mom has a ton to do for *Magic*'s summer editions once July hits."

I had to wonder what she was really thinking when she brought up the magazine. After all, she and I now knew that her "mom" (mortal friend of her actual parents) was only doing it for the same reason my mom stayed a Hunter for so long after meeting Dad: it paid really well and created a strong cover—in this case, literally. I hate to say it, but *Magic* has fairly eye-catching covers.

"I kind of want to finally set up the prototype of my security system I've been working on since Christmas," Breanne said, walking to the empty white desk in the corner of the room and plopping down into the chair.

"You built a security system?" I asked as I closed the top drawer of the bedside table. "Why?"

She shrugged, mindlessly picking at the hairs on her arm. "It'll distract me and make me feel better about my brother living on his own."

Her older brother had moved to Virginia last year for college, but last I heard, he was wanting to make the jump to Belgium. That wasn't surprising to hear about the brother of a girl who gets a sweet tooth when she's anxious: why *wouldn't* he pick the chocolate capital of the world to expand his career in film production?

Sarah grinned, strolling over to Breanne and squeezing her. "I can't *wait* to see what you're gonna do over the summer. Hey, maybe we can take a trip around the country and visit a ton of colleges at some point."

Sarah Duncan, of *all* people, just said that.

Breanne broke away from her hold. "Uh, what?"

Even Opal's eyes narrowed in skepticism. "Who wants to visit colleges during summer?"

Sarah rolled her eyes, nudging Breanne's shoulder. "I mean so you can get a better idea of where you wanna go. The three of us will be hitting up the downtown boutiques."

That sounded more like her.

"We'll have fun together this summer either way." Opal hugged the curler to her chest. "But my mom's gonna be here any minute, I should probably get going."

"You're not leaving just like that," Sarah said. She took her place back in the center of the room, waving at us each to follow suit.

I'd gotten pretty used to the purple circle rug in the middle of our room, but now we stood on plain beige carpet. If anything, that made our group hug all the more comforting, a familiarity amidst the difference happening in our lives. And with Opal here, it felt like our hug had evolved, like we were growing to a point of being better—expansion.

"Have a great first vacation," Breanne said to her. She turned to me and Sarah on her other side. "Will you guys help me set up the prototype for my security system?"

I bit the inside of my lip. "Next week."

I'd spent the last month preparing to leave the Callistro Academy behind for three months, to temporarily erase the building from my mind. And yet, now that I was standing on the driveway and staring back at the manor, I could practically *feel* a string tying me to it, threatening to pull me straight through the double doors.

"It's so beautiful." Breanne sighed wistfully, resting her chin on top of her hands on her suitcase handle.

"Bye, Callistro," Sarah sang next to me, light-green eyes locked on where I was pretty sure our dorm was. "I'll miss you. I guess."

A few more of our classmates trickled through the propped-open front doors. I stared, reminded of the first day of school when Sarah, Breanne, and I had pushed them open and met Jak already waiting. I'd met Alexa that day.

That day had been the beginning of the year, and today was the end of it.

A gentle, warm wind blew against me as I looked up at Momma standing on my other side. She was already smiling at me, like she was telling me that I'd really done it: I'd survived a year here as a sorceress, after all.

"Bre!" someone called behind us, turning us around with Breanne. Mrs. Shaw scurried ahead of her husband down the driveway, where sedans and SUVs were taking Callistro Girls into the forest and then home.

Mrs. Shaw threw out her arms, and Breanne leaped into them. "Oh, hi, sweetheart! We missed you!"

"I missed you, too!" Breanne released and turned to her father, reaching her arms around his neck. "Now we get the whole summer!"

"You've all grown so much." Mrs. Shaw awed as her young blue eyes glanced between me and Sarah, folded hands pressed against her thin lips. Then her eyes rose to Momma. "It's so good to see you again, Amy. I'm glad they at least had you keeping an eye on them during the year."

"Easier than you'd think." Momma smirked, wrapping an arm around my shoulders. Well, that was true for Sarah and Breanne, and that was all that mattered. "You're taking Sarah home, too, right?"

"Yep," Mr. Shaw replied in a clear voice, taking Breanne's yellow suitcase for her. "She's staying with us for a few days while her parents are out of state. Emma, you're more than welcome to join us at any point."

"She already said no." Sarah rolled her eyes, then nudged me with her elbow. "If you wanna hang out with Jak so badly, you can just tell us."

"Okay," I said, holding up a finger, "first of all—"

"She has a one-visit-a-week rule with boys, don't worry," Momma remarked, patting my shoulder. "We just have a few plans we wanna get to before we fully settle in to summer."

Exactly why I didn't want the hair curler.

Sarah pouted at me. "Don't ignore us for too long please."

"Are you ready to go, pumpkin?" Mr. Shaw asked.

"Yeah—oh!" Breanne exclaimed, grinning like a child. "Can we all eat out tonight? To celebrate?"

I looked up at Momma with the question. A trace of something familiar curved her lips upward. When I named it, our emotions were in sync: nostalgia. Just like the good days, when dinners lacked Hunters as a constant threat.

"Let's do it." Her honey-like eyes met me, her thumb rubbing my shoulder. "Ready?"

Taking my duffel bag off the ground, I started the walk down the driveway with my friends, where the few remaining cars sat parked in front of the tall black gate encompassing the school.

I glanced behind me as another warm breeze fluttered by, when muscle memory told me that we were far enough away to grasp the full image of the manor.

Goodbye, Callistro.

†

When Momma and I got home from dinner that night, Mr. Dawson was already there (in a *sweatshirt*, which was way too weird) with Dad and Aunt Becca. I was ready to make a joke about how we were his only friends to hang out with—until I realized that that was actually probably true. Then I kept my mouth shut and let Momma do the talking.

"That bored, Thomas?" she teased, hanging her coat over the head seat of the dining table. Dad walked out from the kitchen and kissed her cheek.

"Education never sleeps." He smirked from the couch, shoving his hands into his sweatshirt pockets. "Emma gets an academic break, but she can't quit being a magician."

"No!" I groaned, throwing my head back and leaning against the buffet at the front of the room. Seriously? Wasn't yesterday morning's torture enough? "I'm tired, it's been a long day."

"I know." He smiled warmly as if excited to relieve me. "So I wanna get to that tomorrow. Tonight, we're celebrating."

Good choice, Dawson, I thought bitterly.

"To all of you, for surviving an entire school year at that place against *all* odds." Aunt Becca emerged from the kitchen. In her hands rested a china plate with a chocolate cake slathered in rainbow sprinkles. "Great job on not getting arrested or murdered!"

"Becca!" Momma awed as we gathered around her. Then, just as quickly, she arched a brow at her. "Did you bake this?"

Auntie rolled her eyes and nodded to her brother. "Relax. He did."

"Good." Momma took Dad's face into her hands and softly kissed him.

"I'm gonna miss you both so much," he whispered, granting me his kind light-blue eyes.

"It's what's best," Momma said, rubbing his arm. "You know we'll visit the new place as often as we can."

"And Auntie gets to practice baking without burning down our house." I cuddled into Dad, embracing his clean cologne.

"Oh, you think you're funny." Aunt Becca shook the short platinum-blond bangs out of her face. "Fine, I'll have your slice for you as 'practice'."

"You'll miss me," I shot back.

Her smirk melted into a smile. "Lots."

Mr. Dawson cleared his throat, clasping his hands behind his back. "And Thomas is amazing for getting into contact with his magician friend, the real estate agent, and scoring a beautiful, inexpensive one-bedroom."

"Yes," Momma said, nodding curtly, "you are."

Dad fixed his gaze onto me, taking my hand. "I'm so proud of you both. You went through a lot, kiddo. So much more than you give yourself credit for. And you smashed it out of the ballpark."

I wrapped an arm around Momma, and Dad rested a gentle hand on it. Awkward side hugs are better than words. And the warm, chocolatey aroma of the cake only made it better.

"My role was only minor," Mr. Dawson grumbled.

After yesterday, I seriously wish that were true.

Aunt Becca rolled her eyes and probably would've hit him if she weren't holding the cake. "I said 'all of you'. Quit whining and help me cut this."

They walked to the dining table while Momma fetched a knife from the kitchen. Dad's chocolate cake for dessert, spending the night with my family all under one roof, the start of summer vacation—the night felt untouchable. I wanted to enjoy it for the few hours we had, because I knew better.

CHAPTER

ELEVEN

My eyes opened to my elbow jabbing the center of someone's chest as they grabbed me from my bed. *What's happening?*

I fell to the carpet just outside of the streaks of moonlight from my bedroom window. I looked up through my drowsiness. The world spun as an emerald-eyed redhead grinned down at me.

Flash.

Both of us standing now, Alexa held a small velvet box in one hand. Her triumphant eyes loomed over me. "Try this on for—"

I spun into her, ducking as she sprang for my arm.

Flash.

A nightmare, please tell me this is a nightmare!

Alexa had just stood up in front of my closet doors as I sat on my carpet, panting. "Shhh," she said. "Don't wake—"

Flash.

A burning sting radiated on my forearms, warning me of a rug burn as I lay on my back. Alexa swung herself over me, pinned my shoulders with her knees, and grabbed my wrist.

"Model this for me—"

Another blinding flash cut her off. A silver cuff bracelet sat in one hand, her grip firming around my wrist. She stuck the bracelet onto me, shooting a nearly electrocuting shock through my arm—

—and jolting me awake.

I panted in bed, the shock lingering with a tingle in my arm. *Was that... a dream?* That was way too random and nonsensical to have been a vision. Alexa Delphine forcing me to accept a present?

But the flashes... And it happened during summer. I know that—I can feel it.

Wait. That wasn't subconscious dream knowledge. That was... imminence.

I tried to swallow down my heart, but it was stuck in my throat, stirring up nausea that refused to settle long enough for me to fall back asleep. Every beat reminded me that I wasn't in a dream anymore, but reality wasn't any better.

I grabbed my phone off my bedside table and turned on a couple of cat videos. I think it was one of a tabby cat meowing the G major scale that got me back to sleep. (Evidently, cats have soothing voices.) But unfortunately, I couldn't escape last night's Alexa dread for long once morning would arrive: I was supposed to meet Jak, and she was the entire reason for that.

I eventually forced myself to get up and prepare for the drive to Capperson Park, my mind running through all of the what-ifs. This conversation could only go so many ways. And even though Cara was trying to be thoughtful when she texted me, it did anything but calm my nerves:

C: Looking forward to vacation, honey? How did your finals go?

E: Rocky start to vacation… finals were okay

C: I'm sorry. Maybe training with Steven will cheer you up. Does Wednesday still work?

E: That sounds great, thanks

Honestly, I couldn't even think about mage lessons while there was a decent chance that the druid in me had activated last night. Well, if that dream *had* been a vision. Druid visions aren't guaranteed to come true, they only show the possible future. If that dream had somehow been the seer in me, I was in serious trouble.

My mind enjoyed playing cruel jokes on me all the more as I waited for Jak at the gazebo. Jak: the stepson of the nightmare I'd seen last night. And it wasn't like our topic of conversation today would be any comfort.

Don't freak out. Don't panic.

Except, the last few times Jak and I had met up in public, they'd never gone well—at *all*. The night we'd met had introduced me to this whole thing in the first place. The carnival had ended with the two of us in his parents' lair. Then the mall had led to the incident with Ava Baleen and that group of despicable teenage boys. Then there was our final. And that...

I shuddered. Too big a part of me didn't want to remember. "Merlin."

But that nickname would never let me forget.

I stood from the chipping, white-painted steps of the gazebo, where Jak walked up to me with padded footsteps on the grass. A gentle breeze blew through the vibrant-green blades, which barely compensated for the intense sunrays. It was hard to believe that the last time we'd met at the gazebo, the field had been blanketed with crisp snow.

That said, how had this boy walked up to me in his black *hoodie* I'd gotten him for his birthday this year?

"Warm enough?" I teased, stepping down onto the grass.

"Some things are worth melting for." He stuck his hands into his pockets. "Shorts are a good look on you."

He'd never seen me in anything other than a gray plaid skirt, pajama pants, and jeans. The denim shorts were definitely new— and now, despite wearing them every summer, I was suddenly self-conscious.

"Thanks," I said, more than unaware of the proper response. I wished that I had my own pockets to shove my hands into; the short pockets weren't deep enough.

"No disrespect," he quickly told me, "I just mean... you make any style look good."

I mischievously tilted my head up. "So it doesn't matter what I wear because it all looks good and putting in any effort is worthless?"

His eyes doubled in size as he pulled his hands out of his pockets, holding them up in defense. "No, no, I meant—well, no, it's not that you don't—I mean, not that you shouldn't—"

I broke down in laughter, the tips of the grass blades poking where my sandals left my feet exposed. "Okay, you stuttering, never disappoints!"

Jak bit his lip, a scab left over from our final. Just like that, my laughter died. A chill branched out in my chest, replacing it. In a couple of ways, especially physically, that final had been more real to him than it had been to me.

"Okay," he said, "I'm considering that as you getting even for—"

"Teasing me in front of my friends? *Kissing* me in front of my school? Showing up at my final and scaring me to death?"

He opened his mouth, even took the breath to speak, until his lips closed into a thin line with a grimace. There was something he didn't want to tell me. Again.

The light atmosphere dropped with my smile. I couldn't wait for him to be ready this time. "So—do you know why they were there?"

He sighed, his eyes falling to the grass. "Merlin..."

"No, not that," I told him, shaking my head. "You only call me that to either joke around or soften the blow, and I can't afford anything sugarcoated right now."

"Okay." He locked eyes with me. Kept his jaw and words strong as he said, "The pack has a new mission. Alexa's going solo for research, and they found some reason to stay here for summer after they're done with their current hunt. They're moving back into the Capperson base right now."

A pit hardened to stone in my stomach. Somehow, no matter how many times I tried—even forced myself—to breathe, my lungs seemed to lock up. Here? Again? The only reason the entire pack would set up here again was if they'd found something—some*one*—here to investigate!

"Em?" Jak said, as if making sure that I was still there. He reached out to take my arm. "Em—"

I stepped back, forcing myself to rip off the Band-Aid and confront it: Alexa had managed to persuade the pack to be as close to me as possible again, and the mission—the hunt—was going straight back into effect. But there was no way that they'd send themselves on another goose chase like last year. This time around, they had to have a plan. They probably knew exactly how to catch me—if the rest of the pack knew that Alexa was still after me.

"I'm sorry," Jak said, like he'd warned me beforehand. Which, to my dismay, he kind of had. "I didn't mean to freak you out, but that's what's happening right now."

"But—why?" I said, hugging myself despite the heat.

"Well, my dad's shipping me off to stay with Adrien and Wyatt for the summer while the pack stays here. So when I caught him and Alexa at the final—I could explain it, but do I need to?"

He didn't. I hated how easy it was for me to piece together by myself.

I swallowed, somehow steadying my breath. My chest was collapsing under the weight of the heat, my mind was lost on whatever stray end of a thought it could grasp, and I'd lost all control over my fingers as they fidgeted with my locket.

Why was it so hot outside?

It's almost summer, that's why. That was stupid, of course it's hot. I can't believe I'd even—

How, how am I supposed to survive these people again? I couldn't even handle Alexa when she was playing two other people, let alone her entire pack again! She told them, she had to have told them, would Jak have warned me if she'd told him? I can't spend the whole summer trying to figure out—

"Merlin?"

I looked up at Jak. Comfort. That's the third reason he calls me that.

We'd known each other for almost a year; nothing made me hesitate to walk straight into his arms and let him hold me as my mind sifted through whatever emotion was flinging itself at it. At least I wasn't alone. At least I didn't have to hold myself up. At least I didn't have to hide being hunted.

I have to fix this.

"Why do you have to know everything?" I whispered.

He chuckled. "Perks of a dad who wants me in the business that badly. You're right. I know more than I'm supposed to because of him."

"You're staying with Wyatt and Adrien for the *entire* summer?"

Silence. That hesitant silence. I hated that hesitant silence.

"They want me to. Stay with Adrien for a while, then stay with Wyatt for a while. My dad could bring me back here earlier, but it's a slim chance."

"How do I hide her?" I caught myself asking. Because all Jak could ever know was that I was Tristan's daughter's protector, and he had to trust that I could take care of her.

His arms tightened around my back. "You find her before Alexa does."

Well, that wouldn't be hard. And I honest to goodness wanted to tell him that so he wouldn't worry.

"Do you need help?"

I looked up into his round eyes. In the space of a glance, I saw the same boy pointing at the Hall of Generations in January.

I smirked. "Nice try. I got it... Thanks."

A soft smile stretched his lips. "Okay. You have her back, and I'll have yours."

TWELVE

I was awake, yet my eyes stayed closed. Then, my bedroom lock jiggled.

Flash.

—*How did you know?*— Alexa asked, standing in the middle of my room. Her eyes, even in the dim moonlight, burned with an all-too-familiar spite. Anger. Patience that had snapped.

My own seemed to follow. —*Get out.*—

Flash.

"—do you want?!"

—*Nores can't lie, Emmalynn. You know*——

Flash.

I lay on my carpet, moonlight pooling onto the floor. Alexa's silhouette towered above me as she gripped my wrists. "Cooperate for *once* in your life and—"

"*Mom!*" I shouted as she tore out a velvet box from her jacket pocket.

Flash.

I sat shaking against my bedside table, watching as my mother and Alexa threw fist after kick after block after fist.

Flash.

Momma reached for Alexa's neck as Alexa's fingers wrapped around hers. She slammed Momma into my closet door—

Flash.

The closet door had been knocked off its hinges. Alexa's eyes shone with amber as she pushed Momma in my direction. She missed me by a foot and flew straight through my window, shattering the glass.

"MOM!"

Black shrouded my vision until I shot upright in bed, opening my eyes. Harsh breaths racked my chest, my vision struggling to adjust to the darkness swallowing it. It was all I could do to not start flailing my arms and legs around in case I was about to be attacked. Then, I realized what was trapping me: blankets. My blankets. On my bed.

Momma's name echoed, not just in my subconscious, but in my ears. This world was real; I'd actually cried out the word.

It's okay. It's okay. I released each breath with the imagined tick of a clock. *Jak said last night that the pack went to Asheville. Alexa's doing a solo mission somewhere. North Carolina is a big state. They're hours away. They're not here.*

Mr. Dawson was even able to confirm Jak's information by looking through a database. (Don't ask how we gained access to the database.) No pack. No Alexa.

Deep breath.

Realizing all of that, though, that I was in my room, that the pack wasn't here, wasn't enough to lay me back down. I still couldn't relax enough to fall back asleep. Something was blocking me, holding me up—if not the subtlest force of magic. Like the instinct magic had built in me by that point was warning me.

I'd had the same dream three times now. That was too many times for it to just be a dream. The druid in me was showing me the possible future. The *extremely* possible future—

As if fear weren't already wrenching my gut, terror blinded me the second my bedroom doorknob twisted.

I stiffened. *No. No. No—!*

In walked Jak in a black hoodie.

Wait—Jak?

He jumped in surprise, almost bumping into the doorway. "Oh," he whispered, closing the door behind him. "Did... did I wake you up?"

"What're you doing here?!" I whisper-screamed. When the shock finally settled, I threw off my covers and swung my legs over the side of the mattress to standing. Not even drowsiness could suppress my teenage girl instincts, and I ran my hands through my hair to neaten it as much as possible. "Did you seriously just break into my house?"

Jak stifled his laughter as he took a step away from the door. "Uh... not my smartest idea?"

"No! How did you get—?"

Wait. Jak was in my house. The house he'd never been to before.

I'd never told him where I'd grown up.

He may know how to find that out, but Alexa has the means and motive.

I forced myself to steady my breath. Right now, I needed my greatest control to stay calm and ahead of my enemy. No matter how close she was to me.

I sat myself back down onto my bed, sheets still warm from my body heat. Even my legs, left mostly bare from my pajama shorts, were experiencing enough of an anxiety rush to keep themselves warm. I fiddled with the locket around my neck as I asked, "She's still after me, isn't she?"

"Jak" pressed his lips together and nodded. He even had the scab on his lip. A chill snaked down my spine.

"Why?" I said. For the first time since the night Jak and I met, eye contact was a struggle. I kept my stare on his chin.

"Your guess is as good as mine." He ambled closer to the center of my room. "That's... that's why I'm here. I had to warn you. It was important."

The atmosphere twinged. We were mere feet away from each other. I could almost feel the cold blade of a knife against my back.

"I don't know," he said, "did you give away anything new about Tristan's descendant?"

"Descendant". Jak and I had swapped that for "daughter" long ago.

"You know what I told you," I said, trying to conjure a plan—and an escape—in my head. The bracelet, that bracelet had been consistent in my visions, and Alexa had tried to force it onto my wrist. If that was reality, I needed to keep it away from me at all costs before Momma was thrown out the window.

Wait. My whole family, including Mr. Dawson, was in the house right now. Alexa had snuck right by them! What if she had backup waiting in case I didn't cooperate? What if, if I didn't play this out correctly, this was the night my family would land at Caldwell's feet?

"Then"—Jak shook his head and lightly shrugged—"I guess I don't know why she's after you."

"I find that hard to believe." The words escaped my mouth too quickly for me to stop them. "How am I supposed to know *you* didn't tell?"

Honestly, those were the words I'd wanted to say to Alexa for a while now.

Jak scrunched his face in confusion and... almost offense. "You know I'd *never* do that to you, what are you talking about?"

I scoffed, my anxiety ready to shove the words out of my mouth, but I didn't have a lot of options that wouldn't let my enemy know that I knew. I stood there, silently begging for some kind of direction to appear for me.

Jak's lips parted but stayed open, like he had no words left to test. The corner was shrinking, even as he asked, "Are you feeling okay?"

I dropped the locket and made myself stand. As much as I wanted to believe otherwise, perpetuating this wasn't going to fix anything. I just had to rip off the Band-Aid: "Take off the spell."

Jak took a step toward me, reaching for my arm. "Emma—"

Wrong answer.

I jerked away. "I know you're Alexa!"

His soft features contorted in hatred—maybe even fallen pride—as his eyes folded into deeper darkness. "Already?" he sneered. "You're good, Atera."

My body winced; I never thought I'd hear him, of all people, address me with that.

"Either you're good, or I'm getting rusty."

Pulling the hood up, Alexa lowered her head. A spell I was pretty sure I'd heard from her before left her lips in a whisper. When she raised her head, her emerald-green eyes stared back at me.

—Okay,— she said, my very spine shuddering. —*How did you know? What gave it away?*—

I couldn't step back. I couldn't let her win again. I couldn't be afraid no matter how much anxiety was burning in my chest and numbing my limbs.

I locked my jaw to stop it from shaking. —Get out.—

—*Well, that's rude.*— She smirked, putting her hands in her hoodie pockets. Only then did I realize the absence of the purple rose that was supposed to be on Jak's real one. —*I just wanted to catch up, it's been a while. I even got you a present.*—

The bracelet, she was reaching for the bracelet! I had to either get it or avoid it no matter how tonight ended!

With no control over my emotions, they waived that of my volume. "Get out, or I'm waking everyone up!"

—*You wouldn't do that.*— Alexa snickered. I could practically see her fiddling with the box in her pocket. —*Not unless you want this house compromised.*—

It was happening. My vision was happening, I was losing control. I couldn't stop it!

Get a grip, I commanded myself. *Don't let her control you again!*

I only had one thing to defend myself with without touching

her. But—could I afford the risk? After what I'd done to Marcus, and then to Alexa in the forest... could I really wield my magic as a sword against another magician again?

Alexa grinned, biting her lip like I was her favorite thing to marvel at. —*Oh, hang on. You* are *scared.*— She stepped into the first streams of moonlight through my window. —*Why? What's scaring you right now? Mind amusing me?*—

—*Just go, don't make me force you! I don't want to, but I will if you take one more step!*—

Her grin dropped with her hand in her pocket. —*You're getting too brave for your own good, Atera. Now you're threatening me again?*—

The mood in her eyes shifted, straightening her stance and stiffening my body. —*I think I get it,*— she said. —*You had a vision about this because you're a hybrid, didn't you? You know what's in my pocket, you know what I'm here to do.*—

—*I'm giving you one more chance to get out.*—

"Oh, you really do." Alexa shook her head, clicking her tongue. "Do you wanna go ahead and tell me, or is interrogation still your love language?"

This woman was on anything *but* sanity!

"What else do you want?" I whispered. "Please, just tell me!"

—*Unlike you, Emmalynn, nores can't lie. I don't know how you did it, but you lied under that truth spell in the forest. You know more about Adara than just her name, and it's your mistake if you think I won't spend this entire summer looking for her.*—

Who told her? Who could've—no, Moren wouldn't have... He was on our... What nore on this planet preferred helping *Alexa Delphine* over me?

How did a nore's magic not reveal that I am Adara?

My fingers curled. My locket wasn't an option for comfort right now. It felt like out loud was the only way she'd hear my desperation as I said, "Please. Go."

—You're not denying it?—

"Get *out!*"

"You need to get rid of this belief that you hold any power over me!" she snarled, tearing the velvet box out of her pocket. "You're in MY field, Emmalynn, and now you're gonna listen to me when I tell you to—!"

"*Obliviscor!*"

Alexa's eyes glazed over as they rolled into the back of her head. The small box dropped to the floor, her lean body crumpling after.

THIRTEEN

Shallow breaths caught in my throat one at a time. With a magic will as strong as that, had I used any other offensive spell, I could've killed her. *I could've killed her,* I kept thinking. As if what I'd just done wasn't bad as long as I *hadn't* killed her.

—Mr. Dawson. Mr. Dawson!—

It was barely past 1 in the morning, but I leaped over Alexa's limp body to dart into the living room. Mr. Dawson was sleeping on the couch bed in there. Part of me was still bitter about the final, but he was the best option to come to about this.

She doesn't remember. The thought ruthlessly beat in my head. *She doesn't know anything. She doesn't remember.*

She didn't remember anything. I'd done that.

I rounded the hallway corner and stepped into the pitch-black living room. I turned on the lamp sitting on the table next to the couch, yellow light illuminating a sleeping Mr. Dawson. My eyes blinked against the sudden brightness, straining to adjust. Despite the sheets and blankets that covered the man, a strong chest visibly rose and fell with his breaths. I almost felt guilty for ruining it, but disrupting his beauty sleep wasn't really on my list of concerns anymore.

My chest tightened, realizing that I didn't have time for telepathy to fail again. I timidly reached over the bed to shake Mr. Dawson's shoulders.

"Mr. Dawson," I whispered.

The metal frame of the bed creaked with my shaking. Grimacing as I tried again, I prayed for the noise to stop as I surrendered my full voice. "Mr. Dawson?"

A grumble and sharp inhale later, his diamond-blue eyes blinked open and gravitated toward me.

"Emma? What're you doing up?" he asked groggily, squinting against the light.

I didn't have enough patience or time to wait for him to fully wake up: "Alexa's in my room."

I bet he would've sooner believed that he was dreaming in that moment, until seconds passed and I still hadn't broken eye contact. I matched his hard stare with nonconforming truth, and then he woke up.

The couch bed's creak seemed to resonate throughout the house as he threw the covers off and jumped up. I followed him as he darted down the hallway and then through my bedroom doorway. He skid to a stop before he could trip over Alexa's body lying in the middle of my room.

And I know it wasn't the most appropriate time to notice, but the two were *totally* matching in their baggy sleepwear.

Mr. Dawson stammered for words, his eyes constantly switching between me and Alexa. —*What happened?!*—

I closed the door behind me, cursing the shakiness stuck in my breath. I had to be braver than this, I couldn't run away from this.

"I had a vision about Alexa," I whispered, too exhausted for telepathy now. "She tried to put on this bracelet—" I found the box sitting in front of my hanging chair in the corner, and picked it up. "This. She put it on me and it sent this—some kind of shock through me. But tonight, when I woke up—I woke up and *Jak* came in, but it was Alexa under some kind of appearance spell, I told her to take it off—"

"Honey, calm down." Mr. Dawson took my shoulders, rubbing them. "She didn't get it on you and you defended yourself."

"No, no!" I stammered, shaking my head. "I—I didn't put her to sleep, I made her forget! I made her forget everything, it was strong enough to knock her out!"

"Emma. Calm down." Mr. Dawson gently emphasized each word, a mild tension holding them. "What do you mean by 'everything'?"

"*Everything!*" I whispered, gripping my bare arms like it would protect me. "Her whole life, her memories, I felt it, the spell was so strong that she passed out! She won't remember *anything* when she wakes up!"

Mr. Dawson's lips parted as if, any second now, he'd have the solution. I waited and waited for that to happen, for him to gather every last thought and organize them so that he wouldn't forget even one.

"You used magic to *completely* wipe her memory and then knock her out?"

I swallowed hard. When he said it, it sounded so much worse.

He glimpsed the box in my hand and then took it. Leaning back slightly, he rotated it around in the moonlight streaming from the window and then opened it. A silver cuff bracelet sat inside with a diamond in the middle. "If putting this on you was all she came here to do, she would've put it on you in your sleep and then left."

Ha. Great.

"She knows I know something about Adara," I rasped. "She spoke to a nore. She wants everything I know about her."

"So she was gonna put the bracelet on you, kidnap you in the middle of the night, and then debrief you on an anonymous sorceress?"

"I guess..."

"And you said she came in as *Jak?*"

I took a breath in to speak, but the blanks had yet to be filled. Knowing Jak and his habits, he would've given me his gift, sent me off to bed, and then left. Knowing Alexa and what she'd already tried to do through Jak with the trust spell last year, she was probably planning on gathering as much intel as she could with his appearance. And if that didn't work, she was probably going to kidnap me anyway.

It almost sounded like... Alexa wanted to give me a *choice.* When had that ever mattered before?

"She wanted the bracelet handoff to seem natural." I fiddled with the charm around my neck. "And whatever other information she wanted was supposed to be naturally discussed, too. But Adara..."

"Unless she wasn't coming for everything in one night," Mr. Dawson mused, looking up at me from the box. "She's a really patient woman. Always... always has been."

Chills ran from the center of my chest: give me the bracelet as Jak tonight. Find out whatever she wanted to about Adara when it had done its job later. Possibly get my magic in the process.

I looked down at the still woman lying at our feet. "She had it all planned."

As usual.

Mr. Dawson nodded, reserving a few seconds to himself. "And erasing her entire memory is a bad thing *how?*"

My brows furrowed. "William and their pack will question where she is! She has nowhere to go, she's leaving behind a whole life of intel that could change the world!"

"Sure, if you wanna think negatively about it," he replied. I wished that he'd offer a smile to make it feel more like the joke that it was supposed to be. "You said the pack is in Asheville for a couple of weeks, and she's meant to be on a private research mission during that time, too."

I didn't want to believe that this was that simple to solve. Probably because I knew better now: *I* was Alexa's private research mission.

"I'll take care of her for now." Mr. Dawson bent down and picked up Alexa—bridal style. "In the morning, you need to tell your parents what happened and then meet me at my place with your mom. Shoot for, let's say, 10 o'clock."

"Do you have a plan?" I asked as he turned around, Alexa's head resting peacefully against his chest.

He looked over his shoulder to match our eyes, giving me the smirk I'd been waiting for. "Where's your trust?"

Just like that, he'd ruined it. *It died when you betrayed me Thursday morning and thought it'd be okay.* He might've been sorry about how he'd done it, and I might've been trying to forgive him, but none of that meant that my trust in his decision-making hadn't suffered a serious blow. Because this? This was *miles* beyond precarious. I almost trusted myself more to take care of Alexa.

"But where is she gonna go?" I asked. "How are we dealing with her?"

His smile relaxed, his lips pressing together. With uncertainty, hope, or strain, I couldn't tell. "Tomorrow morning. 10 o'clock."

CHAPTER

FOURTEEN

I wanted to be anywhere *but* with Mr. Dawson on Saturday morning, and that was a scary first—but only because of the woman that would probably be answering the door with him. As Momma and I walked up the porch in the tepid late-spring air, my stomach turned while my mind reeled. I was about to see Alexa Delphine, but who was the *woman* I was about to meet?

The front door eased open, and Mr. Dawson stepped aside for us. "Good morning," he whispered, making me wonder how close by Alexa was. "You doing okay, Amy?"

"Emma's gonna hold me back while I try not to strangle her," she spat as he closed the door behind us—which was a pretty good summary of it.

"I figured as much."

"I've never met her before, Thomas," she said, resting her hands on my shoulders. "All this time, all these months, I've never once met the woman who kidnapped my daughter. What kind of a mother am I to have never caught her *once*, to have just let her get away with it?"

"Well, if it helps, you've never gone on a mission *to* hunt her. Not to mention you were running classes while she was traveling around the state." His deep-set eyes landed on me. "And honesty regarding just *how much* she's really been in our lives played a significant role."

I wondered how much time had to pass before they'd let that go. And when Mr. Dawson would stop staring at me after that sentence.

"It's not as if you knew what she was doing this year up until recently," he eventually told Momma. "By the time you did, she was gone. And last year... Look, none of us could've predicted that she would *stay* in our lives. You can't blame yourself."

"Then what kind of a Hunter does that make me?" Momma stated. "To know that my enemy wasn't done with her target and yet completely surrender my defense?"

"You're human." Mr. Dawson crossed his arms, casual against her emotions. "You don't have a tracker on her all hours of the day. But now"—he gestured down the hallway—"you practically do."

I looked next to me, where the humble, minimalistic living room lay. The wooden coffee table had been pushed farther away from the couch, where a couple of fleece blankets and a white pillow messily sat. Which meant that Alexa was sleeping in Mr. Dawson's bed.

"There are a few things we need to discuss," he began, holding up his hands. "First, we don't know exactly how powerful this memory-wiping spell is yet. Emma, you know it erased everything because of how it felt, but do you have any idea as to how strong it is?"

"I was scared." I tightly crossed my arms as if to protect myself against any accusations. "It was self-defense, I knew what I wanted to do—but I don't know if…"

"If?"

I paused, unsure of how I felt about my next words. "I don't know if she can recover."

Momma stayed silent beside me. Mr. Dawson pressed his lips together, pensive eyes cast down.

"This is a seriously dangerous game," he told me. "We don't know if even the slightest trigger will get her memories back. We have to keep everything from her old life as far away from her as possible." He glimpsed me from toe to head. "Unfortunately, some things, we just can't hide. And we have to pray that they don't give everything away."

"Did she have anything on her?" Momma asked. "Her phone? Hunter badge, any weapons?"

"Just her phone. I turned it off and it's staying in my car until further notice."

"Are we…" I asked, digging my feet into the linoleum of the entry foyer, "gonna go through it?"

"It's not the phone we need—based on the wallpaper, it's her personal one." Mr. Dawson tiredly sighed, rubbing his face with both of his hands. "If there's any device that would have useful information, it'd be her phone assigned by the agency or in a drive *at* the agency. Still, that personal phone is a one-way ticket to her memories."

"Just in case," Momma began tentatively, "what if it's bugged?"

"It'd be warm even turned off. It's cold."

My gaze rested on the coffee table in the living room. "How are we gonna make it seem like we're trying to help her when we wanna make sure she *doesn't* remember?"

"Exactly," Momma said, "you can't just keep her here for nobody knows how long without making any efforts toward finding who she really is. She'll definitely suspect something."

Mr. Dawson pressed his lips together. "I was thinking Tristan or Becca could show up with an appearance spell and a cop outfit somewhere down the line."

Momma paused, and I dully stared at him. Unfortunately for us, though, that plan was most likely our best bet, and Mr. Dawson knew it.

I prayed that he'd have a definitive answer to my next question: "What if someone traces her back here?"

"We're gonna take every precaution possible to make sure that doesn't happen," he said. "And if it does, we'll do what's necessary. But that depends on who finds her and when."

Not good enough, I thought, but he was already walking straight past us and then down the hallway. Momma and I followed in trepidation, our footsteps swallowed by the carpet.

The two of us stayed in the doorway when Mr. Dawson walked into his bedroom. He moved aside, revealing a sleeping Alexa on the bed in front of us. Plush white pillows cradled her head, a navy-blue comforter trapping her. Despite the fact that she was completely defenseless, my stomach churned at her red hair and soft, slim features.

How does she have such subtle wrinkles? Hunting's one of the most stressful careers there are.

Mr. Dawson looked back at me and Momma. "I don't have time to tell you the whole story, so here's the short version: you're going to follow my lead *exactly* and only speak when spoken to."

"Oh, really?" Momma said flatly, her hands resting on her hips.

The power this woman holds over everyone around her is terrifying and inspiring.

Mr. Dawson sighed. "Not like that. It's just a plan. I'm gonna wake her up, and it's crucial that no matter what I say, you don't look confused or surprised. Got it?"

Momma exhaled and nodded once.

"Yeah," I told him, reaching for my locket.

"Are you *sure*, Emma?" He tilted his head of dark hair down, his stare weighing heavily on me. "This is a one-hundred-percent performance, and if you let that drop to even ninety-nine, it's over. I ask you again:"—he leaned toward me, the weight of the room pressing down on my shoulders—"can you do this?"

I shouldn't have had to think about it, but I did. Within those few seconds, Mr. Dawson's wavering faith in me was palpable.

"Yes." I even dropped my hand from my locket to prove my point.

His eyes fell onto Alexa, glowing amber a second later. I took a step forward, away from Momma, who flinched. With my breath locked in my lungs, I waited for Alexa's eyes to flutter open.

I'm meeting her for the first time all over again.

She deeply inhaled, her eyes squinting against the natural lighting the window behind her gave. When she tried to prop herself up on her elbows, her eyes widened, transitioning between the three of us. "Who are you, what's going on?"

"You don't remember?" Mr. Dawson asked in the manner of someone who'd just spent the past few hours with her (which, I realized in horror, was true). "We took you to the hospital, the doctors diagnosed you with retrograde amnesia and told us to take you back here, and then you fell asleep."

"Wait." Alexa glimpsed her delicate hands, then down at the blankets, then at her surroundings, and then at us. "No, I don't... I don't remember that. I've never been here before, I've never seen any of you before."

Her voice, I quickly realized, sounded a *lot* different—deeper and fuller—without the sympathetic tone she usually laid on when speaking to me. I couldn't figure out if it was a good different or not. I had to wonder if it was how she'd spoken to Mr. Dawson back when they were dating—how she used to speak when she was... well, normal.

Mr. Dawson crossed his arms, tightening his jaw. For a moment, I actually believed the lie that came from his lips: "The doctor said that your condition is so severe that it might or might not, for the time being, affect your ability to remember as you come in and out of consciousness. Would you like us to explain what happened again?"

"Um..." Alexa used both of her hands to sit up straight. "Yes, please."

Mr. Dawson rested one hand on the headboard, gesturing to

himself. "I'm Julian. Rachael and her daughter, Morgan,"—he nodded to us at the foot of the bed—"found you wandering the road on their way over here yesterday. When Rachael called out to you, you passed out. The doctors gave us the diagnosis once you woke up, and we introduced ourselves to you."

New names. Okay, smart, but in no way was I getting used to that soon.

"Oh," Alexa said simply, gazing at the covers. "I'm... I'm sorry. I don't remember any of that."

The worst part was that she sounded *sincere*. A wave of guilt slammed against my chest.

Mr. Dawson laid a careful hand on the comforter, mindful of where she lay. "It's not your fault. But we were told that you should be resting as much as possible. There's a small chance you'll get your memories back quickly, but—they warned us not to hold our breaths."

"So I..." Alexa began unsteadily. Something brand new twinged in her defined eyes: worry. "There's a chance I might never remember who I am? Did anybody at the hospital recognize me? Were they able to pull up any records or files?"

"They're not even sure you're from around here," Mr. Dawson replied. "You were found with no car, wallet, phone, or I.D. We were hoping you'd remember something that could help us determine your identity, at least. The police should be stopping by within the next few days with a progress report. You can tell them if you remember anything then."

Still one of the best liars I know. But for the first time in my life, I wasn't as sure anymore that that was a good thing.

"So,"—Alexa straightened in realization—"this is your house?"

Mr. Dawson took a deep breath in as if this were the most challenging acting gig he'd ever taken on. "Yep. Forest City, North Carolina. Does that ring a bell?"

She reserved a few seconds to herself before pressing her lips together. Then, she shook her head in defeat.

"Um…" I said. And even when memory-rid Alexa's attention landed on me, the panic from the day we'd met reignited in my chest. "Is there anything you *do* remember?"

She thought on it. The room was ominously quiet, ready to shatter at any moment, for what felt like minutes until her brows furrowed and her lips parted. "Does anybody know my name?"

Mr. Dawson's jaw dropped slightly open again, but this time, Momma and I didn't hesitate to follow. I'd wiped this woman's memory to the point where she couldn't even remember her own name?

"Well, obviously you *have* one," Mr. Dawson said, crossing his arms again. I couldn't even tell if this was part of his act or if he genuinely hadn't thought this part through yet. "Is there… a name you'd like?"

She was silent again, as if debating whether her thoughts were telling her the truth. "'Alexandra' is coming to mind for some reason." Her lean build finally relaxed into the pillows. "I guess I'll go with that."

I stopped myself in time from tilting my head. "For some reason" was right—why "Alexandra"? Why would she remember a name so close to her real one instead of her actual name or one that was completely different?

"It fits you," Mr. Dawson said softly, nodding in approval.

Hang on. That was a smile twitching on the corners of his

mouth. What was going on? Was he just happy that Alexa didn't remember her real name?

Not with that tone. Momma and I need to keep an eye on him.

"Thank you." Alexa smiled, color returning to her fair cheeks. "I hope I'm not being rude by asking if—if you know where I'm staying until everything comes back to me."

"We wanted to discuss it with you." Mr. Dawson stood up straight, pulling my eyes to him. Momma rested a hand on my shoulder like she was helping me brace myself. "The local motel is nearby, but—"

"Oh, no, I couldn't ask that of you," Alexa rushed to say, pushing herself farther up in bed. "Even if I could, I can't promise I'll be able to pay you back within a reasonable time."

"We didn't want to leave you alone there, anyway. So if you're comfortable with it…"—Mr. Dawson purposely kept his eyes away from us, I just knew it—"as Rachael and Morgan have relatives visiting them for the summer, you're welcome to stay with me."

What!

—I told you, you can't act surprised.—

I knew my eyes widening had given me away, but I ignored it as I told him, *—Stay with you? Who told you that was a good idea? They were lying!—*

—There is no telling when she'll get her memories back. I'm not gonna leave her loose in a motel when it does happen, and there are too many leads at your house. She's safest here.—

Alexa took another breath to speak, interrupting my next thought. She glanced at me and Momma as if we had the right answer—like we could verify whether she could trust Mr. Dawson that deeply so quickly. A small part of me wanted to tell her that she couldn't. But, as much as I hated to admit it, if she got her memories back at a motel without us there, or if she stayed with me and Mom and got her memories back while we were out or visiting Dad and Aunt Becca—

Yeah. Neither was happening.

"Morgan and I actually need to visit a friend today," Momma said, her hands rubbing my shoulders.

We do?

"But maybe you and Julian can get acquainted at the nearby café while we do that. Afterwards, we were planning on visiting him for the weekend before family arrives. So we could stay with you here for a day or two—"

Don't act surprised, don't act surprised.

"—and then you can decide what to do from there. How does that sound?"

The woman lying in the bed in front of me had mentally, physically, and emotionally tormented us for almost a year, yet it still felt wrong to subject her to a situation of even the slightest discomfort right now. I guess it was because we weren't talking to that woman anymore.

The corners of Alexa's lips slightly turned upward. "I'd be really grateful. I appreciate everything you're doing for me. I just hope I get my memories back soon so I won't have to impose for too long."

"It's no trouble," Mr. Dawson said, holding up a polite hand.

I mentally scoffed. *Maybe not for you, Romeo.*

Alexa's eyes landed on me again, and I had to stop myself from setting into the basic starting position of self-defense.

"You're Morgan, right? And this is your mom, Rachael?"

"Yeah," I replied timidly, "but you can call me 'Mo'."

I had no idea where the lie had come from; I was probably just so used to a nickname that I had to apply it even in a lie so it'd feel more natural. It comforted me a little bit about lying in the first place.

Alexa's words struggled to escape her again for a couple of seconds. "I really... I'm thankful that you found me. And thank you for taking me to the hospital. I don't know where I'd be right now had it not been for you guys, so thank you."

I do. She wouldn't even be in this bed right now if it hadn't been for me, and I wasn't sure which situation I preferred: one where she was free as herself and after me, or one where she was innocent but at my mercy because of what I'd done to her.

"It was our pleasure." Momma's smile almost looked genuine, but I knew the truth. And I was too scared to read through the raw emotions that had built that lie.

So we were staying with Mr. Dawson and Alexa for the weekend? There wasn't... I couldn't... They expected me to live under the same roof as this woman for *two days*? I—

—had two best friends who could totally get me out of this.

"Uh..." I was only brave enough to face Momma as I said, "I was hoping I could have a sleepover with Sarah and Breanne tonight."

I think Momma more than liked the idea; it meant that she could unapologetically analyze Alexa, memories or none, without worrying about traumatizing me. (I've yet to recover from the story of when she had to sedate and then tie up a runaway magician in the deep end of a public swimming pool in Nashville. You'd think being underwater would make it *easier* to pretzel someone, but Momma… lost her grip a few times.)

"Sure," she said. "After we visit a friend."

When Momma starts being ominous, I've learned to take the hidden message: buckle up; don't ask; and, most importantly, don't be afraid. That was the last thing I could afford to be right now.

C H A P T E R

FIFTEEN

oren was the only one who could tell us the purpose of the bracelet. It was a purpose promising enough for Alexa to have been willing to literally fight to put it on me and then *still* kidnap me. We weren't going to get anywhere without this answer.

That, and I had to interrogate him about who'd told Alexa that I knew something about Adara—and make sure that it hadn't been him.

He opened the door with an impish grin, dark-brown eyes twinkling. "It's my special company!" he chirped in that high-pitched mixture of an English and Scottish accent. "What brings you two along?"

"It's urgent." Momma tightened her hold on my shoulders

like she was trying to prepare me. "We're sorry to bother you so suddenly, but—this is need-to-know."

"Is it about..."—he brought his hand to my ear and then pulled out the small velvet box—"this?"

Momma didn't bother asking. "Yep."

"Do come in," Moren said, moving aside to allow me. Upon Momma taking a step forward to follow, he instantly stepped back into the doorway.

"Tut, tut, tut!" His dark finger danced with each repetition of the word. "Unless you want to pay the price as well, I'm only taking one customer today."

"Emma will tell us your answer anyway," Momma stated, patience already thinning. "What about what you did for us last time we needed you?"

"My dear Emma will tell you an answer that *she* paid for. A birthday cake needs only one purchaser to be shared."

Momma's lips pressed themselves tightly together in what I recognized as her humility.

"As for last time, I was being generous, dearie. You'd just lost your loved ones to those government savages chasing them out of town, and I had to make a good first impression. Now you can see your family whenever you'd like—in fact, they're moving into their new home soon, aren't they?"

"Fine. I'll ask you what we came here for."

"All right," Moren said, his inflection rising suspiciously at the end, "but be warned, I won't be able to tell you everything if you do. There are some answers your daughter unlocks simply with her..."—he gestured grandly to me, his accent brightening his tone—"personality."

With another glance in my direction, Momma sighed heavily. "Fine. But if you—"

"No need to worry, Mrs. Atera." He grinned, half-bowing with the bracelet box still in hand. "She'll be safe with me."

Momma reluctantly gave way, her gaze landing on me one last time with her traditional loving concern. "Be quick."

Moren waited for her to walk back to the car before closing the door, trapping me in the warm aroma of simmering beef stew and fresh bread. His dark and curly hair, almost down to his shoulders, swung as he turned, facing me and keeping the box safe in his hold.

"Hello, savior." His lips curled upward in mischief like we were about to play his favorite board game. "How are you?"

I crossed my arms against my nerves that wanted nothing to do with this conversation. "I'd be a lot better if a *nore* hadn't told Alexa that I knew something about Adara."

Okay—I kind of hadn't expected the furrowed brows and wide eyes he gave me after that.

"Care to elaborate for me?" he asked, tilting his head and leaning forward as if to hear me better.

"You're a nore. Do you know how many there are in Capperson?"

His movements slowed, like he was trying to piece together my thoughts as he went. Eventually, he stilled like a statue. "Admittedly, I'm the only other one."

I was pretty sure I already had the answer to my own question, and yet I needed to hear it from him all the more: "Were you the one who told her?"

"No." His features contorted in the most genuine emotion

I'd ever seen from him—and of course, it had to be offense. "No, of course not. What makes you think I'd confess something like that to her?"

"Other than the fact that you have no choice but to answer, and nores are neutral in all affairs?" I said, tightening my crossed arms. "Because what matters most is information you can exchange and sell to other buyers? You're Mr. Dawson's friend, but that doesn't mean anything for you and me. You don't have a reason to protect me."

He immediately opened his mouth, but nothing came out, almost like he'd had to make a sudden U-turn with his reply. "No, savior," he told me. "Nobody's asked me anything about the matter."

I didn't know how or why this worked—maybe it was the way he'd said one of those words, or the fact that he'd let his voice down into its normal register for those words—but despite how this wasn't an official "nore transaction" and he wasn't under its truth spell... I couldn't help but believe him.

I dragged my eyes to the bare brown wall behind him. "Apparently all the nore said was that I knew something. I don't get it, why wouldn't Alexa just ask directly if I'm Adara?"

Moren lightly shrugged, setting the box down onto the table against the wall. "Thomas is the only reason I know at all. It seems that magic has reserved some answers for itself until due time." He pulled out his chair from the table, inviting me to follow. "Why don't we see what we can do to fight back?"

"Did you mean it when you said not every answer would be revealed if my mom asked the question?" I asked, pulling out the chair across from him. "Don't you usually *want* a lot of people to ask you something so you have more info to 'sell'?"

He gestured to my chair. "You'll have your answers, savior, I promise."

I tensed before sitting down. Honestly, my chest tightened a little more every time he called me that. It wasn't like I wasn't willing to fulfill Adara's fate one day, but the constant reminder, the sheer weight of a title like "savior", was starting to press me into the ground rather than push me up to the sky.

"You don't have a reason to protect me."

Was that why he went to immediately respond but then had to stop himself? He *did?*

"Why do you call me that?"

As he sat down, his hands made a "why not" gesture, a gameshow host-like grin attached to his face again. "That is what you call one who saves the world, isn't it?"

That depended on whose lens you looked through. Adara was a destructive nightmare for people like Alexa and President Caldwell, but she was a savior to people like Dad, Aunt Becca, even Opal. People like... Moren.

Wait a minute.

He was out of a nore's character. Nores are allegedly neutral in any and all affairs *because* of their ability; they have more power if they stay neutral. If Moren knew of my destiny, if he really believed that I could help our people, and if he *wanted* to answer my question, that meant...

"You're on my side," I said in realization. "You're *not* neutral in this, are you?"

His smile hung on for only a second before it flattened. For the first time since I met him, I watched him back into a shell that

I never even knew existed. He hung his head, pressing his lips together. I wondered if I'd unlocked something that he kept caged for a reason.

"My people have been enslaved and exploited for centuries, Miss Atera," he began lowly. Too lowly for it to be Moren's voice. He took his words with him when he stood from his chair and started wandering past me, toward the living room. "Centuries. Are you able to comprehend the amount of days in that span of time? Each one spent in misery and suffering, only to fast forward to the modern era and realize that not even time, not even *centuries*, could save us? Today—today is no different than yesterday! If we aren't killed like every other class of magic once we're found,"— he turned around to face me, his voice crescendoing into... *anger*— "we're held against our will to provide our knowledge. Beaten, abused, tortured, *slaughtered* if we don't comply! We're easily replaceable, they think. If one of us is killed, they have others in stock. They use us to gain whatever they need." A heavy hand landed on his chest as he walked back up to the table. "My people were convinced that that was the way we would live for the rest of our days on Earth. That was our purpose. And we believed that there was no escape."

He sat back down across from me and took my hands into his. And yet, it felt safe to stay sitting where I was. "And then we hear of a young sorceress meant to help unite our two worlds, meant to ensure the safety of the people of magic. We hear that someone will finally have the power to save us, to change the way things are,"—he gestured all around him—"to take us all out of hiding! And now I know that it's you, young Atera, *you* are the one meant to save my people—*your* people!"

When he took another break in, his mouth clamped shut. His thin lips pressed into a line so tight, I was scared his teeth would penetrate straight through. He wanted to continue, he wanted to tell me so much more—but we didn't have the time.

"Yes," he finally said with a calm breath. "I stray from the center this time. But it will be the first and only time."

I exhaled slowly in hopes to not blast my... well, awe and shock—but, most prominent, my fear. Not that it would've helped, but a "no pressure" at the end of all of that would've made it a bit easier to digest.

I thought about Annisa, what she'd told me earlier this year when we first met—our job. It was *our* job to do those things one day, and I only had one comfort with that thought: at the very least, the responsibility didn't rest on me alone.

Without letting me reply, Moren faced the jewelry box in my direction and opened it. The silver cuff bracelet stared back at me, cast in the shadows of the edge of the room.

Moren offered his hand, and I placed mine on top of it. Amber ignited through his irises as he put his other hand on mine.

"So, my dear," he began quietly, "about this bracelet—what would you like to know?"

I let out a shaky breath, feeling safe to expose my heart, especially after he'd done so with me. "Alexa wanted this on my wrist so badly, she was willing to literally fight for it. What does it do?"

He took a few seconds to look at me, as if taking a mental image of his hero. Then came a subtle nod. "You did the right thing in avoiding this bracelet's will. Its enchantment is strong and rare: once put on, only the one who placed it on your wrist may take it off until it finishes its task of draining your magic, turning its white diamond orange. The next person who wears it will absorb the magic it collected from you."

What...? No, completely extracting a magician's magic was a dangerous process, sometimes even fatal! It was why Dad had asked Mr. Dawson to take *most* of his magic when he had to leave the country before I was born—how could Alexa have gotten something like this that could do it so easily, like it was nothing?

That's why the enchantment is so powerful.

I froze in my seat. That close. I'd been *that* close to losing it all last night. If I hadn't had those visions, I would've lost everything.

"She found a way to do it," I whispered.

"And you escaped her," Moren said. "I'd expect nothing less from a hybrid."

I looked up at him, about to ask, but then remembered.

I shook my head, also remembering that Momma was outside, the she-devil herself was alone with Mr. Dawson at his house, and time was more limited now than ever. "What's your question to me?"

To my surprise, Moren had to think about it first.

With the amber still flowing freely in his irises, his eyes narrowed slightly as he asked, "Are you wholeheartedly willing to become Adara and eventually free your people?"

"Yeah, of course I am. But you already knew that."

He patted the top of my hand. "This one's on the house, dearie. How about that?"

I opened my mouth to argue, but I wasn't sure if I should; Momma's always told me that I can't deny a gift more than once, but I couldn't let him get away with that!

"Then let me ask one more question, and you can ask me a real one."

His lips pressed themselves together again with a grimace. The wooden chair beneath him creaked as he shifted his weight. "What would you like to know?"

"Mr. Dawson doesn't have his dreams back yet." I thought back to the day he'd willingly given up the attribute that made him a druid, when we'd learned from Ingrid what the future had in store. But despite all that had come to pass according to her prophecy, Mr. Dawson still hadn't had a single vision. "It means Ingrid's prediction hasn't completely happened yet, but everything else has..."

Moren tilted his head down. "What was the seer's prophecy *exactly?*"

I took a few seconds to remember that late-August day, honing my memory. "My nightmare about Alexa capturing us would come true. It'd be the first step of me admitting the truth and my greatest enemy revealing herself. But both happened when I found my dad at the beach house. I revealed myself as his daughter in front of Alexa, but before that, she'd revealed herself as a—"

A revelation nine months in the making finally dawned on me, stealing a beat from my heart: that wasn't true. Alexa had *never* revealed the truth about herself; Caralyn Callistro had exposed her first in her letter. But Alexa had revealed herself in other ways since then, right? As Julia? As Hunter? Even as Jak! Right?!

Mr. Dawson doesn't have his visions back because Ingrid's prophecy hasn't fully come to pass yet.

"I think you know what to ask, savior."

I looked up at Moren, my mouth hanging open. "Who is my

greatest enemy?"

"I can't tell you that,"—he smally shrugged—"because she doesn't exist."

I instinctually took my hand out of his. "What?"

His irises faded to black. "The seer prophesied that your dream would come to pass, you'd reveal the truth about yourself, and your greatest enemy would reveal herself—"

"When I reach my 'ultimate destination'." I exhaled slowly. I couldn't believe it. I had to be imagining this conversation.

"Which is the only event that hasn't come to happen yet. Meaning that the final event of Ingrid's prophecy has also yet to pass."

"I..."

...was at a complete loss for words. What was there to say?

"B—but if... How can I not have a greatest enemy when—?"

"I can't predict the future." Moren softly tapped the top of my hand. "I can't tell you anything about someone who doesn't exist, this is all I know. Alexa Delphine has lost her memory, meaning she has no idea of the power she has. For all we know, during the time she's at a loss for memories, you might just grow into your power completely."

I didn't want to believe it. I really didn't want to believe it. "Alexa isn't my greatest enemy?"

As terrible as she was, at least she was *familiar*.

"If you want that answer," Moren replied quietly, his Scottish-English accent heavier, "you're going to have to ask the seer."

Well, we all knew why I couldn't do that: I kind of *needed* my magic! And if it wasn't what I depended on most in this world anymore, I really didn't want to find out what had replaced it.

I leaned back in my seat. "Um... what was your question for me?"

He held out his hand again. I took it. As his eyes ignited with amber again, they now carried something I never even knew they could hold: sorrow. It was like he didn't want to do this.

"What is the one promise of your life that you regret making?"

As of then, I was basically under a truth spell. Maybe that was why I had no fear in answering, able to trust that my next words were really the truth: "That nothing will tear me and my family apart again."

Moren abruptly took his hand out from mine, both of our chairs creaking. His magic dissipated from his irises, his thin lips stuck in a confused "o".

Although my honesty was no longer promised, he still asked, "Why?"

"Because I have no control over if I can keep it," I said, realizing the words as they escaped. I rested my hands on the rough wooden table. "It's the one promise I made that didn't belong to me. And I'll live with the guilt for the rest of my life if something ever happens to us."

Moren tilted his head up slightly in understanding, his silence giving way to his thoughts.

"Know this." He took my hands into his, gently squeezing them. "Not one promise belongs to us. But our effort to keep them, no matter what they are, we own that completely."

Sixteen

I regretted not putting my phone on silent before bed as its ringing bled into my dreams. I regretted it even more when I registered that a ringing phone is *loud* and I'd just gotten home from Sarah's birthday party that night; Momma was going to kill me if she woke up.

My eyes squinted against the brightness of my phone screen. The contact name simultaneously drove worry and intrigue into my chest. I answered to stop the ringing, took a deep breath in, and put the phone to my ear.

A dry scratchiness clawed at my throat as I asked, "What time is it?"

"Early enough," Jak replied. Even half-asleep, my brain could register his smirk by his tone alone. "Sorry, I didn't mean to wake you up."

I pulled my phone away and checked the time at the top. I scoffed in disbelief, which actually helped clear a little of the throat pain. "It's 4 in the morning! You thought you could call and not wake me up?"

His chuckle on the other end surprised me. "I called because I thought you weren't gonna pick up."

"What?"

"I knew just calling you would make me feel a little better. It was a comfort call."

I plopped down onto my back, my tiredness barely holding up the phone. Jak's hesitance shifted within a second, like his narrative had to change because I *had* picked up.

"It's..." he said after a brief pause. "You'll relax me even though you're all the way over there. Sorry for waking you up."

I waited a few seconds until the heavy pull of sleep became dangerously strong. I regretted not filling a glass of water to leave on my bedside table as I said, "It's—it's fine. I usually put my phone on silent but forgot to last night. Maybe it was for a reason. Are you okay?"

Silence. And if there was anything I'd learned by that point, it was that Jak's hesitance *never* meant anything good.

"I don't trust Alexa."

It was good to know that I wasn't the only one she was mentally torturing from afar. But Jak didn't have the reasons that I did...

My heart started to unsteadily pulse. "What do you mean?"

"Well, Merlin, they're a *pack* for a reason. They hunt together, and now the leader's gone for a solo 'research' mission?"

I propped myself up on my elbow, fiddling with the locket around my neck. "Didn't the agency assign them their missions?"

"I still don't trust her. Do you? How do we know that research assignment isn't going undercover to investigate a lead on Tristan's daughter?"

Chills swept across my body, even under the warm sheet and comforter. No, not again. She wouldn't use the same trick twice.

I swallowed. At least I could be grateful that Jak was still using "Tristan's daughter" even though I'd given him Adara's name just before Redway left Callistro earlier this year. It was like he understood as well as I did the risks of just mentioning her name, even when we were the only two around.

"She's fine," I assured him. "I promise."

The silence shifted. There went his hesitance again.

Finally, a quiet remnant of a sigh. "If Alexa gets to her, that means she got to you first."

"We'll be prepared. We have you giving us all the warnings. And I trust his daughter's magic to tell us something we need to know ahead of time, too."

Again, nothing. Why was he so quiet tonight? Was he really that worried?

"I can't stay with you and Mom over the summer?"

A snort exploded from my nose, my hand instantly covering my mouth. Jak's whispered, uncontrollable giggling from the other line pushed me to the same laughter until it eventually grew too much for me to throw anywhere else but into my pillow. My mattress bounced with every breath until I felt like I was about to fall straight through it from bouncing it too much.

With a tight breath in, a grin pulled my lips wide apart.

"You're terrible, you're so cruel."

"I'm taking that as you want it just as much as I do."

I rolled my eyes. "Never make me laugh again."

"Not even magic can stop that, Merlin."

I shook my head with a helpless smile. *One of these days, I'll make him pay.*

I traced the rectangular outline of my closet in front of me with my eyes. My chest tightened, bracing me for whatever part of the conversation we were entering next. I despised it: my instincts like that are usually warning me.

"So you haven't seen Alexa?" Jak asked next. "She hasn't come after you?"

The lie was already bitter on my tongue. "No. Not since the final."

Our conversation at the gazebo rang in my head. I swallowed and prayed that he couldn't hear it.

With the ending of laughter, sleep was trying to take me off the phone again. Meanwhile, my throat was encouraging my heavy legs to take me to the kitchen for water.

I exhaled, closing my eyes. "I hope I was somewhat helpful in making you feel better."

"Yeah. You were, I needed the laugh."

It'd been a while since I'd last heard it.

"I miss you, Merlin."

My eyes shot open. We'd never said those words to each other before! It was the closest thing to a couple's phrase we'd ever gotten! Why tonight, why now?

Maybe it was the fact that it was 4 in the morning, the fact that I hadn't heard from Jak in longer than I cared for, the fact that I'd wondered for a long time what it was like to hear those words from and have these late-night calls with a teenage boy—but all I could feel in my chest was the amount of courage I needed to say, "I miss you, too."

I felt it: Jak's smile. Or maybe I only felt it because I was smiling, too.

"Sleep well. Sorry to disturb it."

"I don't mind when it's you."

What was the early morning doing to me? Who *was* I?

Jak chuckled before submitting a final good-night and letting me hang up the call.

That was a good question, I thought, recalling all of the good parts of the conversation and every lie. I repeated that question as I remembered the entire school year of deception I'd pulled off and thought about the amnesiac staying with Mr. Dawson because of that deceitfulness: who *was* I?

SEVENTEEN

The morning weather had been merciful so far, at least for mid-June. With a blazing sun, cloudless sky, and cool breeze, a practice hunt in Capperson Forest was actually how Sarah, Breanne, and I *wanted* to spend one of our summer vacation mornings. Without the pressure of grades, hunting is a more intense version of hide-and-seek—as long as you can pretend that you weren't traumatized by your last hunt.

"Sarah," Momma began in my ear as I pressed my back against a redwood tree, "you just passed two redwoods, one on each side of you: which was infected by a red spider mite?"

"The left," Sarah said instantly.

"Which one had a bird's nest?"

"The left."

"Was the branch it sat on infected or healthy?"

"Healthy."

I almost wished that Opal were here to play with us, but between this and scuba diving in Hawaii, she was probably winning.

I made my way to a pile of leaves and fallen branches. With another glance at my surroundings, I memorized the pattern of the trees that stood tall around me, finding the quickest hiding spots near them.

"Emma," Momma said. "Name the three methods of sneaking in nature and which one you're currently using."

"The Alexeev Method, Halabi's Skulk…" I crouched behind the bushes on my left and crept to a tree, using the lower branches to hang my cardigan. Lightly pressing my back against the trunk, I sneaked around it, rolled forward, and landed behind a small hill with rotting logs. "…and the Russo Diversion. Currently using the Russo."

"Why?"

My gaze landed on the figure in front of me lying flat on the forest floor, on her stomach, as still as the piles of logs she was using as cover: the Alexeev Method.

"I have eyes on a target," I whispered. "She's hesitant to move. I need something different from her surroundings to draw her out and distract her so I can get her."

"Good," Momma said, her grin audible. For some reason, my head wouldn't stop praying that she wouldn't suddenly go silent again.

Because if that happens here, *it would be for real.*

I shook myself out of those thoughts to focus. Dry, dusty wood and fresh leaves inflamed the air as I locked my body with my gaze on my target. Straight blond hair shone under the beaming rays of sunlight peeking through the canopy of tree branches.

I skulked over to the bushes on my right, keeping my eyes locked on Breanne. "*Spiro*," I whispered.

A breeze blew past me and then past her hiding spot, knocking over a few of the smaller branches. Her head perked up. I used the wind spell again on the tree a few feet away from me, the one carrying my sweater. Breanne propped herself up a bit, the logs on top of the hill hiding her face. She took a few seconds before darting out from her spot, taking cover behind everything that gave her an opportunity. Going back to back with the tree, she reached for my sweater and then snatched it.

Knowing that it was mine, her stance stiffened. Round, attentive eyes carefully moved across the forest.

I rolled on my shoulder in the direction of the tree and crouched low. The only thing separating us now was the trunk.

Breanne's nearly inaudible gasp told me that she was glancing in the direction of my previous hiding spot, but I was already gone. I rounded the trunk, pulled her in front of me by her wrist, and then twisted her arm behind her back. My foot tripped her leg and forced her to her knees while I took her other arm and forced it behind her.

"Em—?"

I didn't give her time to speak as I laid her down on the forest floor.

"That's one down," I said, smiling at her.

"I hear that," Momma said, satisfied. "Now, see if you can catch your other target."

I muted my earpiece, and Breanne followed on the ground.

"You're good," she said breathily, her body relaxing as she turned over onto her back. "How?"

I stood up straight and offered her my hand. "It's my mom's fault. I'm more of an on-field Hunter. You wanna go behind the scenes, anyway."

"Yeah, but"—Breanne took my hand and hoisted herself up with a grunt—"it'd still be cool to be able to do what you and Sarah can do."

"You *can*." I rubbed her arm as we took our first few steps in the forest together. "I've seen you."

"It's not as natural for me," she said, her soft features scrunching in doubt. "Great job, though."

She dusted off her blouse and denim shorts. Something foreign hung in the air between us, though, and I wasn't sure if she'd meant to hide it or not.

"What's wrong?" I asked, stopping with her.

She gave a small sigh. "I'm just thinking about our junior trip. The one Sarah mentioned earlier this year."

Huh—I'd forgotten all about that.

"Do you realize that it's only a few months away and we know next to nothing about it except that we'll be graded? On a *trip*? And Sarah said that it's a huge part of training, it's not a vacation... I seriously hope it's not like the final."

You're telling me. If Momma and Mr. Dawson even DARED pull another spring final situation for the junior trip, I was turning them in to President Caldwell myself.

Breanne mindlessly picked at the hair on her pale arms. "This isn't the first time I've been caught on a hunt. And I seriously don't want to fail whatever the trip is going to be."

"You passed the final, remember?" I told her. "Whatever the trip is, you're gonna knock it out of the park."

Her lips stretched into a smile, poking a subtle dimple into her cheek. "Thanks. You, too."

Except, little did she know that she had my mind falling down the rabbit hole of our junior trip, too. And if it was gonna be anything like our pass-or-fail hunt, that only brought up startling questions: did Momma think I could do it again? Did she already know everything about the trip? Had she known that the Hunter's Room would reopen the same year she'd enrolled me at Callistro? And did she have any other plans for me this year...?

My phone chimed in my back pocket, and I reached for it a little too eagerly. *Perfect timing.*

J: So. Did YOU know that Alexa's staying at
Dawson's house?

No—no, how did Jak know about that? How had he found out about that?! If he knew, didn't that mean Alexa's pack did, too? When had any of them tracked her down? Why hadn't Mr. Dawson called us?

He doesn't know yet. He could be in danger.

"What's wrong?" Breanne asked, thin brows scrunching.

I shook my head as I typed. "Nothing."

E: What? Tell me you're joking. Please tell me
you're joking.

J: Cool, you didn't. Now you do.

I'd look into it. ASAP.

†

I didn't know if it was more to my relief or worry when we called Mr. Dawson at Dad and Auntie's place and he didn't know what was wrong.

"They know," I told him. "They must've seen you guys."

I could *feel* my parents tense next to me on the couch as I held up the phone. Dad and Aunt Becca's new apartment was small but cozy, and at the moment, we needed cozy. Even if it was the four of us crammed on the couch, staring at an empty entertainment center with a small window overlooking the other apartments.

We waited for Mr. Dawson's reply after his heavy sigh. I wondered how many nights Auntie and Dad had here—until someone found them.

"My place is compromised," Mr. Dawson finally said in defeat.

"So if they know, why hasn't anyone come for either of you yet?" Momma asked, her brows knitting together in skepticism. "They finished their hunt but she *still* hasn't come back from her solo mission, and they've located her. Nothing's stopping them from grabbing her."

Mr. Dawson's silence changed, like a revelation had dawned on him. What could've possibly—?

"Unless they think *I'm* her mission and she's trying to seduce me."

Aunt Becca couldn't stifle her snort in time. Even Dad fell

victim to the humor in it, covering his grin with a strong hand and shaking his head. Momma and I, on the other hand, were in the same boat as each other, because *what?* That was ridiculous!

Well—okay, the man is handsome for forty. So especially if Alexa had a *solo* "research" mission? If anyone in the pack knew of her history with Mr. Dawson, all it took was one member to convince the rest of the theory.

"In other words," Mr. Dawson added, "they've bought us time."

"But how much time?" Momma asked, drumming her fingers on her crossed thighs.

"Not enough. But it's something. I have to get that bracelet on her ASAP."

Momma's eyes matched mine, thoughts in sync: there was no way we were letting this go by without investigating for ourselves. We were visiting soon.

EIGHTEEN

riday—a week. Alexa had managed to stay with Mr. Dawson for a whole week without getting caught. Most importantly, without Mr. Dawson getting caught. But that was probably thanks to Dad showing up at his house on Wednesday in a cop costume and under an appearance spell, saying that nothing had "come up yet" but they were "doing their best to find a lead". A whole week with Mr. Dawson and not a single memory had returned to the woman.

I sat back in the passenger seat of Momma's car as we drove over, and updated Cara and Steven.

S: Well if she's still mentally gone after a week
I'd say you're in the clear

E: I can't stop thinking she's just pretending…
she's a powerful magician who's spent her entire life lying and acting

C: Put a truth spell on her. If you're still good,
just do your best to keep it that way. We're
here if you need anything.

S: Yeah or we can ship her to Italy

C: How is Italy going to help?

S: It's not America

Thanks for the smile, I wanted to tell Steven, but we were too far away for a telepathic connection.

I dropped my phone into my lap, looking down at my hands as Momma drove into Forest City. My hands weren't what had caused the damage, but they were as much a part of me as my magic was. And I wanted to shun myself for causing so much damage—harm, even—to another life as I had. Even one who'd already spent a fraction of hers trying to destroy mine.

Why did I feel so guilty?

You've done worse, a wicked voice taunted in my head. *A lot worse. You had no problem with that.*

Except, I did. In fact, I was pretty sure that choking Marcus and Alexa were *why* I felt so guilty this time; not only was I carrying the delayed remorse of that, but now I was so out of control that I didn't even have the reins over my own power.

"Em," Momma said next to me as we turned down Mr. Dawson's street. I looked up, meeting her careful eyes. "Prepare yourself. You have no reason to be afraid of her, okay?"

Alexa can't suspect a thing. She can't suspect a single thing. I have to be completely normal.

The thought pounded harder with every repeat. The command was trying to force itself into an unaccepting mind; all my mind knew were the consequences of Alexa's knowledge in the past. That was the only experience, the only foundation, it had to trust. How does someone eradicate the only thing they've ever known just to throw themselves into a new truth?

I took a deep breath and looked out at Mr. Dawson's garage door growing bigger in front of us as we drove up. "Okay," I told Momma, forcing myself out of the rabbit hole my subconscious wanted to leap back into. I told myself to focus on my breathing instead, to focus on anything steady. Alexa couldn't suspect anything—I couldn't be the girl she'd tormented for the last eight months.

Momma and I walked up to the front door, and she knocked. To my disappointment, she looked down at me right after.

"Hey," she crooned. "You okay?"

I nodded. I wanted to be the brave daughter she'd raised.

The door squeaked open, regaining our attention.

"Hello, strangers," Mr. Dawson chimed, grinning at us. For a second, my fear disappeared, because whoa—what had him in such a good mood? Was this his façade for Alexa?

Momma seemed taken aback, too, but she's always been better than me at suppressing her true feelings. "Good afternoon to you, too. May we come in?"

"Of course, come on in." He swung the door open all the way and stepped aside.

Momma almost seemed to hesitate before she walked in, but ironically, I was the one able to step inside with stability; if Mr. Dawson is ever in a good mood, let alone THIS good a mood, everything's fine. Everything's (usually) under control.

The linoleum in the entry foyer gave way to the carpeted living room on our left. Through the wooden archway, Alexa sat with picture-perfect posture on the couch, a glass of lemonade in hand. Her red hair was as sleek as ever, and for once, her eyes didn't stare me down with hatred, but an excited welcome.

"Hi there." She set her glass down onto a brown coaster on the coffee table. "How've you guys been?"

She's gonna remember. She's gonna remember.

"It's been a relaxing week." Momma exhaled contentedly as if she and Alexa had been friends for the better half of their lives. If not for Alexa's primary life goal and the conflict of interest, they probably could have been. "So, you decided to stay with Julian?"

"Oh, yeah." Alexa's tone sank like it was something to be embarrassed about. She glanced at Mr. Dawson as he stepped through the archway and into the living room. Momma and I followed. "It felt comfortable."

"Comfortable"?

I sat on the arm of the reading chair Momma settled down into, adjacent to the couch. Mr. Dawson took a comfy seat next to Alexa, his arm lying on the armrest. After a week, he played his comfort around her... really well.

Unless...

I glimpsed Alexa's wrist. No bracelet. Was he building trust with her first?

—*When are you putting the bracelet on her?*—

—*In due time,*— he said, softly smiling in my direction like he was threatening me to be quiet. —*I'm still just a stranger doing her a favor. When I become her friend, then I give her the gift.*—

"What all have you been up to this week?" Momma asked.

Mr. Dawson nodded casually as he said, "I've shown her around town a bit. It's been pretty calm."

"Sometimes we'll go for inspiration while he tries to figure out the upcoming school year," Alexa said.

"Oh, right," Momma said in realization. "I need to get on that, too."

My head jerked back. Isn't there such a thing as too much work?

"It's definitely gonna be bigger than last year," Mr. Dawson said. "There's a lot to settle before September."

He briefly met his eyes with mine as he said this. Momma fell in line, but if they'd passed a message, I didn't get it.

Alexa glanced between the two of them. "What's going on next year, if I may ask?"

"The juniors are going on a trip." Mr. Dawson turned to her, his sharp jaw tense every time he glanced at me. "But it's supposed to stay classified until the beginning of the school year. Morgan's a junior next year, so we're keeping it under wraps around her."

"We also have staff positions to figure out," Momma added. "A couple of new members are coming, old ones are switching or changing subjects, there's a lot."

The words were sinisterly familiar: it was the same situation we'd found ourselves in when Alexa had come on board with the

Callistro Academy staff as Julia.

My eyes fell onto her at the memory. I chewed on the inside of my cheek. What if she *was* acting like she couldn't remember? Like Julia had acted like she didn't know who I was?

"I didn't know about that," I said to Momma, knowing that I couldn't stare for long.

"Mhm." Her lips pulled upward in a cheeky smile. "That's the point. Because one rumor always leads to another."

"Do you like your mom working at your school, Morgan—I'm sorry, 'Mo', right?" Alexa said, every word sickeningly genuine.

Even for her concern, I couldn't help a smile. "Um, either's fine. Yeah, I love it, I get free test answers."

Momma smacked my knee. "She's kidding."

"As far as you know," I said, shifting in my spot.

Another smack.

Alexa grinned at me. A true grin. A sincere Alexa grin that I would've never seen from the real her. It was radiantly beautiful.

The anxiety was slowly dripping away with every second that her "amnesia" stayed. Her demeanor was too... naturally unlike her to suggest that she was pretending. She couldn't fake the candid warmth in her eyes. She couldn't pretend the curiosity in her thumbs as they brushed her thighs. She couldn't feign the way the corners of her mouth slightly turned up every time she heard something remotely positive about our lives.

If this was the Alexa without her experiences and only her heart, what had *happened* to her?

I didn't realize that I'd missed out on the last couple of minutes of conversation until Alexa's eyes lit up at me, mouth agape. "I love your locket, Mo! Is that a sapphire?"

I realized that my twirling it was what had made her notice. I dropped it like I couldn't cheat while I answered, and then I realized that the wrong name was engraved into it. My fingers went back to twirling it, covering it. "Yeah, that's my birthstone."

"That's beautiful. Who gave it to you?"

Your stepson—

"I gave it to her for her birthday last year," Momma said, placing a hand on my back and rubbing it: keep quiet.

Thank goodness.

"Wow." Alexa nodded in understanding. "Your relationship is something to be admired."

Silence fell over the room, and Cara's text repeated itself to me: the truth spell. Now was my chance.

I waited until Alexa looked at Mr. Dawson. *Veritatem dicere.*

He just as quickly eyed me with a scold; he'd definitely seen the amber flash, but what mattered was that Alexa hadn't.

"You said you guys have been going into town," I began, turning Alexa's attention back to me. "Has that managed to jog any memories, or anything familiar?"

She pressed her defined lips together and shook her head. "I wish, but no. I can't remember a thing."

I exhaled a silent breath of relief. Mr. Dawson rubbed her arm, turning her back to him and letting me release her from the spell.

"The police came by earlier this week, and it honestly... put everything into perspective for me." An unfamiliar melancholy clung to her words now. "I caught myself starting to think about the chance that I probably have a family, maybe a husband and even kids, we never know—and then I started wondering if my mind would actually let me forget them just because of amnesia." She softly shook her head. "I don't want to think that I'd forget them so easily."

I thought about Jak as I looked at Momma, whose eyes had turned pensive as she twisted her golden wedding band. Then, she sat up. "You know, I think you're right about that." Familiar tender eyes found mine. "Maybe you can rule kids out. The connection I have with Morgan, not even amnesia could bury my maternal instinct. Nothing could make me forget her as a part of my life."

Before I knew it, a smile formed on my lips. I stared into the kind love, the protective instinct, rooted deep in Momma's honey-like irises. In moments like these, it was impossible to remember her mistakes—and mine—the moments that made it feel like we didn't understand each other or even cared. That protective instinct that I saw in her right now had felt completely absent during our final, but I couldn't deny that it was there. If I'm being honest, I think I just hated that my mother was capable of *making* mistakes—but she had tried her best during that exam, and I knew that she always did.

I gave her a side hug from my spot on the arm of the chair.

Alexa gestured loosely to us like her point had been proven. "A relationship to be admired."

"Speaking of jewelry," Mr. Dawson said thoughtfully, turning to face Alexa more, "do you like to wear any?"

CHAPTER

I had all the more motivation to get through mage lessons with Steven that night after a high success rate. (His cinnamon rolls probably had something to do with it.) But with the end of June, the hair on my neck was constantly standing on end. Did Alexa's pack really think that a seduction plan took this long?

Too big a part of me said that I was smarter than to believe that.

I wondered if even Jak knew what was really happening with them as I spent the first day of July with Dad on Momma's bed, watching an episode of *Tom and Jerry*. With Steven's appearance spell, Aunt Becca was able to accept a brunch invitation with her friends back in Charlotte, so it was safer for us to bring Dad back to our place and spend the morning indoors.

A sigh of contentment deflated in his chest under my cheek. My arm was wrapped around him like a seatbelt, and his heart beat a strong yet soothing rhythm under my ear. His dark-green T-shirt smelled of his clean cologne, relaxing me in everything reminiscent of my dad.

"Em?"

I hummed in reply.

He took the TV remote lying next to him and turned down the volume. "I've been thinking about the whole Alexa situation. How she finally found a way to take your magic. How close she was to it. It just makes me—I'm a bit..."

He released a tight breath. Momma's memory foam topper seemed to swallow me a little. "Honey, Mr. Dawson is living with the enemy. He's living with a powerful magician who's dead set on *murdering* not just us, but her own people."

"Everything was fine with William when the Redway Boys stayed at Callistro," I told him. "And he never had *his* memory wiped. Alexa doesn't even know she has magic. And she's never been in Mr. Dawson's house before, so it's not like there's an easy trigger."

"*He's* an easy trigger. So are you."

I wished I had an argument against that. Why, I didn't know how to answer, either.

"We can only pray that her pack still thinks she's on her solo mission," Dad said. "Because if they come for her, she risks revealing everything to them with a simple question of who they are. Do you know what she remembers about the magic war?"

I rested my eyes on Momma's tall mahogany dresser sitting in front of us, the flatscreen TV on top of it. "She knows magic is real and that the war is real. And she knows Hunters get rid of magicians."

"She doesn't know what side her blood has put her on?"

"No. I know that for a fact."

He gently rubbed my shoulder with his thumb, looking at me with the fatherly gaze I'd seen a thousand times from him by now. "I know you're careful. You'd have been caught by now if you weren't. But I always worry about you whenever you're away."

"I know." *I worry about you, too.*

I studied him: his strong nose, the faint trace of a dark-brown stubble on his square chin, the straight eyebrows above his icy-blue eyes. I wanted to make it easier on him in some way. Somehow. But what option was there?

"Do you know why your mom enrolled you in Callistro?"

"She said she wanted me to know how to defend myself. But then I realized it was also a cover."

His arm felt heavier around my shoulders as he asked, "Did you *want* to go there?"

I mentally drew back; it was the first time anyone had ever asked me the question. I actually didn't know how I'd felt back then—I only knew how I felt now.

"I was excited to go to school with Sarah and Breanne." After finding that part, the rest flowed like someone was feeding me the words. "I don't know about back then. I do wanna graduate from there, though."

Dad paused for a second. "And you feel safe there? You really believe that school is best for you?"

"I think..." With that one question, I felt the words I never knew I'd been searching for all this time: "I think the key is to grow close to Callistro. Not the people there."

He lightly chuckled, squeezing my shoulder. "You're wise beyond your years, kiddo. Don't lose that."

I closed my eyes and reminded myself of the person I was with right now—all that had been sacrificed and had to have happened for us to have this moment. Not one of them was guaranteed, and we had to fight for each day we did get with Dad.

"I love you," I caught myself saying.

A deep smile stretched his lips. The tenderness in his eyes seemed to restore itself twofold. "I love you, too, sweetheart."

He kissed the top of my head, and I was content enough to get up and grab another serving of the coffee frappes we'd made after Auntie left (something that she was jealous of for more-than-obvious reasons).

I walked through the doorway as Dad turned the volume of the TV back up. Taking only a few steps into the carpeted hallway, my feet nearly stumbled over Mr. Dawson's voice: "I honestly think none of it would've happened had we told her sooner."

I hear "she" or "her" in a private conversation and, call it only child syndrome, I automatically assume that the conversation is about me.

Wait. *What's Mr. Dawson doing here?*

This one time, I almost wanted to be wrong as Momma's voice came in a hushed reply. "Her magic was exactly what she lost when she talked to Ingrid. She depends on it too much to begin with! I don't need to give her another reason to."

"Do you really believe that, or is that just guilt eating at you?"

Whoa. What were they *talking* about?

Seconds passed before Momma's hiss: "Don't lecture me

about how to protect my daughter."

Okay. They were definitely talking about me.

Hang on. Where was Alexa? Had Mr. Dawson seriously left her *alone* at his house?

I carefully pressed my back against the wall and inched closer until the dining table next to the kitchen was visible.

Momma continued. "I need her to be careful around anyone she meets regardless of what she can do. I do not need her skipping steps and automatically placing trust based on title—like she's been known to do."

I wanted to be offended, but I was pretty sure that I wasn't allowed to be.

"I trust her enough to handle it," Mr. Dawson replied. "She's been through enough, and she's learned from her fatal mistakes. You don't think it's fair to give her a little help?"

"Keep your voice down. They'll know you're here."

I fiddled with my locket the slowest I ever had, careful for not even the chain to make a sound. A small voice whispered in the back of my mind, *Is this why Dad wanted to watch something with me?*

"And she's a hybrid," Momma said flatly. "How much more help can she get? Tristan agrees, we want her to get used to what she already has on her plate before she handles anything more. It's too much right now. I can't believe you don't think so."

"I don't, and I'll tell you the one reason why." I imagined Mr. Dawson, if they were on the couch, shifting to face Momma better with a pointed finger. "She should've started growing into it a long time ago, and the only reason she hasn't is because she was never actively looking for it. So whether you want her to have it or not, only time is going to determine at this point *when* she gets it."

I imagined Momma shaking her head. Then I wondered if I was getting any of this right.

"If that's the case, then let her magic tell her. It will let her know when she's ready."

"That's not how it—"

Mr. Dawson's sigh was long and tired.

How long had they been discussing this? Since I went to go hang out with Dad? Seriously, where was Alexa? Mr. Dawson wasn't dumb enough to leave her alone at his house or in the car in front of ours.

He was crazy enough, though, to tell her to get in the car for an outing and then put a sleeping spell on her.

Don't tell me he actually did that.

How much of this *was* I getting right? How long had they been keeping whatever they were talking about from me? I tried desperately to believe otherwise, but it sounded like my entire life!

There's no way. They wouldn't...

I stepped forward, ready to demand the truth, but Mr. Dawson's voice made me stiffen. "I'm withholding it from her out of respect for you and Tristan. But you won't be able to hide it from her for long. It is her *entire* identity as a sorceress."

C H A P T E R

TWENTY

"**P**rofessor Gene was *very* happy with my proposal and prototype." Breanne beamed like a proud child at us, sitting back in the brown vinyl booth at Joe's House. Opal playfully rolled her eyes next to her, diagonally across from me, as Breanne continued. "He says once I perfect the formula, he's going to turn it into an extra credit project for his seniors."

We weren't even officially in Professor Gene's class yet; Breanne was just too fascinated (and bored) to wait for the whole summer until he'd actually be our biomedical instructor, so this was one of her extra credit projects for the summer. Because when you go to a Hunter school, concocting a serum to make someone resemble a dead person isn't a concerning extra credit experiment—it's practice for real life.

"Why not an extra credit project for his juniors?" Sarah asked, taking a sip from her iced latte.

"Because"—Breanne shrugged happily—"he thinks that the seniors should have enough expertise by then to attempt it. He said that I was the 'special example'."

Which is what all of Breanne's teachers have said about her since the third grade, but I wouldn't spoil her joy.

"And thanks for asking your mom to be my test subject, Emmy." She pushed her blond hair out of her face, crossing her arms on the glazed table surface. "After you and Sarah refused."

"I would've volunteered had I gotten back earlier," Opal said, twiddling her thumbs under her green sweater sleeves that were too long. "You can test the final draft on me, though."

"*See?*" Breanne glanced between me and Sarah, taking her glass of chocolate milk. "*This* is what I need from you two!"

Sarah and I looked at each other, unamused, and then went back to our coffee. The air conditioning was practically cold enough to keep the drinks iced, but nothing hits better than actual ice.

My gaze fell to my phone's black screen. Sarah had been the last person to text me, telling me where she, Breanne, and Opal were in Joe's House. But I wondered about Alexa's phone sitting in Mr. Dawson's car, and the paranoid part of me wondered how long it'd be until she found it there.

"Hey," I heard Opal say.

I looked up to find her and Breanne's concerned eyes.

"Is everything okay?" Opal asked.

"Yeah," I said cautiously. "Why?"

Sarah folded her hands on the table. "You keep looking at

your phone like someone's gonna catch you being here."

They've noticed every time I've looked at my phone?

"I'm kind of..." I began timidly, "waiting on a text from my mom. About when the family's going back."

"Then what're you doing here?" Sarah asked, furrowing her brows and turning in her spot to better face me. "Emmy, we don't wanna take you away from something important. We're still gonna be right here at the end of summer, your family won't be."

We were almost halfway through vacation, and I'd only hung out with the girls three times because of the Alexa situation, which I covered as "family business". Except, right now, the last place I wanted to be was anywhere around a Grand Hunter—and any-where around my parents, who were keeping a critical piece of information about my identity as a sorceress from me.

"Basically, is everything okay?" Opal asked me. "You *can* be here right now, right?"

I licked my lips, stopping myself from turning my phone over so that the screen rested on the table. "Yeah, everything's fine. They're leaving soon, but that's why I've spent so much time with them already. Opal just got back, they get why I'm here."

Besides, I had a mission for today: I was going to finally in-troduce Opal to the whole Alexa business. With her becoming a regular in our group, she deserved to know as much as Sarah and Breanne knew. The topic still came up every once in a while in passing between me, Sarah, and Breanne, and the last thing I wanted was a secret separating all *four* of us.

Opal placed her pale hand on top of mine, smiling softly. Then, she took her handbag sitting between her and Breanne. "Okay. Well, I really hate to do this after that, but I have to get home and pack for our next trip. We leave in two days."

Shoot. How was this already backfiring?

I opened my mouth, but Breanne was already sliding out of the booth to let her out, and Sarah was wishing her a safe trip.

I mentally facepalmed. I was *not* used to telling the truth about the magician-Hunter stuff in my life, and it definitely wasn't like I could drop the story in two easily digestible sentences. Well, I guess it was better to not do it in a public place where the Callistro gossip girl could let something slip out a little too loudly.

Upon watching Opal walk out the front doors, Sarah immediately spun back around to face me. "Okay. What's actually going on?"

At least Opal couldn't read me as well as these two could yet. Because in all honesty? I was also thinking about the boy who'd called me at 4 in the morning, and that had been about Alexa business that Opal didn't know about yet.

I told them the first half because these girls *could* know some of the Alexa story right now. And just like with the first week of first semester, if I wanted to stay trustworthy to them and have as little to hide as possible, I needed to let them in somewhat.

Sarah gasped, bare arms crossed. "*What?* Why? What was Jak doing up so early?"

"Exactly what I asked." I braced myself for my next words. "He was worried about Alexa. She went from a solo mission to kind of going MIA."

Breanne's doe-like eyes widened with fear, Sarah's narrowing with concern. No matter which girl I looked at, I could almost see the reflection of a girl from last August who'd felt that same panic after finding out that Alexa was after her in the first place.

I looked around the café for any eavesdropping café-goers. "Jak said he didn't trust that she wasn't after me. Then he texted a few days later saying she was... gone."

Translation: she was staying with Mr. Dawson.

"She's just gone?" Breanne asked, her voice thin.

I took a deep breath. "No."

Sarah arched a sharp brow. "What do you mean 'no'?"

"I mean..." I looked around us again, leaned even closer in, and felt my heart jump into my throat as it pumped with adrenaline. "Not here. In my car."

"Why?" Sarah asked.

Ripping off the Band-Aid was the only way to get them to obey: "She's staying with Mr. Dawson."

✝

"Em," Sarah snapped as we walked out of Joe's, stepping aside to let new customers in, "what is she doing at Dawson's *house?*"

I stopped and nodded at my car parked in front of us. "Get in. I can't tell you with people around."

The girls eyed each other, passing notes in that silent language I wasn't fluent in, before they stepped down from the curb and followed me to the car. Sarah climbed into the passenger seat and put our lattes in the cup holders, Breanne in the back and holding her chocolate milk.

I closed my door in the driver's seat. "Don't hate me for this." I exhaled, my body weighed down by every lie I'd told them since we met and all the ones I was about to spew. "A couple weeks ago, my mom and I found Alexa walking around town alone. She looked completely disoriented, and when we walked up to her, she had no idea who we were. She just looked at us and then... passed out."

Sarah pushed a black wave behind her ear. "Wait. She lost her memory and you thought the best thing to do was to bring her to Dawson's *house?*"

"Yeah!" Breanne blurted, finding her words. "Why did you get him involved to begin with?"

I was going to tell them the story Mr. Dawson had given to Alexa, but the circumstances of that one were too separated—impersonal. More plausible for someone who had no idea who we were, but the girls needed a story that still connected Alexa to me somehow.

"Who else were we supposed to get?" I told them. "It's not like the cops were an option!"

"But..." Breanne stammered, concern contorting her features. "But Mr. Dawson—"

"We figured he was more—*obligated* to help. As a concerned citizen not as directly involved as my mom."

Our words didn't have the right space to resonate in the air, and that only made them feel all the more suffocating. They were too loud. They were absorbing straight back into me as the three of us gave way to silence again. At least the ocean breeze car freshener hanging from my rear-view mirror was still fully effective; that was some comfort.

Sarah crossed her arms, her grave pear-green eyes telling me to continue.

"We took her to the hospital, and they diagnosed her with amnesia. She can't remember anything. Like *anything*-anything."

"Her entire life is gone from her memories?" Sarah asked.

"They don't even know if she can recover."

"Meaning"—Breanne was wary, as if she'd be giving me false hope by speaking—"you're *actually*, finally safe?"

The truth shushed me almost a second too late: all these two knew was that I'd been Alexa Delphine and William Bleu's target first semester, but they had absolutely NO intel regarding second. And yet Breanne had felt the need to ask that question, as if... as if they'd never really believed that I was safe.

"Weren't you guys the ones telling me that nobody was out to get me?"

"You found the Grand Hunter who hunted you last year wandering around *your* town, almost right on top of your home," Sarah replied flatly. "It's alarming. Especially because you don't even know what she was doing there in the first place."

"That's just it." I dropped my hand onto the gear shift. "Was she dropped off there after coming down with amnesia? Was she already in town beforehand? Was she coming for me first and then somehow got it before she could reach me?"

"I think all of those situations..." Sarah began, her eyes falling to the dark-gray mat under her feet, "require someone to have used magic."

She was right. And I even knew the perpetrator.

"We don't know how it happened," I said, fiddling with my locket, "but she has no idea what she was doing in Capperson, who I am, or even who *she* is. So I'm pretty sure we're safe."

Sarah's head bounced up, brows knitted together in thought. Her interrogative gaze locked on me again. "You said Jak was worried she was still after you. And she was found in Capperson: *your* town."

Instinct sounded an unnamed alarm in my head. "Yeah."

"Why would she still be after you?"

I prayed and hoped that my words would suffice, because they were improvised from the start. "That's the scariest part. I don't know. But she came here."

Sarah's and Breanne's sighs were practically in sync, and I let my own join them. If Alexa was going to be a prevalent problem in my life for much longer, I needed a cover story—or maybe even a version of the truth—to explain why I was still her target. But for now, I got away. My friends were as worried as I was, and that was what mattered.

Sarah leaned back in her seat with her arms tightly crossed. Breanne rested her cheek on the shoulder of my fabric seat, dangerously quiet.

"You're staying away from her, right?" Sarah asked me. I'd never seen her bright eyes held down by so much solemnity. "Em, this is seriously dangerous. I can't even put it into words."

"Her pack is going to be looking for her," Breanne added softly behind me.

I rolled my lips together, nodding subconsciously. "Yeah. Mr. Dawson said he had a plan. And he always has a plan." Flashes of the beach house burned in my memory and sent a wicked chill down my back. The spring final was next in my mind. I buried it all the same.

I swallowed. "It'll be okay."

I wasn't kidding anyone. *I* wasn't even convinced of that, yet here I was lying to my best friends about it.

C H A P T E R

Twenty-One

We had our swim unit in Defensive Calisthenics for a reason: either for cases that Momma experienced as a Master, where she chased a magician directly into the otter tank at the Monterey Bay Aquarium (another long story that I can never tell with a straight face), or for cases like Opal's when she got back a week later—vacation. Because when you know what you're doing in the water, you can swim with sharks with absolute abandon.

It probably helped that she could stop the sharks at any moment with her mind. Speaking of...

From my hanging chair in the corner of my room, a sneaky smirk slithered to my lips. I asked the question that was the reason Sarah and Breanne couldn't join us this time: "Did you manage to sneak in any magic?"

"This one time," Opal simpered on my bed, fiddling with her thumbs in her lap. She leaned against the wall. "I tipped over the kayak of these kids who'd been bullying the kids behind them."

"What?" I asked, my jaw falling open. "Isn't that *really* dangerous?"

She shook her head, her brows knitting in a no. "They had life vests on and the water was shallow."

I smiled. "Geez. Superhero potential."

When the quiet overtook us, the debate with myself was all the louder even in my head: tell Opal about Alexa now? Wait until Sarah and Breanne were with us so that they could back me up and verify that this was top secret and I had to be extra careful with the people I told? I mean, since the school year ended, Opal wasn't really involved in magic gossip anymore. She'd shed one identity to take on another. And she'd taken on that identity fully aware that it was bigger than herself. She'd definitely treated it as such ever since...

I had to test the waters first. "Can I ask you something?"

"Shoot."

"With—what you found out about yourself this year, how do you feel about the Atera situation now? Like, has your view on them changed at all?"

I wondered if I'd caught her off guard—no, I had definitely caught her off guard, because her mouth opened to respond, but her words hesitated for too long. Almost like she was afraid to answer.

"I don't think..." she began slowly, "that I ever *wanted* them to be caught, to be honest. I just liked the situation as a whole because it was something to talk about. But I guess—if they ever *are* caught, I want their sentence, whatever it is, to be given on the account of them committing an actual crime. Not because they have magic."

I nodded. "Yeah. Me, too."

A tense silence settled over us, but I didn't know how to fill it this time. The tip of my foot scraped the carpet as I slightly swayed in the chair.

"Actually, Em, about that..." Opal shifted on my bed, slouching against the wall. Her voice slid into a high lilt. "I... There's something I've never told anyone before that I... I'm tired of keeping it to myself. I could never tell Caroline or Amelia but you understand the whole magic thing, so... c—can you keep this a secret?"

Whoa. What kind of secrets could the Callistro gossip girl be hiding that she *didn't* want anyone else knowing about?

I nodded. "Of course."

"So—*I* was..." Her voice remained high and airy as she struggled with her words. "I was suspected of being Tristan Atera's descendant."

Wait. *What?* Opal was... That wasn't—how could she have—?

"Yeah." She twiddled with her thumbs, laughing at herself like the memory was too ridiculous for even her to believe. "I don't like to think about it. Obviously. Still, it just—it feels so good to finally get that off my chest."

And here I was, about to be stupid enough to say that Jak had never mentioned anything about her when he was trying to protect *me* from his parents.

Hang on, why had he never mentioned anything about Opal?

Did she already know about me and Alexa? Was this her way of trying to get it out of me? Were she and Jak... *familiar* with each other beyond ex-classmates from when the Redway Boys had stayed with us?

Wait a second. *Didn't Opal even say the day they left that she and Jak had talked a couple of times?* In the Grand Foyer, after he'd kissed me in front of everyone—had they talked about the hunt...?

"I don't even know what to say," I finally said, which was the dead-honest truth.

"You don't have to. I'm really sorry if that was out of the blue, I just—I really needed an outlet for that."

Yeah. I know how that feels.

I wanted to say those words so badly. But for the first time since Opal had found out about her identity as a druid, red flags were popping up. Something wasn't right about this. I was missing a piece somewhere, stopping the others from connecting.

I'll have to ask Jak about it.

"How long has Uncle Thomas known your family?" Opal asked next.

"As long as I can remember, to be honest," I said, because it wasn't like I could tell her that Mr. Dawson met my dad when he was fourteen at Redway Academy and had visions that revealed how their destinies were intertwined. "I don't really have the story."

Opal chuckled and focused on her thumbs again. We sat in silence for longer than what was comfortable, and I wondered how to break it. Opal's confession had inflicted more damage than I'd initially realized.

"Has Mr. Dawson taught you anything else about druids?" I

asked, buying the time my head needed as she lit up and started rattling off everything I already knew. I mean, up until two minutes ago, I was almost convinced that I was going to tell this girl my second-darkest secret. She'd laid all of her cards out on the table; I thought that the least I could do after the honest friendship she'd given me the last few months was be honest with her. She was a magician. We were bound together by magic.

Why did it feel like something had grown between those lines?

"That's really cool," I told her, even though I had no idea what she'd just said.

She scoffed, my bed comforter stealing her gaze. "Yeah, except now I don't even get why we're called 'magicians'. It's weird. I don't like it."

This, I perked up for, sitting up straight in my seat. "Really?"

"Yeah. I mean, sure, we all have magic, but... Okay. What would you call us?"

That's the question I've been asking myself for a while. I quietly laughed to myself, careful with every thought.

Opal rolled her eyes and stretched her legs out across my bed. "I mean, some of us have specific abilities others don't. We all—have magic... I don't know. It's hard to group *every* single wielder of magic under one—"

I froze, pointing at her. That was it—it was so simple, why hadn't it come to me before? "Wait. That's it, that's the word."

"What is?"

"'Wielder'," I said, a grin stretching my lips. "Wielders, you're all *wielders of magic.*"

Opal's jaw hung open slightly as she stared at me in awe.

"Hey! Nice! That's good, I like that. I'm gonna use that from now on!"

It made me wonder who'd come up with "magician" to begin with. I was never the biggest fan of the connotation—considering the profession for kids' parties and Vegas when *we* weren't allowed to show off our tricks—but nobody had ever been brave or crazy enough to break the mold, I guess.

I like that, too. For once, this was a change I could gladly accept.

†

There's something to be said about double agents. Sure, they're untrustworthy, they usually have intel that could start World War Three, and they're just about the most unpredictable professionals on the planet. But they can easily survive in enemy territory. They're the ones who can tread through grounds unknown to either of their agencies, and they manage to lie throughout their entire lives without ever being caught (if they're good enough).

But if there's anything to remember about double agents, it's that their most important tool is each other. Depending on the situation, depending on the people, they can use each other as either a weapon or a tool. The person you find the most comfort in can turn your friendship against you in a snap.

That was why, when Momma and I visited Mr. Dawson Friday night, Alexa was sitting on his couch as always—but she was grinning this time. Why was she grinning this time?

"Ladies," Mr. Dawson said as Momma and I walked inside, a smile sewn to his own face, "how are you doing?"

"Good, thanks." Momma led me into the living room, greeting Alexa with a superficial smile. "What about you?"

Alexa was rubbing something silver around her wrist, trapping my words in my head: the bracelet. The bracelet was around *her wrist!*

"Oh!" Momma gasped, but her high pitch strained to tame her joy. "That's beautiful, Alexandra, where did you get it?"

Alexa dropped her hands into her lap, glancing at Mr. Dawson as if for permission to tell us. My eyes jumped to analyze him: he didn't leave me a nod or even movement of his lips to translate. I rushed back to Alexa before I could miss something.

"Julian gave it to me."

He did it!

"Really?" Momma asked, ambling to her. Alexa offered her wrist as I followed Momma, peering from behind her arm.

"Turning its white diamond orange", Moren had said. The diamond in front of me gleamed white.

Not for long.

Momma smirked, looking behind her shoulder at Mr. Dawson. "You have good taste, Jules."

While I stifled a laugh at the nickname, Alexa was the only one in the room who couldn't translate the message.

I nodded in approval. "It looks great on you."

"Thank you!" Alexa's fair cheeks flushed as she glanced at Mr. Dawson like he was a lifeline and the only thing keeping her sitting upright. I'd never seen her so... uneasy. Nervous?

Alexa Delphine, nervous. I can't believe I lived to see the day.

I shook my head. What mattered was that Mr. Dawson had finally given her the bracelet. He'd taken her magic away. He'd just solved one of the biggest threats we'd encountered in the last year, if not *the* biggest!

—Nice job,— I told him. —*I'm guessing you even managed to excuse the jolt it probably sent her when she put it on.*—

For a second, his brows flinched as he leaned against the living room archway. —*The most difficult part, but not impossible. You don't sound too thrilled about it, though.*—

No—my heart was jumping up and down with thrill. The problem was that it was conflicting with my mind, which refused to let my joy show through for a few reasons. One being that I'd experienced too much by now and knew that our successes, like magic, always came at some kind of price.

I eyed him carefully before smiling again at Alexa. —*Kinda hard to swallow everything we're keeping from her at once, the bracelet included now. I'm almost expecting something to... blow up.*—

—*Don't worry too much about that. Your mom and I got it.*—

—Yeah,— I said before I could stop myself. I locked eyes with him, my pettiness enticed all the more. —*I know. You guys are great at keeping things.*—

He stilled. Anybody else, I don't think they would've caught on, but at least an ex-Master knows how to pick up the clues. Or at least suspect that they're there.

He took himself away from the archway. "Morgan," he said, a soft smile on his lips, "didn't you say you wanted to see how the roses are doing?"

It was night, but the message was loud and clear.

I looked back at Momma, tacitly verifying that she'd be okay with Alexa on her own. Scratch that—that Alexa would be okay left alone with Momma.

Mr. Dawson guided me through the kitchen and dining area, to the sliding glass door that led to the backyard. Crickets chirped softly in the background, echoing into the humid night. Gnats flew all around the outdoor lanterns and lamps stuck in the dirt of his garden along the perimeter of the fence. The red, white, and yellow roses were in full bloom, but as I stepped off the concrete patio and met Mr. Dawson on the cool grass, I didn't really want to stop and smell them.

Evidently, he felt the same way, crossing his bare arms. "What did you hear?"

"You were talking to my mom about keeping my identity as a sorceress from me."

He pressed his lips together, releasing his breath. "I don't like it, either, Em."

"Really?" I said, my chest tightening with impatience. "I really thought the final was as far as you'd ever go with me, that was the first time you ever challenged my trust in you like that. I finally almost got over it, but—but then..."

I wanted to shake my head. *My whole life.* Kept from me my whole life, and not even as my mentor in magic had he ever confessed to me what they were hiding about *my* magic identity.

I exhaled. "Then I find out that the final was never even the beginning. You've been lying to me about this for, what, my whole life?"

"I haven't lied to you about anything," he said, holding his hand out as if to pause me. Tiredness dulled his irises, even in the light the lantern hanging from the patio cover cast. "I've kept it from you out of respect for your parents. Mostly your mom. When your magic first started showing, she asked me to keep this from you. I never liked it, I never have. But I won't go against your mother and my best friend as long as they believe they're doing what's right for their daughter—my goddaughter. I love them and I love you too much to do what I want just because I disagree."

"But you disagree to a valid extent. And this has to do with *my* identity!"

A lump passed in his throat, but Mr. Dawson's resolve has always been stronger than a teenage girl begging. He nodded toward the house. "Inside please. You're just gonna have to accept for now that we're both not happy about this."

Twenty-Two

As I put on some yoga pants and a tank top for a much-needed walk Tuesday morning, I wanted to figure out how I'd get my answer out of Momma regarding what she was keeping from me. Her resolve against my teenage girl tactics is even stronger than Mr. Dawson's, and I'm actually scared of her; I'm not really scared of Mr. Dawson. So when I asked her if she wanted to come walking with me, I thought that I'd built a solid plan to get her alone in a public place to ask her about it, meaning she wouldn't be able to retaliate against me that much for pushing her—but she said no to the walk because she wanted to go grocery shopping before it got too hot.

I tried thinking of another plan as I stuck my phone into my pocket and opened the front door. The morning atmosphere was already warm, warning of a hot afternoon. Stepping down the concrete steps of the walkway seemed to amplify the air by one degree per step.

I knew I should've worn my white leggings instead of the dark ones.

—Help! I need your help!—

I stopped in the middle of the sidewalk. Who was THIS?

—Anyone, *if you can hear me, I'm in the Callistro Forest, a mile south of the school. I don't have much time, somebody, please hurry!*—

I slowed my pace on the sidewalk, trying not to look into my neighbors' windows as their houses gradually passed by. This was a man's voice in my head, but it wasn't any of the men I knew—which was a red flag in itself. If the last year had taught me anything, it was that "magician" did not equal "friend". This guy was asking for help, but following his voice could turn *me* into a victim just as quickly.

Wait. "Anyone"? "Somebody"?

This guy didn't know that he was calling *me*? But didn't telepathy only work with a specific target in mind?

I hate it when Mr. Dawson is right: I do *need to brush up on the magic basics.*

—Please! A Master Hunter is closing in on me!—

The air left my lungs, sinister memories wrapping around me. A Master Hunter right here in Capperson. Another one of my people was suffering from the rule of President Caldwell right in front of me. I had to at least see from a distance if I could do something, to see if it was even real. And if it was, I *had* to help!

I came across no signs of a kidnapping as I turned onto Main Street. Not one sedan rushing down the street, no mysterious Hunter following me between buildings or behind the trees as I entered the forest...

—Hurry, please! He's right behind me, he's blocking my magic!—

Whether it was the warm breeze whistling through the branches of the tall trees or the rustling of the leaves and twigs on the ground, my stomach flipped at every sound. Even though I wasn't the hunted this time, an instinct was still thrumming as if I were.

Finally, knowing the forest as I did, I stopped when I deep enough in. If someone was trying to lure people into their van in the Callistro Forest, at least I had my magic to defend me. Then again, this person had his, too... but what was one wielder to a hybrid?

—Hello? I heard your call, I'm here to help.—

Nothing. But I didn't know if that was because I didn't know the person I was talking to or if he'd just been... silenced.

I crouched behind a pile of boulders, taking note of my surroundings: dirt and moss sprinkled the stone, which housed small insects ranging from ants to tiny red spiders. (I was *so* not okay with that, but I highly doubt that a Hunter will let you find a new hiding spot because you're afraid of spiders.) Old branches, dead pine needles, and fallen leaves littered the ground. The trees stood tall and wide, swaying in the morning breeze. The sun was already hot and high in the air—

WHOA!

I was flying through the air!

Nanoseconds away from hitting the ground, I bent my knees and let my body tumble down, rolling on my shoulder.

Good thing I didn't wear white, I thought, trying to steady my breath. I turned my head to my previous hiding spot. I'd already known that I'd be dealing with someone who had magic; I just didn't know that *I* was their target, after all!

Mistake, mistake, mistake, I knew this would happen. I need to leave, now.

I stood and faced the pile of boulders, eyes darting every which way. A figure moved out from behind a tree in the corner of my eye. I turned. Dressed in jeans, a T-shirt, and a dark-green blazer, the man's young and clean-shaven face was rather stolid for someone who'd just cried for help. He strolled with his hands behind his back until he stood in front of me, yards away. Then, he faced me with forest-green eyes and umber hair.

I'd never seen him before in my life.

This was such a mistake. Run.

"You're quick on your feet," he remarked. Other than the sturdy confidence now, he matched the telepathic voice identically. "I'm kind of impressed. Is that what they teach you at the Callistro Academy?"

"Who are you?" I asked, carefully straightening and ready to unsheathe my magic.

"Tell me something first," he said, which told me that he was going to ignore all of my questions. "Does anyone at your school know who you are?"

"Who are you?!"

He nodded once, taking a step toward me. "I'll tell you. Once you tell me what in her right mind Alexa thinks she's doing."

I stepped back. This was it. Alexa's pack had known the entire time that she'd been gone for too long for a solo mission—she'd been borderline kidnapped for the last month—but how had this guy traced just me as the culprit?

And why had he lured me all the way out here with no witnesses around?

Fighting him was the last thing I wanted to do, not with someone who hadn't exposed just how powerful he was yet. My magic was ready, but a fight had to be my last resort. I had to keep him calm.

"What're you talking about?" I said. "How am I supposed to know that?"

His defined green eyes flashed amber. "Okay, we're trying this again."

I stepped back again and opened my mouth until the weight of the truth spell fell flat onto me. Shoot. There had to be a way I could manipulate the falsehoods into truths!

A wicked smirk slithered to the young man's face. "There we go. Go ahead: what is Alexa actually doing at Thomas Dawson's house right now?"

"I'm serious," I replied, noting my foot inching back farther, "what do you want? Her plan? What she's *literally* doing right this second?"

"I'm not in the mood to play dumb," he said, hardening his scowl. When amber flashed in his irises again, my body flew into the tree behind me. A hard blow struck the back of my head, and I yelped as the man advanced toward me. "And you don't want me to prove it to you, *believe* me."

That's it.

Lungs recovering from the impact, I glanced at the four-foot-long branch hanging high above his head. *Distraho!*

His gaze darted up at the branch cracking. Just in time, he jumped back as it crashed onto the ground.

"Threats don't mean anything to you, do they?"

"If you attack me—I fight back!" I spat with strain.

"I'm not an empty threat, Emmalynn." At the next flash of amber, the branch flew to the right, far from my sight. "You get one more sentence."

That warning was all I had left, I knew that. And yet, when I met his eyes again, it was with a challenge. I wouldn't give up that easily when I had what he did—if not more of it!

"You think I'm some little girl who just plays with her magic?" I said, pushing myself away from the tree trunk. "We're equal. Tell me who you are, and I'll tell you what I know."

His lips grinned with impatience, a laugh whispering under his breath. "No, see, that's not how this works."

His eyes held their glowing amber this time. An invisible force seized my body, freezing me in my spot as he met me at the tree. "I'm already being generous. You're gonna tell me what you know,"—he gripped my neck and pushed me back into the rough bark—"or I'll arrest you right now as a magician."

"You don't have proof," I hissed, throat tight against the pressure of his hand.

"All I have to do is say that I used a magician to telepathically lure you out here. Any lie detector will note that as the God-honest truth."

My throat itched from his fingers pressing into my neck. For dear life, I shoved my tears of anger, fear, and frustration far down. He'd trapped me.

Come on! Trap him back!

I hadn't had to say the telekinesis spell out loud for a few months, but pride was the last thing on my mind right now. "*Ite procul!*"

The man forcefully dropped my neck, giving me the confidence to silently throw him back.

"I told you," I hissed, a couple of coughs escaping. "I'm not some little girl. Arrest me, go ahead, but the second they put me under a lie detector, they'll know what you are. If you're so loyal to Alexa, you'll let me go!"

"You *are* brave." He propped himself up from the ground, shaking his head with a soft smirk. Like he pitied me. "Too brave for your own good."

Standing, he didn't give me a second to blink as his eyes returned to amber. My throat tightened at his whim, slowly closing up on me.

"Go ahead," the man said, stretching his arms out wide. "Do the same thing to me. Make another branch fall on me. Throw me fifty feet away! Do it."

I tried to, but the second he saw my chest lift to breathe, his magic tightened around my esophagus.

"You're the almighty sorceress challenging Alexa Delphine, aren't you? Prove it. Show me how powerful you are."

But all I could do was press my body against the tree, rest my hands on the textured bark, and pray that he'd release me before I went unconscious. Spells muddled together in my mind. I could only remember the last one I'd said, but there was no strength to give it power. The pressure in my head was building up and up until I had to shut my eyes. Without warning, my knees fell to the ground. Only then did the man finally release his hold.

I gasped and coughed for dear life, inhaling the fresh oxygen all around me. Footsteps drew closer and closer in front of me until I was at the man's feet.

He kneeled down and took my chin with strong fingers, lifting my head. "Well?"

"She doesn't—remember!" I rasped, a cough between almost every word. He'd stripped me of my confidence. *Now* he was too much for me.

But for whatever reason that I was grateful for, he gave me the seconds I needed to regain my breath's composure. "She lost... her mem—ories," I breathed, each word a stab in my throat. "She thinks—Dawson's helping—her."

He dropped my chin. "She lost her—?"

An eerie quiet enveloped us amidst the hums of the wind and chants of distant birds. When I was finally brave enough to look up at the man still standing tall and proud above me, his eyes were almost... wary of me. His dark hair fluttered in the light breeze as he hummed his response.

"She *lost* her memories," he spat. The words were spoken too slowly to give me any reassurance, as if he knew that I was the one who'd taken those memories.

I sat up against the tree as he finally turned away. My every breath burned my throat.

He knows. What is he gonna do? Is this where someone's gonna find me after days of—?

"We have eyes, Emmalynn," he told me as I took a hard, painful swallow. "I'd be watching my back at all times."

Eyes... eyes, had they seen the bracelet on Alexa's wrist? Did they even know what it did? How much had Alexa kept a secret from even her own pack?

The man turned around to face me. "Anthony," he said

simply. "Anthony Delphine."

Against my desire to land on anything else, my gaze froze on him. "What?"

He shrugged. "It's okay. You're not gonna remember any of this, anyway."

His eyes flashed amber a final time. The last few minutes became nothing but black in my memory, the world around me following suit.

Twenty-Three

One second I'd been on a walk around my neighborhood, the next I was waking up in the Callistro Forest—of all places—with a throat that *seared* me every time I breathed!

And there were mysterious dirt stains on my leggings!

Good thing I didn't wear the white ones.

That was all I remembered. There was no in-between, just a blank spot between then and now.

With my neck sore for whatever reason, I walked around the forest and then a bit of Capperson, trying to figure out what on Earth I'd been doing before the blank spot hit me. That ended up only accomplishing my goal of a walk. Thanks to the heat exponentially rising by the half hour, I had to cut it short by convincing myself that I was going crazy because of the Alexa business.

There's no way. I'm not that crazy. I know something happened, how else did I end up falling asleep in the forest? Something inside my mind was tingling, almost burning to be called by memory but meeting a brick wall every time it tried to come forward.

Gently rubbing my neck, I walked through my front door in a daze. I pressed my back against it, closing it, and exhaled, muscles in my neck straining.

How did...? Why does my throat...?

That lack of an in-between was slowly fading into nothing more than a lack of detail, like how all memories eventually become.

Did something actually happen, or am I just not remembering what I did?

Is this what Alexa feels like right now?

I froze. Had I put myself under a forgetting spell? I knew nobody else had, I'd been alone for the entire walk. But that didn't explain the strained throat, unless my mind had chosen to block out an *awful* singing session.

Maybe that's why I was in the forest: privacy. I like to sing, but that doesn't mean I'm good at it. Had I screamed my frustrations out into the forest air?

I shook my head. Upon the pounding sensation forming in it from too many flawed theories and questions, I brought out my phone and found Momma's new message:

M: Please make some ice in the ice cube trays
and drink LOTS of water when you get back
from your walk!

I couldn't help but smile at her motherly instinct. Sure, it was built in, but intent means nothing without proper execution. And Momma did a pretty good job of executing her intent every time.

A new notification went off at the top of my screen.

Wait a second, what? Wasn't Jak still staying with his friends in Topa? How was he already here in Capperson?

No, this was rather sudden and impulsive, even for him. If he wanted to surprise me with a date, he would've shown up without warning and then asked. Why was he warning me now that he was on his way?

If Alexa and William had managed to spy on us throughout the final, the pack still hadn't made any advancements, and Jak was in Capperson... I wanted more than anything to prove myself wrong, but he had said so himself that they were setting up base in town. Were they really back just to monitor us? Or was Jak coming over simply because? Did he have something outside of Hunter matters to talk about?

To my impatient dismay, as I sent Jak my address, all I could do now was wait.

†

"Are you okay?" was Jak's first question when he walked through the door. "Did anything happen this morning?"

"What's wrong?" I asked, throat straining against my voice.

Okay. Talking was going to be difficult.

"So you're not hurt?" he asked, his brown-eyed stare heavy. "Nothing... nothing happened?"

"No," I said, shutting the door behind him and cursing every word that left my mouth. I followed him to the living room. "Why? Should... some—thing—have happened?"

He paused. "Why do you sound like that?"

My mouth stayed open, trying to think of an excuse. I didn't even have one for myself, let alone him.

I also *seriously* didn't want to talk. I shrugged.

He walked up to me, succumbing to his worry that I still didn't have context for. "What's wrong, what happened?"

"I don't—know."

"You don't—?" He cut himself off like he didn't want to press me, rubbing the bottom half of his face. His breath out was too heavy, tired. What was going on with him?

He dropped his hands to his sides, turning and planting himself on the couch. "I'm gonna be straightforward: has someone named 'Anthony' come after you?"

My confusion sweltered. I tilted my head slightly, like that would help me hear him better. "Who?"

He sighed. "Em..."

Come *after* me? This was why Jak had come over? Why would some guy—that he knew—be after me? Did Jak know something I didn't?

"Why would—he come after—me?" I forced myself to ask. "Does he... have a reason?"

"It was just a question, I wanted to make sure—"

Tears from the pain burned in my eyes as I barked, "Who is

he, Jak?"

"He's in Alexa's pack, drop it!"

It was the very first time in the time we'd known each other that Jakson Bleu had snapped at me. Needless to say, every inch of me despised it.

"He was assigned to piece together what Alexa's doing since she hasn't updated them, and figure out why she's staying at Dawson's, I was just... He was indirectly involved with what happened last year. I figured he'd come after you."

Jak had made it his personal mission to protect the kids suspected of being my father's descendant. That was what his mom had wanted: for magicians and mortals to coexist. And now that Jak knew that I was his closest lead to the most wanted kid in America, protecting me was the closest thing to protecting her and fulfilling part of his mother's dying wish.

Speaking of... why had he never told me about Opal being a suspect?

I took in a breath to ask, but my throat shushed me with a searing pain. Yet another price I'd paid since Alexa had come into my life—I didn't know what had happened, but I could almost bet my magic that she had something to do with it. I followed Jak's tired sigh, sick of the way things were. I was sick of any and every Hunter chasing me for any and every reason, sick of Jak randomly popping up only if it was about the Hunter business, and sick of being Alexa's sole target.

"Thanks. For checking in," I finally said, lowering my voice to a near whisper. I crossed my arms and met my stare with the carpet below my feet. I wanted to sit in the recliner, but my body didn't want to be trapped right now.

"You're back," I said next. "In town."

Jak's eyes met the floor again. "Yeah. This morning. The second I got through the front door, Anthony was missing. Then my dad updated me on the missions and I just... assumed the worst."

I nodded. The words weren't exactly friendly to me, either. Now I knew that there was a fairly decent possibility that this Anthony guy *would* come after me.

"You need to—leave," I said, swallowing with a wince. "Mom will be back."

"I'm sorry I freaked you out—and snapped." Jak stood from the couch and came up to me. "I worry about you."

I rolled my eyes. "That's Mom's job."

"And mine."

I cursed my lips for turning upward.

His eyes trickled down to my neck, and a soft smile touched him. "I don't know why I'm surprised every time I see you wearing that." He took my locket into his fingers, scrutinizing it. "I'm honored that you love it so much."

"It's a symbol. We made it—out." I shrugged it off. "Perfect reward."

He wrapped his arms around my waist, resting his hands on my lower back. "You don't sound good. At all. Stop talking and drink some tea."

He rested his forehead against mine, taking a deep breath in and closing his eyes. I followed suit, letting the stillness stretch between us until he softly chuckled.

"What?" I asked, biting back my own laughter lest we encountered another 4 A.M. situation and my throat started bleeding.

"Nothing. Just..."—he broke away to look up, glancing all

around at the living room and dining area on the other side of him—"I've been here this whole time without knowing what this place looks like." His eyes felt full of intent as they landed back on me. "You were actually all I saw for a couple of minutes."

Can I just say, even though I didn't grow up around normal girls and I'm not even going to a school with normal girls now, I'm pretty sure that they don't get to hear something like that from the most perfect boy who's ever walked the face of the planet?

I brought my hands to his neck, my thumbs brushing his light-brown cheeks. "Mom will be back," I whispered.

He hummed in acknowledgement, dropping his voice to a whisper with mine. "Stop talking."

"Jak."

He locked our hands together and closed the gap between our chests, his subtly musky cologne lingering in the air. He quietly sighed. "Yeah. I guess I have to go."

He leaned forward before hesitating, like he had to make a detour. Instead, his lips moved to the side of my face and placed a long, soft peck on my cheek.

"See you later, Merlin," he said, stepping backwards and in the direction of the door.

"You're a cruel tease, you know."

"Good," he said, his hand resting on the doorknob. "Then Beanie Boy can't steal you away."

Oh boy. He didn't even need to know the finished story of *that* because he already knew how good he was. He was just making sure that I knew it, too, and he got exactly what he wanted when my smile betrayed me.

CHAPTER

Twenty-Four

No matter how much Moren wanted to believe otherwise the next day, "activating the nore within me upon contact with my buyer's hand" wasn't any easier to understand than any of his other attempts at explaining my nore magic to me.

"Simple," he repeated, gesturing with wide arms as he walked across his living room. "Their hand rests between yours, your nore magic senses this, and every answer in the world is bestowed upon you from it."

From my seat at his "nore table", as I liked to call it, my arm rested lazily on the surface. I blinked as if, with every second, I got closer to understanding.

"Y'know," I began, propping my chin on my hand, "for a guy

who knows everything, you're not great at teaching."

His head of shoulder-length curls swung to the side as he looked at me, his eyes narrowed. "For the savior of the world, you're not great at your magic."

"That term is slightly inaccurate," I replied bitterly, "and that was a low blow."

If Moren was amused by my inability to bite back, he did a good job of hiding it. He approached the table. "May we continue?"

"I've only known about this part of me for a few months," my pride said. "I deserve credit."

"You *deserve* access to every part of you," he said. He held out his hand. "I won't give up on the one that I can help."

As eccentric as he can be, at the end of the day, the man knows how to reach the heart.

He took his seat across from me. I exhaled and placed my hand into his. If he wasn't going to give up on me, then I had double the reasons not to.

"Close your eyes," he told me.

I obeyed. In those seconds filled with the hum of the whirling fan in the living room, circulating the moist air, the savory aroma of the simmering vegetable soup in his kitchen swelled.

"Tap into the still, small sensation of when my magic accesses the events of your life," he said. "When you understand your result, you'll know better the steps to achieve it."

Since our mentoring sessions began in April, I'd had a few successful attempts, but they were few and far between—and way too short to actually absorb any of the information I was looking for. But with Alexa's memory gone and my anxiety debilitating my ability to read her, I *needed* this power. It was a survival tool now.

I discreetly bit my lip as Moren's hand rested on top of mine. A subtle, vacuum-like suction drained from my head as Moren activated his power.

"Keep your eyes closed," he said. "Ask me any question you already know the answer to."

"Where is Alexa Delphine right now?"

"Thomas Dawson's living room," he answered simply. "Now, when I ask my question, indulge yourself in the temporary truth spell. Let it take hold of the same veins your magic flows through. Then you will know what you're meant to feel as a nore."

It almost felt like I was in a self-defense class all over again.

"Who are your biological parents?"

All instincts of deception and lies were locked as the nore's effect gripped my brain. Practicing Moren's words, I let my magic amplify it until I knew I was ready to embrace what was happening inside.

"Amy Dalbert-Marie and Tristan Atera."

With the fading of the truth spell and Moren's release of my hand, I opened my eyes and sat up straight in my chair. Moren's eyes bored into me with patience and readiness.

"Don't let your grip falter," he warned.

You already have the power, I told myself.

Chewing on my lip, I offered him my hand. No distractions, only concentration. I had nothing to be afraid of.

I closed my eyes, remembering the vacuum from when he'd placed his hand on top of mine. I willed myself to send it to him, telling my magic to suspend me in truth. My other hand went on top of his.

My will commanded my magic to reach into Moren's mind, pulling out the events of his life. With the first flash of an image, magic gripped it for dear life. I let my mind cherish Moren's memories as they played across the screen in my head.

Until one.

In a split second played one full event in Moren's perspective. Twelve years old, hiding under a couch. A man with dark skin and black curls—his father, Isayas—was making sure that Moren was safely tucked under. Moren threw the hood of an invisibility cloak over his head as the front door, across from them in the sunlit living room, banged open. Isayas stood with his hands up. Masked agents, armed and armored, stormed inside.

"I don't want trouble, please," Isayas began calmly in a deep voice.

Two agents charged forward, five at the door with their weapons aimed.

"No, please, we can talk!" Isayas exclaimed, his hands shoved behind his back and cuffed. "Wait!"

Nobody listened to him. Unwisely of Isayas, he writhed in the agents' hold.

"Listen, please!" he cried. "Don't take me away, I'm just like you! I'm one of you, don't!"

An agent from the door charged forward and grabbed Isayas's feet when he started violently kicking.

"I'm a man like you!" Airy, dry sobs erupted from his chest. "Don't take me away, please! *Listen to me!*"

His cries fell to the wooden floor. Moren watched the agents force his father out of their home. Heavy footsteps pounded on the asphalt pathway at the front of the house.

Isayas's shouts bellowed into the air. "I'm one of you! *Please!*"

Moren stayed under the couch with shallow, trembling breaths. His finger rose to his teeth, and he chewed. Outside, grunts of struggle pursued his father's screams—not just from one man. A couple of bodies hit the ground. Fast footsteps battered on the asphalt and away from the house.

Three gunshots echoed in the air.

Young Moren's eyes squeezed shut. I yanked my hand away.

If I was breathing, I couldn't feel it. The throbbing, dull ache was suffocating my chest so tightly that I was almost numb. I cursed my tears, cursed the agents, cursed my powers and mortality...

I sat still in my chair, hands resting heavily on the table's surface. "Why," I whispered shakily, "did you show me that?"

"I didn't," Moren replied, all too quietly. I wasn't surprised that he knew what I was referring to. "Your magic did."

"You were twelve."

His mom was found out at work when he was six and her own coworkers killed her. He was orphaned that day.

Maybe Moren nodded in response. I didn't see it. My eyes were focused on something in front of me, but fresh memory held my vision.

Things... were making a lot more sense.

The heat from my cheeks seemed to radiate into the temperature of the house. "I'm sorry."

His lips pressed together as his only response. The fan over the living room whirled louder.

"You've never accessed so much before and for so long," he said. He was ready to change gears, but my chest stayed anchored to his memory of that day. "It seemed to come naturally to you today. What was different?"

I swallowed. I knew that our people suffered at the hands of our government every day, I knew that they were killed because of what they were. But I'd never even remotely witnessed it before. I'd never heard it.

Before Moren could speak again, I forced my voice back into my throat. "I've had a lot of practice."

Things were making a lot more sense.

I thought back to the woman who was the reason I was so determined to solidify this part of my magic at all. If this was part of Moren's story, what was Alexa's? What was the difference stark enough to turn one into a mass murderer and the other a silent ally? What drove Alexa to kill and Moren to sit and be patient?

And beyond her, what had driven Alexa's family to join her besides legacy? According to what she'd told me on our way to the beach house last year, the Delphines were the ones who'd *founded* the Hunter career. Was that really enough to keep every generation in it since the beginning? And if they were so dead set on the mission, why hadn't they come for her yet?

"You seem to have a question."

At Moren's words, I finally looked up. "I need to know about Alexa's pack. The solo research and seduction theory aren't enough. There's a reason they haven't come for her yet. It's been weeks."

"I could search for that answer with a simple touch," he said, leaning forward, "but I've given you too many passes. I'd need to ask a real question. And I don't want anyone to be able to use me against you."

I nodded softly. Moren's layers were concise and separate; that was how I knew exactly how many he'd peeled back to show me as much as he had today.

"With my deepest apologies, savior," he began, standing from his seat, "you'll need to find this answer yourself."

"Please, no."

I couldn't give this up. The name, the situation, Alexa's whole pack were too opaque in my mind to be erased or brushed aside. It'd been a month. The Callistro Academy wasn't a school to teach the art or game of seduction, but even I knew it was suspicious when that game lasted for that long without any intel back to headquarters.

Especially when the seducer was married.

"I don't have the time or confidence for you to ask me, so please, let me ask it."

Moren paused as if I were trying to trap him in a game of loyalty. As if whether he'd tell me this would alter our entire relationship.

He pressed the tips of his fingers together. "I'll need to ask a real question. I'll need real payment."

"Then let me pay it."

He slowly sat himself back down—the same way I'd done the day we'd met, like there were spikes sticking up from the seat. He held out his hand, and I placed mine on top of it.

"Are you sure that you don't want to practice with this question?" he asked, dark-brown eyes encouraging me with wisdom.

"I don't have time to fail."

He nodded and then placed his other hand on top of mine. Amber flooded into his irises, maintaining its glow. "What would you like to know?"

"Why hasn't Alexa's pack come for her yet?"

In the second that the answer revealed itself to him, his lips parted. I silently begged for the information flooding into his mind when his hands, surprisingly, stayed still on top of and under mine.

"So many…" he began, astonished, as if he were overwhelmed by the sheer multitude of reasons. He lightly shook his head, eyes staying with our hands. "In order: during the pack's time away, she had promised them the results of a private mission. Upon the pack returning without their leader's report, a member was sent yesterday to you."

"What?"

He shook his head at me. I knew to seal my lips like a watertight door.

"Finding that she's lost her memories, the pack believes that she's still undercover. They think she needs more time, that she's being smart about her approach by ignoring them—pretending to have forgotten them."

Reserving a few seconds to catch up, I repeated every sentence in my head. Hang on. Magic was obviously involved in all of that. So that had to mean…

"Doesn't that mean her pack is her family? Or at least other magicians? Don't we have more time because of that?"

"One question at a time, dearie. You know that."

I sighed. If only one closed door didn't lead to a room of open windows. "Okay."

"This is my question to you: who are you hundredth generations of your family, with abilities impossible for even magic?"

A protective instinct clawed my chest. Annisa—I'd spoken her name aloud before and tied it to Morgana, another sacred name in the magic world like Adara's. Alexa was already hunting Adara, and now that Moren knew who Morgana was, anyone could get that intel out of him if they were looking for it. Annisa was vulnerable now because of me.

He's gotten that piece of information every time I've asked him a question since then.

Before regret could cripple me any further, Moren's question buzzed in my head. Who were we? Annisa and I were asking each other that every time we texted! I might've been under the nore's truth spell right now, but that didn't mean I had the answer.

"I don't know," I admitted. "We only know that we have the same destiny to help unite the mortal and magic worlds. We don't know why it's us."

Moren's eyes faded to dark brown. He released my hands, setting his own down on the rough table. "I'm glad," he said quietly. "Hold on to it when you find out."

I guess that went as well as it could've. But now I had to tell Annisa that someone else knew her identity in the magic world. Didn't I?

I'd definitely want to know if the roles were reversed.

I stood, already preparing that conversation in my head. "Thanks for today," I told Moren, turning and walking to the table next to the door to grab my keys. "I know where I need to go now."

C H A P T E R

Twenty-Five

I spent a good few minutes of silence in my car in front of Moren's house out of respect for his father. It's one thing to know of how nores are kidnapped and imprisoned so that the government can exploit their power, but to witness history rise to reality—for its sinister roots to wrap around your own vision...

I couldn't let that reality persist. In fact, never in my life had Adara felt like such a possibility, a future actually within reach now that I had the determination.

My phone finally buzzed in my cup holder with Annisa's reply.

A: i understand... it's kinda on me too for not telepathically telling you that part. i just hope

After Moren's house, I went to Mr. Dawson's. Now that I had more information about the pack, I knew exactly what kind of conversation I needed to have with him.

I stepped out of the car and onto his driveway, wondering how I'd get Alexa out of earshot and for long enough. Maybe I could put her under a sleeping spell. That might be too risky... Maybe we could slip another forgetting spell in—no, that was definitely too risky. Maybe—

Wow, he's good, I thought when the front door opened just as I walked up. But then I processed Alexa standing next to him in the doorway. In a red evening dress. Hanging on to Mr. Dawson's arm. Who was in a navy-blue suit. Both had been laughing until their startled eyes fell onto me.

There was no way. An intrusive thought was making me hallucinate. I was jumping to conclusions, wasn't I? I had to be. I had to be! I was!

"Em—Mo," Mr. Dawson said, too rushed to have been expecting me. I almost wanted to congratulate him for the natural save: a "stutter" in the beginning before he used my fake name. But he *hadn't* been expecting me. He'd had no idea that I'd catch him. And the stammer tripping over his words only fueled my anger.

With her red lips stuck open, Alexa glanced between the two of us in wary anticipation. Her usually wavy hair had been curled into loose ringlets. It shouldn't have looked so captivating on her.

Her eyes settled on me. "Are you okay, honey?" she asked, too sincerely for my comfort.

I had to stay my center of gravity so that I wouldn't stumble backwards and fall down the porch steps. "Mr. Dawson?" I whispered. I couldn't understand why his name was the only thing comfortable on my tongue. The smallest part of me wondered if I'd blown his cover by using it. A bigger part of me didn't even care.

"It's not what it looks like," he said, far too calmly. "We're just going out to dinner, that's all."

Just "going out to dinner"?

At Alexa's panged glance at him, my own darted to his sharp jaw: clenched. He was lying.

The summer sun's heat on my back intensified as I tamed the narrowing of my eyes, bringing them up to his. —*I know you better.*—

The smallest lump of a swallow passed in his throat. "Okay, um..." he murmured hoarsely, slightly turning to Alexa. "I'm so sorry, can you give us a minute, please?"

She drew her arm out from his, promptly nodded, and turned around. Her black heels—*Where did she get those?*—clicked on the linoleum in the entry foyer as she went back into the house and shut the door behind her.

My eyes were ready to laser a hole straight through Mr. Dawson's head, fury blurring my sight. The shade of the overhead cooled my clothes as my arms crossed firmly in front of my chest. We were out of the sun, but it was still too bright outside. Such a beautiful day wasted.

This brilliant man. How could he be so stupid?

"Emma," he finally began, his eyes finding mine only after he could speak my name. "I know you're jumping to conclusions—"

"*Jumping* to *conclusions?*" I spat, the words venomous to even my own tongue. I fought to keep my voice hushed. "Are you kidding me? You're in a suit, she's in a skintight dress, it's 5 o'clock on a Wednesday night, and she was clinging to you like a puppy! Was I supposed to think you're going grocery shopping?"

"It's not what it—"

"Oh, it's *not* a date? Tell me it's not a date, do it!"

It just felt right. Every word felt right. First the spring final, then him hiding something from me, and now this.

Most of me still didn't want to cry in front of him. But the remaining part—the small part letting my nose redden and eyes water—wanted him to see just how much he had hurt me this summer.

Because of that, maybe, just maybe, a small fraction of him knew that everything I was saying *was* right. Because he didn't give me anything in response.

"You're going on a date with Alexa Delphine. A *married* Alexa Delphine! You said your feelings for her died a long time ago!"

"Say it a *little* louder, I don't think the woman on the other side of the door heard you," he hissed, finally giving me the authoritative eyes of a headmaster.

I instinctually glimpsed the street beside me. As much as I hated to admit it, the neighbors could have been listening in, too. His house was at the end of the court, so every house on either side felt like another pair of eyes watching us. I wondered if any were as I wiped a runaway tear from my cheek.

"My feelings for her died when she became a Grand Hunter,"

Mr. Dawson said next, resetting his volume to just above a whisper. "They died when she *was* Alexa Delphine."

What's wrong with him?

"Who do you think is staying with you?" I snapped quietly, anger starting to singe my tears. "That's the same woman who almost killed you last year."

"I'm the one who set the fire," he said bitterly. The guilt on my tongue was sour. "And that's my whole point: she's not the same woman."

Am I the only sane one in this situation?

My mind replayed his lies over and over as screams and shouts and yells strained my throat, stuck in it like a fly in honey; Alexa was just on the other side of the door. And I hated that. I didn't want to believe that she was here, I didn't want to believe that he'd *let* her be here.

I bit down hard on my lip and monitored the silver SUV parked in the next-door driveway. The whisper of a horrific memory snaked around my mind. That morning... I didn't understand—*Mr. Dawson* had saved me from it. He was supposed to be the adult. I couldn't think of any other question: how? How could one of my foundations of trust betray me so selfishly? *Again*, for the third time in a row?

Anger burned away every fear. I held myself high and my voice low, dragging my eyes to the wooden floor of the porch. "When did you stop caring about me?"

"Emmalynn—"

"No, don't," I snapped, surprising even myself. This bitterness was foreign, and yet so right, so deserved. "You told me that betraying me, even pretending to, was the hardest thing you've ever had to do. But here we are,"—I counted each time on my fingers—"one, two, three! You've managed to pull it off three times in ONE summer!"

My fingers itched to fiddle with my locket, but I refused to show any weakness in front of him right now as I struggled for a semblance of stability. "This is—this is Alexa!" I whispered airily, voice giving way to those cries. "How could you go back, she's—she was just a childhood fling—!"

"No," he retorted, pointing an accusatory finger at me. "She is *not* a fling and she's not the Alexa who hunted you all year! She's finally back to the woman I fell in love with!"

I stumbled into the porch pole behind me. Somehow, my mouth hung open yet no air passed through.

He rubbed his face with both hands, his lips pressed so tightly together that they turned white. I'd caught him. Those words had told me everything.

His jaw clenched again. "I didn't—" he breathed. Every step he paced on the porch echoed with a wooden click that was too loud. "I didn't mean that."

"You *did*." I pushed myself back up. "You still have feelings for her. You're not using her for our gain, you're just trying to convince yourself you are. You're falling for her again."

A gently shaking head. A hand rubbing his neck.

I didn't care what I said anymore. "I can't even say I'm surprised."

"You know why 'Alexandra' was the name she remembered?"

My head caught back in surprise. *That* was what mattered to him right now? "Because she doesn't remember anything?"

"Because that's her real name."

What...?

"She was Alexandra when we were together in high school. The next time I heard anything about her, she was a Grand Hunter and had changed her name to 'Alexa'. Now she doesn't remember any of that—she's back to Alexandra. Back to..."

Back to the woman he fell in love with. In every sense. I despised that he actually had some kind of foundation for this.

"But that's not who she actually is," I told him, like he really needed to be reminded of that, because I was pretty sure that he did. "It's a miracle she didn't try to kill you in the fire!"

"She saved me from the fire."

Wait. *What?*

"Okay," he said, holding up both of his hands as if to will my patience, "we saved each other. We brought each other out of the basement and through the house and then..."

There was no way. No way. But he'd acted surprised when I'd told him this year that Alexa was still alive! He'd been faking? Had he seriously pretended that he'd had nothing to do with that?

As if reading my thoughts, he gently nodded. "She let me go. Like I let her."

Did... did Alexa still have feelings for him? Before all of this? How long had this been going on?

"Maybe I did fall for her again," Mr. Dawson finally whispered, too ashamed to maintain eye contact now. "Maybe I want to live my fantasies for once. Maybe I want to forget, just for *so* briefly. But you have to know me better than that, Emma. I want to, but I'd *never* act on it. I'm not doing any of this to hurt you, this is not happening for the reason you think. Even now, I can't bring myself to be that stupid."

I sniffed, wiping another stray tear from my cheek. *Could you if you knew how she really felt?*

The corner of the porch pole dug into my back, but I couldn't care. "If you even wanna *think* about making me trust you again, you have to tell me your plan. If this were our regular Alexa, you know she'd have an ulterior motive, so what's yours?"

"You *have* to trust me," he said, finally returning to his gentleness. To that father-like figure I'd come to know. "If you believe it, so will she. I know how everything looks. I know I've made mistakes this summer. But please—please trust me on this, Emmalynn. Please."

I scoffed, shaking my head and drying my eyes. Those words meant less to me than what I felt I meant to him.

"It's easy to believe when it's the truth," I muttered. Especially when all Alexa knew right now were her unburied feelings.

Alexa's the entire reason Mr. Dawson is even alive. And he was hers.

Anger resurfaced. —*I'm honestly scared you've lost your mind,*— I finally told him, eyeing the elderly woman in a pink 80's tracksuit who'd just turned down the street. —*You have to give me something that'll let me know you're not completely blind in this and aren't just throwing away my safety for her. Can you really blame me for thinking that way?*—

He softly shook his head again. He wasn't going to tell me his plan. His honesty was nonexistent unless I violated our boundaries and cast a truth spell (which was more than tempting). So whatever he was planning, he didn't want me knowing. And if he really did have feelings for her now, he didn't want me judging.

Too late.

The front doorknob twisted. Mr. Dawson and I froze in defense, careful as if Alexa's pack had broken into the house and was about to catch us on the porch.

Alexa's defined, delicate face with that perfectly done eye makeup peeked out from the door. "Sorry, am I interrupting—?"

When her eyes landed on me, her jaw fell open. "Mo, honey, what's wrong?"

Oh, that concern. That genuine care and concern and pet name coming from *her*, of all people. It reminded me too much of Julia. Another person who'd betrayed me, who'd lied about who she was. And she was standing right in front of me.

"Nothing," I whispered with a soft smile, rubbing my nose. "Just talking about... school."

"You're not interrupting," a calm Mr. Dawson said. "We were just about finished."

"Don't worry, I didn't hear anything," she said, glancing back and forth between us and then sticking with me again. "But are you sure you're okay?"

There was a sincerity to her that not even Grand Hunter Alexa Delphine could feign; she was telling the truth as Alexandra Delphine. Picking up on her mannerisms since she'd been with Mr. Dawson was promising me that.

I nodded. "I'm fine. Enjoy your night."

I fought to keep my honesty inside. Mr. Dawson had always been a smart man up until this summer, but this was too far. Plan or not, he *had* to see the reality of the situation. His heart had to be stronger—strong enough to never let this actually happen. His emotions couldn't make him lower his guard. His life depended on it, he knew that.

How can love be so strong yet make you so weak?

I took a deep breath in, turned away, and stepped down the porch steps, homing my focus on him. —*I pray you know what you're doing. For all our sakes.*—

Twenty-Six

Thirteen, I was thirteen. Nothing other than my head was telling me that. Little thirteen-year-old Emmalynn had managed to get herself kidnapped.

I sat in a big wooden chair, unable to rip the thick duct tape strapping down my wrists and ankles. That tape was nailed to the chair.

Momma?

Momma wasn't there. Nobody was there in that large, white-walled, black-carpeted room. Nobody was there except fifteen-year-old Emmalynn's memories: Alexa and William's underground lair from the Capperson Fall Carnival.

The realization swept an invisible wave of magic throughout the room. I grew to sixteen-year-old me. William Bleu, with dark-brown hair and eyes that matched Jak's too well, appeared in front of me. He was talking away and pacing the width of the room. Dream Emmalynn knew to look to her right: a trolly with files, pictures, and small jars filled with blue fluid.

"Emmalynn," William hissed. He bent down and grabbed my chin.

No! "No!"

His body flew across the room and into the wall on the other side. Somehow, the duct tape had weakened with my telekinesis. I tore my wrists free, but my ankles were practically glued to the chair.

"Mom!" I cried.

A gloved hand covered my mouth. "Shush, darling," a sweet voice crooned behind me, whispering a prickly chill down my body. In my peripheral loomed what I could only pray wasn't a gloved hand holding a godforsaken syringe.

"No, please! Don't, I can't!"

My voice was muffled behind the glove, but my subconscious told Alexa exactly what I'd said.

"*Shhh.*" She pushed my head back, pressing harder against my mouth. Emerald-green eyes, red hair, and all came into view against the harsh, fluorescent lights above. "It won't hurt if you stay still."

"STOP!" I screamed, forcing my head forward as if to shake away her hand. "Mom! Please!"

William appeared beside me, grabbing my chin in his strong hand. His fingernails dug into my skin. The room was too bright. "Stop struggling and tell us!" he snarled.

"I don't know!" I cried, a sliver of the room in my peripheral vision the only safe space from this nightmare. "Stop, I don't know!"

"Tell me the truth, Emmalynn," Alexa growled, pulling my hair down to force my face upward.

Prick. My scream amplified the sting of the needle sinking into my neck.

William grabbed a hold of my neck with fire in his fingers, squeezing with unshakeable force. "I'm not letting you go until you tell me!"

"I know—!" I gasped. "I know where—she's hiding!"

"*Who*, Atera?" Alexa demanded.

"Adara!"

"Who is she?"

I shut my eyes against the white lights, absorbing every ounce of pain from William's fingers and Alexa's syringe.

"Who is she—?!"

"I AM!"

All shut to black, shrouding my vision. When I opened my eyes again, my body sprang up in bed. My bed.

Thank God, my bed!

With my breath barely able to slow itself, lying down was useless; if I lay back down, I'd be subjected to sleep. I'd be subjected to the world I'd just narrowly escaped.

Mom. Momma.

Momma was here.

I threw off my covers, jumped out of bed, almost tripped on my bedroom carpet, and then leaped across the hallway to Momma's open bedroom door.

Walking to the mahogany foot of her bed, I realized that being careful was stupid—I was her daughter, and I needed her. I hurried to the right side of her bed, moved the pink satin comforter, and crawled into the cool sheets. I nestled up next to Momma sleeping on her back.

She jumped, gasping as her head turned to find me lying beside her. "Emma?" she whispered frantically. "What's wrong?"

That thirteen-year-old Emmalynn that had disappeared in the nightmare ran home at Momma's call. I hugged her arm. Too afraid to hear my voice, I whispered, "I had a nightmare."

She exhaled and then swallowed, turning toward me and propping herself up on her elbow. "Turn over, honey."

I did as I was told and lay on my side, facing the window overlooking our backyard. Moonlight pooled onto the wooden floor below it. I focused on what little I could make out of the bushes lining our fence as Momma's arm slid around my waist. Her body stuck closely to mine.

I'd been tortured with visions since early this year. I'd been tortured with the potential future—let alone the definite—for months now. I wanted to believe that my nightmare had just been that, a nightmare. It had had all of the characteristics of a normal dream and hadn't been as immersive as my visions. But...

At this point, I almost *wanted* to go to Ingrid to know my future so I could pay her price and deactivate my magic for a little while. I couldn't believe that it was torturing me like this—even when I hadn't activated it, when I wasn't using it.

"You're safe," Momma whispered behind me, as if she could hear my thoughts. "I got you."

I squeezed her arm in thanks. A firefly blinked into existence outside as her promise soothed me enough to close my eyes. I was safe. Momma was here.

†

Summer vacation means that kids can do absolutely whatever they want whenever they want. Here's the fine print of that, though: if you want to spend those days *with* anyone, you *all* have to be available at the exact same time. I'm pretty sure that was why I hadn't seen the girls nearly as often as I'd thought we would, because they were always off on other vacations or with family, and I was always on Atera *and* Alexa duty now.

I could come up with a whole list on what Jak's excuses were, so when he actually answered my call the next day, it was all the more a pleasant surprise—especially when the first thing he asked me was how I was feeling after my mysteriously sore throat.

"Better, thanks," I told him, pacing the outline of the sunlight that my bedroom window left on the floor. "I have no idea where a sore throat came from, but it's okay now."

I'd especially had no idea when I'd looked in the mirror after Jak had left that day and found no marks on my neck. Maybe it was a cold that had been scared away by the sun before it could fully manifest.

I didn't know, and I didn't really care. "I need to ask you something. Your parents' pack, did they hunt *all* of the suspects of Tristan's descendant?"

Hesitance. "The ones in North Carolina, yeah."

"Do you remember everyone that was on their list? You tried to protect them, right?"

"Yeah,"—he laughed—"but I probably don't remember *every* single one."

"Was Opal Dubois a suspect?"

Another pause, but this one wasn't because of uneasiness. I knew him well enough by then. "Okay, yeah, I'd definitely remember her," he said.

She was telling the truth...?

"But no, she wasn't a suspect."

Wait. What?

I couldn't figure out what was going on in my head. Something had shattered, yet I felt something build itself back up at the same time. Why would Opal lie about that? Why would Opal *lie?*

"Just curious, are you guys friends?" I asked Jak next.

"Not really..." The curiosity in his hesitance was mounting by the second. "I saw her around school when Redway stayed with Callistro, but—geez, I think the first and last *real* conversation we had was the first time I spent the night at the school, last year."

Opal had lied about talking to him a few times, too...? Why?

Something's definitely going on, this doesn't make any sense. I'm missing something.

"Em," Momma called from the living room before I could even start trying to put the pieces together. "Important message from Mr. Dawson."

Ugh, great—that meant that it actually *was* important.

"I have to go," I told Jak. "But thanks, I was just wondering."

"Um..." Jak breathily chuckled. "Sure. Stay out of trouble with that info."

I'll honestly *try to.*

I hung up and darted out of my room, down the hall and

into the living room. Momma looked up from her phone once I stopped in front of her at the couch.

"He wants to meet up at Dad and Auntie's," she said. She stood up, sliding her phone into her back pocket. "Let's go."

Despite the betrayal that still lingered from Wednesday night, I followed her without argument into the car. She said nothing in regards to *what* Mr. Dawson wanted to discuss; either he hadn't said anything to her, or she didn't trust me with the information.

She doesn't trust me with a lot of information, it seems.

When Mr. Dawson walked into Dad and Auntie's apartment, I tried to forget our last conversation. There was a reason he'd called us all here, and it definitely wasn't to talk about his date. And for some reason, I couldn't bring myself to expose it. But I also couldn't bring myself to overcome my disappointment in him, either.

He closed the front door behind him. Momma and Dad sat next to each other on the couch, Aunt Becca was rocking in the recliner with a mug of coffee, and I was deliberately disobeying Momma and sitting on the arm of the couch anyway.

"What's up?" Dad asked. "Where's Alexa?"

"Napping at my place," he said, taking a spot in front of us, the entertainment center behind him. "I used a weakening spell to make her feel tired, then put her under a sleeping spell when she lay down."

"Did you steal the bracelet off her while she was sleeping?" Auntie asked, partly like she didn't believe it and partly like she was proud.

"No," he replied. "But that *is* why I'm here."

He dug out a velvet jewelry box from his pocket and opened it. A silver cuff bracelet sat inside—with an *orange* diamond!

My family sprang from their seats, and instinct brought me up with them. *He got it!*

"I managed to ask for this back without suspicion, long story," Mr. Dawson said. "What matters is that she's still an amnesiac, and we have this."

I couldn't believe it. I wanted to run straight up to him and throw my arms around him in gratitude—but emotions were still running high in light of Wednesday night. Not even right now did he match the secure father figure I'd spent my whole life knowing him as.

But I couldn't deny that the diamond on that bracelet had never glimmered more.

"Wow," I said instead, my breath escaping me in relief.

"Yep." He eyed me with caution and almost remorse, but I wasn't sure if that was real or what I *wanted* to see.

"Alexa doesn't have her magic anymore."

The fact struck me like a lightning bolt when the words left Auntie's lips. That was right. Alexa wasn't a magician anymore!

"I'm glad we realize that," Mr. Dawson said. "Because we need to find a safe place for this. If *anyone* puts it on, I don't need to explain how catastrophic the consequences would be. God only knows how much time we have before she remembers something or when her pack will come for her. So this isn't safe at my house."

I was almost tempted to put the bracelet on myself, but the *last* thing Alexa needed was another reason to hunt me down.

Mr. Dawson shut the box and then extended it to me. "Guard this with your *life*, Emmalynn. I will never be able to stress that enough."

What? Me? What was he thinking?! Was this his way of trying to smooth things over? Some kind of peace offering?

"Thomas," Momma began warily.

I matched her amber eyes with the same concern. "Yeah!" I stammered. "I can't protect this, there has to be somewhere we can put it. Or even a way to destroy it, or at *least* make it impossible to reach."

"There has to be," Mr. Dawson said, "but I don't have the time or privacy to think of it right now. The second Alexa gets her memories back, she's gonna rip my house apart looking for this. Emma, keep it in your room for now, and if the worst happens, I'll warn you so you can grab the bracelet and get a head start. She won't be able to track you with her magic, so start thinking of your best hiding spot right now and be ready to sprint to it."

He had everything planned out. He'd already prepared for any and all outcomes the situation could have. Was this his way of making up for Wednesday? Or was Wednesday just an unfortunate byproduct like—?

Like he'd told me?

I sighed under my breath in defeat. He'd planned everything. He'd had a plan like always.

Great—out of everyone in the room now, I trusted myself the least with this. "Can't Mom hide—?"

She shook her head, pursing her lips. "You're able to leave at the drop of a hat much easier than I am. As long as that bracelet stays here, you're our best option."

Her other hand rested on Dad's arm, seeming to hold on to it for dear life. Aunt Becca stood in front of the recliner, her pursed lips telling me that she was practicing every virtue of patience in her body to keep her thoughts to herself.

I chewed the inside of my cheek, turning back to Mr. Dawson as if he'd give me a different answer.

"Your family's fate—*your* fate—is resting on this," he said. He held the bracelet out to me again. "Can you do this?"

Man, did I want the story: how had he gotten the bracelet back? Had the date had anything to do with this? Had Alexa noticed the diamond's change in color?

Well, none of that mattered. My family's entire legacy depended on this bracelet staying out of the Delphines' hands. Not even trying was an option now—I just had to do it.

"Okay. I'll guard this with my life."

Because, unfortunately, I also knew that I didn't have another choice.

Twenty-Seven

By now, I'd been alone with Alexa way more times than I wanted to admit. And the only times I'd had good moments with her were moments that I hadn't even known it *was* her.

Now I have a good moment where I did. And I never, ever thought for a second in my life that I'd ever write those words.

After a fake phone call between "the police" and Mr. Dawson verifying that nobody had found a lead on her, it was his genius idea to leave us alone while he went to grab a few emergency items from the store. (Momma was going to KILL him, and I was looking forward to that.) At first I thought that Alexa had actually remembered everything and was going to try and kidnap me for revenge once he was far enough away. But then, as we sat on the couch, she asked if she could do my makeup. And if I'd ever had a boyfriend.

"What?" I ended up replying with as she set her drugstore makeup on the coffee table. Something about the artificial yellow glow of the room and closed window blinds made the atmosphere a *lot* friendlier than I wanted it to be.

"I'm sorry," she said shyly, pausing as she grabbed her four-shade eyeshadow palette. "Did I overstep?"

"No, not at all." I quickly shook my head, frozen on the couch as if she'd get her memories back if I moved. "I just wasn't expecting it."

"Oh!" She chuckled as she took a blending brush and opened the palette. "Well, you're a pretty girl. You have a bright personality. I just figured I'd ask."

I was smiling. *Why am I smiling?*

I reached for my locket but caught myself in time. "My friends bother me about this all the time—well, with this one guy. But there was this other, and..."

"Almost sounds like he was kept a pretty little secret," Alexa simpered in a manner that reminded me hauntingly well of Julia. She dipped the blending brush into a neutral shade close to my skin tone and told me to close my eyes.

"No, they just thought that..." I began awkwardly, every warning alarm in my head blaring, scolding me for keeping my eyes closed in her company. "They figured it was nothing special."

Translation: they'd figured that I'd completely forgotten about Nolan after the nasty rejection I had to give him thanks to Jak also pining after me in a simultaneous attempt to protect me from Alexa and her husband.

"*Was* it nothing special?" Alexa asked, like she actually wanted to know, the brush's bristles tickling my eyelid.

I chewed on my cheek. "No."

"What? What happened?"

I chuckled, as if it'd be enough to fill the horrible silence.

The brush drew away from my face, and I opened my eyes to a frowning Alexa.

"I'm sorry," she said again. And I believed her because, well, she probably meant it. "Was he cute?"

I covered my grin but then dropped my hand to my locket. "Yeah. And he liked to wear beanies, which is always cute."

She shared a smile with me, re-dipping the brush into the same shadow and then moving on to my other eye. "I hope it's okay that I asked, I didn't mean to pry."

"You didn't."

"Can I ask you a possibly less invasive question?"

"Sure," I said, my walls already halfway down.

"Why does your locket say 'Emma'?"

My hand froze around it.

She definitely just felt my eye twitch. I just gave away too much. We're dead. She's gonna—

Say something, idiot!

"My grandma," I finally said. Wait. That was actually the truth. "My grandma's name was 'Emma'."

Wait—we already had a backstory for this. How was I supposed to incorporate it?

Stop, don't freak out—just say something.

"She meant a lot to me but I didn't get to see her much before she died. So my mom had her name engraved in the locket before she gave it to me for my birthday. To remember her by."

I opened my eyes as the brush drew away again. A reminiscent, almost comforting smile stretched Alexa's lips.

It was all I could do to smile back and then close my eyes for her to resume her work.

I did it. Even from the afterlife, Grandma Atera was working her magic.

The brush met my eye again, and Momma's tactic came flooding back to memory. I bit my lip as the brush moved in small circles on my lid. I was ready to do my own hunting.

"What about you? Do you remember any past relationships?"

Alexa released the tiniest snort, and I opened my eyes in surprise. We shared a giggle that caused a wave of guilt in my chest, but then a giddy apology ran from her lips. I closed my eyes again as she dabbed the brush in a darker shade in the palette.

She quietly hummed like she was searching the depths of her mind again. "No, but, I mean, I've probably had them. I don't even know how old I am, but I'm guessing I'm not... around your age."

We shared another laugh.

"I don't know,"—she sighed—"I wish I could remember. I know the police said they're doing whatever they can, I know they have practically no leads. I don't blame them for not finding anything. But I feel like... like my relationships affected me in one way or the other—I mean, obviously, right? The effects are there in my memory. But relationships affect everyone, you know?"

"Yeah." I nodded ever so slightly so as to not disturb the flow of the brush in the corner of my eye. "Relationships can be a key to anyone's story. Sometimes, those relationships *are* your story. I know a couple of people like that."

The brush lifted from my eye again—but the intent was different. A second later, I opened my eyes. Alexa sat frozen in front of me, firmly gripping the brush with her mouth hanging open. Something had clicked in her.

"What's wrong?" I dared to ask.

"I remember something," she whispered, eyes stuck somewhere behind me. "I remember something."

No. Not now. I'm alone, I'm not ready, I can't defend myself—!

She opened her mouth to speak, but drew in a breath instead. It was easy to tell that whatever memory she'd just unearthed, it wasn't pleasant. And I had to *pray* that it wasn't about me.

"Are you okay?" I murmured.

She sat in silence for a few seconds, like she was gathering details with every one that passed. "It wasn't a relationship. But it did affect me." Her delicate hand lightly twirled the brush in the darker eyeshadow. Then, she held up the brush, looking at me with eyes asking for permission to continue.

"Are you sure—?"

"Please?" she asked in a soft voice that I couldn't refuse. "It'll—help me relax."

I closed my eyes, heart pulsating.

The brush touched the corner of my left eye. Alexa took a few more seconds to herself, the bristles tracing a circle pattern on my skin. "I was... seventeen. I was walking in town, some kind of town, when this boy walked up to me and started a conversation. He offered to walk around with me, so we did, and then..."—the brush moved to my right eye as Alexa exhaled—"I found myself in this alley. I went to ask why he'd taken me there, but when I turned around, he...”

I stilled at the sound of her swallow, like even she couldn’t believe the words escaping her lips.

“He knocked me out without even touching me.”

“What?” I asked, accidentally opening my eyes and instinctually leaning backwards.

“He...” Alexa’s furrowed brows relaxed, and her lips slowly rubbed against each other. She brought her eyes back to me. For the first time in weeks, I saw the old Alexa Delphine in them. “He had magic. His eyes flashed amber right before I was knocked out.”

I cursed that my own swallow was as loud as hers. I hated that every muscle in my neck had probably moved with it and she’d probably seen it all.

“When I woke up—” She gripped the makeup brush so tight, I half expected it to snap in half. Alexa’s head dropped, her hand falling into her lap. Anger and defeat laced her tone. “I’m not sure I should be telling you this story.”

“You don’t have to,” I said, almost reaching for her arm.

She exhaled, slouching and shaking her head as she raised the brush again. I closed my eyes, and she blended my left eye. “I woke up to him taking advantage of me.”

My eyes shot open. The words exploded in my mind and yet froze in the air. My memory was so desperate to erase them that they almost sounded like a different language in my head. And because I had nothing to reply with that would ever do those words justice—because they *were* real—I closed my eyes again.

I don’t wanna believe it. She can’t mean...

“I was out of it,” Alexa said next. The brush’s bristles shook against my eyelid. "I was so out of it, like he drugged me. I wasn't conscious enough to defend myself, if I even could've, but I could see around his room. It was dark, the curtains were closed, and… he had a lot of college gear. But I saw a duffel bag sitting on his dresser with a racket hanging out of it—that was some kind of wake-up call to me, like the sign I needed to start yelling at myself to snap out of it.

"I tried to defend myself, but he used magic to shut my mouth and freeze me in place. And then…"—she released another breath—"I somehow escaped. I don't know, one minute I was frozen, the next I was shoving him off me. When I threw him off, the impact knocked him out."

She chuckled under her breath. I couldn't believe she'd found it within herself to chuckle at all. "I guess my parents signed me up for self-defense class."

There was only one reason she'd been able to escape that boy's immobility spell that day. Alexa's magic had saved her.

That was her story. That was her motive for being what she was today. That was why she was out for the blood of magic, not just my family's—because she needed my family's blood to make her powerful enough to wipe out the rest of her kind.

No… that wasn't right. There had to be more to it. Why take vengeance on an entire kind when only one person severely wronged you? Could… could more wielders have wronged her in the past? Was there even more to her story?

"Alexa…" I caught myself whispering. The brush had long since moved away from my eye again, and I stared at what I had to admit was one of the strongest women I knew.

"It's over now." She timidly shook her head. The makeup

rested in her lap. "It may have been an awful experience, for an extreme lack of better words, but I'm in charge of what comes out of it. And I feel like I've let it turn me into a stronger person."

Wait. Hang on—what was I doing? *What're you doing?*

I was wrapping my arms around her.

The weight of anxiety and fear pressed down on my chest, but the rest of my heart was reaching out to a woman who needed it. If that was what had started her reign of evil, it had to be because nobody back then had been around to hug her. Comfort her. Let her know that it wasn't her fault.

"Thank you," she whispered into my ear.

I swallowed at the words. So she *did* need someone like that. She always had.

I pulled away when anxiety threatened to overwhelm my very breath. "You get one of your memories back," I said, "and *that's* the one you remember."

"No, no, I needed a memory, no matter what it was," she assured me, placing a gentle hand on my knee. It almost reminded me of Cara's touch. "It gave me a key to my past, and to who I am. You had nothing to do with back then. It's not your fault, darling."

The pet name slammed into me like a straight punch. I prayed that Alexa hadn't heard the way my breath had tightened, because that was her pet name for me—what she called me as the ruthless Grand Hunter after my blood and magic. A glimpse of Alexa Delphine had broken the surface, and I had to face the truth that her absence wouldn't last for much longer.

Don't freak out—we have the bracelet. It's okay. She's powerless.

After the story I'd just heard, I cursed myself for my wording.

I almost made the mistake of glancing up in realization: Alexa had actually remembered something. Her memories *were* being triggered, and that meant that anything could trigger more!

Including the entire town of Capperson. Including Mr. Dawson. Including me!

—*You need to come back, now,*— I told him.

—*What's wrong? Did she get her memories back? Is she looking for the bracelet?*—

—*It's too much to explain right now. You just have to come back.*—

I bit the inside of my lip as my thoughts tried to take over. I went with the only truthful one that Alexa could hear: "I still can't believe you went through that. I *never* would've thought that…"

"You just never really know who you're talking to," she said, putting the makeup brush on the coffee table and then rubbing her middle finger in a shimmery eyeshadow. "Everyone has a story. I just needed to remember that to remember part of mine."

I closed my eyes as her warm finger went to my right eye, catching one last glance at the woman in front of me. I thought back to the conversation we'd had with Mr. Dawson the night she'd kidnapped the two of us. We'd tried to get her story out of her because it was the only way to answer our last question: why she was doing all of this when she was a magician herself. We'd always thought that it was for power.

But then I realized that a magician who wants power alone doesn't kill those they steal it from. A vengeful magician kills those they steal it from.

Mr. Dawson seemed to have no trouble connecting this when he got back and settled into the armchair next to the couch. What surprised me the most, though, even though it probably shouldn't have, was his face as Alexa revealed to him what that boy had done to her. His concern and wonderment melded into shock, disgust, and...

Grief.

His posture sank, less than ideal for a headmaster and more ideal for, well, a loved one.

I scolded myself for not remembering it sooner: Mr. Dawson and Alexa had been dating when all of that had happened. And based on his reaction, he'd never known about that day until tonight.

"Alexandra..." he whispered, his saddened, dull eyes meeting hers. The name sounded as heavy as iron chains on his lips. For the first time ever, it sounded like he was addressing her instead of her cover. And, I realized, he actually was. "I'm—I can't believe..."

"It's okay," she said gently. "I'm not letting it take over. Right now, I'm glad I can't remember the aftermath. But still, that memory told me a lot."

I fiddled with my locket as I looked at Mr. Dawson. —*Are you okay?*—

His lips pressed together even tighter. He couldn't meet my eyes. —*I don't want to talk about it.*—

Mr. Dawson has always been a protector. I couldn't even begin to imagine what his protective instincts were undergoing then, how violated they must have felt to have failed so miserably at keeping the woman who had once been his entire world safe. What kind of guilty weight he was carrying.

It wasn't until seconds later that he met my eyes. —*If she remembered that entire story based on that one vague sentence you said...*—

—I know.— I swallowed a sigh. *—We don't have much longer.—*

—No, we don't. Tonight's a warning.—

Alexa was already speaking as he told me this. "There's something else. What happened that day marked the beginning of my life. A little after that, I remember dedicating myself to exposing that boy. No matter what, I wanted to make sure he'd... suffer for what he did. That day, I decided to become a Hunter."

I was almost confused at first, but I remembered that we were all born into a legacy, including her. She might have gone to the Callistro Academy to fulfill a familial obligation, but that never meant that she wanted to. Not until that day.

"And," Mr. Dawson dared to ask, "did you?"

"I don't know." Alexa took a deep breath in and rested her hands on her knees. "I don't even know if I knew how to actually do that. I just remember swearing all I was to it. I wanted to make sure that boy would never hurt someone like that again. I needed him to pay, to hurt worse than I did."

Wait. "Him". Just him? She wanted revenge on just him—not all magicians of the world?

I looked up and caught the sadness clouding Mr. Dawson's diamond-blue eyes. Somehow, I just knew that he felt like he'd lost Alexa all over again.

"I have a bit of insight as to who I am now," she added. "I have a small taste of what my personality was like back then. And the rest of it feels so close, like I can physically reach it. I just can't see it yet."

The knock at the front door was timed almost perfectly. Mr. Dawson stood and walked into the entry foyer to open it.

"Hi," a sweet yet shy voice faintly said from outside. "I need to talk to you about something."

Opal.

"Honey, I'm kind of—"

Opal stepped into the house and peered her head into the living room, purple eyes widening when they landed on me and Alexa.

"Hey," I said timidly. All of a sudden, the elephant in the room expanded enough to suffocate.

"Oh, I'm sorry," Opal said daintily, looking back at Mr. Dawson. "Should I come back?"

"No, actually. She was just about to head home."

—Do you mean me?— I asked.

—Yes. And I'm hoping to get Opal to do the same before she exposes your real name.—

Opal took a quick glance in Alexa's direction and then back at her uncle. "I wanted to talk for a few minutes, is that okay?"

"Oh, don't let me stop you." Alexa insisted the words with that perfect, gentle smile the amnesiac in her had developed over the last month. She stood up and walked into the foyer, offering her hand to Opal. "You're Opal, Julian's niece, right?"

I restrained my wince as Opal's brows knitted in confusion. She hadn't exposed my real name, but Alexa *had* just exposed our use of a cover at all.

"Yep," she replied anyway, shaking her hand.

"That's beautiful, just like your eyes! I'm Alexandra—I'll, um, leave your uncle to tell you the story."

"Thanks," Mr. Dawson said, rubbing his neck with a strained smile on his face.

"Good night, Julian."

Yeah. Never getting used to that.

I didn't expect the long, awkward silence that followed the second after Alexa's door (which was really Mr. Dawson's door) shut—mostly because I was expecting Mr. Dawson to fill it with an explanation. So why were we all quiet? Why couldn't any of us figure out what to say next?

Mr. Dawson meandered back into the living room. "Story time, Opal."

Of course I was able to tell Sarah and Breanne about Alexa staying here, but not her. Then again, Opal had kind of thrown me a curveball the last time she'd hung out with me at my house.

"Why did she call you by your middle name?" she asked, sitting down in the armchair as he sat beside me on the arm of the couch. "Who is she?"

"She's a woman who needs my help right now, and I didn't want to use my real name. She lost her memory last month, and I'm trying to help her remember her life so she can get back to it."

"Oh," Opal said simply. Too simply. I couldn't read it. "Nice."

Sarah and Breanne were only allowed to know that Alexa was Alexa *Delphine* because they knew the drama that had gone on last year and half of the drama that had gone on second semester. Even though Opal was biologically closer to me than they'd ever be because of magic, I couldn't help but feel that, if we told her who was actually staying here right now, she'd ask why we were housing a Grand Hunter. And until I had the truth of if she'd *actually* been suspected of being my father's descendant last year, I wanted to keep the truth of last year to myself, which meant we'd have to make up *another* story for why Alexa was here. And, well,

I was already having a hard time keeping track of all of the stories we were telling people.

"So," Mr. Dawson said, "what brings you here at this hour?"

She perked up, her eyes sparkling. "Oh—my visions are getting clearer and longer. But there's been an ongoing theme in them lately, and I had this one question about them."

"I'm probably not gonna be much help there," I said, readying myself to stand. "I have to get going, anyway—"

"No, stay! This might be important," Opal chirped. She looked back at Mr. Dawson. "Uncle Thomas, do you, um... do you know who Adara is?"

CHAPTER

Twenty-Eight

Of course, my first instinct was to lie—to show Opal how supposedly confused I was at the name of "Adara", to bury my panic that Opal actually knew something about her—but Mr. Dawson had completely different plans.

"So you've finally started dreaming about her."

My gaze locked on him. *What is he doing?!*

"What do you mean?" Opal asked before I could.

"Druids and seers have known about Adara for centuries. We're the only classes of magicians able to see the future. It's up to us to inform others about what she's meant to accomplish."

"But I don't even know what she looks like," Opal said, leaning forward in the armchair. "Do you?"

"Nobody does. Her face is vague like an extra in a regular dream. Magic itself protects her identity. All we know is what she's meant to do. Have you dreamed that part yet?"

—*You're giving away too much!*—

—*Not now. If she's dreaming about Adara, it's every bit her right to know who she is like it is for every other magician who knows about her.*—

You don't know that she lied, I managed to keep to myself.

"I haven't dreamed anything about what she's meant to do," Opal replied. "Everyone just keeps talking about her in my visions, either saying how excited they are for her to come, being thankful for whatever she did, or..."

"Or?" I asked, heart beating so fast that I was scared she could hear it. And I couldn't convince myself that I was overreacting with the conclusions I was already jumping to in my head.

"Or they're mourning her and her 'unfinished work'."

At least I was wearing long sleeves, because I *really* didn't want her to see the goosebumps running up my arms.

Mr. Dawson jolted upward in his seat on the arm of the couch. Having the freedom of expressing how he felt, he gawked at his niece. "You've had dreams where she dies?"

"I haven't *seen* her die." She shrugged shyly, stealing a glance in my direction. "But from the looks and sounds of it, and based on what you've told me about our visions, there's a possibility it'll happen, right? Why?"

He ran a hand through his tousled dark-brown hair, heavily sighing. "It's about her 'unfinished work'. Adara is an extremely powerful sorceress and destined to help unite the mortal and magic worlds. But if you had a vision where she dies before that..."

"It was just one or two," Opal was quick to say, scooting to the edge of her seat. "All the others were where she was alive, some where she *did* do that."

With her eyes locked on Mr. Dawson, I couldn't help but put in my own two cents. —*You've never had a vision where I die before I become Adara?*—

He glanced between the two of us, trying to decide which to answer first. "That's all we need to know, that it's possible," he told Opal. "The only way to know for sure is if we visit a seer."

"But we'd have to pay the price," Opal finished quietly, folding her arms against her chest.

Mr. Dawson blindly stared at the coffee table. —No,— he said. —*Not even one. But that's not to say that other druids haven't gotten those dreams before.*—

Other druids... other druids having dreams about *me*. Druids like Mr. Dawson, like Annisa—both of which had actually seen my face in their dreams. Why? How? If magic was letting *them* see me, what was stopping it from showing other druids, like Opal? Would magic be the first thing to expose me to her...?

I swallowed hard, my fingers lacing themselves around my locket. Anything, *anything* to not show Opal how terrified I was right now.

"So," I added, hoping to distract myself, "do you know *when* Adara will show up?"

"No." She said it as if I should've known that. "All of my visions that involve her are full of people I've never seen before. So I don't know if we'll be grown up when it happens or if we're a month away or something."

"Her identity is unknown," Mr. Dawson said, resting his hands on his knees, "and it's meant to stay unknown until she reveals herself.”

Opal pressed her thin lips together. She glimpsed me again like I had the answers to her questions. Like she knew that I was holding out on her.

I felt myself temporarily revert to the girl I'd been when Jak had shown up at Momma's classroom in the gym and told me that Grand Hunters thought I was my father's descendant: *Don't let your face give it away. Don't let her know anything with your expression. Everything's only a possibility right now.*

I was too anxious. I couldn't keep it inside.

"Well, I have to get going," I said, standing before Opal could have another second to read me. "Good night, you guys."

"Night, Emma," she said. Mr. Dawson echoed her as I passed the entryway and reached the front door. With another superficial smile, I opened it and stepped out into the heat.

My heart raced like a rabbit's. Alexa had remembered something, Opal had had one of our secrets revealed to her, there was a chance I'd die before I could accomplish Adara's destiny... What was I supposed to do? Why was everything so out of my control?

Don't cry. Don't cry.

What was I supposed to do? *Not* cry?

Tears filled my vision and rolled down my face as I walked to my car and threw open the door.

†

On a happier note, as much as I adored the meals at the Callistro Academy, summer vacation offered even greater possibilities. If I didn't go out to eat with Sarah, Breanne, and Opal, Momma and

I stayed in and cooked together. Today it was homemade chicken Alfredo, so spirits were especially high when we finished eating and took our plates to the kitchen.

"You know," she mused, passing the archway, "it's a tragedy that Alexa became what she did. Without the pain of her memories, she seems like a wonderful person."

"You do realize who you're talking about, right?" I said flatly, mind foreign to something positive about that woman. After Mr. Dawson had found it within himself to actually go out with her, the *last* thing I needed was my mother, of all people, changing her mind about her, too.

"Yes," Momma said skeptically, slowing when she placed our dishes into the sink. "The Alexa who's *not* a Grand Hunter, Alexandra. The woman behind the career."

I'm sorry—how did her having amnesia suddenly excuse everything she'd become?

I shook my head, leaning against the granite countertop. "Whatever."

Momma froze. "Excuse me?"

"I didn't mean it like that," I said, straightening with respect. "I just—apparently I'm the only one who remembers who she really is and what she's done."

"Em," Momma said, scoffing as she turned on the faucet, "of course we remember who she is and what she's done! But we're not talking about her, we're talking about the woman staying with Mr. Dawson."

"They're the—"

—*same thing!* I was ready to scream it until discipline somehow stopped me. I couldn't do it. I couldn't have this conversation again. I couldn't have someone else go against me just because they could forget so easily.

"I can't talk about this right now." I turned away and left the kitchen for the living room.

"Em," Momma called, turning off the faucet. She followed me to the couch and took a seat next to me, even though I refused to look anywhere else but ahead of me. Her hand rested on my back as she told me, "I know. I was there through everything she did to you. But whenever we visit, we talk to a normal person who has her own fears, her own goals, her own story—"

"First of all, no, you *weren't* there!" I stood back up, walking around the coffee table. My body refused to be still, feet pacing the width of the table as I chewed on the inside of my cheek. Mom was doing it: she was casting aside every last thing Alexa had done to me, to my family, for almost a year. Alexa not remembering what she'd done didn't change the fact that she'd done it!

If everything could be forgotten so easily... were any of my feelings, any last resentments or fears, even valid?

"You may *know* about everything, but you weren't there," I said, facing Momma. "*I* was. *I* experienced everything, I still am!"

Silence. Blind staring.

And despite everything that Alexa had done to me—especially after my last visit with her—I *still* felt guilty.

Like I'd done this to myself.

"I can't," I cried, darting out of the living room, down the hallway, and into my room.

"Emma!" Momma called again. I practically heard her stand up, but I prayed that she'd stay in the living room and let me be alone right now. The world was swaying. My heart was throbbing.

The oxygen around me was deteriorating. My vision was blacking out on me in guilt, fury, and a hundred trapped screams.

I shut my bedroom door and leaned against it, stomach rocking with nausea. Remorse. Rage. Combating each other.

Why would she say that, why would she do that to me?

I had to face it: I was still angry. I thought I'd forgiven Momma, but that only applied to the spring final. In truth, part of me had been silently resenting her and Mr. Dawson ever since I'd found out that they were keeping something from me that was supposed to *help* me with all of this, whatever it even was. Now they were forgiving the monster in my life while I was still picking up the pieces of myself that she had broken.

Maybe because she deserves it, a wicked voice taunted. You know what she's been through. All you've done is take away her entire life and manipulate her.

The blood in my head seemed to drain to my feet. My back slid down my bedroom door as I took deep, futile breath after deep, futile breath.

She was about to take my magic!

But all I've done since is make her helpless.

She's put me through hell! *I'm like this now because of her!*

But did that give me the right to strip her of everything? And keep it?

I didn't just make her helpless. I made her powerless.

"Stop!" I whispered to myself, grabbing my head as if to shake out the two sides ripping me apart. "Stop it, stop, stop!"

"Emma, open the door!"

"I'm sorry," I cried. "I didn't mean to, I didn't mean to do it, I'm sorry!"

I didn't know if I meant it for Momma or Alexa.

I buried my face into my hands. The carpet seemed to burn under me. I could feel Momma's presence on the other side of my door. She could hear me, I knew. I prayed that she wouldn't try anything. I prayed that she'd go away. My heart was beating too fast, and if she came in, it'd implode.

"Emmy... honey, I'm sorry."

Why was she saying that? What was she apologizing for?

Stop it. Stop it, stop it, stop it.

"It's okay, baby girl. I'm here."

She understands after what I said to her?

She understood after I'd said to her.

Deep breath. Deep breath. It was okay.

Momma stayed on the other side of the door. Momma stayed no matter how many seconds passed, no matter how long the door stayed shut.

Eventually, I finally exhaled, shakily stood up, and opened my door. She stood still, gracing me with gentle, honey-like eyes, ready to comfort me on my command. I walked into her arms, and she embraced me wholeheartedly.

"I'm sorry," I whispered with a tear-soaked voice. "I'm—I'm scared. But everyone is—accepting her so easily because—she doesn't remember."

"Who is, honey?"

Heart still beating too fast for me, I couldn't keep another secret. "Mr. Dawson. He's treating her normally."

Momma smoothed my hair. "He's playing a part, my love. But even then, he probably has a bit of the same reasoning I do after hearing what she's been through."

You don't get it.

"How am I supposed—to not be scared? You can't just—erase trauma." I took another wobbly deep breath. At my words, Momma rested her hand on the back of my head. "A part of me will—will always be afraid of her. No matter who her target is."

"You're right." She sighed. "I'm sorry, I *never* expected you to get over your experiences like that. I was just... observing how deeply affected Alexa had been for her to wind up like how she is right now without the harm of her memories."

I nodded. It was the only thing I could do.

But did it secretly change my loved ones' perceptions of Alexa? And should it change mine? Were any of my feelings valid anymore after what *I'd* caused in the first place?

The question repeated itself ruthlessly in my head. Validity. I wanted some shape or form of validity for my fear.

But didn't Alexa have it worse than I did? And what had she done to me *recently*? She'd been nothing but kind.

I swallowed again in Momma's arms. I just wanted to know what was valid.

†

Alexa had set up a comfy spot at the front of my mind by the end of the week. At least it forced me to pick, evaluate, and secure a safe spot for the bracelet. The gazebo steps had just been redone in the park a couple of weeks ago, so it'd be a long while before someone would lift them. It would at least buy me enough time to find a more permanent place for—

"Emmy!" Breanne exclaimed next to me, softly smacking my

arm as she bounced on the pillows at the front of her bed. "Come on, you said you'd start paying attention!"

"I am!" I said, leaning against the wall her bed sat against. I gestured to her laptop sitting in her lap. "Your serum's only draining color from a person's face instead of their whole body."

"And?"

"It's not cooling their skin temperature."

She smiled at me. "Okay. Thanks."

I looked at Sarah and Opal, who sat at the foot of the bed. Sarah was typing furiously on her bedazzled phone, and Opal was leaning against the headboard with her legs stretched out.

"What do you think?" I asked.

Opal shrugged. "Sounds solid."

Sarah glanced up from her screen. "Yeah, your dead-person serum sounds cool."

"It's not—" Breanne sighed. "*Juliet* serum."

I laughed, hugging my knees closer to my chest. "I'm scared of you sometimes. I'm not letting you test this on anyone we know."

Seriously. The only reason this girl isn't in a position of power yet is because she *chooses* the humble academic life.

She pouted at me with doe-like eyes. "But Opal said—"

Sarah jumped up from the bed act, eyes stuck to her phone like a cat's stuck to a red dot. "Be right back, I need to call Adrien."

She scurried into Breanne's bathroom on the other side of the room and shut the door behind her.

Opal and I looked back at Breanne.

She closed her laptop, huffing. "I think Adrien's been going through something," she whispered. She picked at the fuzz on her bed's comforter. "Any time I call Sarah now, eight times out of ten, she tells me a couple of minutes into the conversation that she has to get back to him. And it's never happy like it was before."

"Oh." I stared after the bathroom door ahead of me. "Poor Sarah... You don't think they're fighting, do you?"

Breanne scrunched her soft features in doubt, shaking her head. "No. They're good. Always are."

Unfortunately, I knew a thing or two about guises and disguises. Enough to know that Sarah was going through even more than we'd thought during second semester, and she felt like she couldn't confide in her closest friends about it. If I was hiding a federal secret, what on Earth was that girl keeping from us?

My phone buzzed in my lap, pulling my attention down:

J: Pack left for a new hunt yesterday. Thought knowing would help you relax a little :)

E: You know way too much

J: Son of two Grand Hunters and a desperate dad

Jak got points for one thing: the update did help me relax. Only for a moment, though, because paranoia had checked back in to stay for a while and was daring me to believe that that new hunt was for me.

C H A P T E R

Twenty-Nine

A couple of days later, I heard Momma's phone ring from my room with a foreboding sense. Sitting in my hanging chair, I continued texting the girls and tried not to let the suddenly unnerving silence get under my skin. But as the seconds passed, for some reason, all I could think about was how much I wanted to enjoy the last month of summer—and how that probably wasn't going to happen.

"Emmy?" Momma soon called from the living room, in the same tone she'd use when I was a kid and had broken something but she didn't want to snap at me *just* yet.

I don't remember doing anything, I thought. The sooner I faced her, though, the better.

E: Pray for me, I think I'm in trouble

S: oh no

should we come over later then ?

O: Do whatever you have to to keep her happy
and don't die

E: It should be okay, I can probably talk her out
of whatever it is, gimme 5 minutes

B: Please do! I want to show you guys the updated serum!

Is that supposed to serve as motivation?

I walked out of my room, finding Momma sitting at the dining table. Her phone rested in her hand and faced the ceiling—so someone was on speaker.

This can't be good.

"Mr. Dawson," she mouthed, patting the surface of the table in front of the head seat.

This definitely can't be good.

I took my spot, and Momma set down her phone. "She's here," she said, crossing her arms and leaning forward.

"Emmalynn?" Mr. Dawson began.

Okay, now I was nauseous. "Yeah?"

"I pray to God you've thought of a place for that bracelet."

Momma and I locked eyes. No. We were out of time.

Mom shook away the assumptions, shifting in her seat. "Are you saying—?"

"I came back into the kitchen and she was gone."

My eyes shut the world away. With every muscle in my throat tense, I refused to let Momma see my eyes until I knew the tears were in the back of my head.

"Okay, hang on," she said, "why don't you just track her with a locator spell?"

"I don't have anything that belongs to her," he stated. Too firmly for the man who never freaked out about anything outside of his control, like he was overcompensating. "Everything's gone. Everything she ever owned while she was here, even her phone in my car."

Momma bit her lip, sliding her wedding ring up and down her finger. Deep breath after deep breath.

I wish we still had Steven's mental locator spell.

"Okay," Mom finally muttered. Dragon-like eyes moved up to me. "Go get it, now."

I stood from the table and darted back down the hall, into my bedroom. My shaking hands grabbed the velvet box off my nightstand and opened it. I tried to steady my booming heart at the sight of the cuff bracelet inside.

The doorbell rang.

"Emma?" Momma called—this time in a *much* firmer mom tone.

So much for talking her out of being mad at me.

I set the box back down onto my nightstand and ran down the hall.

"I know what you're gonna say," I began, holding my hands

up in defense.

I hoped that Mr. Dawson was off the phone as she stood at the dining table. "You invited the girls over *now* of all times?"

"How was I supposed to know this was gonna happen?" I said, walking to the front door as if that would prevent my friends from hearing us. "It's fine. I'm gonna go with them and hide it."

"Where?"

"Under one of the gazebo steps."

Her lips pursed in doubt. "If they ever try to repair—"

"They were just done a couple weeks ago. That's why I chose it."

"So you're gonna ruin a new job so they'll have to redo it and find the bracelet there?"

The doorbell rang again. I gently pressed myself against the door. "With magic," I mouthed. "Nobody will ever know."

Momma's nostrils flared as she exhaled, shaking her head and twisting her wedding ring. "This is a temporary spot. We need to find something more permanent."

I nodded and then turned around to open the door.

"*Hi!*" Sarah sang, smiling awkwardly as she waved. "Everything okay?"

"Yeah!" I told her. "Just let me use the bathroom first."

"Oh, me, too!" she said, stepping inside. "I forgot to go before I left."

"*Thank* you," Opal breathed, eagerly walking by her and basking in the living room. "It's so hot today."

"Hi, Mrs. Marie!" Breanne smiled sweetly as I shut the door behind her. "How are you?"

Momma breathily chuckled. "It's a headache day today. I love you all, but I need to lie down."

Wish I had that option.

Breanne hummed in sympathy, waving at her as we passed. "Feel better!"

"Thank you, honey," Momma said as I turned into the bathroom down the hallway. The girls continued on into my room.

For some reason, as I shut the bathroom door behind me, the shower tub straight ahead was calling to me. I wanted to take a bath with rose petals and lavender bath salts, soak for two hours, and forget the kind of school I went to and the kind of people I knew. But time was scarce enough as it was, and I'd only have the luxury of rest after hiding the bracelet.

I have to figure out how to excuse staying behind at the gazebo long enough to actually do that. And then I have to do it without getting caught.

I filed through every last excuse in my head to give my best friends this time. The lies were starting to taste acidic even in prep now. I hated being such a close friend to lying. I hated that the longer my hands stayed under the cold running water in the sink, the longer I stared at myself in the mirror, the more I couldn't recognize myself. The more I started wondering who I'd be if absolutely none of it was a lie, and if I'd ever get to explore that girl.

I walked into my room, my friends sitting (more like bouncing) on my bed. "Go ahead, Sarah," I told her.

"Thanks!" she said, a little too enthusiastically for a bathroom trip, leaping off the bed and darting past me.

I smirked at Breanne as I heard the bathroom door shut. "Is the sugar still wearing off from last night?"

Dad and Aunt Becca no longer living here had its pros and

cons. Con: I missed out on more outings (and chaos) with Sarah, Breanne, and Opal so that I could visit them instead.

"*Ugh.*" Breanne fell flat on her back on my bed. "It was *so* much fun, I really wish you'd come!"

"Yeah!" Opal beamed next to her, eyes wide. "Em, no, you don't understand, we almost got kicked out of the grocery store."

My head shot back in surprise as I sat myself in my hanging chair in the corner of the room. "*Breanne* almost got kicked out of somewhere?"

She sat straight up and pointed an accusing finger at Opal. "Because of them! So I made us go to Dom's Bakery instead—"

Opal cackled. "Em, Sarah had WAY too many desserts there."

"You guys, she *never* gets sugar highs," Breanne said, blue-hazel eyes wide, "but she was *gone* last night. And remember, Opal, then we had to stay outside for most of the night because she kept being too loud, and then she started a dance mob in front of the movie theater, and then—"

Opal and I burst out laughing, but I shouldn't have been surprised: Sarah Duncan is the only person I know who's capable of pulling off something like that using the loaned courage of a few pastries. Plus, well, she's flat out model material, so if I knew Sarah as well as I thought I did, Opal was about to say—

Her hand just as quickly flew to her mouth when the bathroom door opened down the hall. The three of us exchanged suppressed laughter and faced the doorway just as Sarah walked through.

"Okay, gang!" she chirped, oblivious. "Let's hit the road!"

In an atmosphere all too familiar to January's "bucket list" adventure to commemorate our last weekend with the Redway Boys, Breanne and I smiled at each other with the same message: *Strap in for the ride.*

†

Forty-eight hours passed with no sign of Alexa. Even though the bracelet was safely hidden, I was terrified every minute of the day, and that wasn't just because Sarah had made me, Breanne, and Opal do tightrope walking from ten feet high at an interactive science museum the day before.

My family and I quickly decided that we didn't want to let the bracelet survive *at all* as long as any Delphine was alive, at least if we could help it. On the slim chance that Dad and Aunt Becca could destroy an object harnessing powerful magic, Momma took it to their apartment to give it a try. And they were *actually* able to destroy it with an obliteration spell!

Now, whether Alexa's magic had been destroyed with it was an issue we were ready to temporarily set aside—only because we knew that we definitely couldn't find it now. If it had somehow transferred back to her by default, we'd find out pretty quickly, anyway.

I'd barely shaken off those thoughts the next morning when my phone rang on my nightstand. I reached over and took it.

Unknown number.

A familiar chill slithered down my spine. I couldn't help but think of all the other times an unknown number had been a lot more than a scam or wrong number.

I lay back down on my bed, took in a breath, and forced my

voice to sound steadier than I felt. "Hello?"

"You were right."

My heart slammed against my chest, my fingers almost dropping my phone.

Alexa's falsely sympathetic tone had returned full force. "Nolan's a cutie. Why didn't you go for it?"

I shot up, squeezing my phone. "Where are you?"

"I really thought your threat was empty," she told me curiously. "But *you* managed to pull something like that off? Huh. I'm starting to think I'm underestimating you—"

"Where are you?!"

"I'm enjoying a nice afternoon in the square. Nolan's having a good time with his friends right now. Did you know how popular he is? He looks like a nice boy. He looks like the kind of boy who'd give his girlfriend presents, like a bracelet. What do you think, darling?"

I swallowed hard, gaze digging into the uneven coating of paint on my bedroom wall next to me. My throat strained to keep my breaths quiet. I refused to let Alexa know how pitifully weak and afraid I was.

"Actually, come to think of it," she said, her voice maintaining that sweet lilt, "I think I've misplaced mine. I wonder if he knows where it is. I should go ask him—"

"Don't touch him!"

"But I need to find my bracelet," she said innocently. "Unless *you* know where it is. Do you?"

I bit the inside of my cheek until I tasted iron. I wondered how long I could hold off on the truth. I needed more time.

"Where is it, Emmalynn?"

I couldn't hold it off anymore.

With another swallow, my white flag went up. My eyes traced the foot of my bed in what little comfort I could squeeze out. "We don't have it."

A terrifying pause ensued on the other line, but I knew better than to speak.

"What?" Alexa stated.

"It's…"

Her whisper hardened to stone. "So help me, Emmalynn, unless you want me drawing a knife to your mother's throat tonight, you're gonna tell me where you put my—!"

"We destroyed it with a spell, it's gone!"

One. Two. Three. Four. The silence ticked by, screaming its presence in my head until the call went dead.

My phone stayed pressed against my ear, stare stuck on the end of my bed. Thoughts beat against my mind a hundred per second, uncontrollable, desperate. What-ifs and worst-cases and taunts and bad memories. And nothing to prove any of them wrong.

My arm dropped onto my bed. My phone's home screen stared back at me, asking me what to do next. But I didn't know. I had no idea what to do next, and if I'm being completely honest, I had no idea how much time left on this earth I really had after that call.

My phone dinged. This time, a name came with it.

B: Hi, hi! What're you up to~?

Breanne's chipper self couldn't have asked at a worse time.

E: Hanging in there is pretty accurate, what's
up

B: One, are you up to hanging out this weekend
since Sarah's going on vacation to Egypt next
week?

E: Of course, I'll meet you guys at Joe's

B: Cool, I'll let her know.

Two, I've been meaning to ask this for a few
days now, but where did you get that bracelet
sitting on your nightstand?

Wait. Wait—*what?*

This wasn't happening right after that conversation with Alexa. This wasn't happening.

Dial tone. Dial tone. Pick up, Breanne!

My fingers entangled themselves with the chain my locket hung from. Breanne finally answered, and I had to force steadiness into my voice again.

"Emmy?"

"You mean the silver cuff bracelet?" I asked, questioning if I'd actually read the words or if I'd just hallucinated. For the first time in my life, I *prayed* that I was starting to hallucinate.

"Yeah."

I quietly drew out my breath, the lie heavy on my tongue and threatening to snowball down the hill. "That was my mom's. She doesn't wear it anymore, so she gave it to me, I don't know where she got it from." I swallowed so hard that I could almost feel my larynx being shoved out of my throat. "Why?"

"I hope you don't mind, I tried it on for a sec while you were in the bathroom. It looked really nice, I want something like it for my birthday this year!"

No. She didn't. Alexa's magic—

"You tried it on?" I asked, fighting an uphill battle to stop my voice from trembling, to keep my breathing even.

"Just for a second," she said softly, innocently. Poor Breanne. She was feeling the guilt for unlocking the gates of the Underworld, but I was the one who'd given her the key. "I'm sorry if that was wrong."

It was so, so wrong.

I wiped a runaway tear from my cheek, breathing through my mouth to prevent my nose from exposing my tears. My entire life depended on this performance. "No, don't worry, you're fine—you should be able to find something like it at the jewelry store in the square."

"Oh, cool, thanks!"

Her cheery voice rang in one ear and out the other. I wanted her to know. I wanted to spill myself to her and every secret I'd kept from her since the beginning of our friendship. I wanted her to know that she was just like me now. But above all else, every fiber in my body hoped against hope that she wouldn't ask—

"Also, what color was the diamond?"

I mentally facepalmed, wondering if my fingernails had managed to scratch the silver of my locket at this point.

"Um—white or orange." Another swallow. I dried another

tear. "I could never really tell, to be honest, it depends on the lighting."

"Oh, yeah, same. Good to know, though."

That bracelet was the only thing able to fix this mess, and Dad and Aunt Becca had destroyed it the day before. That was why they'd been able *to* destroy it, because there hadn't been an ounce of magic in it, after all!

They didn't notice the white diamond? How could they've not noticed the white diamond?

"Okay, Mom's calling," Breanne said next. "I'll see you Friday!"

She said it so casually, like the conversation was totally normal. And as she hung up the call, I envied her more than I ever had in my life, because to her, it was.

For once, it was my turn to reach out to Momma. I threw open my bedroom door and ran into the living room.

THIRTY

Teenage girls generally feel like the world is caving in on them, but this week had *nothing* to do with hormones. My world really was falling apart. Alexa had gotten her memories back, Breanne had inherited Alexa's magic, and I was supposed to pretend that I was okay?

I wasn't okay!

I was fed up with keeping every secret to myself, falsely figuring that my control, as limited as it was, was better than everyone freaking out and thinking that I couldn't handle it. But maybe they were right. Maybe I couldn't.

I can't.

Momma's hand rubbed my back as we sat on the couch. I sobbed in her arms, begging her embrace to fix things like it always used to. She gently swayed us back and forth, my sniffs and gasps the only sounds traveling through the room.

"We'll figure it out, honey," Momma whispered. She kissed the side of my head. "It's okay, we'll figure it out."

My heart staggered. She didn't sound like she believed it.

"How did they not notice the diamond?" I managed between sobs.

Seconds of cruel silence passed. Momma paused.

"If I just remembered that, you know they probably forgot, too," she replied. "We were all too caught up, they were focused on destroying the bracelet. And white diamonds are so common on jewelry—we never thought to question it."

They're not supposed to make stupid mistakes like that.

Like how you left the bracelet unattended?

"Do we... tell everyone about Breanne?"

Momma swayed us even gentler. "They need to know. We have to do something ASAP."

I didn't want my family to know. I didn't want them to know that I'd been that stupid and careless after Mr. Dawson had specifically told me not to be. Maybe them knowing was my punishment.

"What're they gonna do?"

"Well—Steven can try to put the same enchantment on another bracelet. Then you just have to figure out how to give it to Breanne and make sure she doesn't take it off."

Except, problem number one: Breanne didn't wear jewelry, ever, unless it was for special occasions, so giving her something that she couldn't take off for a while would make her suspicious.

Problem number two: Breanne couldn't be the one to put it

on because she would constantly be taking it off and we'd never get Alexa's magic back. But if I put it on her, Breanne wouldn't be able to take it off, which would make her even *more* suspicious.

Problem number three: if the enchantment on the bracelet were anything easy, people would be stealing magic left and right. Steven could take days, if not a couple of weeks, to master the enchantment, like he had with his mental locator spell.

Problem number four: even if we *were* to execute the plan perfectly, if we didn't get to Breanne first once the bracelet was done with its job, we'd just be doing Alexa a favor.

I gripped Momma even tighter. How had it all come to this? How could I have cost us everything with my stupidity?

"Em?" she whispered into my ear. "Honey, what's wrong?"

"I hate this," I cried, breaths growing raspy but deep all over again. "I hate this, I hate it, I wanna go back!"

She tried smoothing my hair. "Go back to where—?"

"*Anywhere* but here! Home, not here, *home!*"

I wanted to go back to the days when mornings rose without a constant need for hope. I wanted to go back to a place where I was completely my own, I wasn't anyone's to hunt and pursue. My real home didn't have Hunters. My best friends were mortals in my home. Adara didn't exist in my home. I was anywhere but home, I couldn't have been further from it.

For the first time ever, Momma didn't know what to say.

I was anywhere but home.

As soon as I was ready a couple of hours later (or, at least, I *forced*

myself to be ready a couple of hours later), Momma took me to
Dad and Aunt Becca's apartment to explain things. Mr. Dawson
met us there. It was twice as hard as I'd thought it was going to be.
Just as I'd expected, Momma had to take over for me for most of
the story.

The absolute *last* thing I'd expected, though, was Mr. Dawson's suggestion to come clean to Breanne.

"Really, Thomas?" Momma crossed her arms and sat back in
her seat on the couch. "Tell me why Opal doesn't know that
Emma's a magician, and I'll tell you why Breanne can't know anything."

Mr. Dawson paused in the middle of the living area. "Funny
you bring that up. How about you remind me why Opal doesn't
know about Emma?" He counted each point on his fingers: "Both
magicians, both using Callistro as a cover, both in need of someone their age to confide in—"

"Thomas," Dad said tiredly, softly shaking his head between
me and Momma. "Emma's not just a magician, she's an Atera.
She's unofficially being hunted by the federal government. And
she has a sacred identity in the magic world. If Opal knew—"

Mr. Dawson's hands dropped to his sides. "She'd understand
all of that!"

"That's just the problem, you *know* that," Aunt Becca said
from her usual spot in the recliner, holding a hot mug of coffee
(even though it was ninety degrees outside). She brushed a piece
of her blond hair out of her eyes. "Her understanding will make
her as protective over Emma as any of us are. When people *really*
start to come for Emma, Opal's gonna be one of their top leads,
and she's gonna wanna do everything she can to protect her."

"We're not trying to gatekeep her," Momma said, her hands resting in her lap. "We're trying to protect her. She's already a target just by having magic—we're not putting another one on her back."

At the heavy sigh that escaped Mr. Dawson, I looked up at him. He'd buried his face in his hands. I'd never heard such a defeated sound from him before.

"None of you see the look on her face when we finish training," he finally said, resting his hands on his hips. "You have no idea what this is doing to her. She *needs* a magician that's not an adult to lean on." He gestured loosely to me. "Emma's had her whole life to adjust to that. Opal's had months. And now Breanne's... what? Never gonna find out? Rely on Opal? Rely on Emma?"

No. Telling either of them wasn't right. I needed to remind him of that.

"Alexa used you to get to me the morning she took me to the beach house," I said. "You were taken, too. But you were a trained agent. Opal's not. I wouldn't be able to live with myself if that happened to her because of *my* secret."

A long exhale withdrew from his lips. Everything we'd said so far was just speculation, but in our world, risk is to be respected as fact—especially when the outcome could make or break our lives.

"Then Breanne shouldn't know about either of them?" Mr. Dawson asked.

Momma shook her head. "Not about Emma. But she and Opal can know this: Alexa's a magician, Emma found out, and that's why she's still after her. So because of that, Alexa came after

Emma, you put a forgetting spell on her as defense, you enchanted a bracelet to take away her magic, and Breanne accidentally put it on before we could get it to the authorities."

"So Breanne will know about me," he said flatly, looking out the small window.

I locked my jaw as Momma let a beat of silence pass. "I think it's best," she said, nodding. Dad rubbed her arm as if in approval.

That meant that I had to tell Opal about first semester. But I still wasn't on board with that when, as far as I knew right now, she'd lied about being hunted for whatever reason she'd somehow conjured. I wasn't even sure if I wanted to mention that part right now, not until I knew the full story. Maybe Jak just hadn't known that Opal was a suspect. Or maybe she was lying. I had nothing except their contradicting testimonies, and that really wasn't enough to propose a potential "situation".

Mr. Dawson pressed his lips together. "Fine," he muttered.

With no other choice, I sank into Dad's embrace on the couch with our plan tucked into my mind. Facing a day where I was actually *set* to tell my friends the truth was terrifyingly brand new. I always knew that the truth would come out eventually, but to plan the day when I'd blatantly come forth with it...

A hard pit dropped into my stomach that not even magic could make disappear, and it stayed there for a couple of days. But whether I liked it or not, August was in full swing with an even brighter sun, more humid heat, and higher temperatures. Sarah left for vacation to Egypt, and after Breanne and I saw her and her family off at the airport and grabbed a pastry (or three, thanks to Breanne's anxious sweet tooth), I had seer lessons with Ingrid for the first time in a while. Today's lesson was more important now than ever: with everything going on, I needed to know if I could activate my seer abilities for myself without having to pay the price.

"No," Ingrid told me from her loveseat, her posture picture perfect as always and pencil skirt as smooth as a flatscreen TV. "Seers can't afford that luxury. You must be answering someone's question about the future."

I leaned back in the couch, the cushions pushing the air out of my lungs. "I can't answer my own question?"

"Afraid not." Ingrid's intensely dark-brown eyes, blind to the world, stayed just above my head. "The gifts you've been given aren't for you. They're for those around you."

"I know, but—I don't want to involuntarily rip what people depend on most away from them."

The words whipped me across the face the second they left my mouth. A subtle lump passed in Ingrid's throat. She bent her head down and pushed a dark curl behind her ear.

"No, I'm sorry, I didn't mean that," I said quickly, sitting back up.

"You did," she said gently, resting her umber hands on her skirt. "But you didn't mean their effect. For that, I forgive you."

I discreetly bit the inside of my lip, forgetting that she couldn't see it. Still, I refused to move.

"I'm sorry," I repeated.

Ingrid passed a soft smile and nodded in acknowledgement. "It's good that you know to respect the power you wield. There's no room to mistake it: magic is a double-edged sword. If not wielded responsibly and carefully, its owner will hurt themselves one way or another."

Considering how miserable I'd been after losing my magic, I wondered if I would believe her if I hadn't experienced those words firsthand so many times. Even that one time at the mall earlier this year, when my magic had practically attacked me while Jak and I were walking and shown me my druid vision out of the blue...

Wait a minute.

"Can I ask you something else before we start?"

"Of course."

I shifted my position on the sofa, gathering the story. "Earlier this year, when the hybrid part of me was 'waking up' and I was having druid visions—I got flashes of one of my visions while I was walking. But I was *awake.* They were really fast fragments, but it was obvious that... it was just about to happen. And then it did a couple of minutes later. But druids don't get visions while they're awake."

Ingrid pressed her full lips together, humming. "Seers need an enquirer to have any prophecy of the future. But I wonder if, as it continued to awaken in you the stronger you became, it needed an 'outlet' of sorts. And it combined with the druid part of you to lend you an answer of the future. The druid in you may be the only reason the seer part was able to find a means at all to manifest through."

I wasn't even sure if that was possible—but then again, *I* wasn't supposed to be possible.

"That's really interesting..." Ingrid mused, like her own words were simmering in her head. "Let's see if we can awaken the seer in you again. I want you to try executing everything I've already taught you. I'll ask you a temporary question again. Are you ready?"

For some reason, I couldn't help but stay still in her presence; moving felt like it would shatter any and everything in the room, and I seriously didn't want to break anything in this woman's house.

I let myself exhale. "Yep."

She gestured with a graceful hand to the grandfather clock in front of me, on the other side of the room. "No cheating. What will the clock read in sixty seconds?"

With a deep breath in, I closed my eyes and started homing my magic. Ingrid's instructions echoed with every second:

Your magic will grasp the sentence of the future. Let it grab the future's parts. Allow it to bestow them. Your magic is the teller; you are just the messenger.

One by one, all of our past lessons and lectures pieced themselves together like the perfect puzzle, guiding my magic through my veins.

The fog in my black vision began to fade. An arrowhead. No, a *metal arrowhead*—

I shot up in my seat as if someone had jolted me awake. "I saw something!"

Ingrid reached out a hand with caution as if she'd puncture a hole in the air. Her eyes flashed amber for a split second.

"I don't feel your prophesying state of magic," she said pensively. "You saw a fragment, but you're too focused on the results of your magic rather than maintaining the process of it. You're interrupting it and not letting it speak through you."

You are the messenger.

"I'll ask you again." She rested her hand back in her lap.

"What time will my clock read in sixty seconds?"

I closed my eyes again. This time, with my deep breath in, I realized that I was the one who had to surrender to the will of my magic—not vice versa.

The arrowhead faded into view again, shrouded in a white-and-black fog. It pointed to the top half of a letter: V.

Now... lines. Multiple vertical lines an equal, short distance from each other. Every fifth one longer than the rest. A skinnier arrowhead pointed at the second small line between... VI and VII.

As if magic itself controlled my body, my eyes pried themselves open. My voice spoke despite my mind not knowing the words first: "Your grandfather clock will read 5:37."

Then, as gently as it had come, my magic receded back into wherever it kept itself hidden in my blood.

I blinked a few times, shaking off whatever remained of the seer's trance. Had those words been *mine*?

I looked ahead at the mahogany clock sitting against the wall: 5:36.

Goosebumps spread up and down my arms. I'd done it!

When I turned to Ingrid, her full lips were spread into a grin. She reached out her hand again, this time to me, and I wholeheartedly took it. Her mouth opened to speak, even took a breath in, but no words followed.

Her shoulders relaxed in realization, and she squeezed my hand. —*You just prophesied, my dear.*—

My head jolted back. "You can't speak?"

No response. I waited for some kind of reaction, but moments passed before her head finally raised slightly. —*If you said something, I can't hear you unless it's through telepathy. What I rely on most is my hearing.—*

A much different chill snaked into my chest. How cruel.

—It's why I chose the question I did,— Ingrid said next, my hand still in hers. *—Losing my hearing for a minute in exchange for your growth as a seer is a decision that needs no thought. I'm tremendously proud of you.—*

Stunned that my magic was the cause of her losing her hearing—honestly disbelieving that my prophecy had done this—I couldn't help but need some kind of confirmation.

—I wanna hear you say it out loud.—

Another soft smile spread across her full face.

We waited out the rest of the minute until she released my hand. Beaming, she pushed another dark curl behind her ear. "You just prophesied, Emma."

CHAPTER

Thirty-One

Sure, the seer's price was too steep for any of us to pay, so it wasn't like I'd be prophesying anytime soon—but what mattered was that, if a time came when I had to be a seer, I could be a seer.

Except, I was still upset that I couldn't look into the future for myself. Maybe then I would've been able to stay calm the next day when Jak asked to meet up at the gazebo in Capperson Park—rather than internally panic out of fear that he had an Alexa update.

"Before you say anything," I began, approaching the gazebo steps, "does this have anything to do with the pack?"

In all of the dorkiness of his cocky grin, Jak stood on the top step in his black purple-rose hoodie, gazing down at me. He is the only person on the planet who can make me feel short at five-foot-four.

"Nope," he said.

So that's why he's smiling. We're safe for now.

I walked up the steps to him. "Does that mean they're finally packing up and moving somewhere else?"

He pressed his lips together, a warm breeze subtly ruffling the curled-upward tips of his brown hair. "I didn't say that. But you're just as okay, they're working on a different case. We should celebrate."

My movements instinctually slowed. Hang on. This was too... familiar. I'd been here before—that moment in the Hunter's Room, when Jak had told me that Alexa was still alive and the pack had gone off to look for Tristan's descendant somewhere else. I'd thought that I'd killed the old Alexa Delphine, I'd thought that I was finally off the pack's list of priorities, and I'd been dead wrong about both. With Alexa now out for revenge on us, there was no way I could believe Jak so easily this time.

"I don't think them working on a different case means I'm okay."

"Well, Alexa's been back for a few days and she's made no advancements toward you. They're not here for you, I promise."

"You can't *know* that, Jak..." I turned my head, gazing out at the vibrant field, at the people strolling through. I cursed how I still wanted to tell Jak everything. I wanted to spill everything I had in my head. I wanted him to be my safe space, because all I had on my own were fear and anxiety. And all they ever did was squeeze long, bony fingers around my mind, holding me captive and stopping me from thinking anything through.

"Em," Jak muttered softly, sticking his hands inside his hoodie pockets. I couldn't find an accusation in those round eyes as he asked, "Do you know something I don't?"

Just like that, my chest locked with the words, and I remembered every reason he didn't know anything about the situation: for the same reasons my friends didn't.

"You can't blame me for being scared." I leaned against one of the support beams, loosely crossing my arms against my chest and fiddling with my locket. "You're *sure* they're focused on something else right now?"

"I promise."

I wasn't sure how seriously I could take that, considering even Momma had broken one of those this year—but Jak had been worried about me when his parents had breached the final, and nothing had happened—not because of them, at least. If he wasn't worried now... I guess I was allowed to relax a little, just while I was with him.

"Okay," I said, nodding. "So you wanna celebrate. Dare I ask how?"

Thankfully, he smiled at me. "That depends. Will you go out with me?"

Whoa, whoa, whoa, *what?* Had he really just asked me that? Directly? *Before* we went on the date?

"*That's* why you wanted to meet up?" I asked with a laugh that he shared.

"I'm still getting the hang of getting the timing right," he teased. "You're supposed to ask *before* you go on the date."

"Interesting," I simpered, tightening my crossed arms and mulling the last two minutes over in my head. Honestly? I'd spent practically my entire summer scared and tackling Hunter business. I wanted to live in my fantasies, too, and I deserved a day off on my summer vacation.

"Okay," I said, standing from the support beam. "I'd love to go out with you."

Jak slapped on that million-dollar grin, dimples prominent as he took my hand. "Good. Because it's cooler underground."

I instinctively withdrew my hand, stumbling into the support beam behind me. "You're gonna kill me, I knew it—"

Jak threw his head back in sheer amusement, laughing. "No, no, I'm not! I just figured—honestly, the hideout seemed like a cool place, and it'd be nice to check it out without the pressure of... saving anyone."

I bit my lip. There? He wanted to go *there*?

I couldn't blame him for not knowing the full reason I'd been so furious about our final. I could, though, blame him for suggesting that place when he knew how angry it'd made *both* of us. He may be suave, handsome, loyal, and caring, but Jakson Bleu does not know how to read a room.

There was also the fact that the hideout had been properly prepared just for the final, and it was an official historical site, so if anything happened to it while Jak and I were down there...

"You're ready to go back?" I asked.

He lightly shrugged, taking my hand again. "Only if you are. I know what was real now. And this time, it'll be a lot more special than a stupid test."

I rolled my lips together in thought, his words repeating like a record in my head. *"I know what was real now."* He had a point there—Alexa and William had had nothing to do with what had happened in the mine. To my disappointment, that had *all* been Momma and Mr. Dawson, and every part of it had been planned. In actuality, *none* of it had been real...

Okay. Going under better circumstances, enjoying the hideout for the history of it and not because I'd literally been run into the ground? It at least *sounded* doable, which was a start.

"We can start with a peek," I finally said, squeezing Jak's hand. "Let's see how far we get."

With one of his confident smiles assuring me that everything really was right with the world, at least for now, he reached out his arm. I linked mine through it and followed his lead as we stepped down the gazebo and through the field.

The aroma of grass tickled my nose, the sun radiating its beams in a spotless sky. Jak rested his other hand in his hoodie. I couldn't believe that he was still wearing a *black* hoodie in summer, and yet, I was all the more tempted to stay close to him and hug his arm.

Passing every store and business on the sidewalk—even the mechanic shop I'd ducked into in June—fear burned in my chest for only a moment now. Now I knew what had been real, too: none of it. And as much as I hated to admit it, I was going to be dealing with things like this for the rest of high school, the rest of my life. If I didn't figure out how to jump the hurdle now and handle it next time, I'd just get stuck.

I think Jak felt the same way, because he kept the conversation pretty lighthearted the entire way—like he was making sure we wouldn't get stuck. I had to appreciate how he was able to read my mind so easily in those moments.

We got through the mine entrance a little too easily for two people who weren't supposed to be there—yet another perk of Hunter schools. Pebbles and specks of dust rained down as we slipped through the ajar door. Somehow, while we crept down the tunnel and toward the first staircase, the silence was even more intense than it had been during the final. Despite knowing that we were alone, we were still careful to keep quiet as we made our way down and toward the bottom floor.

Jak looked down the five tunnels that stretched out in front of us before glancing down the far-right one. "Which one did you take when you first got here?"

"That one," I said, pointing at the one next to me. "What about you?"

"Straight down." One corner of his mouth turned upward at me. It was nice to see his smile down here without the busted lip. "Show me your side."

I looked down the far-right tunnel, remembering the study area lying at the end. Considering that he wanted me to show him "my side", he hadn't seen it yet—but I knew he'd like it.

"Well, okay," I simpered, pulling him down the tunnel.

The walls made of old wood and dirt sandwiched us, dust disturbed with every step. Soon it gave way to stone, and Jak and I stumbled into the study-like space that led to the wooden bridge I'd jumped down to hide from my Hunter—or, I guess, Mr. Dawson.

I still can't believe that that had been him.

"Whoa." Jak exhaled in awe as he turned his head all around. "I can't believe I completely missed this."

Against the wall in front of us sat the desk, its books, papers, and writing tools just as dusty and untouched as last time. Jak walked around, absorbing every inch his eyes caught. He traced the walls with his hands, then the surface of the desk, and then the arms of the two chairs in the middle.

"We sure someone didn't used to live here?" he asked.

"Well, it was a magician hideout," I said. Curiosity pushed past my instincts and turned my gaze to the portrait hanging above the desk.

John Melicent-Marie Atera, 1787.

John's eyes pulled mine into them yet again: what a blue. But the paint's vibrancy stuck out most in his oak-brown hair.

My family history.

It didn't take long to hear Jak's footsteps approach from behind me. I spun around as if he were coming to turn me in then and there, but then I remembered that he was allowed to be curious, too.

"He looks like Tristan Atera."

I watched his brown eyes shift ever so slightly as they scanned the details of the portrait. Then, they fell to the bottom-right corner stating my ancestor's name.

"Oh," Jak said, blinking. "That's why."

"Crazy," I whispered, because at least I could express *some* of my true thoughts with him like I hadn't been able to do with my classmates. "They've been at it for that long."

Jak reached out a cautious hand toward the cracked canvas until rationality got the better of him, and he drew back. He put both hands into his pockets and took a step back. "Man, the lighting really sets up the atmosphere—"

I glanced back at him and noticed his still eyes. He wasn't staring at the portrait anymore; thought had finally gripped him, like the Hunter part of his brain was at work.

He turned around, eyeing the lantern hanging in the center of the area. "The lights are still on."

Wait a minute. The lights.

I glanced back down the tunnel, then at the lantern above Jak's head, then down the bridge. They were all lit. Why were they all still on? Hadn't the school turned them off after the exams?

"I guess the school forgot to shut them off," I said curiously.

"Oh, no, you don't know?" Jak's eyes fell back onto me. "The school doesn't control the electrical system down here."

I crossed my arms and smirked. "Then who does?"

"The fairies that keep this place running. Duh."

"Uh huh." I stayed put as he approached me, sliding his arms around my waist. "Those don't exist."

"There's probably an alternate universe where people think magic doesn't exist, either."

He ever so slightly started to lean in. Just as I was ready to close my eyes and wait for his soft lips to meet mine, his eyes darted back to the portrait behind me. Then, he pulled away.

"I just realized something," he murmured. "That's her *grandfather*."

"Yes..."

"Do you think she knows this place exists? She might want that painting. Or, you know, a safe place to hide from time to time."

Okay, about anyone else, I would've jumped right on board with this conversation—but secretly about me? I had every right to try and guide Jak's focus back onto, well, me.

I leaned back, arching a brow. "You're asking about another

girl on a date?"

His eyes fell back onto me, mouth stuck open. I could practically see the thoughts competing to be voiced. "No, Em, I didn't mean—I'm sorry, I just..."

"No, no," I told him gently, rubbing his arm, "it's okay. But you don't have to worry about her. She's fine. Like how you told me I'm safe."

He nodded. It kind of felt like he only believed me because he had to.

"No, you're right," he admitted. "I shouldn't've brought her up *now* of all times. But it's hard sometimes. I don't know everything about her, you do. I can't protect her directly. You can. My mom used her dying breaths to tell me to keep her safe, but you're the only one who can do that, y'know?"

"Me and my mom," I told him. "Trust me. We're able to keep a better eye out than you think."

He rolled his lips together again and then took in a breath to speak. But whatever he'd almost decided on saying, he kept it to himself.

"You doing okay so far?" he asked, nodding toward the bridge stretching out beside us.

"Yeah," I said, grateful that I meant it. "It's not bad. You?"

"Yeah." He conducted his signature arms-around-the-waist move, then reaching up and brushing a piece of my hair out of my face. "What do you know—a *lot* better than I imagined."

I grinned, prayed that he couldn't smell my breath as I did, and then let him meet our lips in a soft kiss. After a couple of seconds, he deepened it, the tips of his lips breaking away only briefly before taking my bottom lip into them. His arms tightened around my waist while my hands rose up to his neck, fingers tracing his jaw.

I could get used to dates.

I couldn't understand how it felt so natural with him.

With fluttering butterflies already swarming in my stomach, Jak's hands moved up and found my neck. His lips never left mine.

I could get really used to dates.

I threw my arms around his neck, heart only speeding up. His musky cologne inflamed my senses, our grips on each other tightening. I'd barely broken away to take his lips with mine when the ground beneath us trembled.

Jak and I stumbled into each other, his arms a firm frame for me to balance myself on. Had the earth really just...?

"No way," I whispered, carefully looking up at him.

"No, I don't think—" he began before another rumble rattled the mine.

"This place is supposed to be safe," I said, red flags flying in my chest. I glanced around until looking across the bridge, begging for nature to lend me an answer.

"If there's an earthquake happening right now, we need to get out of here," Jak urged, motioning for me to follow him as he turned around and darted back down the tunnel.

I took a step to follow after him before an unnatural force gripped me. My body froze, pinned to its spot on the stone floor.

Something deep and buried in my mind was telling me that I'd experienced this before. When and where, though, I couldn't remember.

My eyes darted all around the cave before landing on two

figures emerging on the other side of the bridge from behind a stone wall: Alexa and a slim man with a young face, forest-green eyes, and umber hair, who matched her in height.

They followed us here. How, why?

The young man's eyes flashed amber, setting me free and in sync with another earthquake that made me stumble forward.

He released another flash from those piercing eyes. Fire erupted on their side of the bridge.

He had turned on the lights! Alexa had known that Jak and I were coming here!

Footsteps echoed down the tunnel Jak had just run into. Alexa and the man ran and disappeared behind the wall on the other side of the bridge's width.

"Emma! What're you doing?" Jak shouted, grabbing my wrist. The growing orange glow of the fire grabbed his attention, consuming the bridge.

I looked down at his grip, almost pulling away. With another glance at the bridge and then at the portrait of John Atera, another quake rumbled. "Wait—" I began, but Jak was already pulling me into the tunnel.

The world was literally tumbling down around us as we pushed through the narrow hall of dirt and old wood. Splinters were the last thing on my mind as dust poured down by the bucket. I held up my arm to shield my eyes, heart pulsing with every new thought invading the excitement and even peace I'd felt minutes ago.

She's here, she's here, she's here.

Who was that man?

The portrait, the hideout, they're destroying everything!

"Are you okay?" Jak asked when we stumbled out onto the other side.

It was all I could do to nod, which let him drag me up the stairs.

The rest was a blur until I detected the familiar brightness of daylight and I had to shield my eyes against it. My chest finally expanded with a breath, a full breath. Fresh air filled my lungs as Jak pulled me into the Capperson Forest beside the mine entrance.

I stumbled into a nearby tree. Panting, Jak firmly took hold of my shoulders and held me against the trunk like he was trying to help stabilize me.

"That was—way—too close." Every word was a pant as he monitored the way we'd come like a hawk. Almost like he'd seen Alexa and that young man.

All that lay in front of us now were the pinecones, leaves, pebbles, and fallen branches of the forest floor. Only then did I realize that the ground was still shaking underneath me. My body was still trembling. I wondered if anybody in town had felt the earthquakes, if the crumbling of the hideout had been audible. I tried and tried to tune my ears to anything else but the whistling birds and creaking tree branches.

With my next breath, the shaking stopped.

The air was cleaner up here, but I struggled to inhale enough of it. I couldn't. I couldn't breathe. That woman had survived a house fire from a basement, and this was practically no different.

The house. The house—the fire had completely destroyed the house. The hideout *might* be able to support itself after the earthquake that man had inflicted on it, but he was also setting fire to every wooden board in it! They were *destroying* it!

Another part of my family. Destroyed.

"Hey." Jak finally looked at me as his panting started to slow. When I found his soft gaze, he was wiping a tear from my cheek.

When did I start crying?

"Are you okay?"

I turned my eyes back toward the mine like it would hide my tears, but every single one was flowing over without my control.

I don't... I don't understand what I'm feeling. Mostly because I could hardly feel *anything.*

My tears grew hotter, amplified by the stinging of my nose. I don't know how much time passed before an audible crash resounded from the mine entrance. A sword of realization plunged into me: the hideout was gone.

Sobs pierced my chest, stealing my breath. Jak caught me as I fell forward and onto my knees.

John Atera. That portrait. I *had* wanted that portrait. I'd wanted to take that portrait and keep it at home. I'd wanted that portrait, my family history. Everything was gone.

"Em?"

I'd lost the battle with my emotions long ago. I wondered just *how* long ago as my hands rose to my mouth and nose. Jak kept me in his arms as I crumpled against him, crying. Grieving.

Why had Alexa followed us to the hideout? Why was she wasting her time and energy on me and destroying the good things in my life instead of forming a plan? I'd told her that the bracelet was destroyed! Did that actually create grounds for punishing me like this?

I might as well have expressed all of that out loud through

incoherent sobs, because now Jak was holding me and swaying with me. "What's wrong?" he murmured.

I wished that even a single part of me *didn't* hurt. Even now, though, I had to come up with an excuse, because there was no way that he could know why that hideout had been so important to me.

"I can't—" I gasped between cries. "I c—can't—tell."

The other thing I love about Jak: he knows me. He can read me. He knew that calling me "Merlin" was reserved for moments the complete opposite of this, and he knew then that the comfort of his presence was the only relief my heart had access to. And he gave it wholeheartedly, hugging me tighter when I buried my face into his chest and cried.

An earthquake. Like what I—

Like what I'd done during the final. With my *warlock* side.

Warlocks are the only class of magic that can control nature. They're a rare, powerful class. And if that man was related to Alexa in any way—something that I had to assume because they looked too similar—in a way, the Delphines were dead equal with the Ateras. I'd never been dealing with someone whose strength I simply had to grow to match; I was dealing with someone who was my equal and would be until I somehow defeated her.

Alexa Delphine, you just made the biggest mistake of your life.

My sobs finally calmed, transfiguring into anger locked in every fiber of my being. I lightly shook in Jak's hold, but not for the same reasons anymore, not for the reasons he thought. That witch and that man had to still be alive. For the first time ever, that ignited a fire in my veins.

I'll turn myself in before I let you get away with that.

Thirty-Two

Confessing to my family that the Delphines were probably warlocks (much to their disappointment) wasn't as hard as telling them about the attack on the wielder hideout. Momma and Mr. Dawson had known that the hideout was founded by a John Atera—so hearing why Jak and I had wanted to explore it and what had resulted from it was a weight of guilt for them, too. The story even showed up on local news the next day, which felt like a rub in our faces.

It felt like I'd had no time to process even a few days later, when Sarah called from Egypt while Momma and I were blending coffee frappes. Evidently, despite her relationship with Adrien, this girl never takes a break from scouting out the "good ones" for her friends, not even while on vacation.

Emma!" she squealed, already speaking ninety miles a minute. "You never told us you knew such a cutie in Egypt!"

Thank goodness she wasn't there in person, because my blank stare would've given me away in a heartbeat. What was she talking about?

"I'm... sorry?" I said as Momma grabbed a giant glass from the cabinet and curiously glanced at me.

"You should be!" she exclaimed. "He could've flown out here and visited us all this time! Why'd you keep him a secret?"

Because he was a secret to me until now.

"Um... sorry."

I mentally facepalmed, and Momma's deadpan at me didn't help that embarrassment.

"Whatever." Sarah finally slowed down, pausing. "Are you okay? You don't sound like you're okay."

"Oh, yeah!" I replied, shaking myself out of the confusion and into my cover. "Sorry, I'm finally remembering. It's been a while, we weren't able to keep in touch."

If there was a boy in Egypt claiming to know me, he had probably used magic to find me. So if Sarah knew that I didn't know who he was, she'd definitely start asking the questions I wasn't allowed to answer.

"Oh! Great!" she chirped. "I got his number just in case! He said you lost touch after you both got busy with school but you came into mind recently."

I paused. Rationality was telling me that that wasn't code, yet the paranoid part of me had interpreted it as such. For the first time, though, my paranoia was actually giving me an *answer*:

"*In mind*". How could someone all the way in Egypt know

who I was when we'd never met before? Unless he had a way of finding me with his mind—or what his mind had shown him about me...

...with magic. He was *definitely* a wielder.

"Yeah, send it over." I motioned at Momma with my hand to follow me out of the kitchen. "Thanks!"

I spent the walk down the hallway in goodbyes with Sarah and then stared down at the international contact she'd sent: someone named "Kamose". Momma was a step behind me, placing a gentle hand on my shoulder. That was the first time in my life that I cursed her phone plan having free international calling.

"Who's that?" she asked as we entered my room.

"He says... he knows me."

Momma stayed silent. I dialed the number, put it on speaker, and then sat down on my bed.

It only took a few dial tones before a sonorous voice in a thick Egyptian accent came clearly on the other line. "Emmalynn?"

My blood stopped, the oxygen in my lungs freezing. Even Momma sat up straighter, stilling into a statue.

"Who's this?" I asked.

"Oh, right. I forgot, we are strangers. Sorry."

I glanced at Momma in utter bafflement, fiddling with my locket as he reserved a few seconds.

"Well, I'm Kamose, but I'll be known to the magic world as 'Ezranai'."

The magic world... He had a name that he was known by in the magic world just like Annisa and I did!

I looked at Momma, our minds already in sync. She'd tested my Hunter abilities during the final, but now she was testing my abilities as a magician to handle a conversation with someone like me as safely—and non-stupidly—as possible.

"If magic doesn't deceive me," Kamose said next, "you're Adara. The magic world's sorceress."

For the first time, someone had put it into words that I loved.

I fiddled with my locket. "Then what are you?"

"Their nore."

Sorceress, druid, nore.

I blinked as if this were the first time that I was hearing about a nore's existence. I wondered what was going through Momma's head as I tried plucking the most prominent questions from the marathon of them in my head.

"How do you know about me? How did you know Sarah was my friend?"

"That's a tricky one, commander." He chuckled, humming thoughtfully. "Would I get away with telling you that I can manipulate the present and its circumstances?"

Wait—what?

"What does that mean?" I asked.

"I figured not, but it was worth a shot. It means that when I gain access to the world's present circumstances, I can manipulate them with my magic. Change them in the blink of an eye to whatever I need them to be. And I don't need an enquirer to do so."

Oh, this guy was *dangerous.*

That was why he'd used Sarah: manipulating present circumstances so that I had his number would've been about as terrible of an introduction as Cara and Steven had given me.

"Do you have any limitations with that?" I asked, the question transparent in Momma's mind. Her eyes turned golden in the setting sunlight coming from my window, which brought little comfort as my stomach growled for the coffee frappes we'd left on the kitchen counter.

"Of course, just as you have limitations with your ability as a hybrid."

Never before had I felt so seen—but not in a good way. In a very naked way. I did not like feeling so naked.

"I also can't teleport myself or anyone else somewhere. I can't manipulate time, such as what hour or day it is. Whatever else might be there, only *time* itself will tell." He snickered. "See what I did there?"

My brain was running too far with my own questions to reply to that. "Did you manipulate Sarah's vacation? So she would meet you?"

"The only thing I manipulated was the airport they landed in. I wasn't willing to drive a few hours to make sure we met."

Almost every question I had—how he knew who I was, how he'd known that Sarah and I were best friends, how he'd known exactly how to time it all—was most likely going to meet the same answer: he just knew. Nores know. I shouldn't have been that surprised.

Wait. I was a hybrid, Annisa could time travel, and this boy could manipulate present circumstances at whim. We all had powers that went beyond magic's boundaries, all known to the magic world by a different name... What was going on?

I paused again. "Are you... the next one hundredth generation of your family?"

"And the Nasirs are proud of it," he said. I wanted to say that I heard a smile, and I couldn't blame him if so: the Nasirs were one of the first families of nores in existence. Known for their humanitarianism, they also have the privilege of owning their identities and titles as wielders. Egypt spent a couple of centuries in an on-and-off war of legalizing magic, and the Nasirs played a sizeable role in finalizing its legality there. Now their son would work alongside me in the construction of a new world.

"So," I began carefully, eyeing Momma's curious stare, "but what made you contact me now?"

"We're meant to be allies in saving our world, aren't we?"

Kamose said the words so casually, as if there were no weight to them. I wanted more than anything to believe that, that we were just kids meeting for the first time and playing pretend. But I'd grown out of those childhood fantasies way too soon, and it was too late to go back to them. He was serious, and I had to take him as such.

"That's the rumor." I begged Momma with my eyes to stay quiet and trust me before taking the reins for herself. "Have you met anyone else?"

"As a matter of fact, you are destined to tell me about the next one, commander."

"Nice try," I teased, leaning back and supporting myself with my arm. "You don't know future circumstances."

"I like to play games," he said. I wondered what his smile looked like, because it was definitely on his face then. "I'm good at winning them, too."

Because that's what you should tell someone you just met whom you also want to trust you.

"You're hesitant to trust me," he said after a second. Don't tell me he could read minds, too! "Good. That's how we survive."

Momma nodded her head to the side, her brows cocking in silent agreement.

"Wait," I said, "if you know all present circumstances, don't you know about anyone else like us?"

"If there are more," he replied, "magic keeps them a secret, us too. That's how so little people do know who we are, whereas we are anonymous to the world. The only reason I found out about you is because a druid friend of mine had a vision of you—visiting me right here in Aswan. He thought nothing of it at first, until he had it again. And then we conducted our own investigation, which isn't hard for someone who knows all present things."

Annisa had a nore friend tell her about me, and Kamose had a druid. At this point, I wouldn't have been surprised if they'd been each other's friends.

How are people having visions about me when they don't even know me? Visions usually only relayed events about ourselves and the people around us at the time of a predicted event. There had to be some kind of pattern going on here, because when and how would I find myself in *Egypt?*

"So," Kamose said, "does that mean that there *are* more like us?"

Annisa. I'd already exposed her to Moren; I needed to update her on this before I told Kamose about her.

"I'll get back to you on that," I told him with uncertainty. "But if you and I exist, I don't think we should rule the possibility out."

"True. It's a miracle I started keeping track of you around the time your friend was coming here. I had to take my chance. The opportunity was too... rare. When is the next time you will be on my side of the pond? Except for my friend's vision, of course."

That was a great question, and I was almost scared of the answer.

"Then we'll keep in touch," I said. Momma nodded in approval. "Something crazy is going on."

"Yes, but I think it's a good crazy," he said. "We may not know how much time we have before our alter egos surface, but we should spend the time until then for our benefit."

It took me a second to process that before my hand finally released my locket. I sat up straight, unable to think about anything else but Alexa. "Agreed."

"Enjoy the rest of your summer vacation, Miss Atera. And hello to you, too, Mrs. Atera. Take my word for it: your husband and his sister are safe at their apartment."

My jaw dropped as Momma gaped at the phone, conflict waging a war in her eyes. She started twisting the golden band around her left ring finger.

"Thank you," she said, and I followed suit, meaning it.

Kamose hung up.

Silence rested between me and Momma after that, either in gratitude or fear that if we said anything, it'd break that promise of safety over Dad's and Aunt Becca's lives. It was definitely a fragile promise.

But Momma's always been braver than me. She spoke first: "I'm proud of you for not being immediately trusting of a boy just because he's a magician, especially one who lives on the other side of the world and *manipulated* the circumstances around him for you two to meet. And I'm especially proud of you for including me in on this and not keeping it a secret like you did with Annisa."

Her hand rested on my back, soft eyes shimmering in the setting sun's rays. "I'm glad you've learned at least one thing after all this time."

"Um… thanks." I wondered if that was actually as much of a compliment as I wanted it to be.

Hang on. She was proud of *me* for finally learning something? For learning my lesson in being honest with her, in being transparent about what was happening in my life with magic affairs? She was proud of me for that when *she* knew something about my own identity that I didn't, and was keeping that locked up tighter than the Declaration of Independence.

"Mom?"

"Yes?"

I didn't know what to say. I didn't know how to communicate my brewing emotions.

When I didn't say anything, she leaned toward me, wrapped her arms around me, and squeezed me with the love I'd grown up with. Back when everything—and I mean everything—was normal. When I didn't have so much to hide from her, not even how scared I was and how badly I wanted her arms to work in fixing me.

They just didn't.

She can say all that and hug me while lying to me.

I swallowed. Mr. Dawson had made me drop the topic out of respect for my parents—but if anything, Kamose's call had given me the courage to finally confront her, because even he had been honest with me. My own mother hadn't been for my entire life.

"I heard you and Mr. Dawson talking. About my identity as a sorceress."

She broke away, her arms hanging loosely around me. There it was: that frozen moment of realization, the deer-caught-in-the-headlights eyes.

"I'm not talking about this with you right now, okay?"

At least she wasn't denying that she *was* keeping something from me, but I couldn't figure out which was worse: lying and saying that she wasn't, or being open and confident about how she was.

"This is about *me*, though," I said, already testing the waters as I scooted away from her. "This *is* me we're talking about, how are you gonna withhold my entire identity from me?"

"Emma," she said, "everything I do is *for* you. And this time, I have your father's agreement that this is something we will keep to ourselves until you are ready and it can *benefit* you. Right now, we only see it doing harm. You need to wait for this to develop. You don't cash out a savings bond a year after getting it."

If keeping it was for my own benefit, why did Mr. Dawson so heavily disagree with it? Just a difference of opinion or prediction of outcome?

"Don't question my decisions when they regard your safety and well-being," Mom said next, standing from my bed and walking to my door. She turned around to face me. "Please don't bring this up again. We'll tell you when we all agree that you're ready."

She walked out. The smallest voice in my head hoped that she'd serve up the frappes.

I bit my tongue and twirled my locket, left in the airy silence of my bedroom. To this day, patience isn't my strong suit.

THIRTY-THREE

Not only was my family kind enough to start a group chat the next day and remind me of Momma's birthday in a couple of weeks, but Annisa also started a group chat between us and Kamose. I had a lot more confidence in her trustworthiness detector than my own; if she trusted him, I could, too. Plus, it was always nice to know that my family was safe with a nore's knowledge.

Speaking of safe loved ones, I knew that Alexa hadn't done anything to Nolan when I never got a creepy sentiment from her implying that tragedy had befallen him or something. Still, when he texted me Sunday evening asking to meet behind Dom's Bakery, it still came as a surprise. After all, we hadn't seen each other all summer, not since his father had threatened us to stay away from each other.

Knowing the risks with Marcus, I went because I knew that Nolan wouldn't defy him after all this time if it weren't important. But the other part of me dreaded going, because what could've possibly prompted Nolan to text me out of the blue after two solid months, asking to meet up like normal?

Part of me wanted to live in ignorance of him for the rest of my life. By the time I finished my cronut and took the back door out, I already wanted to reverse the clock and stick to that desire—because for the first time ever, seeing Nolan with a blue beanie covering his shaggy, dark hair, in his T-shirt and flannel, created a storm of anxiety instead of butterflies.

I swallowed and forced every step forward toward the bench.

His head bounced up from his fiddling thumbs when he heard me approach. "You made it."

"You asked me to." I took a seat on the bench across from him. "I know it's a risk, I wouldn't let you waste it."

"Do you wanna tell me why it's a risk, then?" His pear-green eyes sharpened, the anger in them unsheathing like a sword. He rested his forearms on his knees and folded his pale hands to-gether. "Why am I banned from seeing you? What did you do to my dad, what's he so scared of?"

Nothing, not even a flower box, stood between us. There was no barrier between us. I hated being so open in front of him, es-pecially because tonight was the *one* cool night of the hottest month of the year and I was almost shivering.

It's none of your business, I wanted to tell him. But it was about a girl he cared about and his dad, so it kind of was.

"Hello?" he said, wearing an unfamiliarly firm tone.

The worst part? He had every right to be angry and skeptical.

"What did you do for my dad to go from wanting you over for dinner one night to thinking he's *saving my life* by keeping me away from you? You told me you're not a criminal, but it's all you, apparently! Who are you, Emmalynn, WHAT are you?"

"A sor—!" I began, gluing my mouth shut just in time. I tore my eyes away from his, eyeing the trees lined up along the edge of the area. The Callistro Forest lay just beyond them with Caralyn's own dark secrets. I'd never in my life been so close to admitting my identity to someone, not even in front of Sarah and Breanne. And I'd almost sacrificed everything for this one boy.

"A magician."

No. I hadn't just heard that. He hadn't—he wasn't talking to me anymore, he hadn't just said that to me.

I forced—really forced—myself to look at him in pure disgust, with betrayal. At least neither was fake. "What did you just say?"

This was dangerous: I couldn't read his eyes anymore. The mixture was too rich, too abundant in ingredients for me to pick them out. All he did was stare back and study me. My reaction.

I wasn't acting well enough.

He nodded to himself, sitting up a little straighter. "You're one of them."

One of them.

I wasn't going to let go of my cover that easily—especially not for someone who thought of my people as an easily disposable "them".

"Say that again, I dare you," I hissed, gripping the edge of the bench. "Look me in the eyes and accuse me of being—!"

"I don't care if you are!" he exclaimed, standing and pushing me back in surprise.

Wait. What?

"I don't care what you are or what you can do, I just wanted *you*, Emma!" His hands firmly gestured to me at the word. "All I wanted was a chance to be with you, to go on a date and show you I cared about you! I just wanted *you*!"

Why is...? Why was he saying everything in past tense?

He stepped away from the benches, throwing his hands up in defeat. "But fine, whatever, you didn't feel the same way. You never felt the same way, you just liked seeing me pine after you while you two-timed me for Jak or whatever—" He spun around on me, eyes narrowing. "Don't think I actually bought that whole 'cousin' story. You two make it more obvious than you think."

Every word. Every word twisted a sword in my gut, searing me with edges of fire.

I swallowed hard, angry at my eyes for exposing its tears. "Don't you dare," I whispered.

"What?"

"Don't you dare say I didn't feel the same way!" I cried, standing with him. "How dare you say I never felt the same way?"

"You didn't act like it! I didn't see you accepting any of my offers to take you out! You barely even let me kiss you!"

I hated that. I hated that I'd so easily given Jak *all* of those opportunities, which just invalidated my own justification saying I'd done the right thing because it wasn't safe to date someone who didn't know. But what had I done at the hideout almost two weeks ago?

And it had ended in fire. Literally.

"You seriously think I've been *two-timing* you with him?" I said instead, my last straw of truth. "I'm not his girlfriend, we were never together in the time I've known you!"

"So how many dates has he taken you on?"

Dominance, I did catch that in Nolan's eyes then. And I despised it, because he had dominated the entire conversation with that one question and he *knew* it.

His lips cracked with a smirk out of unsurprised victory. "Right. Good to know."

"Two. And we never even officially went out on the first—"

"You're REALLY missing the point here! It's not about how many dates we got to take you on, it's how you never put to rest the idea of us when I advanced!" He pointed an accusing finger at me the whole way through. "You had another guy in mind EVERY time I tried to kiss you or tell you I wanted to be with you. You strung me along and, God forbid I'm right when I say, you enjoyed it enough to let me keep going!"

"That's not true!" I exclaimed, but that familiar, acidic taste of a lie fell onto my tongue. I'd never put the idea to rest even though it was a dead end anyway, whether or not Jak was in the picture. I'd always had Jak in mind when I was with Nolan. I *had* strung him along, but...

"You really think I'm despicable enough to enjoy your suffering? You think I'm so horrible to the extent that you're able to accuse me of enjoying all of that?"

"What's your excuse, then?"

Forget it. He already knew.

"I could never be with *either* of you for the same reason. People like me are killed on the spot, and you think I would've been able to have a safe relationship with just anyone?"

"No, I get that, Emma, I really do. You're still not getting it: why did you never shut me up? Why didn't you ever give me a definite no?"

"Because I *did* feel the same way! I wanted to live outside of my bubble for once and enjoy what I wanted, I wanted to pretend I'm not what I am! You were how I forgot everything wrong with the world and could enjoy the last few good things in it!"

He pressed his lips together, as if he really wanted to believe me. Then he started shaking his head.

No. No, that was supposed to make him see.

"See, I'd believe that so easily," he murmured. "But there was always someone else who got what I didn't. I don't care if you were interested in someone else, I care that you led me on. For a *year!* And even then you're doing the exact same thing to him! Have you told him you can't do a relationship? Have you told him it's not gonna happen? I mean, geez, Emma, how many times have you kissed him if you've let him take you out twice?"

"I'm sorry!" I cried, furious at my tears for falling despite every last attempt to cage them. "It's not like I did any of it on purpose, I didn't—*try* to get every step of it wrong! I wanted to tell you, I just—never knew when—"

Nolan glanced up at the blue sky with a sarcastic grin, like it had all of his answers. And maybe it did that evening, because he came back to me with "Fine, I actually get that, too. I just hate that I had to get stuck in the crossfire. I wish I could redo the whole thing, I wish I'd been smart enough to know it wasn't gonna happen. I wouldn't've been as stupid. Honestly? Part of me wants to forget you completely—"

"Then just *forget me!*"

The air shifted, the words echoing harshly in my ears like a spell. Nolan stumbled back and blinked, his anger melting from his demeanor. The wind and heat seemed to settle for just that moment. I dared to study him. He shook his head, falling forward.

"Hey!" I said, holding him up by his shoulders. "Are you okay?"

He looked up at me with empty eyes—eyes that were empty of any memory of me.

"Um, yeah." He straightened, stumbling. "Thanks, I'm fine."

Don't... don't tell me I did what I think I just did.

"Okay," I said carefully, testing the waters. "That's good."

"Sorry, that was probably—really weird," he said, breathily chuckling. "I don't know what just happened, sorry, um—wait, are you okay?"

My eyes. My tears. He could still see those.

I shook my head, wiping my eyes dry. "Right, yeah, I just—I came out for some air. You caught me at a bad time. I'm good, though, seriously."

"Oh. I'm so sorry, I hope things get better."

I softly nodded, the ground stealing my gaze. "Thanks."

"I haven't seen you around here before. Are you new, by any chance?"

He was the same boy he'd been the night we met. Oh, how many nights had passed since then. And he had forgotten every single one that I was in.

I swallowed everything—the memories, the feelings, the tears—down into the pit of my stomach, and plastered on that lie of a smile. "No, I'm visiting on my way to Charlotte. I have to get back to the motel before my mom gets worried."

"Oh." Disappointment drooped his features. I almost wished that I still lived in that reality, one where he'd be disappointed if I had to leave. "Sure thing. Thanks again."

I waved, stepped by him, and walked through the back area and toward Main Street. Everything Nolan had said, almost every accusation was true. And the ones that were, were the ones I was angriest at him for. Why was I so mad about the things I *had* done? And why had it taken me so long to realize how stupid I'd been to not say no earlier? Were my fantasies that powerful? Were my desires that selfish? Did I have a right to any of them?

Even after that, though, I was relieved above all else that my identity was still safe from him. But I was never going to see him again—what would ever make him remember me?

Was I really that selfish?

I shook all of those thoughts away as I stepped onto the sidewalk, hugged myself, and fiddled with my locket. I felt dirty even touching that: it had been a gift from Jak. The other boy I hadn't laid down the hardcore truth to. Ha—I'd even been greedy enough to accept another date from him a couple of weeks ago.

Stupid. Stupid. Stupid.

I had to lay it down. It was only fair. With no possibility of a future with him, I had to put the present to rest. I spent the drive home with every single one of those thoughts, alone.

CHAPTER

Thirty-Four

"**I** get it," Dad said over the phone as I sat in Opal's driveway. "Parents aren't cool. You wanna get off the phone and hang out with your friends."

I laughed, my hand resting on my car door handle. "Shut up. I love you."

"Hey, but seriously, what should I get your mom for her birthday?"

I stopped. "You still haven't gotten her anything?"

"I'm sorry, ma'am, have you?" he simpered.

"I'm her daughter. I have until the day before and can get away with it. *You* should've been thinking about this since you came home last year."

He gave me a warm laugh. "You're right. I'm thinking about

a promise ring. She's always wanted one, but I never got around to it when we were dating. Then we got married and I figured the wedding bands did the trick—but she deserves what she's always wanted. So I wanna get her one with three pink sapphires: one to say I loved her in the past, one to say I love her today, and one to say I'll love her forever."

I all but melted right there in my seat. "That's *perfect.* Do it."

"Thanks, honey. Okay, I'll stop talking your ear off. Have fun with your friends, I love you."

Ha, yeah. "Fun". Not with the conversation I had planned for today.

I hung up, opened the door, and stepped out of the car. Then I realized that the car next to mine was Opal's mom's—not Breanne's.

Breanne's... late?

I mean, Momma's seen her fair share of weird things/things she was probably supposed to go the rest of her life without seeing, like the time she tailed a magician into a mall in Vermont and saw a man in an adult diaper bathing in the fountain. It turned out that the magician had somehow bribed the man into doing it so that she could escape the mall without Momma noticing. (Needless to say, it worked.) So Breanne Shaw, religiously punctual if not ten minutes early altogether, not being here when we were supposed to be at Opal's ten minutes ago? *This* was weird.

Opal greeted me at the front door and warned me that her mom's friend, who didn't feel the same way Leah did about wielders, was visiting in the living room. We sped through quick introductions before Opal guided me upstairs.

"What's up?" she asked, walking me into her purple bedroom

and shutting the door. "You sounded a bit serious in your text. You okay?"

My nerves immediately came out to play. This conversation had to happen, and I'd put it off for too long. The situation with Alexa's magic was bigger than myself, and it was only fair to include Opal in it. Plus, I actually had my family's permission to be honest for once. That spoke volumes. After all, maybe Opal *hadn't* lied about being a suspect for Dad's descendant. Maybe Jak had just never known that she'd been on the list. That was plausible, right?

"No," I told her. "I'm actually not."

That truth alone felt like someone had taken a weighted blanket off my chest.

The purple faux-fur rug was so soft under my feet that I could barely feel it as I walked to her bed in the middle of the wall. "Look, there's... there's so much I need to tell you guys. Do you know where Breanne is?"

Opal's curiosity melded into worry. Waves folded in on themselves in my stomach.

"I haven't heard from her yet," she said.

What could be holding her up?

Whatever. I had the courage now, and I had to act on it. Opal and I could tell her together whenever she did show up.

"What did you need to talk about?" Opal asked.

I glanced at the TV mounted on the wall across from her bed like it would magically turn on and give me cue cards. "Okay. I'm... I'm more knowledgeable about the Hunter-magic war than I've let on. I witnessed it firsthand at the beginning of the school year last year."

"What're you talking about?" she asked slowly, brows scrunching together.

"Remember that conversation we had on the Main Staircase on the first day of school?" I said. Wow. I was speaking to an entirely different girl now. "I was uncomfortable talking about Tristan Atera's possible descendant—because..."

I could practically hear her thoughts, the worst of them, at least: the ones accusing me of being who I really was. But I had my family's permission this time. I was okay.

"I'd just found out that day that I was being hunted by a Grand Hunter pack that thought I was his descendant. Like you."

Opal's eyes doubled in size, her jaw falling agape, but I couldn't let her say a word until I told the full story.

"You already know what they did to their suspects, I won't go over that. But that's not all of it." I swallowed hard, fiddling furiously with my fingers—my locket wasn't an option right now. "Alexa Delphine, the leader of the pack, has been secretly hunting me ever since they moved on."

"Alexa—?" Opal stammered, her voice succumbing to a quiver. "Alexa Delphine was...? But that's—why?"

"Because toward the end of the hunt, I found out her secret. And it's a spark for a global schism, so I *need* you to keep it safe."

She nodded. "I promise."

"The Delphines are warlocks. They always have been, and hunting's just been their cover. Alexa's doing everything she can to make sure I don't tell anyone."

To my fear, Opal didn't move. I couldn't even tell if she was breathing. The truth had rendered her speechless, and her reaction had proven just how fatal it would be if those words ever escaped into the world.

"But—but you just told me!" she cried, fear now marking its place on her face. "What is she gonna do?"

If my family said it was best, it's okay. It's okay.

"That's just it." I plopped down onto her bed's purple comforter. Lighter than air. "Mr. Dawson found out about her, so he got an enchanted bracelet that drains a person's magic when they have it on. The next person who puts it on gets that magic."

"Wait," she said, even paler than usual. "Wait—was she that woman I saw at his house?"

"That was why she was staying with him. She came after me at the beginning of summer, but Mr. Dawson caught her and wiped her memory with a forgetting spell. That's how he got the bracelet on her, she was still amnesiac when he took it back. And then he gave it to me."

"Then, where's...?"

A lump formed in my throat. I viciously fought back the tears, the fear, even my words. "Breanne put it on when you guys came over a couple weeks ago. She has Alexa's magic."

I didn't get to see Opal's reaction because her bedroom door flew open.

The smartest girl I knew, the smartest girl the Callistro Academy has probably ever had, stood in the doorway.

"*What?*" she hissed, her voice nothing but a whisper. Her blue-hazel eyes were on fire.

Opal ran to the door to shut it as I forced myself off the bed, heart stuck in my throat. "Bre," I repeated, my voice trapped in panic, "wait, let me—"

"*That's* why you're still so afraid of Alexa and William?" she said. Opal took a spot behind her, against the door. "*That's* how Alexa lost her memory? That's why the bracelet's diamond turned white when I put it on? Because *I got Alexa's magic?*"

She'd overheard it all.

"Please," I cried as I took another step toward her, but she stepped back in defense, "I came here to tell you—"

"No, don't you DARE try that!" she snapped, keeping her arm up between us. "You lied! You've *been* lying to my face, you've been lying to both of us the whole year, forget this summer!"

"I'm sorry!" Tears were officially out of my control. "You have to understand why I kept it hidden for so long—"

"That's just it, I can't!" She gestured to a timid Opal standing behind her. "You trusted her with the truth but not your two best friends of almost a decade! A *decade*, Emmalynn!"

Silenced by that name of formality that she and Sarah had shunned when we'd become friends, I shut down. I tried in vain to swallow my tears, but that just made a hiccup form in my throat. When Breanne said my name that day, it had been a weapon. It had never sounded so destructive.

Opal firmly stepped up beside Breanne. "Okay, don't blame Emma for this!"

Breanne turned to face her, looking up slightly at her like she'd betrayed her.

"She asked me where you were and I told her I didn't hear from you yet." Opal came to stand between us, our mediator. "She probably figured we'd tell you together once you got here."

I took a deep breath despite the breathy cries interrupting my words. "I knew I had to tell you when—when you told me you put the bracelet on. I talked it over—with my mom and Mr. Dawson.

They told me—to tell you guys."

"You think I don't feel hurt that my own uncle kept something like this from me?" Opal said to Breanne. "Of course I am. But just like he has his secrets he needs to keep,"—she met my eyes, as if warning me of what she was about to do—"I have my own, too. I'm a magician. A druid."

My and Breanne's mouths hung agape. Opal had just disclosed her most fatal secret—Mr. *Dawson's* most fatal secret—seemingly without a second thought.

"I didn't know until a few months ago. I didn't even know my mom wasn't actually my mom until then. My real parents came up to me and told me the truth, and my dad wanted my uncle to be part of my life since he and my mom weren't able to. They were nearly found out. Dawson being my uncle was just... pure coincidence."

"The headmaster has magic," Breanne whispered, blindly staring at somewhere behind me. "Dawson's... Dawson's a *magician?*"

"That's why I have purple eyes. My mom told me to tell everyone I wear contacts so nobody would get suspicious. Only some druids are born with purple eyes. It was a dead giveaway."

Breanne's eyes shifted between the two of us. She didn't even know that she was staring at two wielders right now, but it definitely looked like it. Because betrayal still lingered in her gaze every time she looked back at me.

"I can't." She exhaled, turning away. Burying her face into her hands, she started pacing. I'd never seen her look so small. "I can't, this is too much."

"Bre," I said, my tears finally slowing down, "I *am* sorry for keeping the Alexa story a secret for so long. It was almost as overwhelming for me as it is for you. But I love you guys, you're my entire world. I *never* wanted to lie to you. And I only found out about Opal a few months ago.

"I kept some things from you, but I know you see why. You know the consequences of *anyone* finding out about this, don't you? How would the Delphines react if they found out you guys know their biggest secret, too?"

She whirled on me. "So why are you telling us just now?"

"Because of Alexa's magic," I answered, finally sounding brave. "She..."

I paused, realizing that Breanne had come in before I could tell the complete story. I looked at Opal as though to see if she was still there. Even though she had no idea what I was about to say, her gentle gaze seemed to tell me to continue.

I looked back at Breanne. "Alexa has her memories back. She knows that the bracelet had her magic, but—Mr. Dawson destroyed it."

"*What?*" they exclaimed in unison.

"What would you have done?" I held out my arms, daring them to challenge what my family and I had done. "Do you really wanna live in a world where *that* woman has magic?"

"I don't—I don't get it," Breanne said. "Obviously becoming a Hunter is her family legacy, but why kill her own people?"

"Why did she become a Hunter?" Opal asked beside me, holding herself.

"It's... That's not my story to tell," I said, remembering that cruel night on Mr. Dawson's couch. "But a magician wronged her, and she dedicated her life to hunting them."

"But *she's* one of them." Breanne's inquisitive stare was intent on the purple rug under our feet. Her mental encyclopedia was already flipping through its pages. "It was one magician. It doesn't make sense."

I knew the other reason—how the Delphines were also following in Henry Callistro's footsteps—but enough of the truth had been spilled today, and I had to close the conversation before any more of it could escape.

"Hang on," Opal said. "Does Alexa know that her magic wasn't in the bracelet when it was destroyed?"

I took a deep breath in, because that was the part I was scared of the most. I didn't have an answer for that.

"Emma?" Breanne asked, like I hadn't heard Opal. Fear shook my best friend's every word. "Am I next on Alexa's list?"

"She doesn't know *you* have her magic. As long as she doesn't, you're fine."

"No, that's just it, I *can't* have magic." She stepped back and furiously picked at the hair on her arms. "It feels—I don't feel— right! Especially with *hers*! I don't... No offense, Opal, but I can't do this, I don't wanna do this."

Seconds of numbing silence passed, seconds I braced myself to hear the absolute worst come out of Breanne's mouth.

"This isn't me," she finally whispered. Those doe-like eyes returned for a hard comeback. "I don't want to be this."

"I'm sorry." That was the only thing I felt safe to say as I sat back down on Opal's bed. "I really am. I wanted to tell you, but I had a Grand Hunter at my throat."

"I know..." Breanne sighed. "I get that, but—"

"But, Emma—" She shook her head at me, Opal seeming to

tighten her grip on herself. "I know why you had to do it, I just—I just don't get *how* you managed to do it. So easily."

"You think it was easy for me?"

The words didn't need any thought to escape. I think Breanne sensed that, how strong they were in me, because she swallowed without arguing.

I walked up to her and took her small hands, looking her dead in the eyes. "Lying to you about the biggest weight I've ever had for months on end was one of the hardest things I've ever had to do. I knew I was violating our friendship every single time, and that *killed* me. It was a coat I wanted to rip off the second I put it on—"

My throat caught on the words that were now ringing in my ears with a memory. Their familiarity was bittersweet, and they had rolled so easily off my tongue: that was what Mr. Dawson had said to me about his role in the spring final.

I get it now.

"I'm sorry." Another tear streamed down my cheek without my control. "I'm so sorry."

Seeing the truth—raw, painful truth—in my eyes seemed to be all that Breanne needed to nod and then wrap her arms around me.

Her sweet perfume wafted into my nose with every inhale. I squeezed her tighter every time another cry threatened to bubble up. I'd known for months now that lying to my best friends was becoming a game I'd eventually lose. For whatever reason, though, I was glad about that. I'd given up my victory wholeheartedly in that moment to hold my best friend.

Eventually, she pulled away. "Em,"—she chuckled breathily,

her finger wiping a tear from my cheek—"Sarah told you to get waterproof mascara."

I turned away to laugh, catching Opal still standing behind her. What I wasn't expecting to see were *her* glistening red eyes.

I furrowed my brows in concern. "Are you—?"

She shook her head with a smile. "I'm fine, I'm just—I'm happy. I have *two* friends now that I don't have to hide anything from." She strode to her bedside table and grabbed a tissue from the silver tissue box. "Here, Em."

I graciously took it and wiped under my eyes, thankful that I didn't actually have to care about running mascara in front of these two.

I turned to Breanne, wiping my cheeks. "Why were you late?"

"My brother called from his trip in Belgium. We ended up talking for a while. He's... going through some things right now."

I guess the summer's been difficult for all of us.

"I'm sorry," Opal and I said.

She shrugged, pushing a piece of her straight hair behind her ear. With her deep breath, it sounded like she was releasing every last bit of tension. "I'm sorry I snapped, Em."

"You had every right to."

"Is that all? I mean... is that everything?"

Why? Why did you have to say that?

I looked at Opal, now sitting on her bed crisscross-applesauce. I knew that eventually, the full truth would have to come out. And after today, my heart was too fragile in recovery to give another lie.

I looked back at Breanne, wet tissue in hand. "No. There's one more thing you guys should know, but I can't tell you yet.

Please believe me when I tell you that it's really delicate and I have to tell you at the right time. I promise I will, as soon as I'm allowed to."

Her brows furrowed in what I hope was curiosity. "When will the right time be?"

"I don't know." I swallowed the rest of my confession. "But I know it won't be never."

Breanne's eyes stayed locked with mine, reading the truth for themselves. Then, she finally nodded. "Okay."

"So, what do we do about Alexa's magic?" Opal asked. "Once we somehow... get it out of Breanne, where are we gonna put it where the Delphines can't get it?"

I turned to Breanne, who was back to staring down the rug and picking at the hairs on her arms. "Bre?"

She was too deep in thought to be disturbed. A few moments passed before she took a deep breath in. Fresh eyes landed on me again. "Do you trust me?"

"Of course I do."

"Enough to feel safe around me even if—I have magic?"

My jaw dropped, and I'm pretty sure I saw Opal's in my peripheral follow. She cautiously stood from her bed as I asked, "You wanna keep Alexa's magic?"

"I—I don't know. It might be... safer with me. For now. And I guess I could—see how the other side lives." The words were frail, like she wasn't ready to say them. I don't think she was. "This could've... happened for a reason. Maybe we're, you know—not as different as we think."

"That..." Opal said, tears in her voice. "That means a lot to me. That means *everything* to me."

I suppressed my own tears, because it meant everything to me, too. They meant that my best friend was willing to understand my people, she was finally about to get a grasp of how we lived day by day. It was the answer to my lifelong prayers, yet all I could do was rub her arm with reassurance.

"Of course I trust you."

I could see just how shaken she really was with the tight smile that braced her lips. And that stung because I couldn't do anything about it except hope that she'd be okay.

"I'm guessing," she began timidly, "we're not telling Sarah about any of this."

Just like that, my optimism dropped. "You know we can't."

"Yeah," she whispered. "I just wish I could. We've never lied to each other. I know I have to, and I will, but she's—"

In that moment, I understood exactly why teachers demand that phones be silent during class; they don't want the atmosphere wrecked by someone calling in the middle of an important topic or sermon. That was crystal clear when Breanne's phone rang in her back pocket and it was Sarah calling.

We all love the girl, but her timing has always needed work.

"Hello?" Breanne answered shyly. Note to self: teach her how to better hide her newfound identity.

"Hey!" Sarah chirped on speaker, pausing just as quickly. "Are you okay?"

"Oh, yeah!" Breanne said in a manner that I had to assume resembled my own when Sarah had called me about Kamose. "You caught me off guard, I'm with Emma and Opal."

"Oh, perfect!" Sarah said. "I wanted to tell you guys about the trip so far! Bre, you'll NEVER believe what building I just walked into!"

Don't get me wrong, I wanted to hear about Sarah's vacation. Updates, updates, updates: I wanted them all until I realized that I was due to provide my own soon. It was a terrifying thought, to say the least—to think about the look that would appear on Breanne's and Opal's faces when the day that I knew was coming actually came. When Alexa would find out that Breanne was the one with her magic, when Breanne would become next on her list.

I didn't know if I was more relieved or scared when my phone chimed next.

K: Lend me your thoughts, ladies: we travel
one hundred years into the future and find out
how our paths ultimately cross and we come
to save the world!

A: my ability only extends to the past, sir.

K: How unfortunate. Even magic doesn't want
us to have a head start, it seems.

At least they're still having fun.
I silenced my phone. Breanne, Opal, and I glanced at each other with every bit of news Sarah shared. Every time, I stared into purple and blue-hazel eyes that shared so many unspoken thoughts and emotions I desperately wanted to excavate. With the pieces of the truth unfolding, how much longer did I have?

CHAPTER
THIRTY-FIVE

 white flash burst through my vision. Jak and I stood in the middle of my living room, his back to me.

"Why didn't you tell me?" he snapped, whirling on me. "How did you go months—?"

Flash. His hands were gripping my shoulders.

"If you don't do something, she's gonna die!"

"I—"

Another flash. This time, I sat in an unfamiliar concrete room, cuffed to a chair. William Bleu stood in front of me with an all-too triumphant smirk.

"We finally found her," he said. "She's in—"

Flash.

Breanne and I bolted through the hall of an unknown building, passing signs and boxes with foreign writing on them. My best friend and I didn't stop for anything as we entered an abandoned warehouse and met Alexa—holding a gun to Opal's head.

Flash.

With Opal still in her grip, Alexa had the weapon turned to us. "Take one more step and I'll shoot!"

Everything burst into white. A gunshot boomed from an unknown direction. I hadn't sounded the shot, yet I was the one dropping a gun.

My eyes were open but I wasn't seeing. Muffled screams, muffled cries, and my heartbeat sounded off like an alarm in my head. Someone dragged me down the warehouse.

Flash.

My eyes could barely process the man pulling me.

I should be dead, I thought. *I should... We were almost—*

With another flash, I sat in the back of a van with people I still couldn't see yet knew were my allies. People I loved more than anything in the world.

"Emma?" one of them breathed with a terrified quiver.

"They're..." I whispered, so quietly that even I barely heard it. "They're dead."

The world flashed to black. I shot up in bed.

That word boomeranged around my head, scraping my mind as it flew in every direction. Dead. *Dead.*

Who? I thought desperately, my body soaked in a cold sweat and heart ramming against my chest. *Who's dead, who's "they"? Who's dead?!*

I couldn't feel, I couldn't breathe right. Almost too late, I realized that I was hyperventilating.

I closed my eyes and waited until my breath slowed enough for me to focus on my surroundings. The silhouettes and shadows of my bedroom finally faded into view. I was safe in my home with Momma just across the hall. I could lie back down on my side and take a deep breath in. Then out.

At this point, I missed the days before I knew that I was part druid and seer, because repeating to myself that that nightmare had just been a dream felt like I was lying to myself. There was always a possibility of it being a glance into the definite future, and that was enough to keep me awake.

Just for comfort, just because it had almost always worked before, I took my phone off my nightstand to distract myself. Surprisingly, Breanne's text was first to catch my attention, having come in just barely after midnight.

The girl is *always* asleep by 10. This couldn't be good.

B: I'm stressed I'm so stressed I just made my
cup of water tip over on my nightstand WITH
MY MIND

Opal showed me the telekinesis spell

I feel so weird like this shouldn't be possible it
shouldn't be working but it is

I'm sorry I'm going to bed now I promise I'm
just really freaking out

Aunt Becca's recent text in the group chat sat underneath that conversation:

AB: Ok hear me out, I just woke up from a dream about Amy becoming vegan and long story short, what if we all pitch in and get her a juicer for her birthday?

A reminder of Breanne having Alexa's magic and how I still didn't have a birthday present for my mother and it was in a few days: literally the two worst distractions my phone could've given me. For some reason, I wasn't in the mood for cat videos, either. My mind had put me between a rock and a hard place: I couldn't move on from either situation, let alone put them to rest for now, without knowing what I was going to do about at least one of them first.

Druids see the possible future while seers see the definite; it sounds paradoxical, but it's true, and there is a difference. But if I was a hybrid, who was to say that my seer abilities couldn't activate on their own, even overlap with my druid magic, like it had earlier this year at the mall?

Half of me didn't even want to consider that possibility. That meant that any one of my flashing nightmares had a chance of coming true.

†

I'd invited all three girls to a sleepover Wednesday night, but then Sarah's parents' movie production in New York encountered an unexpected setback that Sarah wanted to tag along for, and Breanne had to go to her cousin's birthday sleepover two towns over. Opal, however, was more than happy to come.

I just wished that I would've known she was going to turn it around on me and make it about boys. Which I wouldn't have minded—I just obviously couldn't tell her that I had to reject the cutest boy to walk our halls because I was a wielder.

"You told me that's his favorite color!" she exclaimed from the middle of my bed. "And it TOTALLY complements your hair."

Standing in front of my closet door, I threw my sheer purple blouse at her. "It makes me look like an old lady. I *know* I have something better." I turned back to my closet to try and find something to wear tomorrow for when we drove to Greenville. They'd just opened a location of Opal's favorite crepe place of all time, which she only ever got to visit when she saw her grandparents in South Carolina, and she was adamant on going with me. She had insisted that I invite Jak, and I was still trying to persuade her otherwise.

Momma loves crepes, too. I should get her one tomorrow—

I gasped, spinning back to Opal. "My mom's birthday is on Friday! I haven't even *thought* about what to get her!"

Her eyes widened, but her laugh burst out only a second later. "You're just now remembering, are you kidding?"

I shushed her, walking to the foot of my bed. "What am I supposed to get her?"

"Just ask my uncle," she said simply. "He knows her like you do, doesn't he?"

Valid point. But I was pretty sure that after ratting him out

to Momma last year about secretly helping me find the underground passageways, he was going to enjoy doing the same to me
about forgetting her present.

"Will you come with me tomorrow to get her something in
Greenville?" I asked, leaning against the bed railing. "I'll be quick,
I promise, especially if you help me."

"Shut up, of course I'll come," she chimed, right in sync with
my phone lighting up beside her.

I graciously thanked her before grabbing it. A new message
notification from an unknown—

An unknown number...

Goosebumps scattered across my arms. I'd been down this
road too many times this year, even once this summer. There was
no way I was letting myself believe that the cycle would break any
time soon.

I quietly exhaled, cursing the fact of the situation: *I have to
answer it now if it is worst case.*

#: So you gave my most valuable possession
to your friend. Not wise. Now you both get to
meet me in the Callistro Forest, the spot where
this all started, and make a deal with me.

You have thirty minutes. You can have Thomas
back once I see you. If not, he's going away for
a long time.

I'm done with this.

Alexa knew. And she had Mr. Dawson.

"Emma?"

I stopped myself from looking up in time—I couldn't let Opal in. I couldn't let either her *or* Breanne in for this exact reason. This was what we'd wanted to avoid, and it was the one thing we'd slammed straight into.

—*Mr. Dawson?*—

No answer.

—*Thomas, I NEED you to say something! Please!*—

Nothing.

I swallowed hard, Opal eyeing me with intense caution in my peripheral. We should've known that Alexa was better. And I would turn myself in to Caldwell before I let her bring any of my friends—let alone Mr. Dawson—into our fight.

"I'm so sorry," I finally said, still denying Opal's eyes. My vision became more and more fixated on Alexa's words on my screen, daring me to defy them. "A family emergency just came up, I have to get this."

"What?" Opal asked, swinging her legs over the bed and onto the floor. I didn't dare look at the concern that I knew was etched in her face. "Is everything okay?"

Sliding my phone into my back pocket, I cursed the hot tears that had brimmed in my eyes at the question. I turned to my bedroom door. An all-too-curious Opal followed close behind.

"Just trust me when I say I need to take care of this ASAP," I told her, straining to hide the panic stuck in my throat.

We walked down the hallway and to the front door. I grabbed my white sneakers and slid them on.

"Without your mom?" Opal asked skeptically, hesitantly

grabbing her shoes.

"She's already there, she's the one who texted me."

But for some reason—just like the girl who'd challenged me on the Main Staircase on the first day of school—Opal defiantly stared into my eyes and was ready to test my walls all over again. "You're lying."

I swallowed, mentally screamed at my throat for not being able to hide it, and scoured every inch of my head for a lie. It would be so easy. It would fall straight off my lips like honey. It would have—if I'd been able to find one.

"I'm sorry," I said, because ignorance is bliss. "I need to take care of this."

"What was that text?"

I turned and opened the front door. "It's none of your business—"

Opal darted to my side and shut the door. "Why are you keeping something from me again? If you're not even letting your mom know what's going on, you really think I'll let you do whatever with no one knowing where you're going?"

I planted my feet in the floor, jaw firm. I had to give her the chance to be mature enough to realize why I was shutting her out right now. And to do that, I had to tell her the truth.

"Alexa," I said. "She wants me and Breanne to meet her in the Callistro Forest. She knows. I don't know how, but I have to meet her in the next half hour—"

"You're *going?*" Opal asked, as if I were stupid for even considering it (which—I don't even know if I was). "Alone? You're gonna get hurt, you have no idea what she has planned!"

I leaned in closer. "She has something on Mr. Dawson."

Opal's face somehow paled past her usual shade. With her being this adamant to come with me just for *my* sake, there was no way that I was going to tell her that Alexa actually had Mr. Dawson himself.

"I have to at *least* get that evidence," I said. "She doesn't have her magic. I'll be fine."

"What about Breanne?"

"I have to go on her behalf. But even if she were here, she's nowhere *near* ready for something like this. Bringing any of you is practically sending you to the hospital, I'm not risking you guys like that."

"This is what we're all being trained to do. If anything, this is just practice for next year."

I scoffed. "'Practice'? If you think this is practice, you're not ready for her, either. You don't know her like I do, she managed to do a *lot* before I ever found out she had magic. If I know her as well as I think I do, she's not gonna go easy just because we're teenagers."

"Then I *am* coming with you." Opal asserted the words with a firmness I'd never heard from her before. It was almost enough to persuade me. "None of us have the experience she does, which means you need more people on your side to compensate. We have to protect Uncle Thomas, and at least you'll have a wielder on your side."

"No! I'm not putting you in danger like that!" I opened the door again, but she grabbed my arm and stood in front of me.

"Opal!"

"No!" she stated, sounding too much like Momma. "If you think I'm gonna go home while knowing what you're doing—"

My anxiety had snapped my patience like a twig. "Where's your phone?"

"In your room..." she replied hesitantly. "Why?"

"Because we don't need Alexa getting a hold of any evidence that we're not against magic."

I took out my phone and texted Momma that we were going out to look for a birthday present. Tossing my phone onto the couch, I locked the doorknob, let Opal walk out first, and then shut the door behind us.

As we stepped down the walkway and toward the sidewalk, I swallowed and gripped my locket for dear life. It was the only thing saving me from an anxiety attack, and it was my last safe place with my family so far away.

But at least *they* were safe. It was time for me to take the bullet for once.

Thirty-Six

"Do you know where you're going?" Opal whispered a few yards into the Callistro Forest. Such familiar grounds had never felt more like treacherous enemy territory. In a way, I guess they'd always been exactly that before I found out the truth about Caralyn Callistro. But Alexa had come and reclaimed them for the night.

"She said to meet her at the spot where it all started. I met her for the first time about halfway through the forest, on this path."

I looked at the girl next to me, something different pumping through me. "Opal—you really shouldn't be here."

"We already talked about this—"

"We didn't talk about it enough." I stopped in my tracks and sternly met her eyes. "This was also why I wasn't honest with you guys about Alexa: I knew you'd wanna help and try to protect me, but like you said, now that I've told you the truth, I have no idea what she's gonna do! You're probably on her list now, too, just because you know!"

To my surprise, she didn't respond immediately; instead, she kept on walking, eyes gripped by thought.

I caught up to her right as she asked, "How did you say she lost her memory again?"

"Mr. Dawson cast a forgetting spell on her."

"Okay, then that's the solution to her problem," she said simply. "She can make me forget that I know anything. If my uncle was able to erase her *entire* memory, then someone from her family can erase that one small event where you told me the truth. It's fine."

I wanted to agree with her, and for a split second, I started to—but then I realized the other side of that sentence, the fatal question hanging off its end. And I prayed that Opal's next words wouldn't be—

"But then..." she mused, as though she were already trying to figure out the answer, "why hasn't she done that to you?"

Because I'd already gone through too much to *not* notice that my memory had suddenly been erased. Because I had so many different ways of getting it back anyway. Because the only reason I'd found out Alexa's secret in the first place was because I had magic. Wiping my memory was a dangerously temporary solution, if one at all.

"What a noteworthy solution, my dear."

Opal and I spun around. Alexa was strolling out from behind

a tree on the side of the path, stopping in the middle of it.

She marveled at the girl next to me with an appraising stare. "Look who it is. The girl with the pretty eyes. Your *uncle* put the forgetting spell on me, did he?"

Momma's lesson last semester played on repeat in my head: never let your opponent know anything that they don't already. Opal was wise and didn't say a thing.

Wait. Something was wrong.

"Where is he?" I asked, because Alexa was definitely alone. "You said—"

"What? I lied to get you over here? What a plot twist," Alexa said. Her brows furrowed, and I just knew it was because her patience was thinning and not because she was mocking me. "What else would've brought you here when I don't have my magic to threaten you?"

She's definitely mad.

"But then why didn't he—?" I began, cutting myself off like a sword had been held up to my throat. Opal didn't know that I could use telepathy.

Too close. Way too close.

"Opal," I said, eyeing her in my peripheral, "telepathically call him."

A sick smile spread across Alexa's lips as she seemed to piece together what had just happened, like she knew every thought in my head. If I didn't play this out exactly right, she'd win tonight.

"Why isn't he answering?" Opal soon asked.

"Couldn't do the sleeping spell myself and Julia owed me another favor," Alexa replied, turning my stomach upside down.

Rage flashed in my vision as I realized that she *had* won: I'd let her trap me.

"Then what do you want?" I exclaimed. "I told you, we don't have the bracelet anymore!"

"Or my magic," she said, the mild strain in her voice warning me that she was holding herself back. "I told you to bring Breanne."

"I chose to come," Opal said, sounding more confident than I really was. "I'm not letting you hurt her."

Alexa gave a high-lilted laugh. "Really? What's your plan for that? You won't be a high priestess for another few years at *least*, what kind of power do you have to defend yourself with right now?"

Opal kept her mouth shut. I wondered if she was debating on threatening Alexa with a spell to prove a point. I almost wanted to tell her not to, because I'd already tried that—it didn't really work out.

Alexa's refined eyes hardened on me. "I told you I was done with this, Emmalynn. I brought you here to make a deal with you and the girl with my magic, not some Callistro Girl in *way* over her head."

"I'm not 'some Callistro Girl'—!"

"Stop," I said, holding up my hand to shush Opal. "Just—just tell me the deal and I'll tell Breanne."

Alexa seemed to stand a little taller as she crossed her arms, smirking. "I can always get another enchanted bracelet. So in exchange for my magic, Breanne only loses the memories about me."

I knew better—there was definitely another catch. By the grin on her face as she gazed at me, I knew that it was probably lethal.

I fought the urge to reach for my locket as I asked, "But then—

why did you need me to come?"

"As perceptive as ever," she remarked. "So in exchange for your knowledge about Adara, I won't expose you."

Before I could open my mouth, Opal spun on me, confusion scrunching her features together. "*You* know something about Adara? How did you—?"

One glimpse at Alexa seemed to remind her of her other question. My body went rigid.

"What does she mean 'expose'?" Opal asked.

I wanted more than anything to erase Alexa's memory again then and there, but it'd be a constant cycle of this summer if I did. And I really didn't want to live that way. An Alexa without magic was a lot less dangerous, anyway, right?

No, I realized, my breath stopping: Alexa needed proof that I had magic before she could turn me in to President Caldwell, but she didn't have any that wouldn't expose herself as a magician, too.

Things were different now.

"She doesn't know?" Alexa asked, as if this were the most awkward conversation in the world. "Yikes. Well, she was bound to find out."

"Don't you dare—"

"Don't be shy, Emmalynn. Come on, I'm still dying to know how *you* managed to erase my memory like that."

She just said that. She'd just said that, and there was no taking it back. I'd just have to deal with her head on now.

"I warned you," I said, too furious to bother remembering that Opal was next to me anymore. "I told you to get out of my house, but you didn't listen!"

"I didn't believe you had it in you to go through with it!" Alexa laughed in disbelief. "You wouldn't even tell me what you'd do if I didn't leave. But you *really* delivered."

"You're a magician?"

That one gentle whisper thrust a sword through me. My identity twisted it in my gut. Those words—how could I have never been ready to hear the truth about myself from one of my closest friends?

With every breath trapped in my lungs and my chest locked with shame—of my actions or who I was, I didn't know—I made myself face Opal. "I wanted to tell you."

"Was that the other thing you were gonna tell us at the 'right time'?"

No. Not another lie. Me being "friends" with Tristan's daughter was what I was going to tell them. I... I couldn't lie... could I? Would I?

"No."

Why were my walls tumbling down? When had the dam broken?

When had I lost the game Momma had spent my entire life training me to play?

Opal's panged purple eyes hardened, her round jaw stiffening. Her brows furrowed in what I could only interpret as hurt and increasing anger.

"This whole time," she finally whispered, stiller than the ancient redwoods around us. "Were you ever gonna tell us?"

"Opal," I said in a weak voice that I resented, stepping toward her, but she held out a defensive hand.

"No, don't!" she demanded, glancing between me and

Alexa—who, I realized, was still standing there, merely watching us. "Why did you lie? To *me*? Why did you keep that from me when you knew how long I've wanted a friend just like me?"

I risked my own glance at Alexa, who, surprisingly, wasn't smiling her signature innocent grin. Dare I say there was a solemn look of "I told you so" on those soft, defined features. Like this was the price every wielder eventually paid, and I should've known better a lot sooner.

My jaw locked. "Her," I said. "Her, *this*, I didn't want you involved because I knew *she* would make you a target if you knew."

With another glimpse of the Grand Hunter standing in front of us, Opal seemed to be shaken back to reality. Our issues right now were bigger than what I had and hadn't told her. And part of her, I wanted to say, knew that.

"Okay," she finally said, her eyes trained on Alexa. "Fine. We'll figure this out later. We're still here for the same reason—"

"I'm curious, Opal," Alexa mused, casually meandering toward us, "did Emmalynn promise you the full truth 'at the right time'?"

Unfortunately, telepathy was no longer an option for Alexa. I had to tell her aloud, "It's none of your business."

When Opal didn't immediately back me up, that red-flag instinct started waving in my chest. Something was wrong. It took all of my courage to look at her and realize that her gaze had frozen on Alexa. She'd caught something in her words that I hadn't.

"If you just told me," Opal began, facing me, "that you having magic wasn't the full truth—does *Alexa* know what it is?"

"I told you, 'at the right time'," I stated, scrambling to find whatever control I could before Alexa did expose me, because I knew her too well. "This isn't the—"

"But Alexa knows?" Opal demanded the question as a statement. "If now isn't the right time, when—?"

"You've lied to her enough, Emmalynn," Alexa simpered. "You can tell her, or I'll gladly take the honor—"

"I'm friends with Tristan's daughter," I barked. "I know who she is. That's what I was gonna tell you."

Even those words seemed to pause the world as Opal gawked at me. I thought back to that wicked night in front of William in the underground lair, when I'd confessed the same thing, stunning the atmosphere with it. After that, Jak had come and helped me escape. Tonight, I was pretty sure that rescue wasn't coming.

"They're a *lot* closer than you think, Opal," Alexa remarked, cocking a brow. "When's the last time you saw a picture of Tristan Atera?"

That's it!

I shouted the spell in my head, releasing the rage that had never seen the light of day since the day I'd met her. Alexa flew down the forest path before crashing, rolling to a stop. If she wanted to push me to my limit until I snapped, I'd give it to her *full* force!

"You?"

I didn't dare face Opal next to me. My eyes stayed stuck on Alexa, grunting as she struggled to prop herself up.

"You're Tristan's descendant," Opal stated. "You're Tristan's daughter."

Furious tears blurred my vision. I spun to her, what little control I had left abandoning me. "Opal—"

"Shut up!" Her arm was stretched out in full defense. "Let

me get this straight: you lied about being a magician and never planned to tell us, there was something you *wanted* to tell us but still couldn't despite lying, and then you lied *about* that one thing you were gonna be honest about?"

"I didn't—"

"Yes, you did!" she cried, her volume dangerously close to a scream. "You just looked me in the eye, lied to me when I demanded the truth, and *Alexa* was the one who told me! What's next, *you're* actually Adara?"

"Go ahead," Alexa called with another grunt, on one knee. "Rip her head off. I wanna see where this goes."

"It was just those things, I promise, and it was all to protect you!" I told Opal, swearing the truth with my eyes. But a familiar disbelief that I'd seen on Nolan's face just a few nights ago etched itself across her face.

"Right, because I can believe a pathological liar."

"Like *you* were so honest when you lied about being hunted last year?" burst from my lips before I could even think the words— and only a small part of me regretted it.

"Wow," she muttered, staring at me blankly. "Are you kidding me?"

"Don't you dare act like I'm the only liar here. Jak knew all the suspects and told me you were never on the list, you even lied about being friends with him! At least I lied about things that *mattered!*"

Her thin lips curved upward in a shaky smile, eyes hardening into something I'd never seen in them before: something that resembled what I saw in Alexa's eyes when she looked at me.

"But lying is *all* you do, Emmalynn," Alexa strained to say, approaching us with a small limp. "All she ever does is lie, Opal. Her entire life is a lie. Who she is, is a lie." Her tone dripped with an enraging arrogance. "All she knows how to do is lie no matter who it is. Whatever she told you about your friendship was a *lie.*"

"No," I stated, "*that* is a lie. Opal's one of my closest—"

Alexa's eyes narrowed. "You'd get rid of her the fastest way possible if you had the chance."

"That's not true—!"

The words had barely left my mouth when the girl next to me flew off the path, her body hurtling into the forestry behind her.

C H A P T E R

Thirty-Seven

I gawked at Opal's body that had landed at the foot of a small hill ten feet into the forest. She trembled bringing herself to her knees, her legs wobbling as she stood.

Even in the dark, her rage was visibly ablaze on her face. "Are you kidding me?" she whispered.

No, no, I hadn't done that! That wasn't my magic!

Was it...?

Was I losing that much control over myself?

"That wasn't me!" I cried, glancing between her and Alexa still on the path—like she'd be on my side and defend me. "Opal, I didn't do that, I wouldn't try to fight you!"

"What other magicians do you see, Emma?" she retorted, limping back toward the path in slow steps. I heard her sniff in the dark.

"That wasn't–!" I cried. But not only did I have no proof–I also had no clue if I *had* involuntarily done that.

Opal limped onto the moonlit path, her eyes glistening with pain. "You know what? I've always been vulnerable with you. I put myself in danger to *protect* you tonight, but you couldn't even tell me the truth, and then you *literally* threw me away!"

"I never wanted to lie, we were protecting you from–!"

"*Shut up!*" she screamed, purple eyes flashing amber.

A powerful force thrust me into the tree on the other side of the path. Lungs heaving from the blow, I steadied myself against the trunk as quickly as I could, feet planted in the ground. I couldn't fight her if I could help it.

"Opal, please–!"

"Don't." A heavy sadness saturated her tone. Her fists clenched, shaking. "Show me what you were 'protecting' me from, *Atera!*"

My body rose from the ground and flew back onto the dirt path. I didn't have the time to be thankful that my head had been last to hit the ground as I propped myself up. Padded footsteps crunched in front of me. I looked up, standing. Opal was running for me.

"Don't do this!" I said, watching her weight shift into her pelvis and then her shoulder for a straight.

"Do what?" she snarled. "Feel hurt? Angry? Thrown away again?!"

"*Again*"?

She pushed her shoulder forward and aimed for the center of my face. I ducked, put myself behind her, and pulled both of her arms behind her back to trip her.

Her body slammed into the ground with a yelp. Before I could plead with her again, she looked up at me, fury burning alive in her irises. "*Ite procul!*"

Amber flashed, and magic flung me straight off the path. The ground swallowed the thud of my body as I crashed, my breath knocked out of me. In the corner of my vision, a boulder rose and flew toward me. My telekinesis caught it just in time and threw it far into the forest.

I darted back to the path. Empty. Where was Opal? Where was *Alexa—*?

When I whirled around again, Opal emerged from the darkness of the forest on the other side.

I looked at the branches of the trees that lined the path. They'd block her path.

Distraho!

The branches snapped off and hurtled toward the ground. Opal yelped, jumping back as they landed just in front of her.

"Wow." She panted, breathless. Mockery dripped from her voice. "Emma's using magic."

"I was surprised the first time I saw it, too."

I didn't have time to face the voice behind me before Alexa grabbed me. I pushed upwards with my elbows, breaking free. Spinning, I tried to elbow her head until her fist slammed into my stomach. She shoved a push kick against my chest, throwing me back down to the ground.

A pounding throbbed in my head as Alexa turned me onto my stomach, ignoring how my feet were caught. I cried out as my right ankle twisted in a way it wasn't supposed to. Both arms were shoved behind my back, pushing the limits of my shoulder sockets. I pictured the woman above me and threw her off with telekinesis. I forced myself to stand up again, stumbling with fear and, well, a twisted ankle. My eyes darted all around for Opal, but she'd turned invisible.

"Opal!" I called out just before someone kicked me hard in the back. I slammed down onto the ground.

Alexa turned me onto my back. Her fingers had too firm a grip on my arms. The pressure in my veins built up and up, like she was commanding each blood vessel to pop.

"I was fair, Atera," she sneered. "I gave you multiple chances to give me what I asked for, I offered you a way out *many* times, yet here you are."

The tree above us!

Distraho!

A heavy branch crashed down, pushing Alexa onto me. I shoved her and the branch to the side with a strengthening spell my will alone cast. Alexa rolled to the middle of the main path, red hair sprawled around her head.

"I will *never* stop fighting you if it means protecting my family and every last magician in this country!" I propped myself up on the ground with a pulsating ache in my chest and arms. With an agonizing burst of effort, I forced myself to my feet.

An unnatural force picked me up and slammed me back down to the ground. I screamed as a crack resonated across my body and I was turned onto my back. The impact seemed to shatter the fibers of my rib cage.

Wh—what? But Alexa—doesn't have—!

I barely had the strength to think. Seconds later, with my

strained breaths echoing throughout the night, Alexa appeared above me.

"Again: look where that's gotten you," she muttered. She pulled me up by my arms and threw me into a tree trunk. My body slammed into it, pushing the oxygen out of my lungs. A sickening crack rippled across my chest again.

"What about—Thomas?" I breathed, holding myself up against the tree. The words were tight in my throat. "He knows—you're better than this—that's why he still loves—!"

"Don't you DARE use him against me again!" Alexa snarled, thrusting another push kick at the center of my stomach. A cry of agony curdled in my throat. Alexa threw a turning kick to my side, shoving me to the ground. "That manipulative sorry excuse for a man spent *weeks* gaslighting me! He took advantage of what we once had and made me tell him things that I always kept from him for a reason! It's a miracle by God I haven't gone back to his house to have him arrested and killed!"

She does *still have feelings for him.*

The thought pulsed in my head with my vision thrusting forward and backwards. My lungs seared me with fire, choking on the lack of air but screaming in protest if I inhaled. It was all I could do to prop myself up on a trembling arm, suffocating.

"You want to *protect* magicians?" Alexa sneered. She grabbed me by my arms. I yelped at the sharp pain that shot through my chest. "Magicians like him? The same magicians who've started wars and only ended them once the mortals surrendered?"

Ite... ite...! I tried the telekinesis spell over and over, but a pang throbbed with every attempt. I was getting to the point where not even my will was brave enough to try my injuries.

Alexa tightened her grip around my skin as if to punish me for trying a spell. "You want to protect the magicians who believe they're so high and mighty with their magic that not only are they invincible, but immune to any law or moral that slaps them across the face? The same laws *they're* trying to enact? The magicians who've harmed their own people because they can do whatever they want?!"

"You decided," I rasped, "to join the mortals' hatred—to *fix* things?"

"You don't know *anything*, Atera!"

She turned me onto my back, pushing me into the ground. The mere idea of resisting her threatened my body into submission.

"Trust me, you want this to end *now*," she hissed, reading my mind. "So? Do we have a—?"

Her weight flew off me, leaving me lying breathless on the ground. My head spun more and more with every heartbeat. My sore stomach churned. My ankle bulged, and my arms were on fire. I couldn't stand—not this time. All my body allowed was keeping my head turned to the left, my fading vision stuck on the path and what lay beyond it—what stood in the right corner of my eye.

"I'm still angry," Opal spat, facing Alexa. "But—I came here to protect her. We're here to protect—*our* people."

"Not a fan of the next generation of Callistro Girls," Alexa growled, pushing herself off the ground. "How did you get so cocky?"

Opal's body flew into the tree behind her like a dummy—but no amber had flashed from Alexa's eyes.

Of course. Of course! She had a magician hiding somewhere!

They had flung Opal into the forest, not my magic!

I tried to prop myself up with shaky, pulsating arms—as if I could warn her—but my strength gave out. My body couldn't do it again. I fell onto my back, staring up at the starry night sky. It was cold for a summer night—but my body was overheating, keeping me awake, forcing me to remember that I was still every bit alive.

"You're making a big mistake, little girl," Alexa hissed, standing in the corner of my eye.

Her body flew into an aerial cartwheel toward Opal. I squeezed my eyes shut at another sickening crack, a gasp of pain, and a body plummeting into the pile of branches I'd broken off the trees.

"Take this as a token of your visit tonight," Alexa said.

Opal's muffled scream distorted the air. A crunchy, blood-curdling snap echoed in horrifying waves as it replayed in my mind. My body winced as I squeezed my eyes shut tighter, stomach folding in on itself. Opal's pained gasps and whimpers followed amidst rustling foliage.

I have no idea what Alexa did to her next, but it silenced her.

—*Opal, please, say... say something!*—

"Tap out, Emmalynn," Alexa demanded. "I'm going until you've had enough."

I need to get up. For Opal. I need to see if she's okay. I have to get up!

I took a few seconds to sit up. A sharp jolt shot into my ribcage. My scream wasn't enough to wake Opal up, wherever she lay. I didn't dare try to shake away the dizzy throbbing in my head.

Alexa grabbed my arms and forced me up, sounding another cry from my throat. "You don't wanna see the state she's in, trust me," she whispered. "Do we have a deal or not?"

I pushed through the excruciating torment and tried to trip her, but her stance was too strong and my leg too weak. "Y—you have—nothing—on me!"

"Guess again, Atera. One of the buttons on my shirt isn't a normal button. This entire night is on film, and I finally have my leverage. Say hi to Anthony."

Anthony. The man Jak had mentioned a few weeks ago—*he* was working behind the scenes somewhere! He was the one who'd kept me on my back minutes ago! HE had started the fight!

"W—why are you doing this?" I cried, my voice nothing but air. "You're one of us. *Your* people are—suffering! Why are you killing—instead of—helping them?!"

Alexa was out of patience. She used my right arm to turn me around and face her. With another hard kick to my chest, she sent me back into a tree. My head slammed against the trunk, sending it swimming. Every fiber of my body's strength had been spent. I crumpled to the ground and rolled onto the path.

Alexa loomed over me. No grin. No smirk. No remorse.

"Don't mind me, darling. I'm just returning the favor."

She tapped something in her ear, emerald-green eyes haunting my last few seconds awake. "Anthony, she's ready for you."

Everything dissolved to black.

CHAPTER

Thirty-Eight

Salty tears burned their paths down my face as each memory swarmed my mind. Guilt and shame stained my body. And with every memory stripped of their hiding place, every last fear I'd had for the past year had come back from the dead.

The quiet trailing my words seemed to reflect back onto me and press against me on all sides. The heart monitor next to me beeped and beeped, reminding me and my family that I was still alive after this summer, after every mistake I'd made. My mother, standing beside the hospital bed, deserved my eyes for what I was about to say, but my remorse was pushing my head down, resisting any words of honor that my family deserved to hear.

"I'm sorry," I whispered. I could only look up to Momma's

chin, but it was enough. "I'm sorry this is how you're spending your birthday."

"Honey." She gently took my hand. "Baby girl, I thought I'd lost you Wednesday night. All day today we didn't even know if you'd wake up. Finally knowing that you're okay is all I could *ever* ask for today."

"But it shouldn't be," I said, shutting my eyes and pressing my head against the pillow. "You should—be expecting a lot better."

"Kiddo, what's done is done," Aunt Becca assured me at the foot of the bed, resting her hands on the plastic headboard. Her invisibility cloak almost hid them. "You made mistakes, but you're growing up a lot faster than the average kid your age. You're taking responsibility a lot faster than the majority of adults, too. Don't beat yourself up, Alexa did enough of that for you. We're okay."

"Exactly," Dad said next to Momma. "There's nothing left to do but heal and move forward. And be grateful that we're even alive *to* heal."

Heal. That word had never been bigger than ourselves before. I was glad that Momma had used "we" with it; that word applied to people who weren't even in this room with us right now.

I looked at Mr. Dawson sitting in the chair under the window. Regret. So much regret dulling those deep-set, startlingly blue eyes.

We'd all kept secrets from each other this summer. Now that they were out in the open, I wasn't sure if any of them would've been best left kept.

"I lied," I whispered. Unfortunately, I didn't have the strength or pain tolerance to wipe away the next tear sliding down my cheek. Momma took care of it for me. "Again. Wednesday night. I'm sorry."

By the tightness in her lips, as gentle as her thumb was, she was mad at me for that, too. For my sake right now, I could bet my magic, she was holding it all in.

Then, her lips released, and she exhaled. It was almost like she was asking me, *Lesson learned?*

I didn't even have enough pride to reject that sentiment, either. Lesson *way* learned.

Dad's eyes shared glimpses of the rest of us around the room. "We need to address a couple of things. First of all, Opal can't get her memories back."

"What?" Mr. Dawson said, standing from the chair.

"Thomas," Momma said flatly. "Our greatest fears were realized once she knew what we *did* allow for. When she found out *everything*, not only was she furious, but she became a target, and look what happened. If she stays knowing the entire truth, we can't continue our lives the way we are, we'd have to adopt another protect-ee."

"Nobody in this room is meant to live the rest of their life the same way they always have," he argued, fearlessly staring back at her. Even Aunt Becca kept her eyes intently on them like they were her favorite soap opera. "Let me ask you something, Amy: what if the night that Tristan proposed to you was the night you found out that he was a sorcerer? What if someone had walked up to you while he was down on one knee and exposed him to you? Would that have stopped you from saying yes?"

Momma didn't respond. I bet we were both trying to figure out where he was going with this.

"I really don't think it would've," Mr. Dawson said, "because you loved him too much by that point. Opal wasn't initially angry, she was hurt. And then she was ready to protect your daughter *twice* once she was given the chance to calm down—once she remembered how much they care about each other. Magic brought them together, and it's not gonna be what tears them apart. A lack of forgiveness and willingness to understand *will*."

Momma's silence changed. She had nothing to argue back with. With a blink, she broke her stare with him, surrendering.

If things were to go differently this time... *could* we get away with Opal knowing the full truth?

"She lied to me."

The words leaped out before I'd even realized that they were in my mind, jumping to answer my own question. And the only thing that told me that I'd spoken them was everyone's eyes falling onto me—but this was the truth, and I was going to run with it.

I looked at Mr. Dawson. "Do you know Opal's tell for when she's lying?"

Caution slowed his steps up to the bed. "She's never lied to me, as far as I know."

"Her voice gets high," I said. "When she told me she was suspected of being Dad's descendant last year, her voice stayed high and airy, and Jak confirmed that she wasn't a suspect. Alexa's pack also handled the suspects from North Carolina, but Opal was surprised when I said Alexa was the one who hunted me last year. On top of that—she told me when the Redway Boys left Callistro that she and Jak talked a few times. Which Jak denied."

Hindsight vision really is 20/20. I couldn't help but wonder what else the girl had lied to me about—how *long* she'd been lying to me. Maybe even her other friends and classmates.

"Thomas, I really don't wanna say it..." Momma said, hugging herself, "but toward the end of the school year, I asked her to come in after school to do some make-up work. She told me she already had an appointment with Goubeaux. Her voice was higher than usual—airy. Goubeaux confirmed that she never had an appointment with him."

Airy. Exactly.

Mr. Dawson closed his eyes. A quiet, heavy sigh drew from him. He pressed his lips so tightly together that I couldn't see them anymore. Like a parent trying to convince themselves that they'd raised their child better than that.

Why would Opal lie?

"Okay," Mr. Dawson said, resting his hands on the hospital bed. "I'll let her forget the parts where Emma used magic and Alexa exposed her, because... admittedly, I don't like knowing that Opal can lie like that, especially about last year's hunt. She does, though, have a right to know everything else that happened this summer. We can't keep it to ourselves forever. She's in this fight now whether we like it or not."

"Okay," Aunt Becca said, nodding. "So who's gonna tell Breanne that she is, too? There's no way Alexa's letting her off the hook with her magic."

"Where is she?" I asked, my stomach churning at the notion. "Are she or Sarah here?"

"Everyone's in the waiting room," Mr. Dawson replied. "But I'd tell Breanne ASAP, Emma. Privately, obviously, but ASAP. We'll start sending them in."

"Who's 'everyone'?" I asked as they all herded toward the

door.

Momma looked over her shoulder at me, lips softly turned upward. "You'll see."

Dad and Aunt Becca threw on their hoods, fading into the room. Mr. Dawson held the door open for them and waited for Momma to walk by before reaching the doorway.

"Wait."

He stopped, looking over at me. Hearing my unspoken message, he told Momma to give us a couple of minutes.

When he closed the heavy door, his hand stayed on the steel handle. I wondered if he knew what I was about to say or if he was wondering what I'd chosen to chew him out for.

"Are you okay?" I asked.

He looked up in surprise, like that was the *last* question he'd expected me to ask. A part of me agreed with him.

He breathily chuckled, strolling to the foot of the hospital bed. "Really? You're asking me that?"

"You lost the woman you love twice."

Okay. I could've found a better way to say that.

He pressed his lips together, like he had to verify that statement for himself. His hands came to rest on the plastic headboard. "Is that really what you want to talk about?" he murmured.

"I just wanna make sure you're okay."

Whatever he was thinking behind that firm jaw and solid stance, whatever he was feeling, he wanted to keep it from me. I couldn't help but think that he *wasn't* okay.

"I was an idiot," he finally said. Too simply for this conversation, as if the circumstances were just that: simple. "I let myself play pretend, knowing that that was all it was, and that fantasy ended. I knew it would, but I'd managed to convince myself that it would last longer, it'd be different, she'd be different. I was stupid enough to try it. Part of me—"

Something hitched in his throat. His grip on the headboard tightened. So much regret.

He looked back up at me. Red inflamed his eyes, yet they still lacked a glisten. "Part of me was stupid enough to enjoy it. Look past everything and let her back in. Give her another chance... And then she did this. Yeah—I was the idiot for pretending for a *second* that it was real. I just wish I was the only one who had to pay the price. But I'm not. I forgave her for everything else, but she physically attacked my family. I will never forgive her for that."

I thought back to Alexa's words in the forest. It was partly *because* of her feelings for Mr. Dawson that she was so hurt by what he'd done. Anyone would've been furious after weeks of that. But Alexa was beyond that: she was in the midst of a shattered dream. Mr. Dawson had probably been the last wholly good thing in her life, and we'd taken even that away from her.

They'd both hurt each other in the same crossfire.

"I'll be okay," Mr. Dawson finally said. "Thank you, Emma. And I'm sorry—truly, for how I hurt you this summer."

Before I could react, he turned around. I swallowed, trying to find the right words anyway. There just wasn't enough room anymore for bitterness and resentment. Something had to go, and I wasn't going to keep the acid.

"I'm sorry, too," I said, stopping him halfway to the door. "And I forgive you."

He nodded, his back to me. "You've already been forgiven."

He pulled open the door and walked out of the room. The

door softly fell shut behind him.

I was alone. Truly alone in that sterile room with nothing but the sore stiffness of my backside, the throbbing across my body, and the memories of the summer to keep me company. It actually reminded me of the afternoon that Alexa had revealed herself as Julia in the nurse's office.

Man, I hated that day. And right now was nowhere near any better.

The enemy had *pulverized* me Wednesday night. If I hadn't been able to win with my magic against a mortal, how was I supposed to keep my family safe? Especially with how many fatal mistakes I'd made the last three months? In full honesty, it was tempting to *purposely* forget everything—how I'd messed up, the person I'd become—from this summer.

No. I closed my eyes, letting that word wash over me. *No. I can't do that.* Because that was just it: in the months of burying my memories and experiences, I'd buried my strength and ability to defend the ones I loved. I'd almost lost my family because of my ignorance—my ruthless denial—because I kept choosing to forget. Never again. I could leave no memory unturned ever again.

†

My next visitor appeared out from behind the opening door. And when I saw his face, on instinct, my heart skipped a hard beat.

"How did you end up here?" Jak all too casually asked, his thumbs in the pockets of his black hoodie.

"You can't make me laugh. My ribs are broken."

"I know," he said, ambling over to the side of my bed. "Your mom told us. No more friendly hugs, huh?"

"Your hugs are anything *but* friendly." My lips lifted into a smile—until I remembered our last few conversations. Then, most painfully, my and Nolan's.

I had to give Jak my definite no like I'd given Nolan. I'd spent too much time leading him on. And I had to pray that he'd forgive me a lot faster than Nolan had—who, I remembered, had never even had the chance *to* forgive me. Even worse.

But he just got here...

My brain switched to the topic that would bring the least amount of pain first: Anthony. He *had* come after me the day Jak had asked about him. The reason there hadn't been any marks on my neck after he'd choked me was that his physical grip hadn't stayed long enough, and his magic had inflicted the damage internally. Jak couldn't know what had really been wrong with me that day—let alone the forgetting spell Anthony had used on me—but Anthony had been there Wednesday night, working behind the scenes and ready to help Alexa when she needed it. That was my ticket in.

"Hey," Jak murmured, sitting down in the chair next to me. "What's wrong?"

Why did he have to make this so hard?

I avoided his eyes now, sticking mine on the hospital sheets. "Remember when you asked me about Anthony?"

"Um..." He almost made me regret the question with that divot between his brow and his scrutinizing tone, like he was already analyzing this conversation. "Yeah."

"Who is he?"

Seconds of pensive silence passed.

"I told you," he said, bringing my eyes up to his. "He's in Alexa's pack."

"He was there Wednesday night—"

Jak sprang from his seat. "*He* did this?"

"No, Alexa's the one who attacked us," I said quickly, "but he was there, hiding somewhere. We never saw him."

Jak's face scrunched in confusion, and then I realized the weight of my words—and how I had to come up with an excuse for Anthony being there because "Alexa doesn't have her magic" wasn't an option.

"Why was *he* helping her?" Jak asked, sitting himself back down.

"What do you mean?"

"I mean my dad's the one who works from a distance while she's out on the field. Anthony's not... He's not even a Grand Hunter, he's only part of the pack because..."

He couldn't tell me the truth while looking me in the eye, but I stared into his anyway as if trying to burn a hole through him. "I know he's a Delphine, Jak. What're you not telling me?"

He leaned forward, resting his elbows on his knees. Never before had his thoughts been so crystal clear, but that was what told me how heavy the situation really was: not only was Jak letting me see what he was thinking, but his thoughts were clashing with one another. They were having a filibuster on top of the other.

His tight jaw stayed shut—until, for the first time ever since we'd known each other, Jakson Bleu looked at me with *interrogative* eyes. "Why did Alexa come after you in the first place?"

I didn't dare try to lie; I was under no circumstances to execute one perfectly.

"Did she tell you why she's been in Capperson?" he asked.

Right, because Alexa would be so generous.

The words barely found me in time: "She was looking for information on Tristan's daughter."

"Alexa's *still*—?"

"Yes, Jak, she is!" I snapped, startling us—but it turned out that I was a lot more fed up with everything than I'd thought as I spoke it all aloud, cementing it. "You're always telling me I'm safe from the pack like I'm always telling you she's safe, but we both just—got it wrong. Alexa told me I had half an hour to meet her in the forest, and when I did, her plan was to beat me half to death to force me into telling her everything."

"Did you?"

"No! I passed out before I could hear her conversation with Anthony."

Jak took a deep breath in as if trying to pick between which thought to voice first. "Anthony's..." He shook his head, dropping the sentence. "It's not for me to say."

"Not for—?" I began. But I couldn't afford him being cryptic right now, nor did I have the patience for it. "Are you scared to tell me he's a Delphine? Because I *know*. But why was *he* the one with Alexa that night? What makes him so special, who is he?"

Just like that, Jak closed off his thoughts to me again and looked away. His very breath out sounded like it was made of fire. Then, his shoulders relaxed—and instinct warned me to steel myself against his next words.

He didn't dare look me in the eyes when he said, "Her son."

THIRTY-NINE

Obviously I knew that Alexa had immediate family, not just the family she'd married into. I knew that she had siblings, just not how many. I knew that she had parents, just not whether they were alive. She had aunts, uncles, and cousins for all I knew, but *never* would I have thought that Alexa Delphine was... a mom!

I mean, she was a stepmom, but nobody had told me that she'd had a son of her own!

"He's..." I stammered. "But he's too... You said—wait, you said he *wasn't* a Grand Hunter. But he's part of the pack?"

"He's technically a Master."

"That *young*? Is he a Redway Boy with a pass or something?"

"No. He graduated four years ago."

"So he's... twenty-two?"

"As of May."

Alexa's story that night on Mr. Dawson's couch flooded back to me and hit me like a tsunami. I almost didn't want to connect the dots. "But Alexa's only—"

"Thirty-nine."

That only left a seventeen-year gap between them.

Seventeen.

"It's not for me to say."

Chills scattered up my arms and legs. The room went dead, neither of us knowing the right words to say. Even after all that Alexa had done to us, we owed her that moment where we simply kept our thoughts to ourselves and, out of everything else, focused on her strength alone.

I'd gotten to know the Alexa before then—Alexandra. I'd gotten to know the woman that Mr. Dawson fell in love with in high school. Her story, her gentleness that had once been there, her words Wednesday night... it was finally hitting me. I'd been last to the line, but it was hitting me.

Anything else—I need to think of anything else.

I forced my voice back up to ask, "How did you know I was here?"

Jak seemed grateful for the subject change, his head perking up slightly. "Sarah called me."

My ribs instantly punished me for my amused breath in. I grunted, carefully sinking into the pillows behind me. "I don't even know why I asked."

"She knew I'd help you feel better." Jak stood from the chair and mindfully sat on the side of the bed. "So on a scale of one to ten, how fragile are you right now?"

"I'd shrug, but I'm scared it'll break my clavicle."

"Okay." He rested his hand on the bed and leaned forward, coming closer. His fingers on his other hand grazed the side of my cheek. The heart monitor beeped faster as he whispered, "Then just tell me if it hurts."

He lightly cupped the side of my face, his hand almost hovering, as his lips brushed against mine. He waited. He waited and even I waited for some kind of denial, but against my body's wishes, I brought my hand up to his neck and returned his lips' touch, closing the distance.

And Jak kissed me with a touch so soft that, solely out of spite, I wanted to press my lips harder against his to reject the state of my body, reject our circumstances. I wanted him to know that he *was* making me feel better, making me forget again, and I never wanted him to stop.

Sharp pain surged through me with every beat of my heart. I still kissed him. The heart monitor sped up by the second. I still kissed him. My heart clenched with the memory of my mistakes this summer. I tried to hold on to him. I held on until my hand slipped, until my arm fell to the hospital sheets, until I had to force myself to pull away.

"Stop, I can't!"

Jak jumped off the bed like I was on fire. "Did I hurt you?"

"No," I said, desperately trying to control my breath for the sake of my crumbling ribcage. "No, I don't—I don't know!"

He glanced at the heart monitor next to us. "Hey, try to calm down," he told me, like it was really that easy. "What's wrong, do you need the nurse?"

"Jak..." I swallowed hard, closing my eyes. I had to face the truth head on. He deserved the respect of eye contact for this conversation, but I couldn't do it. I couldn't, not when such venomous words were falling from my lips.

"It's not..." I whispered anyway, opening my eyes to the hospital sheets. "It... it can't happen."

Silence. Earth-shattering silence.

I wondered if he heard my swallow. I couldn't understand how it could be so loud, and I cursed it.

I dared to raise my eyes, catching just the tip of Jak's nose, his tightly pressed-together lips, and his tense jaw. Finally, the half of his head that I could see nodded.

"Okay. I get it."

That was all he had to say? I needed more than that! I wanted his thoughts, I had to know if he hated me or if he wanted to forget me, too, if he regretted anything that had happened between us in the last year! Why wasn't he telling me any of that?

A nurse pushed open the door and rushed into the room. Jak stepped aside as she came up to the side of my bed and asked with concerned brown eyes, "Honey, are you okay? The heart monitor triggered an alarm at the nurse's station, can you tell me what's wrong?"

"I just—" I began, pushing more volume into my voice, "I just got... I got overwhelmed thinking."

"Oh, I see. Okay." She rested her nitrile-gloved hand on the bed railing. "Your vitals are stabilizing, but try your best to avoid thinking about anything stressful right now. We need you to rest so you can heal." A soft smile touched her face, and I appreciated it more than anything in that moment because it looked like she meant it. "You're okay."

I didn't trust my voice, so I carefully nodded.

She faced Jak next. "Are you done visiting, sweetheart?"

He glanced in my direction for a split second. That was it.

Don't hate me. Let me in again. Please.

"Yeah," he told the nurse with a neutral smile, putting his hands in his hoodie pockets. Then, in the space of a blink, he glanced at me again. "All good."

That code, I could understand. The only problem was that I wasn't sure if I believed it.

"Great. Let's go grab the next visitor," the nurse said, guiding Jak to the door. "Is there anything I can get for you, Miss Emmalynn?"

"I'm okay. Thank you."

Liar.

Jak walked out the door without another glimpse in my direction. The door shut behind him. *That* was why I wasn't sure I could believe his code.

†

"How did you handle introductions out there?" I asked in pleasant surprise as Cara and Steven walked in next, Cara clutching a dark-green book to her chest. "Does everyone know who you are?"

"Your mom introduced us as 'not-so-distant relatives'." Cara chuckled, her distended belly providing difficulty as she sat in the chair Jak had used. She set the book down in her lap.

"Which, um, kind of feels true," Steven added. He rested a dark hand on her shoulder, standing behind her and running his other hand through his feathered black hair. "Your friends are probably gonna be next in. They want as much time with you as possible."

Oh—right. Sarah and Breanne *hadn't* had their memories wiped. They still remembered every detail of summer. Suddenly, I was that much more grateful that I hadn't been able to take Breanne with me Wednesday night.

Steven took a seat on the bed as Cara uncomfortably shifted in the plastic chair. "How are you feeling, honey?" she asked, pushing a lock of fawn hair behind her ear. "Your mom told everyone the diagnoses once she found out."

"I've been a lot better. This summer... sucked. It kind of feels like everything's unraveling and becoming this gigantic mess I'm not even sure I can fix. I'm beginning to think that the problem is a lot more than 'mortal is afraid of and hates magic'."

Alexa's story slithered back into my mind. Cara and Steven waited patiently for me to continue.

I gave myself another stingy breath, mindful of my ribs. "Magicians haven't been perfect, either. We're turning on each other because of it. Magician is hunting magician, they're abusing their power to get what they want. No wonder people are scared of us. If the problem doesn't solely lie with the fact of whether or not someone has magic, where *does* it lie?"

Cara gently took my hand into hers, her defined gray eyes softening. "You're wise and intuitive for your age. But you can't speak for an entire people just because some of them made some mistakes. You and Alexa are polar opposites, but you're still united by magic. And I think your answer's actually right there: people start thinking what you are now, and they give up. Some *don't* care if you're a magician or mortal—they just know that they've been hurt. That's why we need you to help unite all these divisions that have formed over the years."

"*How?*" I asked. "It's impossible for everyone to agree on one thing."

"Well, yeah," Steven said, his head bouncing with the words, "but nobody said they had to. They just have to know that everyone they talk to—magic or no magic—their humanity's the same. Civility goes a long way."

I let myself smile, his words comfortingly warming my chest. I had to wonder what Sarah and Breanne would think of the two people sitting in front of me: the seventh-great granddaughter of Caralyn Callistro and seventh-great grandson of Samuel Baelford, the mage who'd planned to murder Caralyn's corrupt father.

"We actually brought you something that may help you figure things out," Cara said. She took the green book from her lap and held it out to me: a journal.

That's for me?

I slowly took it, careful of my body, and rested it in my lap. Smooth cover, golden corner protectors—even more pages than the one Momma had given me for my birthday last year. A smile helplessly pulled my lips apart.

"Your mom told us that journaling has really helped you get through all this craziness," Cara said, leaning forward as much as she could for a woman due in a month and a half. "We wanted to get you something to cheer you up, and with how this summer went, we figured this would be perfect."

"It is," I said softly, marveling as I flipped through the empty pages. "Thank you. I'm probably gonna start writing in it as soon

as visiting hours are done. This'll probably help me fall asleep tonight when my brain tries to keep me up."

"Glad you like it." Steven smiled, sitting up straighter on the
edge of the bed. "And I really look forward to reading those pages
when you're done and finding out exactly what happened.
Thomas, um... updated me telepathically. About Alexa and
Breanne. *That* is crazy."

And a *long* story. He had a point.

I think my smile fell at the thought, because Cara's slender
hand tightened around mine. The situation was a lot more than
just "crazy". I almost wanted to ask how Alexa had even found out
that Breanne had her magic, but as long as you just *know* a magician—A.K.A. a nore—getting information is pretty easy.

"We're really happy you're okay," Cara said, her thumb rubbing my hand. "But let's get you rested up so you can heal."

I lightly squeezed her fingers. "Thanks."

"Do you want us to get your friends?"

I chuckled under my breath. "Actually... I wanna put off seeing them for as long as I can."

"Because of Breanne?" Steven asked.

"Yeah. A lot happened this summer. She basically knows everything except that I'm a wielder—magician. She was hurt, but she
understood. But now it looks like I trusted Opal with the Alexa
situation more when this whole thing is about her now, too."

Cara leaned back in her chair, resting her hands in her lap
and under her belly. "Just tell her that first part. That complete
honesty is exactly what she wants and needs."

"Which is, um, kind of awkward, considering nobody knows
you're Tristan's daughter," Steven said.

Cara backhanded his stomach.

"It's true!" he retorted.

"Not everything true must be said, my love."

"It's fine." The genuine smile on my face right now was the biggest semblance of relief I'd gotten since waking up. "Thanks for visiting me. And for the journal."

"Of course, honey." Cara gave my hand one last squeeze. "Call or text us if you ever need anything."

I wished that "everything" really meant *everything*; unfortunately, they couldn't be with me for the most terrifying conversation I'd ever had with my best friends.

FORTY

I had five minutes to mentally and emotionally prepare for Sarah and Breanne. By then, the only thing giving me the slightest bit of comfort was that I didn't have to worry about how I looked. You can't really help your appearance when you've been hospitalized after being beaten nearly to death in a forest. (That, and we stopped caring about how each other looks after a mishap with Breanne's at-home chemistry kit she got in fourth grade for Christmas.)

But I was probably never going to be ready for this visit, and the only way to handle it was to do it. The lingering feeling that I'd somehow betrayed *both* of my best friends inhibited the joy I should've felt when they came through the door next. The shock and remorse they shared in their expressions was at least some consolidation, though.

"Emmy!" Sarah carefully approached the left side of the bed. I assumed that one of her parents had taken an emergency flight back from New York with her. "I just—you—*how?*"

"Seriously!" Breanne said, coming to my other side. To my relief, anger was absent from her face. "What did you guys *do?*"

Wait a minute. The only way I'd be able to tell them that this was Alexa's doing was if Sarah knew about the Delphines, too. But I *really* didn't want Alexa to have an even bigger reason to target me—let alone have a reason to target her.

"I... I don't—"

"Do *not* say you don't know," Sarah deadpanned, raising a warning finger. "A moderate concussion, broken ribs, ankle sprain, and bruising? I have to believe you were conscious during all of that."

Agonizingly conscious. We both were.

I looked down at the sheets. Despite everything I'd told everyone else, that was the one update I didn't have, the one topic everyone had managed to avoid: the girl in the room next to mine.

"I need to know what's wrong with Opal first," I said. "Nobody's told me anything since I woke up."

Breanne shifted her weight, sighing as she thought. "Her arm is broken. Her left leg is severely fractured. There's a deep gash across her stomach..."

My body tensed at how effortlessly she'd said "gash", her absolutely least-favorite word in the entire English language. And when she paused, so did my breath. Especially when she looked at Sarah, like she needed someone braver than she was to deliver the news.

"Um..." Sarah told me, "she came in with a severe spinal fracture. She went in for surgery as soon as you guys got here. But there's, like... a fifty percent chance that when she wakes up, she'll be paralyzed from the waist down."

I could've sworn that the heart monitor stopped beeping.

The word repeatedly slashed at my mind like a whip, cutting deeper every time. If *I* hadn't been physically incapacitated, I honestly believe I would've jumped up from that hospital bed to hunt Alexa Delphine down myself and make sure she never walked again.

Even Hunters have a small group of people they trust more than themselves. In the Hunter world, trust is an invaluable tool—and weapon. Because when you care about someone enough, it becomes the sword they use to stab you in the back. As much as nobody wants to admit it, Hunters rely on trust. They *need* it.

And right now, I felt the exact same heartbreak from broken trust: I'd let Opal down. I'd let Mr. Dawson down. I'd brought her into this, I'd let this happen to her, and now there was a chance that Opal Dubois would never get to graduate the Callistro Academy as a Hunter. Or even stand again.

I swallowed my tears. *Be stronger than that. You can't break, too.*

"It's a risk with any spinal surgery," Breanne rushed to say. "We don't have to think the worst."

The quiet that lingered after those words was a little too loud for us to believe otherwise; silence is only ever loud when it's saying whatever we can't admit.

I shouldn't have asked. With Opal's condition looming in my head now, there was no way I could add the Delphine conversation with Sarah on top of that. Not right now, at least.

"I'm—um…" I murmured, my breath shallowing. "I think I've been sworn to secrecy about what happened. I'm sorry."

"You 'think'?" Sarah narrowed her eyes. "Why? Did whoever do this—?"

To my surprise and, well, fear, she just as quickly shook her head after pausing. "I don't even know why I asked. It was Alexa, wasn't it?"

At her words, Breanne's lips parted in surprise. I looked over and remembered that the girl has the entire internet for a brain. She definitely didn't need my help putting the pieces together: Alexa had gone after me and *Opal* after her magic had disappeared? No. Alexa had been looking for me and Breanne.

Her lips closed before Sarah could notice, but her soft, round eyes spoke their message as plain as day: an apology.

I couldn't look at her for too long unless I wanted to start crying, because I couldn't even tell her right now that it wasn't her fault. I had to build up that dam now before I'd come clean with *everything* like I had Wednesday night—look at how well that had turned out.

"Yeah. Alexa," I told Sarah. "That's all I'm saying about it."

"She got her memories back," she said flatly. "And that's *all* you're gonna tell us?"

"I want to," I whispered. I wanted to so badly. I stiffened at the stinging of my nose and heat in my eyes, praying that my tears wouldn't send me on another tormenting round of rib pain. "I want—to tell you. So much."

Sarah shook her head. "What changed? Why can't you trust us with anything now? You used to tell us everything that went on between you and her."

Even that's a lie.

Before I could start crying about how I didn't have the words to respond, Breanne drew in a sharp breath as if out of realization. I looked over again, anticipation begging for something helpful, something that I had an answer to. "Is Alexa... blackmailing you?"

My heart fell with gratitude, and I earnestly thanked her with my eyes. Her question was all Sarah needed to hear.

"What?" A divot formed between her perfectly shaped brows. "With what?"

I laid out discovering the Delphine's biggest secret during the hunt last year (which, thankfully, being that vague was enough and I didn't have to mention finding out in the underground secret passageways). Everything from Alexa hunting me since last semester, to this year's spring final, to her beating me half to death so I'd "keep her secret".

"And then your mom and Dawson found you guys?" Sarah asked.

I nodded. A hiccup formed from suppressing my tears, and I gasped in pain.

"Emmy, no, don't cry!" Breanne said, resting a small hand on top of mine. "It's okay! You're okay now!"

I wondered if she was trying to convince herself of that to make herself feel better.

"Well, you're alive, at least," Sarah said. "But if that's the business between you and Alexa, what was Opal doing there?"

"I *never* meant for her to come. She was just already at my house because of the sleepover when—"

Oh no. I definitely hadn't thought this one through.

"We just... wanted to go through the Callistro Forest for

memory's sake. With the school year around the corner. Alexa met us on the path."

A simple look at Breanne did it for me: she knew I was lying, and she knew that I was lying for the right reasons. But that was just it: I couldn't lie to either of them anymore. It was like my guilt was building a wall against any lie that tried to form.

Any question my best friends asked me next, I was ready to give them the truth—Emmalynn Atera and all.

Sarah paused for a second. "So Alexa's been secretly hunting you all this time? *All* this time?"

"Emmy..." Breanne sighed sorrowfully, rubbing my hand. "It all makes sense now."

"I can't believe it." Sarah's hands went to her hips. "*That's* why you never got over it when the Redway Boys spent January with us—I'm so sorry. Why did you never tell us?"

I could have imploded from the relief. Now both of my best friends knew that Alexa was still in my life—they even knew part of the reason why—and they forgave me for not telling them sooner. They now knew what had always forced me silent around them.

And it just... felt so good for them to know.

"Emma!" Sarah reached for my cheek, drying the tear sliding down. "I'm sorry, please don't cry! It's all out now, it's okay."

I swallowed. That relief had sentenced me to fatal courage. "No. That's not all."

Sarah instinctively retracted her hand, but Breanne seemed to know what I was referring to: she quietly gave me her complete attention.

"There's more to—the situation," I said. "I need to tell you, just—just not right now. But I will, I promise. I'll tell you as soon as the time is right. It's just... not now."

Me "being friends" with Tristan's daughter would've worked on Opal had it not been for Alexa. From now on, I was keeping my best friends on a need-to-know basis, and that secret was going to be my ticket in.

Both girls looked at each other on either side of the bed. Breanne must have given Sarah a look that said they should just trust me on this one, because Sarah rested an ever-so-gentle hand on my shoulder a second later.

"Okay," she said. Like she was truly satisfied with that.

I took her soft hand. "Thanks. Thank you."

I hoped that, one of these days, I'd get to tell her exactly how grateful I was to her right now—I'd get to tell her how that "okay" had honestly let me start the healing process.

FORTY-ONE

You can imagine how sentimental the reunion was when Opal woke up the next afternoon. You can imagine how overjoyed we all were when we found out that she wasn't, in fact, paralyzed from the waist down. You can imagine how relieved we were when Mr. Dawson was able to retrieve all of her memories except certain parts from Wednesday night.

You can imagine how awkward it was when she and I were left alone in her room to "catch up".

Her straight black hair had lost its shine. Her purple eyes had dulled and no longer winked like a vibrant piece of amethyst in the sun. Lying in the hospital bed, Opal looked less like a Callistro Girl and more like a girl waiting to wake up again, to realize that this wasn't actually happening—the girl I'd been at the beginning of first semester.

"I'm sorry," I told her once the nurse shut the door behind me. My arms sat uncomfortably on the armrests of my wheelchair. "And no matter what you say, I'll never think it's not my fault."

"How do you think I feel?" she asked, almost defensively. "*I* chose to come. I knew who was waiting for you. It was my choice."

"And you got *hurt*," I snapped. My nose was already on fire, but I still told myself not to cry. "If I didn't know any better, and I don't, I would've thought Alexa was trying to kill you! You have it so much worse than I do, she dealt with you a *lot* quicker than she did with me!"

I didn't need telepathy to know the one question our minds shared: *why?* First of all, why had Alexa been twice as brutal with Opal as she had been with me? Why had she had our memories wiped when she knew we had so many ways of getting them back? Why erase the *entire* summer? Why had she and Anthony run away when Momma and Mr. Dawson pulled up, like they didn't have the upper hand?

"I'm sorry." Opal's voice was too melancholy for my comfort, nothing like the confident gossiping Callistro Girl I used to know her as. "I'm sorry, I—I just remember being... really scared. I hid from you guys fighting and then somehow forced myself to face her, but you were already on the ground. She was so fast." Sobs caught in her throat again. Her strain to hold them back was painfully clear. "It was a vicious cycle of her being faster than me until I finally passed out.

"I fought so hard to stay awake, Emma," she rasped, meeting my gaze with teary eyes. "I promise, I did. I couldn't leave you alone with her, especially after everything she did to me. And *you* were her target. I didn't know if she was planning on getting rid of you, I just knew I couldn't—leave you to fight on your own."

No high lilt. No airiness. She meant every word. Which also meant that she didn't know that I was a wielder.

But the sting... was less than it usually was.

With extra effort, I wiped a runaway tear from my cheek. "Don't apologize when the whole thing is her fault. We didn't ask for this. She's the one who brought it on us. We have to find a way to fix this and make sure it never happens again."

"So... have you talked to Breanne about things yet? How she's—on Alexa's list?"

"Not alone. I haven't had the chance to."

She stilled, eyes caught on her sheets. Her mind was closed off to me, but I knew it had gripped her. The air buzzed with the anticipation of her next words and then just as quickly shattered when she said, "We're all Alexa's targets now, aren't we?"

I fixed my gaze on my lap in case she'd look back at me; the last thing I wanted was to see her face when I confronted the truth I'd spent too long trying to suppress. "I guess we—"

The words hitched in my throat as my thoughts caught up with them. Targets. We were all her targets now, all enemies that she'd do everything she could to pin down and capture.

The footage from the camera in one of her shirt buttons.

"Emma?"

I couldn't look at Opal. If I looked at her, I'd cry, and my ribs weren't ready to handle more of that. Especially because she couldn't know that I was a wielder.

I was crying.

"Please don't cry, I'm gonna start crying and that really, *really* hurts."

I pressed my lips tightly together, every muscle threatening to quiver. Let Opal think whatever she wanted to. I had every excuse in the world to cry right now. Not one part of her had to know that I was having an actual anxiety attack right now because Alexa Delphine finally had something on me.

†

"She recorded the whole fight with a button camera on her shirt."

Mr. Dawson gently held me up with one hand on my upper arm and the other on my back as I sat on the edge of the hospital bed that night. He was hauntingly still, my parents' and Aunt Becca's eyes heavy on me as they stood at the foot of the bed.

"She has something on me," I said.

Why isn't anyone saying anything? They're supposed to make things better.

Do they really think we've lost?

"How does she plan on excusing the circumstances?" Mr. Dawson asked.

I carefully met his gaze. "What do you mean?"

"She caught your confession of being an Atera *and* two young magicians using their magic on camera." His left hand dropped my back and carefully moved to my shoulder instead. "How does she plan on excusing how she got that? Right place, right time? She just *happened* to know to record finding the number-one target in America right now? How is she gonna justify how she's been hunting you while the rest of her pack moved on?"

"That's why she said she was going on a solo research mission," Momma said in realization, her grip around herself loosening. "She's the leader, next to William. She finds even the slightest hint of a lead that she thinks is worth looking into, conducts her private research for a few weeks, and finds Tristan Atera's daughter at the end of it?"

The crown jewel of America's Hunters' most wanted list. Yeah. That sounded like a pretty worthy risk—especially if you captured the prize.

"Then I'm starting to think most of her pack is her family," I said. "She wouldn't even need to excuse it then—would she?"

"William doesn't know," Mr. Dawson said. "She wouldn't have had to use the pretext of private research. Him and Jak—at least two people don't know. Maybe her family makes up some of the pack, but I don't think they're all involved."

According to Alexa, Julia isn't part of it. Okay. That was some relief... I was pretty sure.

"Sure, she could turn in the footage," Mr. Dawson said next. "But it wouldn't be wise. And I know she knows that."

"Then why would she tell me about it?" I asked, desperation hiding behind each word.

"She *told* you she was recording the whole thing?" Aunt Becca asked skeptically.

"Yeah."

Unfortunately, that only placed us into another deep silence. A wicked silence that I wanted to punch straight through and shatter into a million pieces. I needed something to hit, anything to wreck what was stopping me from reaching the end of this nightmare of a summer.

"She doesn't need to excuse the circumstances of the video if she isn't planning on turning just that in." Mr. Dawson took turns glancing between the four of us. "If she plans on turning that in last."

"Like if... she's gathering multiple pieces of evidence to turn in without trouble," Aunt Becca added in a small voice that didn't fit her.

"Meaning it doesn't matter who's part of her pack." Dad sighed, passing a hand over his face. "If she's gonna turn the footage in to the feds directly, she just needs to cover her own tracks."

"Something deeper is going on here," Mr. Dawson murmured. When I looked back at him, his stare was practically drilling through the ground. "If she really had footage and wanted to turn Emma in, she would've done it without warning her that she had evidence."

"If you can even call it a 'warning'." Momma scoffed, rolling her eyes. Dad squeezed her tighter, pulling her closer to him. "Are you saying she didn't actually record Emma?"

"No. But she has us right where she wants us. We don't know her like we think we do, which means we have no idea what she's doing—and we can't predict it, either." Mr. Dawson looked up, meeting Momma's eyes. "I'm saying she has a plan."

FORTY-TWO

Home is where the heart is, as they say. Except, when I walked through the front door of my childhood home in crutches Monday night, an unfamiliar presence hung in the atmosphere. Something was just... off. I was walking through someplace that *wasn't* home, despite Momma putting a gentle hand on my shoulder as she shut the front door and smiled with the same tenderness.

Even despite her saying, "You're home, Emmy."

"I know," I said. I knew it, but my heart didn't believe it, even though this was where it'd all started. Everything. I was even born here—why did everything feel so far away, out of reach?

That was it: it didn't feel like I *should* be here right now, like I was defying the laws of reality. As morbid and, frankly, crazy as it sounded, why hadn't Alexa just killed me and Opal that night? Why had she physically attacked us at all? What had been her main motive? Did she still want the same things she did at the beginning of summer, or had some items changed?

Momma helped me to the couch and sat us down. I leaned my crutches against it. Despite my anxiety, I was too scared to test the limits of my arm to grab my locket and fiddle with it.

"I have to get used to this," I finally said. "Having to use these things, having everyone ask me a bunch of questions I can't answer once school starts, needing to use the elevator to go from floor to floor..."

"Because that's so terrible." Momma chuckled, resting her hands in her lap. Seconds of pensive silence rested between us, my eyes landing on whatever they could find in front of us: coffee table, entertainment center, or fireplace.

"Remember the first time you ever used that elevator?" Mom asked.

I licked my lips as the steel doors came into mind. That August day replayed in my head in one quick movie. Almost one year exactly had gone by since then.

I bit the inside of my cheek. "Everything seemed so exciting."

Before any of it was real.

"Do the girls know, then?"

"Not all of it, obviously. I can't believe I thought they'd get mad just because I didn't tell them every single detail of my life."

"Why would you ever think that?"

I carefully exhaled. With my arms essentially incapacitated, I settled on fiddling with my fingers. "It's hard to trust people. I didn't wanna put them through—doubt, I guess. I didn't wanna be one of those people they had to question if they could trust."

Momma turned to face me better, brushing a strand of my hair out of my face. "I think this is what you're failing to see: you've been best friends for almost *nine years*. You've never purposely hurt either of them, you've shown countless times that you love them and always have their best interest in mind, and they know your heart is in the right place. Whatever you choose to do, your reasons for it are good. If you involved them in Alexa's secrets, you'd *all* be on her list. You're looking out for them. They know that. At this point, that's the only reason they don't know who your father is."

A large lump passed in my throat, willing that one day I'd hear that speech from my best friends themselves. Based on the conversations in the hospital, that was what they thought, too. But my stomach folded in on itself as my mind snagged on the one error of Momma's words: Breanne *was* on Alexa's list now. So was Opal. As soon as the Delphines found out that Sarah knew about them, she would be, too. And I hadn't budged whatsoever.

Then again, I guess that only reinforced the truth of what Momma was saying. With that, my secrets felt... a little lighter.

I tightly smiled. "You realized all of that before I did."

"Selflessness usually needs these things pointed out."

I didn't feel selfless. A lot of the things I'd done this summer had been quite the opposite.

Momma carefully leaned toward me, kissing my forehead. "Let's get some sleep. It's late."

I nodded and used her help to stand from the couch with my crutches. She guided me down the hall and right into my room, helping me with every step of getting into bed.

"I love you, Emma," she said, throwing the covers over me. She leaned down, careful not to touch me as she kissed my cheek. "Good night."

"I love you, too, Momma."

One last smile passed between us. She turned away, walked out of my room, and shut the door behind her.

I lay in bed and remembered how we had one day left: tomorrow was the last day of summer vacation. Then my junior year would begin. I'd gotten so far this summer and yet had that much further to go.

My exhausted mind knew that I had to let it go for now. There was nothing left to accomplish by worrying anymore, not right now, at least—so I let my eyes close, my body sinking into my bed. I tried to feel excited for the school year. Just for a moment, I willed things to feel a little more normal. I wanted to feel like my friends and I were four girls ending the summer leading into their junior year, and we were ready for it.

With one last listen to the still quiet around me, I slowly exhaled. My body was ready to sleep.

No dreams. No visions. Finally, just peace.

Then the sun peeked through the window. When I opened my eyes, I was still in my room, safe and untouched.

My chest deflated with relief. *The last day.*

Wait. Something was wrong. Why was my chest heavy? Why did I—?

"No, NO!"

Momma. That was Momma, why was she freaking out?

"Mom?"

Quiet.

"Mom!"

Instinct is powerful. Instinct knows what we don't moments before we find out. In all of the mornings I'd spent checking my phone first, I knew something was wrong when instinct told me to do it that morning instead of habit.

Unable to bring myself out of bed and silently cursing Alexa for it, I slid my phone off the nightstand, body as stiff as a brick. Hang on—why were all of my notifications from the news? I didn't get news notifications on my phone…

—*I'm sorry, baby girl,*— said a familiar voice. I looked up from my phone. Dad was getting farther away, why was he getting farther away? —*It's okay.*—

—*Dad?*—

Nothing.

—*Dad, was that you?*—

"Emma?" Momma shouted from down the hall.

She's okay, I thought with relief. But it did little. My heart was already beating a hole through my chest.

Alerts blared on my phone. National headlines were ingrained in my screen. Every notification on my phone had to do with the same subject.

No. No. No.

I searched for the keywords.

Momma pounded on my bedroom door, in sync with my heart. "Emma!"

The results loaded in. Every news article on the internet featured the same subject: my father.

And the same words crowned every last one: TRISTAN ATERA FOUND DEAD IN FOREST CITY, NORTH CAROLINA.

ACKNOWLEDGEMENTS

Strap in, because I owe this book to a *lot* of people. First of all, Mike Diener. This book is dedicated to you because you have been one of my biggest supporters since I first started my author journey. Since then, you've become a teacher to me in writing, friendships, and even my relationship with God. At points, your feedback for this book destroyed me—but it also destroyed its weakest points and turned it into something I am proud of. Thank you for your never-ending patience, guidance, and support. You truly are a real-life Mr. Dawson to me (which, now that I think about it, you're probably gonna take as an insult because you hated him in this book, but hopefully you know what I mean). You having the same middle name as the guy was just the most hilarious and iconic coincidence ever.

I cannot go any further without mentioning my other *phenomenal* beta readers (who, unfortunately, asked for these titles in some of their names): Jack Freeman, Lauren D. Fulter-Delphine,

Colonel McKenna Rowell, Sabrey Moiraine, Official Car Tire Taste Tester Amelia Clawford, Dictator Grace L., Myah R., and Kate W. You guys *transformed* NMU, and its readers will never know just how much. Thank you.

McKenna and Lauren: nobody can deny that God Himself put you both into my life. I needed you long before I knew it. You were fearless in providing me your most professional and honest opinions when beta'ing for me. Thank you a million for fitting in NMU just for me. You added a perspective and voice that it needed.

Momma—you'll kill me if I don't include you in the acknowledgments, but you've also given me astonishing support with my author dreams since I was eleven. Even now, you never treat these dreams like they're a waste of time, you never tell me that I need to "get my head out of the clouds" and "get a real job". Instead, you foster me as I integrate myself into the real world while pursuing this dream. You support me in every aspect of my life, and as our song goes, "[w]hen God made you my mother, He knew what I'd need" (Riley Roth). Thank you for everything you've done for me since the day we met.

Finally, to you, reader—because if you told sixteen-year-old Ariana that this many people would actually read and care about her book series she was starting, she would've cried. She would've only *hoped*. But thanks to you, I don't have to hope. It's reality. I hope you know what you've done for me simply by enjoying this book and its series. Thank you.

About the Author

Ariana Tosado is a 22-year-old author, musician, university student, book editor, and content creator for teen and young-adult audiences. She started pursuing her passion of writing novels in middle school. Today, she's homed her focus on the *Emmalynn Atera* Series, marketing *Thy Kingdom Come*, and producing music. She aims to create relatable and encouraging content through her platforms, all with her cat, Sophie, in one hand and an iced vanilla latte in the other.

You can find out more about what she's up to on her website (www.arianatosado.com) or on Instagram (@thearianatosado).